THE LORD OF STARIEL

Also by AJ Lancaster:

The Prince of Secrets
The Court of Mortals

THE LORD OF STARIEL

STARIEL: BOOK ONE

A.J. LANCASTER

Published in 2018 by Camberion Press, Wellington, New Zealand.

Printed by KDP Print.

A CIP record for this book is available from the National Library of New Zealand.

ISBN 978-0-473-45124-0 (paperback)
ISBN 978-0-473-45125-7 (eBook)

Cover design ©Jennifer Zemanek/Seedlings Design Studio

ajlancaster.com

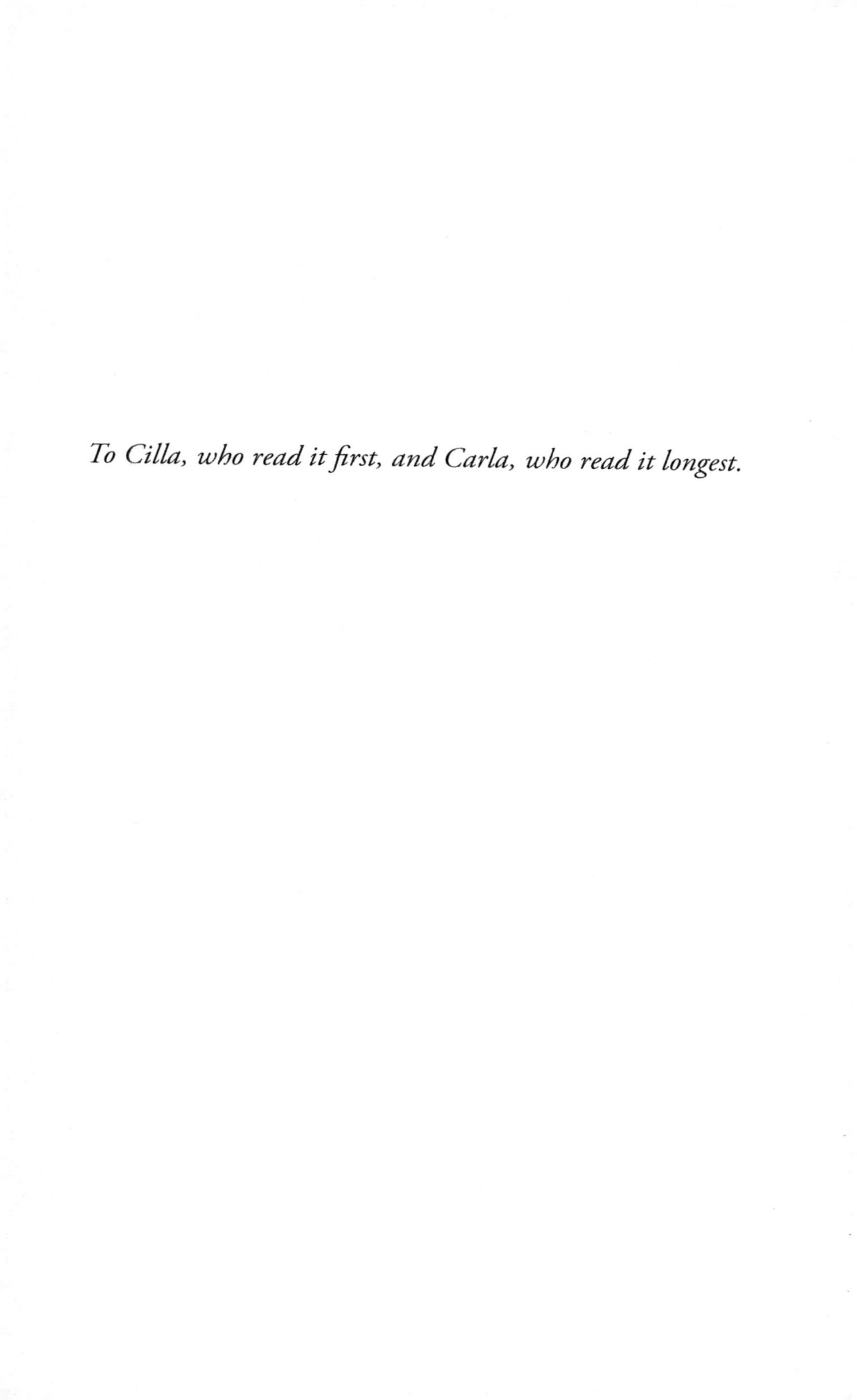

To Cilla, who read it first, and Carla, who read it longest.

AN OMINOUS PROLOGUE

King Aeros approached the Gate, boots echoing on the polished marble floor. For three centuries, the Gate had stood firm against everything he could throw at it. Now, though…

He fanned out his wings in a glory of silver and crimson feathers. Behind him, his court's interest sharpened, but not a wing, tail, horn, or ear among its various members twitched. They knew not to distract him—or risk drawing his ire if the Gate resisted him again. King Aeros smiled. A well-trained court was truly a thing of joy, but they need not have worried. Obviously, he would not try this publicly without being certain of the result; he'd run his own private tests last night.

Still, his court did not need to know that. He ran his fingers down the stone columns, savouring their palpable anticipation, following the pattern of oak leaves. There were no oaks in Faerie, but this Gate did not lead to one of Faerie's many kingdoms.

His touch fell upon a stone acorn buried among the leaves. He drew up ropes of magic, filling the air with his signature of storms and metal, and twisted. The space between the stone columns shimmered.

The Gate activated.

King Aeros paused for effect, taking a moment to sweep his long silver-white hair back from his face, the jewels woven into the braids chiming gently as he did so. Then, with deliberate slowness, he extended his hand. It passed through the shimmer and disappeared. He pulled it back, inspecting the faint hint of moisture on his skin; it was raining on the other side. Mortal rain.

Closing his hand into a fist, he turned back to the court, letting rivulets of storm charge wash over his wings in triumph, the lightning tamed to his will. He spread his primaries to maximise the impact. Drama should accompany this sort of announcement.

"The Iron Law is revoked. The Mortal Realm is open to us once again." His smile widened.

It was not a nice smile.

1

STARIEL HOUSE

Hetta Valstar rummaged through her makeup bag and frowned. Was cherry a sombre enough shade? Or was it too cheerful? Maybe a paler shade would be better. It was easy to visualise a demure rose, which meant it would be equally easy to illuse her lips to appear the same colour. But if someone was rude enough to inspect Hetta with a quizzing glass, they'd know it for illusion. *My aunts will almost certainly be that rude.* In fact, they'd probably disapprove of real lipstick almost as much as the illusory kind; Hetta doubted the North was up to date with Southern fashions. Perhaps no lipstick at all would be preferable.

Hetta began emptying her bag of its contents. She'd just spotted the lipstick tube when the train crossed the border into Stariel Estate. Between one second and the next, a tidal wave of homecoming surged over her. She gasped, dropped the bag, and groped for the side of the bunk bed. The world spun.

Stariel. All the Valstars had at least a touch of the land-sense, but she'd underestimated how it would feel to have that connection snap back into place. A part of her that had lain dormant for years burst into life, as alarming and exhilarating as a second heartbeat. *Home,* it pulsed. *Home,* in direct counterpoint to the fact that the estate *wasn't* home anymore. How could she have forgotten the intensity of it? All those years in the South—where the idea of a land magically connecting with its people would be deemed preposterous—had dimmed the memory.

She leaned against the bunk, heart pounding, and tried to centre herself. *Lipstick. I was searching for lipstick.* It had rolled out of the bag and under her berth. She knelt, cursing the dress's unyielding hemline. The land's vast presence loomed over her, both familiar and alien, as she fished about haphazardly for the lipstick, three-quarters distracted.

Her land-sense slowly settled into its accustomed place, taking that first rush of intensity with it. Despite Hetta's unrelenting—and unwanted—sense of homecoming, the estate itself didn't so much as flicker as it accepted her back. No emotion at all emanated from it. Hetta tried not to feel a tiny bit disappointed at Stariel's lack of reaction, even though it was egotistical to expect otherwise; she was, after all, just one of many Valstars. It probably hadn't even noticed she'd been gone for so long. Did it know why she was here now, why everyone of Valstar blood was swarming back? Her stomach clenched, a slow feeling of dread settling, and she angrily shook her head. Where was the dashed lipstick?

Hetta mentally poked at her land-sense as her fingers brushed the cool metal tube. *Well, at least Stariel accepted me back without a fuss.* Perhaps her family would take their cue from the land; neutral acceptance would be preferable to the disapproving reception she feared was coming.

She stood, weighing the lipstick in one hand. *They have no power over me now,* she reminded herself firmly. *I am a grown and independent woman.* She'd built a life for herself outside Stariel's grasp—a life she'd be returning to in two weeks, after the Choosing. Surely she and her relatives could maintain civility for two weeks? Especially since her father wouldn't be there.

My father is dead. Stariel's lord is dead.

The words struck soft as feathers. They weren't real enough yet to have weight, though they'd hummed in the background for a little over twelve hours now. *Dead.*

She opened her mirror-compact with a snap. This was no time for wool-gathering. The train would reach Stariel Station soon, and she needed to be ready by then. But exactly what form should her readiness take? She drew in a long, steadying breath, filling herself with determination. Her family would see only a confident, put-together young woman when she arrived. *And a fashionable one too*, she decided. Her aunts' sensibilities could go hang. *I don't care what they think of me.*

A tiny voice pointed out that she was spending an awful lot of time worrying about what to wear for someone who didn't care what her relatives thought of her. She ignored it and focused on carefully applying the cherry colour. By the time her lips were painted, the mirror showed a picture of perfect composure. Let Aunt Sybil call the colour vulgar; she wouldn't recognise glamourous sophistication if it bit her on the nose! Hetta pursed her lips in satisfaction and began to pack up her things.

When the train stopped at Stariel Station, Hetta was the only passenger to alight. A handful of assorted goods were unloaded along with her trunk, presumably awaiting pickup, before the train pulled away from the station. Hetta watched it until it curved around a bend and disappeared, taking her tangible connection to the South with it and leaving her entirely alone.

Small sounds magnified with the train's absence—jarringly natural sounds, rather than those of the city she'd become accustomed to. She swallowed, feeling suddenly small and out of place.

Wind rustled in the bracken, and in the distance came the *baaing* of sheep. Stariel Station was some distance from Stariel Village, properly known as Stariel-on-Starwater, and there was only farmland and forest in sight.

It was only then that Hetta realised no one knew she needed collecting from the station.

"Drat." She'd forgotten to arrange it in the scramble to pack and book a ticket on the sleeper train. The telegram notifying her of her father's death had arrived only the day before, in the break between the matinee and evening performances. *I was performing illusions without even knowing he was dead.* The thought slid in, quiet and unsettling as a ghost—and just as unnecessarily morbid. It made not a jot of difference, so why dwell on it?

She arranged her scarf more securely around her neck. In Meridon, the great Southern capital, the weather was still mild, but here in the North the air held the bite of coming winter.

Would any of her family think to meet the sleeper train after sending that telegram? After all, it was the only way for Hetta to return home, and they *must* be expecting her. But she didn't fancy sitting with her luggage in the bitter wind on the strength of that hope. If no one was already here waiting for her, then whoever had sent the telegram hadn't told Wyn, Stariel's butler as well as Hetta's friend, that she'd been summoned. Wyn would never leave her here to wait in the cold. That meant she was probably relying on Aunt Sybil to remember her, since the terseness of the telegram had been very much in that aunt's style.

Aunt Sybil wouldn't *deliberately* forget about Hetta, would she? Perhaps she just hadn't made the logical connection between sending the telegram and the arrival of the sleeper train the next morning. The oversight would be understandable, with everyone preoccupied with funeral and Choosing arrangements.

Perhaps there was a public telephone somewhere nearby. Her spirits lifted at this thought, though she didn't know whether her father had seen fit to install the new technology at Stariel House. There'd been no telephone line when she'd left. But it was worth a try. She burrowed her hands into her coat pockets and went in search.

Ten unfruitful minutes later, she concluded there was no public telephone. But the ticket office would have one inside, surely? She checked her watch again—it was just before eight o'clock on Monday morning. What time did the office open? Memories of the village stores' opening schedules didn't fill her with optimism. Unlike Meridon, where one could depend on stores opening at the same time each day, as advertised, Stariel marched to a more flexible drumbeat.

She went over to examine the goods that had been unloaded from the train. They consisted of such thrilling items as the mailbag and a small crate marked 'Smithson's Manufacturing'. In Meridon, someone would have taken charge of them as soon as they were delivered. Here, it was anyone's guess when someone might be along to collect them. It didn't help her, but she couldn't help smiling at the more lackadaisical attitude of the countryside.

Of course, there was one *other* way she could attract attention. She pulled off her left glove and stared thoughtfully at her palm. Concentrating, she called up an image she'd used in the play yesterday: glittering purple snake-demons writhing in smoke. She'd meant to summon an illusion only a few inches high, more as an idle thought than any serious attempt at a signal, but the snake-demons that emerged were as tall as she was. They burst from her in a riot of colour, their eyes glowing with life, scales realistic enough that they flashed in the weak sunlight. Startled, she snuffed them out of existence and frowned at the space they'd filled. She'd fed the illusion too much power—and a Master of Illusion should not make such a miscalculation. She must be more rattled than she'd realised. That was the first principle of magic, after all: controlling one's emotions.

She took a few deep breaths, though she already felt quite calm. Should she send a giant signal leaping fifty feet into the sky? On the one hand, someone would be bound to come and investigate. On the other, since her decision to train in magic had been a key factor in her exile, it probably wasn't the best way to begin her visit. *Besides, it's childish to deliberately try to shock my family at such a time*, she told herself sternly. *Even if it's still completely nonsensical of them to disapprove of my choices, given how magical Stariel is!* But she knew the cases weren't the same, much as she might rail against the unfairness of it. Quite apart from the magic, Stariel wasn't a well-born woman working in a theatre house. *Dens of iniquity and loose morals*, Hetta thought with a smile. She'd quite enjoyed the loose morals, truth be told.

She'd just decided to walk towards the village in search of someone when the whirring sound of a vehicle came from the road. She went to wave it down, but it proved unnecessary. The vehicle, one of the new kineticars, was clearly heading for the station. The kineticar pulled up, and a man Hetta knew well got out. He was large and broad-shouldered, with cherubic brown curls, warm hazel eyes, and a ready smile that Hetta knew from personal experience could set hearts a-flutter.

"Angus!" she burst out as he came towards the station. "Oh, how glad I am to see you."

It took a few seconds for comprehension to replace confusion on the man's face.

"Henrietta Valstar! I nearly didn't recognise you." His gaze travelled swiftly over her person, from her neatly styled auburn hair to her smart black boots, warming with approval as he took in her trim figure. "By Simulsen, Hetta, you've turned out well."

"Yes, I know." She held out her arms and made a show of making a half-pirouette for his inspection. "Feel free to continue complimenting me." Angus laughed, and her heart gave a traitorous flutter. She'd been hopelessly infatuated with Angus as a gawky teen; he'd been oblivious to the interest of someone he saw as a mere schoolgirl. He wasn't looking at her like a schoolgirl now. "But I ought to call you Lord Penharrow now, hadn't I?" She'd heard he had succeeded his father to Penharrow Estate, Stariel's neighbour, three years ago.

Lord Angus Penharrow broke into a broad grin, showing the dimple in his left cheek. She'd forgotten the unfairly attractive impact of that dimple. "Nay, you'd best call me Angus. It makes me feel ancient to have you calling me 'Lord Penharrow'. Unless you wish me to call you Miss Valstar. I don't want to offend your notions of propriety."

Hetta laughed. "You have no idea, Angus, of the impropriety I've been involved with these last few years. The shoe is on the other foot. No doubt I'll scandalise the locals with my modern ways."

He chuckled. "That I'd like to see." He took in the trunk resting beside her and his expression abruptly sobered. "You've come up from Meridon for the funeral, I suppose." He shook his head. "A sad business. I was sorry to hear of your father's passing. I've always held Lord Valstar in high esteem."

Hetta narrowly avoided raising her eyebrows. The younger Angus had treated her father with disinterested politeness on the rare occasions she'd seen them interact. She doubted their relationship had grown any closer in the intervening years. Her father wasn't an easy man to get along with, even sober, and letters from home had given her the impression that he'd only become more so as age and infirmity caught up with him.

"Thank you," she said diplomatically. "And yes, I'm here for the funeral—and the Choosing." She assumed an expression of self-deprecation. "But I'm afraid in the rush to get here I forgot to inform my family of my arrival." She batted her eyelashes at him with exaggerated motions. "I don't suppose you'd be interested in rescuing a damsel in distress? It is, I know, somewhat out of your way, but you would win my undying gratitude and a warm feeling of virtue from getting to play the white knight."

The dimple made another appearance. "I can hardly leave you stranded here on the platform, can I, with an offer like that?"

She grinned. "Thank you, my lord." She went to gather her luggage. Angus seemed surprised when she deposited her trunk next to the kineticar while he fetched the small crate he'd originally come for.

"You thought I'd turn you into my porter as well," Hetta said shrewdly.

"None of my sisters would carry their own trunks," Angus replied, an odd expression crossing his face. Hetta had the strong impression that he thought her behaviour unnatural. She gave an internal sigh. It wasn't unexpected. The North was more old-fashioned than Meridon. How lowering it was to find that one's childhood hero was only a mortal man after all. However, Angus recovered quickly and stowed her things securely in the vehicle. Determined not to unsettle her rescuer further, Hetta allowed him to open the door for her.

"Your chariot, my lady," he said with a grin.

They conversed amicably as they drove. Angus shook his head as they passed water-logged fields occupied by sad-looking sheep. "Drains are the future of modern farming," he remarked. "My father started them at Penharrow years ago, and I can't say he was wrong to do so. Increases productivity remarkably."

"Father was always very traditional," Hetta said. She knew very little of farming. Father hadn't considered it an appropriate subject for a girl. "But perhaps the new lord will be keen to modernise."

Angus shot her a quick, searching glance. "Perhaps," he said, and Hetta knew he wanted to ask who she thought would be chosen. *Though why he thinks I'd have any insight into it when I haven't set foot here in years is a mystery.* On the other hand, surely her family's dynamics wouldn't have changed that much? She turned the possibilities for the new lord over in her mind; she hadn't yet given it much thought. It was hard to imagine anyone other than Lord Henry Valstar in that role. *My father is dead.* Her chest tightened, and she had to force her fingers not to curl into fists. How dare her father be dead when she was still so very angry at him?

No one ever knew for sure who Stariel would choose, but historically it did often go from father to eldest son. That would mean Marius. Marius had always taken her side. He'd openly risked their father's displeasure, visiting her in the great Southern capital when he could. *Father never thought Marius would be chosen though.* No, unless things had changed significantly, Hetta knew exactly who was expected to inherit: her cousin Jack. He was everything Lord Henry's eldest son was not: blunt and practical, and traditionally masculine in all the ways that counted with the old lord. He had the strongest land-sense in Hetta's generation. Hetta frowned at the passing countryside. Even if Father thought Jack would inherit, it didn't justify treating Marius as a failure. There was more to life than this dashed estate!

They passed through the village of Stariel-on-Starwater. Not much had changed in six years, and Hetta's anger at her father's favouritism faded under a swell of nostalgia. She and Marius had ridden down to the village often. There was the tea shop where they'd frequently over-indulged in clotted cream scones. There was the farrier's workshop. There was the post office with its odd carved owl on the sign, the building impossibly quaint now in comparison to the much larger ones in Meridon. Had the village always been this small? And yet each difference gaped at her like a missing tooth: the apothecary had transformed into a hat shop; the white fence was grey and peeling; and one of the mature walnut trees on the village green had become a rotting stump.

"Have you missed it?" Angus asked.

Hetta started, pulled from her memories. She considered her

answer. "In part," she said after a pause. "How little it has changed since I left! I feel like I've gone back in time."

"We must seem terribly provincial to you," Angus remarked. He said this with an unruffled assurance that belied his words. He did not value the so-called sophistication of the South.

Hetta couldn't resist the urge to tease. "Oh, yes. I confess I don't know how I'll occupy myself in such a backwater until the Choosing. I'm sure there won't be any conversation worth having with anyone here. In fact," she added seriously, "I've become steadily more convinced of this all morning."

Angus snorted, but again that odd look crossed his face. Hetta gave herself a stern mental lecture on appropriate moments for levity, but she couldn't help wishing that one of her Meridon theatre friends were here.

It began to rain as they drove, a sudden downpour typical of the North's climate at this time of year. In seconds, the world faded into greyness, and the sound of rain on the kineticar's roof made conversation difficult. They slowed to cross the Home Bridge, and Hetta knew they were only a few miles away from Stariel House. The kineticar's tyres clattered on the uneven surface.

The rain eased as they rounded a bend and the house came into view. With its trio of turrets, stone walls, and high, arched main entrance, the central part of the structure bore a strong resemblance to a medieval castle. The Valstar crest flew at half-mast from the highest turret, but other than that it was much the same as when she'd left all those years ago. The sight hit Hetta with the force of a blow. *Home*, her land-sense pulsed again. Hetta huffed internally at the sensation. This *wasn't* home anymore, magical connection notwithstanding, and she refused to be sentimental about a building. Stariel House wasn't even a *pretty* building, taken in its entirety, since generations of Valstars had seen fit to add a mish-mash of architectural styles to the central castle core.

Before she could ask him to do otherwise, Angus had pulled

up outside the formal front entrance and switched off the engine. Why had she let herself get so distracted, drinking in the sight of the house? She would've preferred to arrive at the back tradesman's entrance near the kitchens, where she could have slipped in without fuss, but she supposed that was wishful thinking. There was, inevitably, going to be fuss. A strange heaviness formed in her chest. What if they didn't accept her back now Father was gone?

She took a deep breath and got out of the car. Angus followed and lifted out her trunk before she could make a move for it.

"Thank you," she said.

The formal entryway rose before her, familiar and intimidating all at once. Mythical creatures made of stone guarded the bottom of the stairs. Hetta had named them Spot and Reginald in a fit of whimsy long ago. Reginald was a horned greyhound-like creature; Spot was a large cat with three tails. Both came from local fairy stories.

Heart racing, she mustered her courage and marched up the steps to the main door before raising the knocker and bringing it down in a four-beat tattoo. As she stood waiting, oddly dizzy with anticipation, she found herself thinking of a scene from the play where the hero entered the demon's lair. She dismissed the likeness as fanciful, a little annoyed with herself. There were no theatrical snake-demons here. *Unless we count Aunt Sybil,* she thought. Besides, in all probability it would be Wyn opening the door, since he was apparently butler now, and not one of her relatives, so there was no reason for this anxiety in any case.

Despite these reassurances, her nerves stretched, waiting. She was just wondering if she should knock again when the door opened and Hetta found herself staring into her older brother Marius's spectacle-framed eyes.

2

AN OLD FRIEND

"WHY ARE YOU opening the door?" she said inanely as his grey eyes lit up. Thank goodness it wasn't one of her more antagonistic relatives, but, really, Marius shouldn't be manning the front door either. If Wyn wasn't available, it should've been the footman. They did still have a footman, didn't they? The thought felt oddly alien. Hetta-the-no-name-illusionist didn't have servants.

"Hetta! You came!" Marius pulled the door fully open and caught her up in a tight embrace. "Oh, Hetta." He made a noise somewhere between a laugh and a cry, and Hetta could feel his body trembling. Was the excess of emotion purely on her account? *Oh, Marius, what have they been saying to you?* But the knot in her stomach eased a little nonetheless at the warm welcome.

"It's good to see you too, Marius." She returned the embrace before drawing back to examine him. They shared the same long nose and high, flying brows. She'd last seen her oldest brother more than a year ago when he'd come down to Meridon to visit. The silver threading Marius's thick black hair at his temples had grown more pronounced, though Marius was only twenty-seven. Their father had gone grey young too, Hetta remembered being told.

"You look well," she told him fondly, raising a hand to touch the silver. *Though stressed*, she added silently, taking in the circles under his eyes. Was it only Father's death and the funeral arrangements, or was it what came after? Their entire family, like Angus, would be speculating about whether Marius would inherit—hopefully not to his face, but she wouldn't put it past some of them. Even if everyone had somehow managed to be abnormally tactful and refrained from doing so, Marius would still be sensitive to the undercurrents.

Marius looked past her and frowned.

"Whatever is Penharrow doing in our driveway?" he murmured before raising his voice and greeting him. "Lord Penharrow." He nodded politely at Angus.

"Valstar," Angus acknowledged.

It had previously struck Hetta as unfortunate that the two men were civil acquaintances rather than friends, despite their proximity of age, location, and birth. Of course, her younger self had thought it unfortunate mainly because it meant fewer opportunities to see Angus. *Yes, how very unreasonable for two dissimilar personalities not to form a close friendship simply for my convenience,* she thought, hiding a smile.

"Angus was kind enough to drive me from the station," Hetta explained. "I'm afraid I forgot to tell anyone when I was coming. I can't think how I came to be so scatter-brained."

Marius's brows drew together. "That's not like you, Hetta." The delight at her arrival drained from him. "Although I suppose these are hardly usual circumstances." They shared a look, and Hetta could see the echo of her own recurring thought, the same complicated mix of emotions accompanying it: *Father is dead.*

Marius shook himself. "Anyway, thank you, Penharrow, for rescuing my sister. Would you like to come in?" This last was said with a little pause of reluctance.

Angus smiled sympathetically as he gave his refusal. "No, no. I imagine you've enough chaos in the household at the moment, and I really should be getting back."

Marius and Hetta paused to wave as he drove away and out of sight. Marius took in Hetta's trunk.

"You travel lighter than I thought you would."

She shrugged. "I manage. I left my bricks at home."

Marius heaved her trunk under an arm, and Hetta let him. Her brother didn't provoke the same desire to prove her independence as Angus, perhaps because Marius had always taken her seriously. Besides, her bedroom was up two flights of stairs. *And no doubt brotherly solicitude will wear off sooner rather than later once he gets over the novelty of my presence.*

The open, hard-tiled space of the grand entryway amplified sounds, carrying strains of voices from distant rooms, but they met no one as they made their way up the main staircase. Still, her heart pounded, as if they might turn a corner and run straight into one or other of her relatives. It was strange to think the person she dreaded meeting most was the one person she was *guaranteed* not to run into. But it was somehow impossible to convince herself he wasn't here anymore, not while walking these familiar hallways.

"Who else is here?"

"Everyone," Marius said with a sigh. "That's why I answered the door, actually. Wyn is trying to be in sixteen places at once. The footman was supposed to be manning the door for visitors, but he's in the breakfast room with Phoebe." He adjusted his grip on her trunk. "Something Aunt Sybil said about blue china and mourning aesthetics. I *may* have suggested he would be better able to aid her than I."

Hetta raised a brow at him, and he gave a sheepish smile, though it didn't reach his eyes. Poor Marius—and poor Phoebe. Their stepmother hated disapproval and tended to throw herself with frantic earnestness into the effort of avoiding it. Hetta had no doubt Phoebe's nerves would be strung tight as she tried to arrange a funeral with 'helpful' and conflicting suggestions from the rest of her relatives. It would be a losing battle; there was no way to please every single Valstar simultaneously.

"How is Phoebe holding up?" She'd never been sure how much affection her stepmother held for Father. Hetta and Marius's stepmother had married the late Lord Valstar seven years after the death of his first wife, who hadn't survived birthing Hetta. Phoebe had been very young indeed when Lord Valstar married her, at seventeen—only a handful of years older than Marius, in fact. *And younger than I am now.* Hetta wrinkled her nose. What a distasteful thought.

Marius shrugged. "Much as we all are, really." Something very dark flickered in his gaze. "Though I haven't had any hysterics over the china just yet." He didn't say the words *Everyone thinks cousin Jack is going to be chosen rather than me*, but they clamoured unspoken in the air around them nonetheless.

Hetta wanted to hug him but couldn't since he was carrying her trunk. She settled for a bright smile instead. "Well, let me know if you feel some coming on and I'll help you find the dustpan and brush."

He didn't reply as they turned towards the west wing, the intersection marked by a portrait of their deceased grandfather, Lord Marius Valstar II—her brother's namesake. Present-day Marius avoided the portrait's severe gaze.

An unpleasant thought occurred, and Hetta paused.

"My room?" She'd just assumed it would still be hers, but it *had* been years since she'd left, with not much expectation of ever returning. What if Father had decided to expunge any sign of her presence from the house?

"Oh, you're safe," Marius assured her. "Though it was a near thing. We're pretty tightly pressed for bedrooms, what with all our relatives descending upon us."

"I would've thought there were plenty of bedrooms?" Stariel House was enormous.

"Not habitable ones, there aren't." Marius began to tick off names on his fingers and then abandoned the motion since there were far more Valstars than there were digits. "Not counting those of us already in residence, there's all our aunts and uncles, every one of our first cousins, and most of our seconds."

"And Grandmamma?" Hetta would not mind unexpectedly bumping into Grandmamma in the hallway. "Is she still in the Dower House?"

Marius snorted. "No, that's got even less habitable bedrooms than this one. They shut up the Dower House last month. Grandmamma's living here now."

There was no way Hetta could've known that, given the freshness of the news. "Oh." Why had Father shut up the Dower House? Wyn, by far her most reliable correspondent, hadn't mentioned anything in his last letter, but then perhaps he hadn't known at the time. "Is Grandmamma well?"

"She'll outlast us all," Marius reassured her. He picked up on her silent question without prompting; he'd always had a knack for subtext, when he wasn't distracted by his own thoughts. "I think Father was concerned at the ongoing expense of keeping the house open." He examined his own words and frowned, as if it were the first time he'd reflected on the question. "Though I don't know why. I guess it doesn't make sense, running two households rather than just the one."

As Marius said, it *didn't* make sense, but Hetta thought of the grey, peeling fences in the village, and unease stirred. *Most likely Father's steward simply hasn't gotten around to organising the repairs yet,* she told herself. She hoped so, for the new lord's sake. Neither Jack nor Marius deserved to inherit financial woes.

They arrived at her old bedroom, and it took Hetta six years back in time. The walls were still the same pale yellow. The theatre posters and cut-outs she'd pinned up in defiance of respectability remained, the colours faded now with age. A faint smell of cleaning products tickled her nose, and she saw with relief that the linen looked freshly changed. Evidently someone had prepared for her coming despite her lack of communication.

Father didn't change anything at all in my absence. Hetta turned in a slow circle, not sure what to do with that thought. *Maybe he simply closed the door and forgot about me.*

Marius had just deposited her trunk next to the dresser when footsteps sounded in the hallway.

"Marius?" a soft voice inquired, and the door to the bedroom swung open.

There stood the eldest of their half-siblings, and Hetta stared. When had Gregory gotten so *tall*? She performed a rapid mental calculation—he must be seventeen now. Tallness was not so unreasonable, in that context, but she struggled to match her chubby little brother with the gangly youth now rocking uncertainly on the threshold. In general, the Valstars tended towards darker hair, owing to the strong dose of Noorish blood in their lineage, but Gregory had inherited his mother's curling golden locks, pale skin, and delicate features. Only his grey eyes betrayed his Valstar inheritance. As a boy, he'd been rather adorable, like a cherub. No doubt he wouldn't appreciate being referred to as such anymore. *Not that he exactly appreciated it as a boy.*

"Henrietta?" he said unsurely.

"Gregory," she said blankly. "How tall you've grown. I clearly can't keep addressing you as 'little brother' in my correspondence." Gregory now stood half a head taller than Hetta.

"I didn't think you'd come," Gregory blurted out, then flushed. "Oh—sorry, I mean, it's great to see you—" He faltered as he remembered the solemnity of the occasion. "I mean, not great, but—"

"I'm glad to see you again in person too," Hetta interjected kindly. "It's been too long. I hope we'll see more of each other while I'm here."

Gregory recovered his composure enough to ask how long she meant to stay.

"Till the Choosing, of course, brat," Marius said without venom. But he shot Hetta a sharp look nonetheless, and she realised with a start that he would like some reassurance on that point himself. Evidently Hetta had become outrageous enough that even the family member she was closest to wasn't sure whether she would be bound by this last and greatest tradition of their house. For a moment, all she could do was blink at him, unsure if she was annoyed or not by that. It had never crossed her mind that she could simply not come home on such an occasion, but if Marius thought it, then so had everyone else.

A spark of temper flared. "I'll be here for the Choosing, of course." The words came out more defiantly than she'd intended. Why did she care if her family thought her lost to all sense of familial duty?

But Marius didn't pick up on her mood, the mention of the ceremony making him grimace. "Good, good," he said vaguely. He'd gone far away, lost in his own thoughts. It was typical of him—one second intuitive, the next entirely oblivious. She still couldn't tell whether his anxiety about the Choosing Ceremony sprang from a wish to be chosen or a fear of it. Perhaps it was both.

"You're older than cousin Jack," Gregory said, as though the thought were so sudden and strange that he couldn't keep from speaking it.

"Yes." Hetta smiled at her younger brother. "He is two months my junior, though it isn't polite to remind me of it."

"That means you—" Gregory broke off, darting a look at his brother.

Marius came out of his distraction and said sharply: "Yes, Hetta goes before Jack in the ceremony. Though I hope you haven't forgotten cousin Cecily—she's even older than me." The Choosing Ceremony went according to birth order.

"And Aunt Sybil may yet rule over us all," Hetta said lightly, though that wasn't very likely. There had never been a recorded instance of Stariel choosing within the same generation as the deceased lord if the members of younger generations were of age.

Gregory gave a nervous laugh, and Hetta decided it was time for a change to a less fraught subject.

"But what did you come racing in here for, Gregory? You were looking for Marius?" she prompted.

Gregory's eyes widened. "Oh! Yes. I forgot. Grandmamma said the flowers for the casket must be grown at Stariel, but Aunt Sybil said it's more important that they're lilies, even if we have to order them from Greymark, and Grandmamma said ordering flowers from elsewhere would be bad luck for the lord's funeral, and Aunt Sybil said that was ridiculous superstition, and Grandmamma said there was nothing wrong with a little spirituality and her bones told her that lilies were bound to appear if they were wanted, and Aunt Sybil said even the most superstitious fool couldn't conjure lilies outside a hothouse in October, and so I said I would check the greenhouse, but I don't know a lily from lavender."

Marius's lips twitched at this unbroken recitation, but he shook his head. "It wouldn't matter if you did—Aunt Sybil is right. There's no lilies to be had." He said it with regret. Like Gregory, he would clearly have liked to support their often hare-brained but infinitely more sympathetic grandmother. The greenhouse was Marius's domain. Strangely, for one so deeply disinterested in farming, he had a great passion for botany.

"Oh. I guess they'll have to sort it out between them then." A heaviness crept over Gregory, as if he had suddenly remembered *why* they needed lilies. "Do you think it matters if the flowers come from Stariel or not?" It clearly mattered to Gregory, but he looked to his older brother for direction, his face still so *young*, despite the changes time had wrought.

"Well," Hetta said, taking a deep breath to hide her nerves. "There *can* be lilies from Stariel, if you want." She waggled her fingers theatrically. "Or at least, flowers from Stariel that will *appear* to be lilies." Her heart stuck in her throat as she waited for their reaction, and she formulated half a dozen defensive responses as to why she wasn't ashamed of her profession in the time it took for comprehension to dawn in her brothers' faces.

Gregory brightened. "Could you really?"

Hetta was suddenly off-balance. How did you cope with enthusiasm when you'd steeled yourself for disapproval? "Er—yes, I think so, if Marius will direct me to some appropriate stems for the base of the spell. They only need last for a few days."

Gregory practically vibrated with excitement, and she caught a glimpse of the cheerful eleven-year-old she'd known. *Oh—of course Father's denouncement of me would only make my profession more appealing to a teenage boy*, she realised with a lurch of perspective.

Marius wasn't a teenage boy, but he was also the family member most familiar with her abilities. His reaction was somewhere between consternation and amusement.

"I don't know, Hetta...illusory lilies on Father's casket..." He trailed off as she met his eyes.

"Appropriate, though, don't you think?" Gregory missed the sharp subtext, but Marius didn't. His mouth thinned. Their father had always cared more for the look of the thing than the reality below. "But he would have wanted the flowers to come from Stariel, lilies or not." That, Hetta was sure of; Father had always thought anything inside the estate infinitely superior to the rest of the world's offerings.

That darkness from earlier shadowed Marius's face again, but he covered it with a smile. "Very well, Hetta. Let's smuggle you out to the greenhouse before the others realise you're here, or the game will be up when Greg announces there are lilies aplenty."

HETTA HAD IMAGINED MANY scenarios for her return to Stariel House. None had involved illusory lilies, and she had to repress the urge to laugh as they made their way down the hallway and to the back western stairwell. Of course nothing here would be predictable. She ignored the knot of tension gathering in her stomach. Why not simply enjoy the chance to put off confronting her older relatives for a little while more—even if it was for a slightly ridiculous reason?

Gregory eagerly offered himself as a potential distraction, should they encounter any of their aunts, but his willingness wasn't put to the test. They met only a few house servants, who nodded politely as they passed but were otherwise entirely preoccupied with their own tasks. Hetta suffered a sad blow to her sense of self-importance—apparently she didn't warrant more than a flicker of mild interest, even from the servants who had been here before she'd left. *But I suppose they must be busy, given the excessive number of Valstar relatives descending upon them all at once.*

They reached the greenhouse and encountered its sole occupant, a tall, brown-skinned man with pale blond hair. He was crouched, cutting a sprig of mint, and he rose with smooth grace at the sound of their footsteps. His eyes widened slightly as Hetta followed her brothers in. In his surprise, he spoke, she thought, without regard for their presence.

"Henrietta Isadore Valstar," Wyn said, drawing the syllables out as if enjoying the sound of them. His eyes were still the same deep russet-brown of horse chestnuts, his mouth still full and shaped for humour, but everything else was…changed.

Attraction coursed through her, unexpected as a lightning bolt, and shocked Hetta temporarily mute. Wyn Tempest had come to Stariel House several years before Hetta had left home. He'd been a friend to the young, rebellious Hetta, and they'd written to each other in the intervening years—unofficially, of course; young men did not write letters to unmarried ladies to whom they were not related. But Hetta had written those letters with the mental image of a stork-like, wary youth fixed unchanging in her head, not this quietly confident man. The sharp angles that she remembered hadn't softened, but they were somehow transformed into a cut-glass, alien beauty.

How could he have changed so? *Surely* she would have noticed if Wyn had been like this before? She felt both strangely breathless and annoyed at herself for being so.

Wyn's eyes sparkled. Hetta flushed and hoped he hadn't guessed somehow what she'd been thinking.

"Do you not recognise me, Miss Hetta?" he said slowly, each word quivering with amusement. His voice had ripened too; now it made her think of plum brandy. "Allow me to reintroduce myself." He gave a little bow. "You may recall me as a stray who turned up some years ago and who has since proven difficult to dislodge."

"Of course Hetta remembers you, Wyn," Gregory said before Hetta could answer. "What are you doing in the greenhouse?"

Wyn waved the green mint leaves he'd just cut. "Mint-and-berry friands." His eyes met Hetta's. "I'm Acting Assistant Head

Cook at this precise moment," he told her solemnly. "Although it is not my usual role. One of the maidservants is ill."

"I know that!" *I've been exchanging letters with you for years*, she nearly said but managed to snap the words off. She didn't care what people thought of her reputation, but she didn't want to get Wyn in trouble.

Wyn beamed. "So you *do* know who I am! I did not like to assume, Miss Hetta. You looked very surprised just now." His eyes gleamed. He *had* guessed what she'd been thinking. Curse him. She narrowed her eyes at him, in part for that and in part for all the 'Miss Hetta'-ing.

He didn't seem at all repentant as he bowed and excused himself, leaving Hetta alone with her brothers in the greenhouse. Hetta stared thoughtfully after him. *That's two unreasonably attractive men in the space of half an hour*, she thought distantly. *Goodness knows what the next two weeks will bring, if that's a representative sample of the populace now.*

She was recalled by Gregory, who shifted from foot to foot with anticipation.

"Are you going to illuse the lilies or not?"

3

LILIES AND STARFLOWERS

"What would be best for the base, Marius?" Hetta asked, looking around the greenhouse.

Marius considered her request with quiet abstraction, the tight line of his shoulders relaxing slightly. Hetta could imagine him alone here, happily absorbed in recording the growth rates of peas or some such thing, the only sound the gentle creak of the weather against the walls. As if on cue, it began to rain again, and the greenhouse became a cocoon beneath the gentle patter.

Gregory made an impatient noise and Hetta shushed him. She understood that there was significance in this choice, this secret. No one had asked Marius, the botanist, what flowers should go on Father's casket.

Eventually he shook his head. "Not in here."

The rain hung as a fine mist in the air as he beckoned them out of the greenhouse, through the barren flower-beds, now dark and wet, towards the Home Wood. He roved, searching for something, and eventually gave a cry of triumph and swooped down upon a stunted bush. He rose to show them his choice. They were large trumpet-shaped flowers with soft white petals and blue inners, a variety native to Stariel.

"Starflowers," Hetta said.

"Yes." Marius turned one in his palm, expression closed.

"Of course," said Gregory. "Why didn't the two of them think of that?"

"I expect Grandmamma would approve," Hetta said warmly, since Marius seemed too lost in thought to reassure Gregory. Hetta took the damp flowers from him. "Let's go back to the greenhouse." The fine drizzle had probably fluffed her hair out to approximately three times its normal volume already. Would it be shallow to illuse it to look sleeker before she went back into the house?

Illusion had become, if not mundane, at least everyday for Hetta. For Gregory and Marius, it was an altogether different case. Technomancy might be acceptable hidden away in kineticars or in the new elektric lights, but one did not dirty one's own hands practising it openly as a trade if one belonged to the higher classes. In Meridon, society's attitude was slowly changing, but in the isolated North, they still held to their prejudices. The magic of Stariel Estate was a rare exception, made dignified by tradition, and even that was still mainly considered the private business of Stariel's lord. Illusory magic, with no purpose other than to entertain and with its strong association with the theatre houses, dens of promiscuity, and loose morals—well, could there be a more unsuitable occupation for a well-born woman? Hetta had quite enjoyed the loose morals of the Meridon theatre scene, but she had no intention of bringing *that* up in front of her brothers.

Once back within the shelter of the greenhouse's glass walls, she began to craft the illusion. This was a simple enough piece of magic, but there was some added complexity in making the illusion strong enough to last for several days. Most illusionists were limited to casting illusions in the then-and-now; tying off an illusion and giving it enough power to sustain itself when she stopped actively pouring energy into it was part of what gave Hetta her mastery. The lilies would have no scent, or at least only the scent of the starflowers, but hopefully no one would notice or think to check them for illusion. But Hetta wasn't truly worried about the latter. Who would be rude enough to scrutinise funereal flower arrangements through a quizzing glass?

Gregory gasped as Hetta traced her fingers along the starflowers' petals, weaving light in their wake. *They've never seen a master like me*, she thought with professional pride. Travelling fairs and local theatres often included minor illusionists, and even members of the upper classes dabbled in it—for light entertainment between friends, not for a living, of course; *that* would be beneath them—but Hetta had proper training and, just as importantly, *talent*. With untrained illusionists or those of lesser ability, one didn't even need a quizzing glass to be able to tell it wasn't real. But when Hetta had finished with the starflowers, the only way to tell they weren't true lilies was by feeling carefully along the starflowers underneath and noticing the difference in tactility where the fake petals extended slightly past the real ones. Illusion was only light and heat; there was no solidity to it.

She held out the bunch of lilies to Gregory, who examined them in mute awe.

"You can take them in ahead of us. It's probably best if my reappearance doesn't coincide with the 'lilies' if we don't want to give anyone a reason to doubt them."

Gregory grinned. "I won't give the game away; never fear!" He set off, a bounce in his step that hadn't been present before.

It began to drizzle again, the sky a leaden grey. Marius and

Hetta waited in the greenhouse, the silence full of unsaid things. Marius absently traced the edge of a tray of seedlings.

Eventually Hetta said: "I hope Gregory doesn't resent me for my absence."

Marius cocked his head. "If he has, perhaps your presence now will make up for it."

"Are we still speaking of Gregory?"

Marius sighed and ran a hand through his hair. His damp black locks grew increasingly dishevelled, giving him the appearance of a slightly rakish scholar. "I don't begrudge you your escape, Hetta," he said eventually. "The gods only know I'd have been off like a shot if I thought I could manage it."

"It's not my fault you didn't have the chance." They both knew that Hetta being female and younger had made their father able to wash his hands of her when she'd rebelled. The same was not so for Marius, despite Lord Valstar's preference for his nephew over his eldest son. If Marius had announced his intention to pursue some other profession far away, he'd have been brought swiftly to heel.

"I know," he said quietly. He gazed towards the house through the murky walls of the greenhouse. "Are you ready?"

"I have to face them sometime, don't I?"

He grinned. "Unless you plan to sleep out here, yes."

AN AMBUSH AWAITED THEM in the red drawing room. But it could've been worse—it could have contained, oh, thirty relatives rather than merely four: her stepmother Lady Phoebe, Aunt Sybil, and Hetta's two younger half-sisters. The illusory lilies rested in a vase on a side table, but of Gregory there was no sign.

Hetta checked an urge to turn away on the threshold. The room's occupants reacted to her presence with variations of surprise, delight, and disapproval. This last was mainly from Aunt Sybil. She sniffed like a wet dog, as if she resented being unable to lament Hetta's impropriety at not coming home for her father's funeral.

"Henrietta!" Lady Phoebe exclaimed, rising. Time had made her look younger, somehow. She had the appearance of a porcelain doll, with large blue eyes, slightly too widely set, and flaxen ringlets arranged in a neat coiffure. Her hands moved restlessly, like small birds. "You came! You must have got the telegram!"

"Of course she got the telegram," Aunt Sybil said snidely. "What else would bring her here?" She was a tall woman, and her mourning gown and rigid seat on the chesterfield gave her the look of a bad-tempered crow.

Hetta deplored statements of the obvious, but her sympathies immediately went to her stepmother. As a child, Hetta had been unimpressed when her father remarried, but she had more appreciation for her stepmother now. Lady Phoebe had written punctiliously every quarter for the six years she'd been gone, long missives full of small details about her siblings, the names of the latest litter of kittens, and gossip from dinner parties with local gentry. Hetta was sure Father hadn't known about the letters.

"Yes, I did, Phoebe. I'm glad to see you again, although sorry it's under such circumstances." She made a brief nod in Aunt Sybil's direction. "Good morning, Aunt Sybil." She smiled at her two youngest siblings. "And Alexandra and Laurel, although you probably don't remember me very well."

Her half-sister Alexandra blushed, tongue-tied. She was fifteen years old and had also undergone the same disconcerting transition from child to adult as Gregory in Hetta's absence. She had her mother's golden hair, delicate features, and wide blue eyes.

She'd apparently also inherited her mother's indecisive disposition, as she glanced sideways at Lady Phoebe for guidance.

"You sent us the puppets for Wintersol last year," little Laurel said, taking in the details of Hetta's appearance. She was still a child, at least, but no longer the toddler Hetta remembered. "The fairy ones."

"Yes," said Hetta. Then, because something in Laurel reminded her of herself, she added, "They were from a play they ran at the Sun Theatre, where I have lately been working."

Laurel's eyes rounded. "You work at the theatre?"

"Yes," said Hetta, in defiance of Aunt Sybil's growing displeasure. Phoebe made a faint gesture as if to encourage Hetta to retract her words. From the corner of her eye she could see that Marius looked faintly amused, but he remained silent to avoid attracting Aunt Sybil's ire. Traitor. "I'm the illusionist for the troupe." She said the words with exactly the cool confidence she'd wanted, and it hit her then: *they have no power over me.*

She'd repeated the mantra so often that it was a shock to find this was the first time she'd truly believed it. A curious lightness filled her as Aunt Sybil glowered and Lady Phoebe grew flustered. *My father is dead, and my family have no power over me. They cannot trap me here.*

After the funeral and the Choosing, she would leave, back to her own life. She was dependent on her family for neither shelter nor occupation nor affection now; she'd built those things for herself, and her family had no ability to threaten her by withholding them. *And not all of them feel as Aunt Sybil does*, she thought, remembering Gregory's bright eyes and watching her younger sisters, who looked torn between curiosity and the instinct that they ought to share their elders' displeasure. *Perhaps Father's passing is a chance at a new start for all of us.*

All this ran through her between one breath and the next, and

Hetta marvelled that her epiphany wasn't obvious to the entire room. She felt as if the entire world had shifted, rearranging into a new and brighter shape.

Taking pity on Aunt Sybil, she eased the conversation away from her profession. She could afford to be magnanimous. After all, in two weeks she would be gone.

4

THE FUNERAL

THE DAY OF the funeral dawned dark and oppressive as Hetta's family assembled into a loose battalion and descended upon the village of Stariel-upon-Starwater. The funeral itself had been planned to an inch, directed mainly by Aunt Sybil, with Lady Phoebe anxiously carrying out her orders. Grandmamma bobbed above it all, although her usual serenity had taken on a sombre edge. Marius looked close to developing a nervous tic.

As they made their way to the temple, Hetta found herself searching for her cousin Jack. His flame-red locks made him easy to pick out of the crowd of grey-eyed, dark-haired relatives taking up half of the small building. Hetta had seen very little of him since her arrival, as he'd spent most of it out of doors. Jack had probably the strongest land-sense of all the Valstars, and he was probably one of the few genuinely grieving her father's death. It wasn't inconceivable that he might seek solace in Stariel. And, a cynical part of Hetta couldn't help thinking, he probably thought it would increase his chances of being chosen.

The temple was full to overflowing with those who'd come to see her father into the next world. All the surrounding gentry had put in appearances, along with most of the preeminent tradespeople of Stariel-on-Starwater. Angus and his sisters nodded solemnly to Hetta as she took her place in the front pew, reserved for Lord Valstar's children and widow.

Hetta tried to feel something as the druid spoke, but she found her attention so fixed on the great black coffin at the front of the temple that she couldn't afterwards recall what he said. The illusory lilies looked perfect, cool and white against the dark wood. She focused her magesight and the lilies became ghosts, showing the simple starflowers beneath. How odd, was the thought that kept swimming through her mind. How odd that her father was in that box, to go into the ground, to never stir again. She tried to summon tears, but they didn't come.

Marius cried, of course. Hetta had known he would. It didn't truly speak to the depth of his sentiment; he would've cried equally at a stranger's funeral. Jack didn't cry, although his expression was stiff, as if he were wound too tightly for tears. Lady Phoebe wept, along with her three children, even Gregory. Aunt Sybil dabbed at her eyes, her expression severe and daring anyone to comment. Most of Hetta's cousins remained dry-eyed, though their faces were solemn. The children were fractious and sullen, not quite able to absorb the full seriousness of the occasion.

Hetta concentrated on keeping an appropriately sober expression as she struggled with a mix of emotions she couldn't readily identify. Was this grief? Her father was dead, and now they would never reconcile. And yet, she'd never thought they *would* reconcile. Her father's death hadn't changed anything on that count at all, and there was a guilty relief in knowing she didn't have to be weighed down by his disapproval anymore.

The service took forever, with the line of condolences from the other attendees stretching into infinity. Hetta kept her countenance through sheer force of will, determined that no one would know that she wanted to flee into the hills.

The storm had not yet broken as they lowered the coffin into the damp earth, but the wind was rising. The mourners gripped their coats firmly about themselves as the icy wind stole fingers inside buttons and under scarves, trailing cold caresses. A gust swept off little Laurel's hat and carried it up to catch on the branches of one of the graveyard's trees. Aunt Sybil's hissed scold at her carelessness sounded unnaturally loud.

Stariel took its former lord back with such a lack of ceremony that it hardly seemed like magic at all when the grave simply drew closed over the coffin. Hetta stared at the spot where the earth had moved for a long moment, reaching out to Stariel with her land-sense—as she was sure every Valstar was doing at that moment. Stariel wasn't truly capable of human emotions—it was too large and too enduring for such things—but Hetta thought she detected something akin to loss.

The wake withered into the afternoon. Angus made a point of seeking her out, but she was by that point so occupied with maintaining her façade that she barely took in his words. His expression creased towards concern as Hetta excused herself. The impending doom promised by the weather made everyone eager to take their leave early, and it wasn't yet three o'clock when the Valstars saw the last of them off and were free to return to the house.

No one spoke much on the drive back. Hetta shared a horse-drawn carriage with her cousin Jack and her two half-sisters. Lady Phoebe had been so much overcome that Marius had awkwardly taken her in hand, and he and Gregory had bundled her and Aunt Sybil into Father's recently purchased kineticar. Hetta was guiltily grateful not to have to deal with her stepmother's nerves. The rest of their relatives were, thankfully, not Hetta's problem to transport. From what she saw, Wyn had the logistics well under control.

She slipped out of the house almost as soon as they arrived, still unsure what she was feeling, and wandered into the gardens. The last flowers of summer had long since been clipped away, and no gardeners disturbed her solitude as she made her way down to the edges of Starwater. Today the rising wind had stirred the waters of the great lake, and it reflected the mood of the sky above. Thunderclouds gathered in the distance, and between the dark waters and the browning bracken of the surrounding hills, the world was painted in shades of purple.

Henry Valstar, head of the great Valstar family, Lord of Stariel, Defender of Starwater, First of His Name, Father of Marius, Henrietta, Gregory, Alexandra, and Laurel, was dead. This fact finally hit Hetta, with a kind of curious physicality, knocking the air from her lungs.

A memory stirred for the first time in years: large hands helping her onto the back of her first pony. Horsemanship was one of the only activities in which Hetta both excelled and of which her father approved. She remembered his gruff pride when she'd shown no fear of large horsey teeth, and how he'd described her as 'pluck to the backbone'. It was one of the few uncomplicated memories she had of her father. She hadn't allowed herself to recall it for years.

She sighed, expelling tension along with air. Enough brooding. She turned away from the dark waters and made her way back to the house. More time had passed with her contemplating Starwater than she'd realised. In the deepening gloom, she caught a flash of moon-white hair on the uppermost turret of the house: Wyn. As she drew closer, she picked out more than one figure and identified Marius and her cousin Jack as well. She frowned. What were they doing up there? Marius spotted her and waved, inviting her to join them.

5

WINE AND THUNDER

FULL DARK HAD fallen by the time she climbed the stairs up the highest of Stariel's three towers. As she neared the door at the top, she heard low voices. On a still night, voices carried in the outside air, but tonight the wind was enough to muffle the words into meaninglessness.

She emerged to find Marius, Wyn, and her cousin Jack sprawled against the tower wall, each clutching a large mug. Several bottles of wine lay between them. Marius gave her a silent salute, and the three of them shuffled to make space. Wyn handed her a fourth mug.

"Yes, please," she said with a sigh as Wyn held up the bottle and raised an eyebrow. He filled her mug with a hand that was perfectly steady, although he apparently needed to focus rather intently on the task. His hand brushed hers as he handed it over and their eyes met. She blushed. She hadn't spoken to him since that encounter in the greenhouse—easy enough to justify in the chaos of the funeral arrangements, but still smacking of cowardice. He *was* still her friend, wasn't he, regardless of this new and disconcerting pull of attraction?

"How did you all escape?" Hetta asked, since it was clear enough why they were here. The four of them together drinking on the highest tower woke memories of the years before she'd left. They were an odd combination, but they had also been four teenagers of similar ages living in the same house, miles from anywhere.

Marius shrugged. "Most of our lot are camped out in the hall." 'Our lot' being the older set of cousins. "The girls are in bed. Phoebe took to hers with a headache. I left before Aunt Sybil could corner me." He shot a sideways glance at his cousin to see how he took this slight on his mother.

Jack laughed and clonked his glass against Marius's. "And I said I was off for a drink. They assumed I meant the village pub. But I met Marius at the door to the wine cellar, and it seemed the best idea was to slink up here where we wouldn't be heard."

"And you?" Hetta turned to Wyn, amused. He'd dropped much of the formal manner he adopted around the older members of the family or the other servants, which pleased her.

He gave a wry smile. "I'm off duty now, so I have no thrilling tales of avoidance to tell you." His russet eyes glinted in amusement, deep and almost black in the dusk. "But I also possess the key to the wine cellar."

"You're an excellent fellow," Jack agreed, patting Wyn's shoulder. He wasn't intoxicated, but it was clear he'd drunk enough to make him affably expansive to all men. It was one of the things Hetta liked about Jack when compared to her father. Lord Valstar was a mean drunk.

Hetta laughed. "Are we pilfering from the stores, then? It almost makes me feel sixteen again." She drank deeply, and her eyes widened. "Don't tell me you commandeered the Millyard?" She peered into the ruby liquid with reverence.

"Seemed the occasion for it," Marius said.

"Uncle would've appreciated it," Jack said, grief sliding over his face, the flicker of a fish surfacing briefly.

Hetta considered this. "You're probably right. He would hardly want to be associated with an inferior beverage."

"Besides," said Marius, "the wine'll belong to one of us soon enough." He gestured between himself and Jack, and Jack gave an awkward grin.

Oh, Marius. She knew her brother was merely using the wine as an excuse to speak the thought that must have been burning in him for years, and never more so than tonight. He would make peace with it, eventually, if he wasn't chosen, but he couldn't do that until the matter was settled one way or the other.

"Where's Gregory?" Hetta suddenly remembered that she had another brother to account for. But he hadn't been of appropriate drinking age when she'd left home. "You said the children had gone to bed, but surely that doesn't include him, unless he's a very different seventeen-year-old to the ones I am familiar with." And he should be here, part of this smaller, more intimate subset of the vast Valstar family.

Jack shrugged. "No idea."

Marius frowned. "He must have snuck out as well. He wasn't down with the others, and he wasn't in his room when I went past before. I've wondered lately if he's hiding something."

Jack clapped Marius on the shoulder.

"Probably a lass from the village." He didn't seem to think there was anything to be concerned about in Gregory's absence.

Marius was unconvinced. "Not on the night of his father's funeral, surely?"

Jack grew a tad defensive. "Nothing more natural—might have wanted consoling."

"I think he would have mentioned a 'lass from the village', as you call it."

But Jack shook his head. "That age, the last thing a man wants is his brother interfering with his affairs."

They suddenly remembered Hetta's presence. Both turned to her, twin abashed expressions awakening a scrap of family resemblance between them. They did not ordinarily look much alike: Jack was stocky and solid as a mastiff; Marius had Father's gaunt good looks mixed with a greyhound nervousness all his own.

"Begging your pardon, Hetta," Jack said after a beat. "It's not the sort of thing to speak of in front of a lady."

"Yes, because I'm *such* a lady. Please don't treat me like an innocent," Hetta said, amused but also irked. "The possibility of Gregory flirting with one of the village girls neither surprises nor distresses me." For a second, she fought the overwhelming temptation to shock them with a few pithy words concerning the breadth of her own experience, but she resisted with an effort. Like Gregory, she didn't want her relatives to either know of or interfere with her affairs. "I'll admit to sharing Marius's doubts about the timing, but it seems excessive to send out a search party. He's grown enough to dictate his own movements, I suppose."

Jack looked surprised and gave a short laugh. "You're the first female I've heard say as much."

Hetta took this as more of a reflection on his mother and older sister than on womankind in general and chose not to be offended.

"Well," Wyn said out of the silence that had fallen. "It seems a timely moment to bring out these." With that, he rummaged for a tin lying beside him and offered the contents around, revealing half a dozen cheese scones. He looked at them a little sadly. "They'd be better warm." He turned mournful eyes to Hetta.

She gave him a long, steady look. What game was he playing here? But she took the tin from him and focused her will. As a stage illusionist, she more often had call for fake fire than the real kind, but that wasn't her only gift. Pyromancy was a rare talent, frequently confused with the much more common technomancy, which worked on quite different principles of energy transfer but could produce superficially similar results. Hetta had no technomancy, which she'd often thought was a pity, because it was quite a lucrative profession nowadays, powering everything from boilers to kineticars. Hetta couldn't store energy for later use, like a technomancer could do with the right materials, but she could do basic in-the-moment heating spells. She let the barest flicker of fire pass through her, heating the tin, and cradled it in her hands, welcoming the warmth. Then she shook her head at her own foolishness, put the tin aside, and summoned a ball of flame to spin in her palm. She couldn't put it down, lest it turn to real fire and she lose control over it, but it produced heat quite nicely. She thought wistfully of cold nights spent talking to Bradfield, the theatre director, on the roof of the Sun Theatre.

"Are you sure you don't have any technomancy?" Wyn said, though the question was a rhetorical one as he knew very well she didn't. He gave a theatrical sigh. "The boilerstones weren't charged properly last time they came back from the apprentice we use. He'll be a long time earning his mastery at such a rate. It seems a shame to have a trained master in the house and not be able to make use of her."

Was he deliberately reminding the others of Hetta's achievements? Master wasn't a rank conferred on just any mage. She wasn't sure if it would work or if Jack would share too much of her father's disapproval. Still, she responded in the same light tone Wyn had adopted.

"Sadly, no. Fire and illusion are my twin gifts. Which I'm thankful for at this moment, for I've no desire to be bullied into fixing household appliances for you, scoundrel!"

After a few slow blinks, Jack shrugged and held out his hands towards the ball of flame, letting it warm his fingers. "This is still fair useful."

"If only we'd had this when the main chimney cracked last year,"

Marius agreed. "On Wintersol, no less, and snow everywhere. We had to wear ten layers just to open the presents, and we couldn't get it fixed for over a week."

"And it cost an arm and a leg," Jack muttered darkly. Hetta wondered how he knew that. It said a great deal about his access to the estate's accounts. Marius didn't react to the remark, but then it wouldn't exactly surprise him that Father had been preparing Jack to take over management of the estate.

"Do you remember that ancient monstrosity of a dressing gown Grandmamma wore?" Marius said.

The talk turned to pleasant reminiscences, occasionally sliced with thin moments of poignancy, as the late Lord Henry could hardly fail to make an appearance in these. Like Stariel itself, life here revolved around the lord. Hetta listened with something between pain and resignation. She didn't regret her choices, but she felt excluded nonetheless.

Wyn met her eyes and his expression warmed. "Do you remember, Hetta, when you had me serve tea in a dress because I lost a wager to you?"

A slow smiled dawned as she dredged up the memory of a younger Wyn unloading a tea tray with immense dignity. "You looked well in it, if I recall correctly."

Marius overheard the comment and interjected. "I don't remember that." He considered Wyn narrowly. "And I'm fairly certain I would." Even leaning against the tower wall and casually holding a wine-filled mug, Wyn still retained a slight air of neatly pressed butleriness. It had to be some innate feature of waistcoats and starch, because the Wyn she'd known had never been particularly concerned with propriety, at his core.

"No, for I took pity on him and swore Phoebe to secrecy. She thought it a very good joke. But I confess I never expected Wyn to go through with it!" Unspoken had gone the knowledge that her father wouldn't have thought it so, and Hetta wouldn't have put her friend in danger of dismissal over such a small thing.

"How could you think so little of my honour?" Wyn mimed taking a blow to the heart. His remark had turned the conversation to childhood pranks, and Hetta was suddenly a part of things again. She stared at Wyn a moment, wondering if that had been his intention all along.

The third bottle of wine was getting low and all the scones had been eaten when the storm finally rolled over Stariel. They had barely ten seconds' warning between the first ominous rumble of thunder and the sudden deluge. The shrieks they made as the cold rain hit were less indignant than they would've been three bottles prior, but nonetheless they all scrambled for the door to the stairwell. Wyn and Hetta between them scooped up the bottles and mugs—it hadn't occurred to either Marius or Jack that they would need to do so. But Wyn was, technically, a servant, and Hetta had long since been accustomed to waiting on herself.

Spluttering and half-drenched, the four of them began to laugh in the darkened stairwell. Hetta didn't know why it was so funny, but the mood infected them all, and they laughed until they were wobbling against the walls and gasping for breath.

The laughter ebbed, leaving them still squashed in the dark atop the tallest tower. Marius began to fumble for a sconce, but Hetta summoned a ball of light before they could all break their necks. Stariel House hadn't yet had the new elektric wiring installed. The magelight managed to stay impressively steady despite Hetta's inner ear insisting the world was swaying gently. Being the illusionist to a theatre troupe gave one a lot of practice at certain skill sets, though she couldn't reliably cast anything more complicated than illumination under the influence, not if she wanted to convince anyone. Hetta gave a little burble of laughter, remembering some of her more amusing failures.

"Handy, that," Jack remarked, blinking up at the magelight. It threw his face into sharp relief, draining him of colour. Hetta realised she'd cast this time without worrying at all about her audience's reaction, the first time she'd done so at Stariel since her return. The thought warmed her all the way through.

They descended, the tower creaking around them as the weather beat against the stone. The short dash across the courtyard threatened to burst her wine-given bubble of happy numbness, but they stumbled into the house before the cold could truly penetrate. The house was much warmer than the tower had been, and the heat buoyed her up again, even as she ran a hand ruefully through her damp hair.

"Suppose it's time to seek our beds," Marius said, a wisp of regret in his tone. Jack's answering grin was almost a grimace. Darkness and wine had brought camaraderie and nostalgia, but they all knew it would dissipate in the light of day, leaving awkwardness in its place.

"Happen so," Wyn agreed. He held up the wine bottles. "I'll just take this lot down to the kitchen and make it right."

They bade each other good night, and Jack and Marius disappeared into the main part of the house after securing candles for themselves.

"I'll help you," Hetta said, waving the mugs she'd retrieved.

"I appreciate it." Wyn's tone was oddly formal.

They didn't speak as they made their way down to the kitchens. Outside the storm rumbled against the house, but here the world extended no farther than the silvery light. Hetta couldn't make out Wyn's expression in the gloom, and he'd become a creature of strange angles and shadows, his pale hair the most visible part of him.

They reached the kitchen, and Hetta allowed the ball of light to grow and lift towards the ceiling, throwing the room into sudden relief. She put the mugs down on the bench. Wyn didn't look at her, moving rapidly around the room, washing the bottles and storing them, rinsing the mugs out with swift movements. Hetta took them from him with one hand, reaching for a tea towel with the other. Her fingertips brushed his skin, and little quivers of awareness hummed through her, disproportionate to the touch.

"I am glad you are here," Wyn said lightly, his tone at odds with the tension in his body. "We should finish our match in person while we have the opportunity."

"You want to triumph over me in person, you mean," Hetta replied, prodding him sharply in the shoulder.

He smiled mischievously, and all at once Hetta saw in him the young Wyn she'd left behind. "It is, perhaps, a mite more satisfying. You take defeat so very gracefully in writing."

They'd played chess for years via letters. It wasn't Hetta's preferred game—her temperament was more inclined towards cards—but chess was better suited to play at a distance from one's partner. Wyn also had a fondness for the game that he could only rarely indulge with the regular inhabitants of Stariel House. Many of the inhabitants were perfectly willing to play with him, but although he had near-bottomless patience for the unskilled but willing, Hetta knew that he found such games unfulfilling. Marius was probably the most skilled chess player of the usually resident Valstars, but he was prone to putting extreme pressure on himself to perform well, making the exercise a stressful rather than enjoyable one.

Hetta wasn't her brother and could play with both reasonable skill and cheerful emotional detachment. This was fortunate, since she lost far more often than she won.

"You'll find I am just as graceful in person, in both victory and defeat. But it's bad form to presume your triumph is a foregone conclusion."

"Arrogant, isn't it?" Wyn agreed in the mild tone he used when he was being deliberately provoking. He shook his head and added,

"A serious character flaw. It would be much better for a man's character if his chess partners did not lose quite so frequently."

She flicked a tea towel at him. "I thought you were practising servility while I was away? Aren't you head of staff now?"

"Yes, Miss Hetta." His russet eyes gleamed.

The wine had made her just light-headed enough to resort to childish retaliation for the formal address. Besides, part of her wanted to reassure herself once more that this prim butler act really was only skin deep. How long could you play a role before it stopped being one? When did illusion become reality? She shook her head at her muddled thoughts.

Wyn's hair had been mussed every which way by the wind, a hint of wildness at odds with the rest of his appearance. She reached up to tug at it, and he laughed and let her, leaning down obligingly.

"You are impossible," she told him.

"Are you petting me, Miss Hetta?" His eyes looked nearly black in the low lighting. "Is that what current manners dictate must be done in Meridon?" He lifted one long-fingered hand and patted her gently on the head, as if she were a dog. "There, there. Gooood Hetta." His own slight intoxication showed in his overly precise enunciation.

Hetta began to giggle at the utter silliness of the situation, and her laughter set Wyn off. It felt remarkably good, like something unknotting.

"Oh, I've missed you, foolish one."

They grinned at each other. Hetta became aware, all at once, of how close they were standing and of the fact that her hand was resting on Wyn's shoulder. She sucked in a breath. If she went up on tip-toe...

There was a clatter from the stairs leading down into the kitchen, and they sprang apart. The noise came from Marius, who entered with a complaint.

"Where do I find the water jug? I'm parched, and I'll be damned if I can find the one in my room."

"Ah—here," Wyn said, his voice not faltering. He moved to fill a glass for Marius.

Marius abruptly frowned around at them. "What's going on?"

Hetta answered him smoothly. "I just came to help Wyn put the mugs back—remember?" She raised an eyebrow at him. "You've grown worse at handling your liquor, if you can't recall things I told you not five minutes ago."

This slight briefly distracted him, and he grinned. "Unfair aspersion. I'm only slightly touched, and I do remember." His grin faded, and he looked between the two of them again, suspicion returning as he read some invisible current between Hetta and Wyn. "You should go to bed now, though."

Hetta wasn't sure whether to be amused or annoyed at this sudden brotherly concern. "Heavens! I'm not five. But if it makes you feel better, I'll take my leave now." She did so, only fleetingly meeting Wyn's gaze as she said lightly, "I'll see you both tomorrow."

As she mounted the staircase towards her bedroom, she inwardly muttered a curse towards interfering relatives in general and older brothers in particular.

6

GRANDMAMMA'S REMEDY

HETTA WOKE WITH an aching head and a feeling of reluctant gratitude towards her oldest brother. She'd been in a strange mood last night, after the funeral, and who knew what foolishness she might have committed if Marius hadn't interrupted.

Her skull screamed in protest at the transition from horizontal to vertical but slowly subsided into a sullen mutter as she sat on the edge of the bed, contemplating her toes. The floor was pleasantly warm—a pipeline of the central heating system ran under her bedroom. She was glad no one else had realised this and claimed it in her absence. It might be smaller than most of the other chambers, but toasty feet were not to be sniffed at.

Her thoughts kept turning towards Wyn as she got out of bed and chose her dress for the day. It was still disconcerting to realise that she found him attractive. She felt almost indignant. How unreasonable of him to change so while she'd been gone! But more importantly, she wondered, was this new awareness one-sided, or had he too felt that charge between them last night?

Usually Hetta took a rather carefree approach to both flirting and the various enjoyable activities it could lead to, but Wyn was one of her oldest friends. That wasn't something to jeopardise on a whim. *Especially if it turns out to be a one-sided whim*, she thought wryly. Besides, she would be gone from here in only a few days. It would be better to ignore any new impulses in Wyn's direction if she didn't want to complicate matters between them.

Decision made, she fortified herself with a few swallows from the glass of water she'd had the forethought to place on her bedside table the night before and began to dress. She chose a long-sleeved dress with a high, asymmetric collar. She hadn't worn trousers since her return to Stariel. It would cause a stir when she did, since the fashion didn't seem to have spread here yet, but she'd decided it was best not to provoke Aunt Sybil until after the Choosing. Her aunt would be looking for things to criticise until she was sure her son Jack had safely inherited.

The house was bright as Hetta made her way down to breakfast, the storm having passed over in the night. She met no one until she rounded a corner into the east wing and her youngest half-sister dashed past her with a plea: "Don't tell Willow I went this way!" followed thirty seconds later by cousin Willow barrelling into sight, demanding: "Have you seen Laurel? We're playing hide-and-seek." Hetta loyally disavowed all knowledge and continued.

She was smiling as she found her way to the breakfast room, where she encountered Wyn in the corridor just outside, ferrying breakfast dishes. He must be filling in for the sick maidservant again. It was still strange to think of Wyn occupying the position he did at Stariel. Surely he was too young and too irreverent to be head of staff? *He is older than you, though. And far more tactful*, she was forced to admit.

And yet the strangeness wasn't so much because of his position but because Hetta had always had trouble thinking of Wyn as a servant at all. She wasn't the only one. The Valstars had long treated Wyn as occupying a category entirely of his own making, practically ever since he had turned up on their doorstep ten years ago and Lord Henry, with uncharacteristic generosity, had accepted him into the household with no explanation other than that the boy should prove useful. Wyn had never provided any further illumination on the subject, despite Hetta's pestering; he could be maddeningly stubborn about his secrets.

"How's your head?" He looked far too lively for someone who'd imbibed the better part of a bottle of wine the night before. She tried to read his expression for some hint of awkwardness, but there was none to be found. Last night had apparently altered nothing between them, for him. It was unreasonable to be annoyed by this, Hetta told herself sternly, even as she suppressed an urge to glower.

"It's been better," she admitted.

"There's a bottle of Lady Philomena's remedy on the sideboard." He smiled. "You are not the only one so affected." Grandmamma's favoured tonic was a surprisingly effective cure for hangovers, though Hetta couldn't help wishing for the strong coffee she would usually have sought out back in Meridon.

"I'd wager you put it there before you went to bed last night, infernally organised creature."

His eyes were wide and innocent. "I try." He bowed slightly.

"Oh, go away and be smug somewhere else," she told him. He grinned and swept away with his tray.

Gregory appeared at breakfast looking wan but cheerful and promptly had a mild spat with his sister Alexandra over the allocation of blueberry muffins. None of the assorted aunts, uncles, or the newly widowed Lady Phoebe showed, to no one's surprise, since they tended to take advantage of their age and status within the family to command breakfast trays in their rooms. Only a handful of the Valstar cousins had made it down, since they were not, for the most part, a generation of early risers.

Hetta sat down next to Gregory and tried to draw him out. "You missed a rather good bottle of wine on the top tower last night," she told him in a low voice.

His eyes widened, and conflicting emotions flickered in his expression. Hetta read him easily enough: gratitude that she thought him adult enough to include; annoyance that his absence hadn't gone unremarked.

She smiled. "Don't worry, little brother. I'm not going to pry. Your movements are quite your own affair. But you should at least reassure Marius that you don't intend to wander over a cliff in the dark; he worries about you, and he's more sensitive than usual just now."

They both looked across the table at the subject of this remark. Marius wasn't a morning person and frequently didn't make it to breakfast at all. As it was, he didn't appear to have slept well; his hair was even more dishevelled than usual as he sat, wholly engrossed in reading the morning's newspaper, his glasses resting on the bridge of his nose. One hand was held inattentively in mid-air, supporting a teacup at an angle that threatened to spill at any moment. Hetta was certain it contained a good dose of Grandmamma's remedy.

"I'm not about to off myself," Gregory said scornfully, although still in a quiet tone that wouldn't be overheard. "In fact—" But he blushed, and Hetta surmised that Jack's guess as to his activities last night might have some truth in it.

"Just so," she said to spare him further embarrassment. "Well, I'm glad to hear it." She gently turned the conversation to other things, asking him if he rode—which he did—and suggesting that he might help her reacquaint herself with the riding paths of Stariel while she was here. "Though I've no mount, of course. I don't suppose you'd know if there are any appropriate beasts in the stables I might commandeer?"

Gregory began at once to enumerate the various horses' qualities.

He discarded Lady Phoebe's mount outright as being entirely without any merit—her ladyship was a nervous horsewoman—but surprised her by saying thoughtfully that perhaps Alexandra's spare mount would suit. Hetta had assumed that the daughter who bore the most physical resemblance to Lady Phoebe would also share her mother's general nervousness towards animals.

"Alexandra is a keen rider, then?" How did she know so little about her younger siblings' preferences? When had they changed from children into, well, not quite adults, but not children either? Even little Laurel, who *was* still a child, had changed out of all recognition. Last time Hetta had been home, Laurel hadn't been capable of navigating foodstuffs unsupervised; now she calmly piled her plate high with kippers as if daring someone to stop her.

"Oh gods, yes," Gregory said, recalling Hetta from her wool-gathering. "Alex!" This last was addressed to his sister, who was pouring herself tea from the side table. She looked up. Her gold hair hung in a long braid down her back, making her look younger than her fifteen years.

"You shouldn't shout across the room at me, Gregory. It's vulgar."

"Well, you shouldn't have answered me then," Gregory said irrepressibly. "And a fine thing for you to tell me it's vulgar when you—"

Hetta interrupted him to avoid the inevitable disintegration into sibling rivalry. "Gregory has just been telling me you're accounted something of a fine horsewoman, Alexandra."

Alexandra bit her lip. "I do like to ride," she admitted. "Marius told me you hunted."

"I used to." She sighed. "But it's been a long time since I've been astride, I'm afraid. You'll have to be patient with me. Where do you prefer to ride?"

She might have missed six years of their lives, but maybe they could find their way to a stronger relationship now, out of Father's shadow. Hetta was determined to make a start, regardless. It had been her one true regret about leaving, the fact that except for Marius, her other siblings might as well have been strangers.

Talking to Alexandra and Gregory was also a very welcome distraction from Wyn, who continued to be as infuriatingly cheerful and courteous as always as he went back and forth into the room, refilling the sideboard and enquiring if anyone needed anything. The blueberry muffin argument had clearly happened before, because on one of his passes he deposited a fresh one next to Gregory, who'd been the loser in the earlier interplay. He caught Hetta watching and smiled briefly before disappearing again.

The more she spoke with Gregory, the more she began to think that Marius's concern might have some basis. Every now and then a dark expression would cross his face, as if he were remembering something unpleasant, and he would lose track of conversation, returning with a jolt when prompted—usually by Alexandra chiding him on his poor manners. Then he'd grin and refocus, buoyed up by cheerful optimism that was much more in keeping with the enthusiastic boy Hetta had known. But Hetta couldn't help but note the dark circles beneath his eyes. Jack might be correct that there was a girl involved; Gregory was doing an excellent impression of one preoccupied with a strong infatuation. Calf-love in and of itself didn't trouble her, but Gregory's mood swings and air of distraction did. Was the girl toying with him to make him swing so quickly between elation and despair? Hetta had seen plenty of that amongst the actors—their dramatic personalities seemed to lend themselves to equally dramatic personal affairs—and she'd seen the ravages emotional manipulation could wreak on the young and vulnerable.

But it was none of her business, she reminded herself. She would be gone within the week. She'd booked her ticket back on the Monday following; the Choosing Ceremony was to be held on Saturday. She owed it to her company to return as quickly as possible afterwards.

If Marius isn't chosen, it's going to take him a while to get over it, she thought as she watched him absently sip his tea. His nose wrinkled in distaste; Grandmamma's remedy was efficacious but unpleasant. Perhaps she should invite him to come down to Meridon to visit when she left, if he wasn't chosen. She felt guilty for thinking it, but she agreed with the rest of the family that Jack was the much more likely successor to Lord Henry. Marius's land-sense had always been weak. Maybe she could persuade him to bring Gregory with him; if her younger brother's moodiness was because of some misplayed love affair, perhaps distance might give him perspective.

Marius caught her watching him but shied away from meeting her gaze. All his insecurities of the night before had clearly risen again, unmasked by wine, as he folded his paper and got up, shoulders high and tense.

Jack came in just as Marius was leaving, so that they met in the doorway. There was a frozen second of awkwardness where everyone else studiously pretended not to be watching the two of them.

Jack nodded stiffly. "Morning."

Marius nodded back but forgot to reply before he angled his way past. He did that sometimes when he was stressed. A ghostly image of her father stood in the doorway for a second, bellowing at a younger but equally tongue-tied Marius.

Jack's expression was poles apart from Lord Henry's, amused rather than angry as he watched Marius go. The ghost faded. Jack wouldn't be unkind to Marius if he became the new lord, Hetta thought. In fact, it would probably be best for all concerned. It would leave Marius free to escape to pursue his studies and Jack with the running of the estate he loved.

Jack shrugged, coming into the breakfast room and making straight for the sideboard. His cheeks were red with cold; of all the Valstars, Jack was one of the few naturally early risers. He would already have been out and about on the estate before breakfast.

Hetta debated whether to go after Marius right away or not. He could clearly use some support. However, it was also apparent he'd gotten himself into a mood, and sometimes it was better to leave him to muddle his way out again by himself.

Before she could decide, Wyn returned with a note for her.

"Just arrived from Penharrow, Miss Hetta," he said formally, adding in an undertone: "Made a conquest of our noble neighbour, have we? Tsk, tsk." He shook his head sadly, the russet of his eyes gleaming with flecks of brandy-gold. "Does he know you used to doodle 'Henrietta Penharrow' in your notebook?"

"That was only once!" she said indignantly. "And I was *sixteen*."

"Ah, so he doesn't know." He grinned wickedly before he left.

He wasn't at all jealous of the interest of another man, was he? What a fortunate thing that she'd already decided not to pursue this new attraction she felt towards him.

Hetta looked up and found her cousin Caroline considering her curiously. Caroline was only a year younger than Hetta, and the only other proper redhead in the family alongside Jack—Hetta's auburn didn't really count. Caroline inclined her head towards the door through which Wyn had left and raised an eyebrow questioningly, a teasing smile lurking around her mouth. Hetta shook her head, not wishing to discuss it and also annoyed with herself for being so obvious. Although Caroline was both more observant and more discreet than most of the family, so with any luck the rest could carry on being oblivious to Hetta's less-than-strictly-proper interactions with the butler.

The note was a very welcome bolster to her vanity. It was from Angus, inviting her out for lunch.

7

LORD ANGUS PENHARROW

By the time the appointed lunch arrived, Hetta was extremely glad to escape her overstuffed house. The tension in the household had become a palpable thing. Marius gave mumbled, monosyllabic responses to everyday queries. Lady Phoebe complained frequently of headaches. Aunt Sybil oscillated between impatience and smug certainty that her son Jack would surely inherit. She was unbearable towards Marius. Cecily, the eldest cousin, became crotchety and fractious and demanded her husband's attention so completely that even that docile man increasingly made excuses to absent himself. Aunt Maude said whatever she thought was most likely to provoke Aunt Sybil. Uncle Percival attempted to lighten the atmosphere, but since his sense of humour was a somewhat skewed one, he had only minimal success. Second-cousin Randolf caused a stir by arriving with his eldest son in tow, not even pretending he hadn't intended to miss the funeral; he'd had a falling-out with Lord Valstar a decade previous.

Hetta's notoriety became ordinary and uninteresting, as everyone busied themselves reviving feuds and raking over every bit of family gossip since her ancestor had claimed this land nearly a thousand years ago.

The house thronged with multiple generations of Valstars, with cousins of various ages running through hallways, stealing cakes from the kitchens, attempting to slide down the banisters, and generally upsetting the older generations and servants both. Through it all, Wyn remained unruffled, calmly allocating bedrooms and juggling increasingly ridiculous demands with the precision of a general. Grandmamma bobbed above the whole, issuing cheerful and frequently tone-deaf remarks to all and sundry.

Hetta stood outside the house and took a long, steadying breath as she waited for Angus. The day was a fine one, crisp and clear, autumn slowly chilling towards winter. The mountain ranges cut sharply against the blue, blue sky. Filling her lungs, she let her tension fall away. She loved Meridon, but she had to admit that there was more air up here—or at least, *better* air.

Angus picked her up at the back entrance as instructed. He got out of the kineticar to greet her, and she was struck again by how, well, *virile* he appeared. He must be a hands-on estate owner—no one got shoulders like that by pushing paper about. The sun brushed his curls a richer brown and seemed designed to highlight his strong jawline.

His smile widened as he took in her own appearance. "Are these the scandalous modern ways you referred to?"

Hetta had worn trousers, largely to see what kind of reaction they would get. That was another reason for meeting him at the back entrance: to avoid the ire of Aunt Sybil. A certain amount of cursory illusion had still been called for to achieve the escape un-censored.

"Some of," she admitted. She twirled, and the wide ends of the pale trousers flared around her boots. "What do you think?"

Angus smiled down at her, hooking his hands into his belt. "I think you're testing me, lass. But I can't see why any sane man would object to such a fashion. Do I pass?"

"That depends on why, exactly, you think that no sane man should object. I have a suspicion it's nothing at all to do with equality and everything to do with aesthetics."

"Will it land me in trouble if I confess very much to the latter?" The look in his eyes stirred her in a very feminine way. "For you cannot be unaware that they flatter your figure admirably. Though I'll own they look much warmer than skirts and stockings, and I'm generally in favour of practicalities. A happy bonus, that the two should coincide?"

It was impossible not to be charmed, and there was, after all, no reason not to give in to the urge. Nothing serious could come of this, and he must know that as well as she; Hetta was only here for a few days more. Why not let herself be charmed by a good-looking man under those circumstances?

"A point in your favour for the acceptance of modern attire, but I think I shall have to take it away again for impure motives," she said, taking his offered arm.

"Well, at least I am not in the red," Angus said philosophically as he transferred her to the vehicle. "Perhaps I can improve my balance over lunch."

HE TOOK HER TO a picturesque village pub situated on the banks of Deeplake, within the bounds of Penharrow. It appealed very much to Hetta's tastes with its warm wooden interior, hearty fare, and opportunity for privacy in the booths along two of the walls. It wasn't the dainty teashop she'd feared he might think suitable for ladies. Not that she *disliked* teashops, but it was the principle of the thing. He didn't bat an eyelid when she ordered a half-pint of the local beer, dark and malty in flavour. *Points in Angus's favour, indeed.*

Angus asked her about her time in Meridon and listened with every evidence of interest. He himself had spent quite a bit of time in the Southern capital before his father's death. It was a relief to speak of places and people in common with someone who shared the same basic level of understanding.

"I've not had a chance to visit since my father passed," Angus said with a self-deprecating smile. "But you make me want to make the effort again."

Hetta took the opportunity to ask what he'd been doing on his estates. What he'd told her on their initial drive from the station turned out to be the least of it.

"There's so much more to modern farming and estate management than our forebears could've imagined," he enthused, making an encompassing gesture with his arms. Hetta couldn't help noticing their firm muscle, and her insides flipped pleasurably.

He warmed to his subject, and to her surprise, Hetta found his tales of updating machinery and new cross-breeds of sheep highly entertaining. But then, she reflected, Angus had always been articulate. That was at least half his appeal, even if the other half derived a lot from the breadth of his shoulders.

Altogether it was a very pleasant afternoon, and Hetta was somewhat regretful to think that there would be no opportunity to repeat it before she left. Although, she realised with a flash of wonder, her absence need not be nearly as absolute as previously.

"What's made that look come over you, lass?" Angus asked as they strolled along the shore of Deeplake after taking their luncheon. The surrounding hills and clear sky showed perfect reflections in the waters. "You look as if something unexpected just occurred to you." He grinned, hazel eyes almost green in the afternoon sun. "And I suspect you've no recollection of the last few words I spoke."

Hetta had to admit that she didn't. "It just occurred to me that I might visit Stariel more than I've been used to, now." There was no one keeping her from visiting, now; any exile would be entirely self-imposed.

Angus's expression grew more serious, and it was clear that he understood what she meant. Then he smiled again. "I'll confess I'll be glad to see you if you do. The company here is somewhat thin on the ground."

Hetta laughed. "You mean to say that you only tolerate my company because your choices are so limited!"

Angus took this sally as it was intended, chuckling. "Damme if I wouldn't choose to seek you out even amongst all the society of Meridon."

Hetta was flattered, as he'd intended her to be. "That's a very touching sentiment. Why, I almost believe you."

An odd expression crossed Angus's face as he looked down at her, and then he appeared to come to some decision.

"I think I'd better show you some more convincing sign of my affection, then," he said easily. Hetta's heart fluttered as she realised he was about to kiss her, and she obediently tilted her head.

Lord Angus Penharrow kissed her firmly and without hurry, a man who had no doubts about his abilities. *And quite rightly so*, Hetta thought dizzily, as her inner sixteen-year-old punched the air in triumph. Her body felt pleasantly flushed by the time they broke apart.

"Oh!" she said as he twinkled unrepentantly down at her. She had a moment's uncertainty where she hoped that he wasn't about to make it necessary for her to extricate herself from an awkward situation, but he merely gave her that lazy, charming grin again.

"Well," she said. "That was forward of you, but I can't say I didn't enjoy it."

"I rather thought you did," he agreed.

She laughed. "You are outrageous."

"Merely 'forward', I thought you said?" He offered her his arm. "But we should be getting back." He seemed to sense the direction her thoughts had taken and reassured her. "I've no expectations of you, Hetta." His eyes crinkled in amusement. "But you just looked too delectable to resist. Forgive me a moment's weakness."

"Oh, all right then," she said, taking his arm. His forearm felt every bit as firmly muscled as it had looked.

Really, Hetta thought, she needed to leave Stariel before her libido entirely overcame her good sense.

8

THE CHOOSING CEREMONY

EVERYONE WOKE EARLY on Saturday, even though the Choosing wouldn't be until after sunset. The steps of the ceremony had been set out long, long ago, and each and every one of them would be adhered to, no matter how archaic or absurd. Hetta strongly suspected one of her ancestors with a penchant for the melodramatic had deliberately introduced much of the pageantry surrounding the ceremony. *These white robes, for instance, cannot possibly be in any way necessary to the actual event*, she thought, donning hers with resignation. The robes had been designed by someone whose view of history slanted towards the highly romanticised. At least she wouldn't be alone in her ridiculous attire, and it was almost worth it just to see Aunt Sybil, usually so severely dressed, trying to appear dignified whilst wearing the flowing white robe belted with ivy. But she'd underestimated the steel of her aunt and had to admit to reluctant admiration when she saw her don her circlet of starflowers with an expression carved from granite, daring any of their retainers to comment. None did.

Throng was a good way to describe the assorted Valstars as they arranged themselves around the Standing Stones where the ceremony was held, each wearing the prescribed white robes, and each carrying a single white candle. As the sun dipped below the horizon, the candles were lit in a more-or-less synchronised fashion and with more-or-less the solemnity that the occasion called for. Hetta made the mistake of meeting her cousin Caroline's gaze and only just managed to stifle a laugh as Caroline rolled her eyes at their Aunt Maude, who had lit her candle with all the reverence of a priest anointing a holy object.

Hetta's amusement dimmed somewhat as the darkness settled and the atmosphere shifted. The setup might be silly, but the implications of the Choosing were far-reaching. The weight of history, of the long line of Valstars that had ruled over this land for a thousand years, became palpable as Lady Phoebe and Grandmamma arrived with the casket containing the Star Stone. Even Stariel itself felt more awake, the land's focus clearly upon them.

The Star Stone was probably the one part of the ritual that was actually necessary. It was about a hand span across, and made of a deep blue substance that glittered oddly, as if clouds shifted beneath its solid surface. The substance was star indigo, a rare mineral found in the Indigo Mountains within Stariel's borders. Lady Phoebe and Grandmamma took it from the casket and placed it on a stone plinth in the centre of the Standing Stones with slow, careful movements, their hands gloved. The Stone didn't activate without the proper ritual, supposedly, but it was traditional for no one to touch it beforehand.

The Choosing order was well established and very simple: it went in age order. Technically that meant Aunt Sybil was first in line, followed by the remainder of Lord Henry's siblings and cousins, but that was mostly for form's sake; everyone knew Stariel wouldn't choose from its old lord's generation.

Around the inner circle of eligible family members and the outer circle of their wider relations was a crowd made up of those who lived within Stariel's borders as well as some of the neighbouring nobility, come to greet their new neighbour at the earliest opportunity. The night was chill but clear, and small braziers glowed around the field that contained the old stone circle. The smell of roast chestnuts lingered in the air. It put Hetta in mind of a village fair. Her eye caught on a blond man among the villagers, staring intently at Marius. As she watched, his gaze flicked from Marius to Jack and back again. *And we to be the entertainment*, she thought wryly.

Hetta saw Marius's eyes lock onto the blond man for a moment, and she wondered if they knew each other before Marius's gaze moved on over the crowd. Her brother's face was pale but determined. The terrible tension Hetta had observed in him over the last week seemed to have eased. He even smiled when he caught her eye.

"Should I wish you luck?" She reached out to squeeze his hand. Marius shook his head but squeezed back gratefully.

Jack was practically quivering with ill-suppressed excitement and nerves, his attention fixed on the Star Stone. Everyone else was trying, and failing, not to look like they were glancing back and forth between Jack on one side of the circle and Marius on the other, the two most likely candidates for lord.

The small amount of chatter there had been ceased as the moonlight began to inch across the circle. Eventually it touched the Stone, which lit up in iridescent blues and purples, and Aunt Sybil strode forward purposefully. She walked the circle clockwise in a spiral, ending at the Stone, and placed both her hands upon it. Hetta felt a wave of relief pass through the assembled gatherers when nothing happened.

Uncle Percival seemed utterly relaxed as he took his turn next, grinning around at his assembled relations as he too placed his hands on the stone to no effect.

"Ah, well," he said, shrugging as he made his way over to Aunt Sybil. There was a little ripple of amusement, stemming more from a desire to break the increasing tension than from humour. Aunt Maude's passage was more reverent than her older siblings'—she was exactly the sort of person to come up with a ceremony like this in the first place—but she was equally unsuccessful. The rest of Lord Valstar's generation of relatives' turns were perfunctory. They knew they wouldn't be chosen.

And then it was time for the next generation of Valstars. It seemed to take forever for cousin Cecily to take her turn, stroking delicate fingers along the surface of the Stone. She took her place beside her mother and turned to give Marius an encouraging smile.

Marius's face was deathly white as he made his way in the spiral towards the Stone. Hetta held her breath as he reached out in a rapid motion, barely touching its surface. But the result was clear—it didn't respond. He stared at it for a long moment, swaying slightly. For a heartbeat, Hetta worried that he'd faint with the sudden release of tension, but he collected himself and made his way on unsteady legs to where his older relatives waited. Cecily put a hand briefly on his shoulder when he reached her, but he shook it off like a horse dislodging a fly, not looking at anyone.

Hetta couldn't help shooting a glance at Jack. He ignored the many eyes on him, keeping his face impassive, but his colour was high.

Hetta could feel the impatience amongst her relatives now that the conclusion seemed settled. She picked her way through the circle towards the Star Stone. The ritual took place atop a low hill above a wide field, and despite the mass of interested parties spread below and around her, she felt suddenly alone beneath the silver light of the moon, the stars glittering above. Her cumbersome, long-sleeved white robe added to the surrealism, making it difficult to maintain her serious expression, but she managed it by making herself repeat the names for the different branches of illusion silently as she walked.

Chronillism, spatillism, phraenosion, pyrocracy, kinecism… How was Bradfield, the director, getting on without her? Was the new show getting the good reviews it needed to succeed, with whatever slapdash illusionist he could beg, borrow, or steal covering for her?

She reached the Stone and placed her hands matter-of-factly on its surface, her thoughts miles away from Stariel.

The iridescence of the stone exploded outwards, flooding the circle in blue light. Stars glittered, and golden flames roared up around the circle.

The effects lasted for perhaps half a minute, during which Hetta could do nothing but stand there, hands still on the Stone, frozen in shock, thinking of nothing at all.

There was a deep, profound silence. It spread like a pool from the innermost circle outwards, until it included all the gathered servants, villagers, tenants, and neighbouring nobility. It wasn't a peaceful silence. It was an intense, aggressive silence, intently focused on one person—her. She thought wildly of the glare of the stage lights.

Whispers broke out in the outer ranks, hissing in the still night air. None of the Valstars had yet moved, stunned into immobility. It was her cousin Caroline who broke the silence.

"All hail the new Lord of Stariel! Lord Henrietta!" she cried, her voice pitched to carry over the field. The assembled villagers picked up her cue and echoed it back, but the cries sounded weak and lacklustre.

Jack had gone white and red with rage and disbelief, but at this he turned, pushed his way out of the crowd, and stalked out of sight. Aunt Sybil's face was livid.

It fell to Grandmamma to arrange the remainder of the ritual, since the rest of the older generation of Valstars remained rooted to the spot.

Hetta hardly noticed. She looked around helplessly. Marius wouldn't meet her eyes, and the rest of her cousins shuffled their feet, awkward and unwilling to risk Aunt Sybil's wrath. Again, Caroline was the exception, striding forward and steadying her with a hand to one shoulder.

"Just breathe," she said in a low tone. "Everything will be fine." Hetta rather doubted that, but she took her cousin's advice nonetheless.

Suddenly Wyn was at her elbow, and she turned to find him crawling with wild energy, hair pure silver under the starlight.

"My Star," Wyn said quietly, bowing his head. It was an old form of address for the Lord of Stariel, but Hetta was oddly grateful for it at that moment. He smiled at her, a much gentler smile than his normal wicked grin. "Your people await. You know the words?" It steadied her, and she swallowed, nodding and turning her gaze towards the crowd.

The oath words had been imprinted on her memory—as they were for all the Valstars—so long ago that she found herself speaking them without taking in anything of their meaning. She might still have been reciting spell names. Everything felt very far away, and the air had become thick, so that to lift each limb or even open her mouth to speak required a firm effort. She found herself reaching for Stariel. It was there as it had always been: deep, vast, sluggish. Maybe it was the shock, or maybe it needed time to click into place, but her land-sense didn't feel any different than before.

The rest of the evening was a blur. She had no recollection of moving through the crowd, or leaving the stone circle, or of the journey back to Stariel House. She didn't remember anything except suddenly finding herself once again in her yellowing child-hood bedroom and clinging to her blankets as if they were the last real thing left in the world.

MORNING COFFEE

THE SUN WAS still below the horizon when Henrietta Isadore Valstar, First of Her Name, Defender of Starwater, Lord of Stariel, woke and stared up at her bedroom ceiling. It was still dark, but outside, the countryside was quietly waking, the sounds still a jarring difference from her boarding house in Meridon.

Stariel had chosen, and that made Hetta the new Lord of Stariel. The ceiling's peeling plaster whorls seemed inappropriately mundane given the circumstances. She traced the familiar patterns above, very tempted to believe last night's happenings a dream, but knowing they weren't.

She reached out towards Stariel with her land-sense again. Shouldn't she sense something different now? That was the only part of her changed status that held any appeal—the chance to explore new magic—but she couldn't feel any more or less than usual. Maybe it just took time for the bond between land and lord to fully form.

She didn't want to think about any of the other implications of her new title, but it was difficult to avoid. She would need to let her landlady know she was giving up her lease and retrieve her belongings from her boarding house in Meridon. Hetta had, most unfortunately, just paid the next two months' rent. Her lips quirked in pained amusement. And Bradfield; she would have to tell him his illusionist wouldn't be coming back. That realisation was like swallowing a whole bottle of vinegar.

Perhaps she could go back to Meridon, just for a few weeks, to finish out the show's run? But she rejected the idea with a pang even as it occurred to her. It would be impossible to leave Stariel for such a length of time so soon after the Choosing.

It was hard to accept these things, even harder at six o'clock in the morning in the cold and dark. She wanted to shout at someone, but there was no point. How could you argue with something as vast and inhuman as the land itself?

Trying to shake off the spiralling depression, she rose and dressed. Not ten minutes later, she let herself out of the quiet house and into the terraced garden, treading cautiously across the paving stones. The morning was still and cold and clear, ice crystals glittering in the pre-dawn light.

She looked towards Starwater and considered walking down to its glassy waters, but she had on only her slippers, and the ground was heavy with frost. White spread out as far as the eye could see. Hetta's breath plumed in the air as she tucked her hands inside her coat and pondered the strange twists of fate.

Dawn in Stariel was at once a slow and sudden affair. Starwater nestled between mountain ranges, so it was quite light by the time the sun rose above the far range, suddenly flooding the valley below with brilliant gold and reflecting off the waters in a dazzling display.

By the time the sun was fully up, Hetta was no further in her thoughts. She knew there were things she needed to organise, but she felt a strong reluctance to begin. Denial seemed very attractive right now, except that she'd never been good at that. But even her deep core of pragmatism felt as fragile as cracked glass, and she hugged her arms around herself, as if she could hold it forcibly together.

The sound of the side door swinging open made her turn. Wyn stood there, holding a tray upon which rested a gently steaming metal pot and two cups. The smell wafted towards her, and a wave of homesickness washed over her.

"Is that coffee, you marvellous creature? I thought there wasn't any in the house." She took a step towards him, drawn by the smell.

Wyn smiled, bringing the tray over to the outdoor table and setting out the cups. "I took the liberty of ordering some when you came back. You've written of your love affair with the stuff frequently enough. I'll admit the timing of it seems fortuitous."

"I love you," Hetta said fervently as he poured.

His mouth twitched, but when he looked up, his expression was oddly intent. "I may stay, then?"

"Of course you may stay and take coffee with me, my friend." She gestured at the two cups. "But I think you rather anticipated my answer, so I don't know why you bothered to ask."

"No," Wyn clarified. "May I stay at Stariel?"

Hetta blinked at him, looking for some sign of levity, but he seemed in earnest. Eventually she said, "Why are you asking me this?"

Wyn pursed his lips. "You're Lord Valstar now."

Hetta twisted her cup in her hands. "I suppose I am, but what makes you think you need seek my permission to stay?" She tried to follow his mind's path but couldn't.

"Nonetheless, I do seek it."

"Then of course you have it," she said briskly.

Wyn smiled, and his odd intensity drained away. "Excellent."

He poured the coffee and sat down. "It would be terribly inconvenient to have to leave."

"For you or us?" Hetta said with a laugh. "Since you're serving as housekeeper and butler both, as I understand it, since Mabel retired."

Wyn shrugged. "House manager, technically, but butler does well enough for everyday use."

"Thank you," she said, sipping her coffee. It grounded her, this small reminder of Meridon. She wrapped her fingers around the cup and let it warm her hands, the bitter-smooth taste lingering on her tongue.

A comfortable silence fell between them, and the world narrowed into the crisp isolation of the early morning, the steam of the coffee pot and its rich, nutty scent, and the first chirpings of the waking birds.

Then Wyn spoke. "Will you run, Hetta?"

He did not look at her but stared instead out towards Starwater. His tone had not been one of accusation; he had said the words mildly, as if merely inquiring whether she would prefer toast or cereal for breakfast.

"I want to," Hetta admitted, also choosing to avoid the intimacy of facing him. It was easier to admit her fears to the vast landscape. Again, she searched for her land-sense, trying to detect some deeper layer than had been there before, but there was no sudden epiphany to be had. If anything, Stariel seemed to be…waiting. Hetta sighed. "What am I supposed to do? I know nothing about estate management. The people of Stariel know me only as the rebellious daughter who left long ago. I've no claim to their loyalty. Sweet Mother Eostre only knows where the accounts stand—I certainly don't. And everyone sees me as a usurper. Jack couldn't even face me last night."

"Some of these things might be rectified."

"Yes," Hetta agreed unhappily. She swirled the dregs of her cup.

"This isn't how I imagined my homecoming."

"You did imagine it, though?"

Hetta considered the question with a frown. "I don't know. I love my life in Meridon, but it has always felt, not precisely temporary, but…" She struggled to find the words and gestured out towards the hills and forests and glittering lake. "There's a permanence to this place that's hard to deny. It was, I have to admit, comforting to know that it was here, that there were Valstars in Stariel, though I might not be among them."

"That it was there for you to come back to," Wyn suggested.

"Yes."

There didn't seem to be anything else to say, but Wyn's words had loosened some of the tension in her. She knew that there were things she ought to be asking Wyn in his capacity as house manager; things that he ought to be asking her. Yet he stayed silent, and she was grateful for it.

Eventually Wyn began packing up the tray. "I'd best get back. It's the first frost this morning." He gestured out towards the white lawns.

It took Hetta a second to remember what this meant. "Oh. Sloe Day—do we still do that?"

"Indeed we do." He smiled fondly. "We'll have the village children turning up with their baskets by lunchtime, once the sun has dried off the frost."

"I used to love that tradition." Sloe berries were traditionally picked from the hedgerows after the first frost, to sweeten the flavour. They were then used to make everything from sloe gin to chutney. "What's the going rate these days? I remember once making half a crown in a particularly fruitful year."

"Oh you do, do you?" Wyn said, raising his eyebrows. "And was this all on your lonesome? Was there not, perhaps, an impressionable youth involved whom you persuaded to do a lot of running hither and thither to aid your attempt?"

"I cannot say I remember any such thing," Hetta said primly. "But I'm sure you picked plenty of sloe berries in your time too." She reached out to pat his arm consolingly. She'd meant it teasingly, but Wyn looked up and there was a snap of connection, the gesture suddenly more intimate. He inhaled sharply. A sense of fierce otherness clung to him like faint elektricity, and she could feel the warmth of his body through his sleeve. The idea that this wild, beautiful man and the mild-mannered head of staff and the old, comfortable friend of her youth were one and the same person had never seemed more absurd.

Wyn turned his face away and the connection shattered. He rose, nodded in acknowledgement, and left without speaking.

Careful, she cautioned herself as she watched his tall form disappear. *He is technically your employee now as well as your friend.*

Hetta continued to sit, reluctant to make her way back into the house and start the day. There would be unpleasant scenes to face. She tried to be productive and think of which of her illusionist friends might be free and willing to work with Bradfield, but the attempt left her unutterably depressed. She didn't want him to replace her, didn't want to call him and break the news. As long as she put off calling him, a little pocket of the world still existed that hadn't been completely turned upside down.

Distraction came from an unexpected source. The dull thudding of hoofbeats sounded from the forest, and as Hetta watched, a horse and rider appeared. Then the shape resolved itself into two riders on one horse: one fair-haired, one dark. Hetta frowned, trying to make out who it was. As they drew closer, she realised that it was her younger brother Gregory, accompanied by a strange young woman.

A NEW ARRIVAL

HETTA STOOD AND made her way down the small set of steps that opened onto the front lawn from the higher terrace but didn't step onto the grass, conscious of her slippers. She waved and saw Gregory start, making his horse sidle. Gregory quickly controlled it and rode towards Hetta. When he drew close, he dismounted and offered a hand to the girl who'd been seated behind him. He handed her down with the kind of reverence one usually reserves for expensive china. *Here's the source of the calf-love then*, Hetta identified, suppressing the urge to smile.

The mysterious girl wasn't far removed from Gregory in age, and she was entirely, effortlessly lovely. At the theatre, Hetta would have conjured something like her to play the beautiful ingenue, except an illusion that faultless wouldn't be convincing. She had heavenly blue eyes, large and guileless, and dark ringlets, which curled charmingly around her angelic countenance. The top of her head barely reached up to Gregory's shoulder.

Well, this small goddess certainly explained Gregory's infatuation, but why in the nine heavens had he brought her here at this hour? Her jewellery and the cut and fabric of her dress suggested she wasn't a village girl. Where had she come from?

The girl seemed to feel the full force of the moment's awkwardness, for she curtsied and stammered:

"P-p-please don't be angry, my lady. Indeed, I don't wish to trespass, only Mr Valstar here was so kind and…" Her voice grew steadily more inaudible and she trailed off, biting her lip and staring at Hetta's feet.

Hetta looked enquiringly at Gregory, who flushed, but said aggressively, "I told Gwen—I mean, Miss, er, Smith—that she'd be safe here."

"You must forgive me," Hetta said, valiantly keeping her voice from quivering at the melodrama being enacted in front of her. "But I am quite lost. I take it you are Miss Smith?" She smiled reassuringly at the girl, who stole a furtive look up at her but couldn't seem to keep her eyes raised. Miss 'Smith'—if that was her name, which Hetta rather doubted—coloured prettily and said confusedly:

"Oh. Yes, please call me Miss Smith."

"I take it my brother is known to you, although I find his manners at present somewhat lacking. I am Miss Henrietta Valstar." It struck her that she should probably be introducing herself as Lord Valstar, but she soldiered on anyway. "Tell me, why are you a-horse with Gregory here this morning?"

Gregory shifted as if to shield Miss Smith bodily from her questions, putting Hetta in mind of nothing so much as a dog crouching over a bone. "I found her on the road from Stariel."

"On the road from Stariel?" Hetta let astonishment colour her tone. "Need I remind you, Gregory, that kidnapping is a criminal offence?"

"Gregory has not kidnapped me!" the girl broke in, and then flushed again.

With some effort, Hetta prised the story out of the pair. This task was made difficult by the fact that the story was nine-tenths concocted on the spot via the exchange of many meaningful anxious glances.

If Gregory were to be believed, he'd been moved to make an early morning ride and had come upon Miss Smith as he returned. On seeing a young lady walking on the roadside, quite alone and toting a suitcase, he had understandably drawn up and asked if he might be of assistance. Miss Smith had initially maintained that there was nothing amiss, but upon some coaxing had confessed that she was running away. Her guardian was a cruel, cold man, apparently, and now that she was nearly of age, her guardian meant to force her to marry him to secure her fortune for himself. In desperation, she had fled, but as she walked she'd grown bleaker, realising that she had nowhere to go. She knew no one and had no money of her own. Gregory had offered her sanctuary at Stariel.

"For she is of age, next month, Hetta, and might then do as she pleases!" He didn't seem to foresee any problem with a young, unnamed runaway heiress taking up residence at Stariel.

Hetta stared hard at him. It was a very convenient story and reminded her a little too much of the romantic novels she'd read as a teenager.

"And you met Miss Smith only this morning, I am sure?"

Gregory stammered an affirmative. Hetta turned to the subject of their discussion. "Will you tell me your name, for I am quite sure that it isn't Smith?"

The girl wrung her hands awkwardly. "Indeed, I can see that you might think so. But—at least—" She seemed torn between guilt and fear that revealing her name would result in her instant return to her guardian.

Hetta rubbed her forehead with the heel of one hand. "Well, in any case, we cannot keep standing here. Gregory, take your horse back to the stables. I will take Miss Smith up to the house."

When both would have burst into exuberant thanks, she held out a hand to forestall them. "Later," she said tiredly. "I cannot be thanked before breakfast."

Miss Smith obediently followed her back into the house, and Hetta went in search of Wyn. He was uncharacteristically elusive, but fortunately, the senior housemaid appeared while Hetta was contemplating the empty housekeeper's office. The maid paused, clearly in the middle of some mission, with a list clutched in one fist.

"Ms Whitlow! Just the person I was looking for," Hetta said, attempting to inject warmth into her voice. Ms Whitlow had always had a soft spot for both Marius and Jack, but Hetta had never been among her favourites.

"Lord Valstar," the maid acknowledged, her eyes tracking curiously over Miss Smith. It was the first time someone had used her new title in a mundane capacity, and Hetta tried not to twitch. It felt decidedly odd to be called by her father's name.

"This is Miss Smith, who is to stay with us for a few days." Hetta hoped that she would manage to shake the truth free of Gregory well before then. She gave an apologetic smile. "I know that we're rather packed to the rafters at present, but I thought perhaps we might squeeze her in with Alexandra, if you could have someone make up a trestle bed there. Fortunately, many of the family are leaving in the next few days, after which there should be more space in which to put us all."

The housemaid turned her cool gaze onto Miss Smith, who raised pansy-wide eyes and said tremulously: "Oh, I do not wish to cause you so much trouble!"

Her appearance softened the housemaid, for she said: "Don't

worry your head about it. It will be no trouble."

"Thank you, Ms Whitlow," Hetta said, relieved that she hadn't been required to explain Miss Smith's presence. She felt quite exhausted of imagination at that moment. "I shall not take up any more of your valuable time. If you'll follow me, Miss Smith? I'll take you up to my sister."

As they climbed the stairs, Miss Smith said suddenly, "Oh, won't you please call me Gwen? It is so formal to be called 'Miss Smith'."

"I can see that it might be," Hetta agreed, hiding her smile. "Gwen, then. You may call me Hetta."

She expected her half-sister would still be asleep at this hour of the morning—Hetta would've been, at her age—but when Hetta knocked, there was a short pause, the sound of movement, and then a cry to come in. Alexandra was seated at her writing desk, although what she'd been writing wasn't in evidence. Hetta wondered if it was a diary that she'd just then hidden from view and inwardly smiled at the teen's self-consciousness.

"Good morning, Alexandra. I've maligned you—I confess I expected I'd need to wake you. How fortunate that I was wrong."

Alexandra blinked uncertainly, and it occurred to Hetta that this was the first time they'd spoken since the Choosing. It had slipped her mind under the consideration of what to do with Miss Smith.

"May I introduce Miss Gwen Smith to you?" Hetta gestured that damsel into the room. "She has come to stay, but I'm told we are rather pressed for bedrooms at present. Can I prevail upon you to take pity on her and share your room for the night? I'm sure we can arrange a reshuffle tomorrow when people start to leave." And she wouldn't be among those vacating the house. The thought was too disconcerting to be painful.

The two girls eyed each other. Miss Smith was Alexandra's

elder, but not by so many years as to make friendship between them impossible. Otherwise they presented an attractive contrast: one dark, one fair.

"Of course," Alexandra said politely. "I am pleased to make your acquaintance, Miss Smith." She shot a puzzled look at Hetta. "Are you Hetta's friend?"

"I—no—I mean," Miss Smith stumbled, looking beseechingly to Hetta to rescue her.

But Hetta hardened her heart and said serenely: "I'm sure Miss Smith will explain it all to you while she refreshes herself a little. I'll see you both at breakfast." With that, she swept out of the room before either one of them could object. "Blast Gregory!" she muttered under her breath as she went in search of her errant brother.

She wondered if she ought to have concocted some socially acceptable story for her sister. Undoubtedly Miss Smith was at this moment pouring the tale of her woes into Alexandra's willing ears. It seemed unlikely that even Phoebe, doting mother that she was, would approve. But Hetta was neither a hypocrite nor especially burdened with a belief in the delicacy of young female minds. She was also reluctant to spin falsehoods on Gregory's behalf. Untruths, in Hetta's experience, generally made life more rather than less complicated. Gregory could dashed well come up with some explanations himself. After all, it had been his idea to bring Miss Smith to the house, and though Hetta wasn't unsympathetic to whatever misfortunes she might have suffered, Hetta had a hard time believing he'd known nothing of her until this morning.

As she made her way through the house, she overheard voices ahead and froze, unsure whether to announce her presence or not.

"And I cannot bear the thought of that—that *hussy* being in Jack's rightful place."

It was Aunt Sybil. Hetta couldn't think of anyone she would like to encounter less just at this moment, and she looked about for an escape. None presented itself. The only doors along this hallway led to bedrooms, all of them likely occupied at this hour. The sensible course of action would be to walk briskly away, but so strong was her desire not to be seen that Hetta found herself pressing her back into the nearest doorway and concentrating.

An illusionist's abilities were limited by the caster's ability to hold mental images. Hetta had always had an excellent visual memory and the ability to focus on an image in her mind's eye. She did so now, concentrating on the doorway behind her and projecting it over herself.

There was the sound of footsteps, and Aunt Sybil and Uncle Percival came into sight. Hetta held her breath and drew intently on the image of the door. The illusion held. The two passed right by her, the air moving a scant two inches from her in the swish of Aunt Sybil's skirts.

Uncle Percival was frowning. "I know it's been a bit of a shock, but you and Jack will just have to make your peace with it. It's not as if you can argue with Stariel."

"But I can't see why Jack shouldn't have been given his chance—" Aunt Sybil replied mulishly.

"You mean after Stariel had already chosen? What would be the point?"

"She's an illusionist. How do we know what we saw was real?" Aunt Sybil spat.

"You can't go putting that about!"

"I'm just putting two and two together. There's no other explanation for it. Others will say the same. Everyone knows Jack should have been next in line."

"No one ever really knows who will be next in line." Uncle Percival's tone became cold. "And if you think that Henrietta would do such a thing, you've not the sense the gods gave little green apples. It was plain she'd no expectation of it. Never seen anyone look so taken aback."

"That's just what she wanted us to think!"

Their voices faded as they passed down the other end of the corridor. Hetta leaned against the door, letting the illusion dissolve, a bitter taste in her mouth.

TALL TALES

Aunt Sybil's anger was unsurprising; her accusation was another thing entirely. It hadn't occurred to Hetta that her profession could lay her open to accusations of foul play. Winning Stariel's lordship was so far from her desire that it seemed incredible that anyone would believe she'd wanted this to happen. She was slightly reassured by Uncle Percival's rebuttal—he, at least, had thought her shock genuine.

Hetta curled her hands into fists, a fierce determination rising up in her. If she had to be the lord, then she was jolly well going to be a good one. She'd just show them!

Pulling herself together, she made her way to her youngest brother's chamber. Gregory emerged before she could knock. He had changed from his riding habit, but his locks were still in disarray.

Hetta surveyed him critically. "You'd better brush your hair before your mother sees you if you're trying to put her in a good mood."

Gregory reached up a hand to touch his fair curls. "Oh. I was in a hurry. Is Gwe—Miss Smith with you?" He looked around wildly, as if she might suddenly sprout from the worn hallway runner or fading damask wallpaper.

"No. I left her with Alexandra. You'll see her at breakfast, I imagine. But first I want some answers from you, Gregory. If you think I'm about to swallow that tall tale you told me earlier, you must think me a fool indeed!"

"It wasn't a tall tale! Gwe—Miss Smith's guardian is a monster, and she had no choice but to flee!"

"Who is she, Gregory?" Hetta said. "And don't tell me her name is 'Smith'. Really, I'm ashamed you have so little imagination!"

Gregory's mouth assumed a mulish aspect. "I don't know why you say so."

"Yes, you do." She tapped his shoulder lightly. "And you had much better make a clean breast of the affair if you hope for my help. Otherwise you can explain it all to your mother and Aunt Sybil by yourself."

Gregory blanched at this. "You wouldn't!" He turned beseeching grey eyes upon her. But Hetta was accustomed to soulful looks from far more accomplished actors than Gregory and remained unmoved. Gregory's shoulders slumped. "Fine, then. Her name isn't Miss Smith—it was the first thing that came into my head when you asked! But I don't rightly know who she is, except that she has suffered awfully, and I couldn't think what else to do but offer her sanctuary. And you can tell—you met her—that she's not a—" He coloured as he tried to think of a word that meant 'an unvirtuous woman' that he could use in front of his sister. Since his sister was, by some measures, not especially virtuous, she chose not to help him out with any suggestions, and he eventually gave up and made a vague gesture. "She's a good girl," he finished lamely.

"And how long have you known this 'good girl' of mysterious identity?"

Gregory flushed again, but a spark of amusement seemed to seize him now that he was confessing.

"Guessed that as well, did you? Though I don't know how you should have."

"I'm not an idiot," Hetta told him, though she didn't specify more than that. It was clear to her that Gregory was completely infatuated with Miss Gwen 'Smith', and though Hetta currently had a poor opinion of his good sense, even he could surely not have formed so severe a passion after only a few hours!

"Well, I met her just after Father died," Gregory admitted. "I went riding, pretty far out, beyond the estate boundaries, and I found her there, crying. She told me to go away, but I couldn't, could I?" he said disingenuously. "And so I asked if she was lost and she said no, she had ridden from her family house into the forest so that she might be alone for a while, and so I asked her what was wrong and she told me, in bits and pieces, about her guardian. And I couldn't think how to help her, but I promised I would try to think of something, and we arranged to meet again—she wouldn't tell me her full name. I think she was too afraid to. And so I've been meeting with her, and yesterday I told her I thought perhaps Jack would let her visit us, once he was—" He broke off here, in confusion, but Hetta encouraged him on.

"Yes, I know that is what we were all expecting, but do continue, please." Hetta didn't bother inquiring why he thought Jack would be particularly amenable to this scheme. It seemed unlikely, but Gregory viewed Jack with a kind of hero-worship, and his infatuation with Miss Gwen excused a measure of foolishness on his part.

"And I rode out this morning to tell her that things had changed, but she told me that her guardian had obtained a special license and meant to marry her out of hand tomorrow, so I had to act, you see!"

"And you do not know from whom she was fleeing, or, in fact, her name?"

"Well, no. She said to call her Gwen, so I have!" he said defiantly.

Hetta was sure that this tale, too, had some holes in it, but it felt at least half a step closer to the truth. She pinched the bridge of her nose, feeling a headache coming on.

"Well, inventing an acceptable story is quite beyond me, so I suppose the one you came up with must suffice. However, we had better say that it was me who found Miss Smith while out riding, not you, or your mother will never agree to her staying here for the time being." Lady Phoebe might be a doting mother, but Hetta doubted she'd look with favour on Gregory courting a nameless runaway, 'good girl' or not, particularly since he was underage. *Oh gods*, she thought, fighting an urge to laugh, *that means if he takes it into his foolish head that he wants to marry her, it's me he'll need permission from as head of the family.*

Gregory pulled himself upright, glowing with hope. "Oh, will you, Hetta? You are—"

She held out a hand to interrupt him. "Don't thank me just yet. I don't think we can in good conscience steal this girl away from her guardian without a by-your-leave. Her guardian will be quite worried when she is missed. You must find out who he is—"

"But you can't mean to send her back—"

Again, Hetta held up a hand. "If her story is true then of course I will try to help her how I may, but you must see that this cannot be a permanent solution."

"No, but I..." Gregory shuffled his feet awkwardly, and Hetta couldn't resist teasing him.

"And you know, Gregory," she continued as if he hadn't interrupted, "it's bad form to embark on a serious relationship with a girl without even knowing her last name!"

Gregory flushed beet red and stammered a confused negative, but Hetta had already started walking away. "Go brush your hair now, goose!"

Hetta didn't particularly want to approach her stepmother

before breakfast. Lady Phoebe was invariably a late riser and rarely appeared at the breakfast table, preferring to take a tray in her room at a later hour. Perhaps she could simply wait until Miss Gwen and Phoebe encountered each other later in the day, as they were sure to do eventually. The sight of Miss Gwen's tearful countenance might persuade Phoebe better than Hetta's more logical explanation. Yet so many of her relatives were awake abnormally early this morning that Hetta couldn't be confident that Phoebe wouldn't also be shaken out of her usual habits. It also seemed unbearably rude to begin her tenure as lord by not only inviting houseguests but also giving no warning of them whatsoever.

Hetta sighed and steeled herself to the task. Lady Phoebe's soft voice bade her come in when Hetta knocked, but she was still in her nightgown, sitting up in bed and reading a novel that looked of the sort Gregory had borrowed liberally from this morning. She didn't look old enough to be anyone's stepmother, let alone one with three children. She blinked confusedly at Hetta and set the book down on her lap.

"Good morning, dear." Phoebe bit her lip. "How—how are you?"

Hetta wasn't sure if this was a tactful way of referring to yesterday's Choosing or an attempt to ask why Hetta had invaded her bedroom at this hour without pointing out Hetta's rudeness. At least there was nothing of Aunt Sybil's bristling suspicion in her expression.

"Good morning," Hetta said briskly, ignoring both implied questions. She told Lady Phoebe about their new houseguest with cheerful matter-of-factness, as if there were no reason in the world for awkwardness, and it went rather better than she'd hoped. Phoebe only protested weakly: "But wherever shall we put her?" Since this was by far the easiest to answer of the many objections her stepmother might have raised, Hetta assured her that all was well in hand and swept out again before Phoebe had time to think.

She leaned against the wall of the corridor, a headache now in full bloom and pulsing at her temples. Gods, and she still had to tell Bradfield she wasn't coming back. The knowledge sat like a lump of ice in her chest. *After breakfast,* she told herself. *He probably won't even be up yet.* Gods, would Marius and Jack be at breakfast? But perhaps it would be better to face them sooner rather than later.

She was still rubbing at her head when Mr Fisk, her father's steward, appeared in the hallway as if from thin air. The reedy man with thinning hair didn't seem in the least curious about her leaning against the wall outside her stepmother's bedroom, and merely nodded stiffly at her as he passed. Hetta had never previously had much to do with him, and his air of dignified sobriety had intimidated her as a child.

Remembering her earlier vow, Hetta stopped him. "Mr Fisk. I expect we should set up an interview to discuss how the estate stands?"

Mr Fisk looked like he'd swallowed something nasty but nodded again. "Very good, Lord Valstar." Her heart gave a thud of dread, and she had to refrain from checking over her shoulder, as if her father's ghost might be standing behind her.

Forcing her mind away from that unhelpful image, she tried not to think about the fact that she was deliberately putting off speaking to Bradfield. "Will after breakfast suit?"

"As your lordship pleases," Mr Fisk said frostily, and bowed again before retreating.

Hetta blew out a long breath and reached for Stariel again, but there was no comfort to be found there. Her land-sense remained unchanged; Stariel still felt like it was waiting for something. But what, exactly?

12

ACCOUNTS

HETTA BUTTERED A crumpet and found herself thanking the gods for sending her Miss Gwen. Breakfast would have been unbearably awkward without the distraction. Even with Marius, Jack, and Aunt Sybil all absent, she felt the weight of her family's attention at this first shared meal after the Choosing. At least Miss Gwen's abrupt arrival gave them all something to talk about, rather than sitting in bristling silence with no one quite sure what to say. Mealtimes would get less awkward with repetition, once they got past this first one, surely? Hetta took a large bite of crumpet, fortifying herself with that thought.

Alexandra gave her mother a rather garbled account of Miss Gwen's trials while the subject of them blushed and stammered and begged Lady Phoebe to forgive her. Although Lady Phoebe appeared a tad confused, she was clearly touched by the distress of one so young and beautiful and, as Gregory had failed to articulate, respectable. Hetta observed this with a certain amount of ironic enjoyment, wondering how her stepmother would have reacted to someone without the 'respectable' accent, manners, and dress. But she was perhaps being unfair; Lady Phoebe had a kind heart and would've been moved by the girl's story in either case, though she might've been less inclined to welcome her into the house if she'd known of Gregory's involvement.

The single awkward moment came from an entirely unexpected quarter. Grandmamma made one of her erratic appearances at the breakfast table. She was a tall, birdlike woman with oak brown skin and tight iron-grey curls that added several inches to her height. Despite being closer to ninety than eighty, she moved with a sprightliness that belonged to a much younger woman. She greeted Hetta pleasantly enough as she came in, but upon glimpsing Miss Gwen seated at the table, she froze, her dark eyes widening.

"Who is that?" she demanded. She looked at Miss Gwen the way one looks at a snake one has nearly trodden on.

Hetta frowned. "This is Miss Gwen Smith, who has come to stay with us for a time."

Grandmamma's gaze shifted to Hetta. "Is she your guest? Did you invite her? Why is she here?"

Hetta paused. How was she to answer such direct questions? She felt strongly reluctant to lie outright to her grandmother. Fortunately, she did not have to, for Alexandra flared up in Miss Gwen's defence.

"Do not be so uncivil, Grandmamma. Miss Gwen suffered much before she came to us!" Alexandra said fiercely.

Grandmamma rocked back in astonishment at being so addressed by her granddaughter. She opened her mouth to speak, but then she appeared to think better of it and turned and left without excuse or leave-taking. There was a long pause, which the room took several minutes to recover from, aided by Alexandra's efforts to draw out their guest and Hetta taking the time to discuss the latest fashions in Meridon with Phoebe.

AFTER BREAKFAST, HETTA APPROACHED her father's study with a strong sense of approaching the principal's office. It occurred to her that she could put Mr Fisk off and tell him they would discuss business another day. She was technically the ruler of this estate and his employer, wasn't she? But she'd already put off one unpleasant task and delaying another felt too much like shirking. After all, this was her *job* now, and she needed to start somewhere.

She waited for Mr Fisk in her father's study. *Her* study, she amended after a mental pause. There wasn't much of her father's stamp on the room. He'd always preferred outdoor activities to bookwork, and the impersonal arrangement of the room suggested that hadn't changed in recent years. The only decorations were a painting of a prize-winning racehorse several generations past and a moth-eaten stuffed stag head placed above the door, and Hetta suspected both pre-dated her father's tenure. She walked around the large oak desk and bent to open the bottom drawer. The bottle of whisky it contained sloshed gently at the movement. Hetta stared down at the one piece of the room that *did* show evidence of her father's presence. Well, that was useful to know, at least, if this conversation went badly.

A knock on the door made her start, and she hastily slid the drawer shut.

"Come in!"

Mr Fisk entered, holding himself rigidly and carrying a stack of leather-bound volumes. Hetta's stomach sank at the size of the pile.

He didn't seem to notice Hetta's reluctance to sit in her father's chair, putting the files down on the desk and positioning himself across from it. He waited for her to sit before seating himself.

"Shall we make a start then?" she asked, when he seemed ready to remain in awkward silence forever.

He nodded and lifted the first accounts book.

It quickly became apparent that her father hadn't had much time for accounts, relying wholly on Mr Fisk to keep track of things. He seemed to expect much the same attitude from her, pausing in surprise when Hetta asked her first question.

"Do we really spend so little on repairs to the house?" She pointed at a column of numbers that Mr Fisk had been about to turn the page on. She had only the experience of the cost of theatre upkeep to guide her, but the total seemed incongruous.

Mr Fisk chose his words carefully. "Lord Henry was of the opinion that it was unnecessary to maintain the whole of the house when not all of it is required for living purposes."

"Well, these last few days have shown that it definitely is required for living purposes," Hetta said firmly. "And surely the cost of repairs will only get worse the longer they are put off?"

Mr Fisk nodded stiffly. He seemed eager to get this interview over with and only reluctantly stopped turning the pages of the accounts book each time she asked him another question.

"What about the Dower House? I heard it was closed recently?"

Mr Fisk nodded, his face expressionless. "To reduce the expense of maintaining it." He sat uncomfortably upright in his chair. Did he disapprove of her? Had he thought it would be Jack sitting in her father's chair now?

Hetta frowned. "Why was my father trying to reduce expenses?" Maybe frankness might draw him out of his peculiar stiffness.

"The estate's accounts sail very close to the wind, as the saying goes," Mr Fisk said repressively.

"Well, we can't keep living in the last century. We must get the new elektricity up here to the house. And phone lines." She felt on firmer ground here. All of Meridon was wired for elektricity now.

"That will require a great outlay of capital, I imagine."

"Can the estate manage it?"

He paused, delicately. "The capital...it might be raised by selling off some small area of land. Lord Penharrow has stated his interest in purchasing the eastern fields for some years now."

"I see," Hetta said. "I assume my father wasn't keen on the idea of cutting up the estate?"

"He was not. He was...somewhat irrational on the subject, if you will forgive me for saying so."

Hetta found herself agreeing with her father, irrational or not. To sell a piece of Stariel? The thought was not to be borne. She was a little surprised at the strength of her own feelings on the subject.

"But perhaps the bank might be persuaded to give us a loan?" She thought of her overpaid rent in Meridon. "What if we rented out the Dower House?" Warming to her subject, she added, "And aren't there land improvements and suchlike that could increase productivity, maybe?" It was extremely surreal, talking about land improvements as if she had any idea whatsoever how they worked, but she felt surer about the need for elektricity.

Mr Fisk's eyes widened, and he began to object at length to her proposals, turning suddenly loquacious. In the steward's view, it was far better to sell some portion of the estate than to saddle it with debt, though Hetta didn't entirely understand why reducing the estate's land holdings would be a better long-term result.

"I suppose I should also get you to show me around the estate. And I'll need to talk to the tenant farmers as well." Would she? Gods, she had no idea what she was doing. Why had Stariel chosen her when she was ignorant of practically all the skills that might be useful to its lord? She squashed the panic down. There was no point wasting energy railing against Stariel's decision now. She would just have to figure it out. Somehow.

Mr Fisk agreed but added diffidently that Mr Jack was best placed to advise her on the day-to-day running of the estate and the current management practices. He didn't quite manage to meet her eyes as he said this, and Hetta said brightly:

"Well, I suppose I shall just have to ask Mr Jack to give me a tour, then." Jack hadn't shown at breakfast, to Hetta's relief.

She knew she ought to question Mr Fisk further, but she was quite out of temper by this point and summarily dismissed him. He went willingly and would have taken the accounts books back except that she bade him leave them. He did so reluctantly.

After Mr Fisk had vacated the room, Hetta looked glumly at the accounts books in front of her. The prospect of going through them didn't grow any more agreeable. Yet still they seemed more enticing than the task she was putting off: calling Bradfield and informing him that his prize illusionist would not be returning after all.

The door opened just as she was going through the entries for September, and Hetta looked up. As it turned out, the only person she would have been happy to see stood there, holding a tray from which the sweet scent of lemon rose.

13

LEMON CAKE

"I THOUGHT YOU MIGHT require sustenance," Wyn commented, bringing the tray over and setting it on the desk. The lemon smell turned out to be emanating from a slice of fresh cake.

"You are a wonder." Hetta reached for the tea he'd brought. She found it difficult not to linger on the lean lines of him, but she forced herself to maintain a business-like expression. *He is your employee! And your friend!* "I don't suppose you're secretly an accounting genius?"

Wyn perched on the chair that Mr Fisk had recently vacated and looked down at the accounts books with interest. "Do you need one?" He cocked his head to one side, and a few strands of white-blond hair fell over his eyes.

"I'm afraid I do. It seems my inheritance is not an especially solvent one."

Wyn grimaced. "I feared that. I have never been granted access to the estate accounts, but—" He was frowning out the window when something caught his attention. He stiffened. "That should not be possible," he said in quite a different tone, low and menacing.

He got up and stalked closer to the window, every sinew taut. The wildness that sometimes surfaced in him was very much in evidence now, his mild, civilised veneer falling away in an instant. It was, Hetta thought, very much like realising what you had thought was a house cat was, in fact, a tiger.

Hetta stood. "What are you talking about?"

He didn't seem to hear her. "That woman! Do you know who she is?"

She shuffled closer to the window to try to see what had caught his attention. Below, in the winter garden, were Alexandra and Miss Gwen. Alexandra was pointing some feature of the house out to Miss Gwen.

Wyn shifted sharply to the wall beside the window, the movement sudden enough that it made Hetta blink. "She hasn't seen me, has she? Does she know I'm here?"

Miss Gwen continued her consideration of the house and looked up and met Hetta's eyes. She gave a little start, and Hetta waved. Miss Gwen waved back, then turned and said something to Alexandra, who also dutifully returned the gesture. Hetta turned away from the window and narrowed her eyes at Wyn, who was vibrating with repressed anger. Or fear, maybe—she couldn't tell.

"No, I don't think she saw you," she said. "But why on earth—"

"I'm sorry," he said, and moved towards the door, covering the distance in two strides of his long legs. He paused for the briefest instant on the threshold, turning to say: "Please, Hetta, if you value me at all, don't tell that creature of my presence in this house!"

And then he was gone.

"Wyn!" Hetta called after him, infuriated. She followed him out into the corridor, but he had disappeared. She pulled up short halfway along, realising that she had started to run after him. The new lord chasing her butler through the house didn't seem like a good idea. Particularly since the chances of catching Wyn when he was intent on being elusive were nil.

She scowled. While it was like Wyn to be secretive, she'd never seen him display such turbulence before. Why had both he and Grandmamma reacted so oddly to the sight of Miss Gwen? She began to feel a glimmer of apprehension that wasn't related to the awkwardness of housing their mysterious runaway. Wyn's reaction had been one of someone confronted with something not just unpleasant but potentially dangerous. How could Miss Gwen pose a danger to Wyn? Did she know him from before he came to Stariel?

Hetta turned this idea over while absently picking at a peeling piece of wallpaper—they *definitely* needed to find some more money for house maintenance. Perhaps Wyn feared something about his past being revealed? She'd never come up with a satisfactory background for her friend, and he'd been impossible to pin down on the subject. His manners and speech patterns suggested a 'respectable' background, though his striking colouring and faint, un-placeable accent had always made her suppose he hadn't been born in Prydein; she'd vaguely put his origins somewhere on the continent, maybe one of those ever-shifting Balentic principalities. If pressed, she'd have guessed he'd suffered some form of abuse or abandonment from his family that had made him determined to break away from them entirely. Why he'd chosen a menial position in an isolated estate as a vocation, Hetta had no idea.

But Miss Gwen came from somewhere near Stariel Estate, so how could she know anything about Wyn's past? Hetta's frown deepened. Where had Gregory said he'd found her, again?

Before Hetta could make up her mind what to do, she heard footsteps from the other end of the corridor and turned to see

Marius. Her older brother froze, and they contemplated each other in silence for several long seconds, warped reflections of each other. Marius broke first, the tension in him terrible to behold. He came forward in rapid strides, face gaunt with anxiety.

"Hetta, I'm sorry. I'm so sorry. I never meant—"

Of all the reactions Hetta had anticipated, this was not one. She stared at him. "Are you apologising," she said slowly, anger beginning to dawn, "because you think this is your fault?"

Marius jerked to a halt a few feet away. He looked quite wretched, the circles under his eyes even deeper than before. "I'm…I didn't…" he began falteringly.

"Marius Rufus Valstar, are you telling me that you have the truly monumental arrogance to claim that Stariel's choice is somehow your fault? That you have been so utterly self-indulgent and deluded as to think you could have somehow changed this? That this is somehow about *you*?"

Marius went white and opened and closed his mouth several times without speaking. It made him look like nothing so much as a dying goldfish, and with that image, Hetta's gathering anger evaporated and she began to laugh. The laughter had an edge of hysteria to it, but it felt good.

"Oh, Marius, whatever would I do without you and your melodrama?" She stepped forward to embrace him. He relaxed only fractionally, board-stiff and awkward.

When she stepped back, he peered down at her with puzzlement, his glasses slipping to the end of his nose. "I know you didn't want this, Hetta."

She smiled wryly. "Apparently, you're the only one who does." Then she closed her eyes and steeled herself. "Now, will you drive me to the gatehouse so that I can make a phonecall?"

Marius blinked at her. "I—of course." He frowned. "Can't you drive?" This was said with surprise rather than accusation.

"Never learnt," Hetta admitted. "There wasn't much need in Meridon."

"Oh." Marius gave a weak smile. "It seems strange to find something I can do that you can't."

Hetta raised an eyebrow at him. "Don't rest on your laurels for too long, brother mine. I imagine I'll be wanting you to teach me if I'm to stay up here."

There was too much understanding in Marius's eyes. It was the first time Hetta had alluded to her new role and the changes it would mean for her.

"I know this isn't what you imagined," Marius said quietly as they went down to the garage.

"What either of us imagined. Glad to have me as your overlord?" Hetta said sardonically.

Marius gave a true smile at this. He looked her up and down, and some measure of peace came over him. "Time will tell."

14

UNPLEASANT CONVERSATIONS

THE PAST TWENTY-FOUR hours had been difficult, but they paled into insignificance as Hetta contemplated the handset in front of her. She took a deep breath and raised the receiver with fingers that trembled only slightly. After the operator put her through to the Sun Theatre, the phone rang four times before it was picked up, and her heart stuttered in the pause between each one.

"Hello?" a cool young woman's voice answered, familiar but not recognisable from so few syllables.

"This is Henrietta Valstar. I need to speak to Mr Bradfield." Hetta remembered belatedly that she should say 'Lord Valstar'.

"Hetta!" The woman's voice instantly warmed. "It's Angela! I was so sorry to hear about your father, but we'll be glad to have you back. You won't believe what Sally-Ann managed to do to her dress! But Brad's just come in. Wait here."

There was silence on the other end of the telephone before Hetta could reply. She could make out the faint background noises of people talking and moving around, but nothing distinct until Bradfield picked up the phone.

"Hetta! I didn't think to hear from you before your arrival." There was a note of caution in his voice that became overt in his next words. "Is anything the matter?"

"Brad—" Hetta said, and then had to pause to collect herself. In what was now an obvious oversight, she'd neglected to mentally prepare some kind of speech for Bradfield, and her mind had gone blank. The temptation surged in her to say that nothing was wrong at all; that she would see them all tomorrow; that she'd merely wanted to check everything was well.

Her pause had become noticeable. "Hetta?" Bradfield repeated uncertainly.

"I won't be coming back," Hetta said in a rush. The words hurt as they left her lips, and she wanted immediately to recall them. "I mean, I will, to get my things, but not for the show."

She could imagine Bradfield so clearly in her mind's eye, the way his forehead would crease as he frowned, his mouth tightening as the meaning of her words penetrated. Around him would be the chaotic mill of the stage crew, the actors, and the seamstresses, colour and laughter and cheap wine. She yearned so badly to be back there with them all, laughing at Arthur's bad accents and Sally-Ann's dramatics and feeling part of a world where she knew what she was doing; where she *fit*.

"You mean you need more time up there?" Bradfield sounded desperately keen for an affirmative.

"No," Hetta said. "No—I—" She swallowed. "I'm the new Lord of Stariel." She let out a little laugh. "If you can imagine something so ridiculous."

There was a stunned silence at the other end of the line. "I see. There's no chance you could—but, no, I suppose not."

"I don't know how long it will be before I can leave Stariel for any length of time. The estate is in some chaos at present." Now that the worst had been revealed, Hetta found her voice growing steadier. "But I hope to make it down to Meridon later in the year, perhaps. I'm so sorry, Brad. I never meant to put you in such a bind."

"Nonsense," Brad said staunchly. "And, I suppose, congratulations."

At this, Hetta broke. "If you knew how badly I wished things were otherwise—"

"Don't, Hetta," Bradfield interrupted her. "Your duty is with Stariel now. But I hope that you will still consider me a friend?"

"Gods, Brad, you've no idea! Try if you will to stop me descending upon you in all my glory as soon as I can. And you're welcome at Stariel, you know. Always."

"Be careful, or I might just take you up on that," Bradfield said, a smile in his voice. "Might come in handy, having a lord as a friend."

Hetta found herself dabbing furiously at her eyes with her handkerchief, but she laughed through her tears, trying not to sound like she was dying inside.

She could sense Brad's thoughts turning through the phoneline, considering his next course of action. He might sincerely mourn her departure from the company, but he was cursed with the kind of mind that did not cease to consider consequences because of mere emotional considerations. Sure enough, after a few moments, he began:

"I don't suppose you know anyone—" But then the awkwardness of asking her to help find her own replacement caught up with him and he broke off.

She laughed again, this time more genuinely. "You're the absolute worst, Brad. Here I am suffering under the greatest shock of my life and you're already mentally compiling a list of possible replacements for me! You could at least pretend to be too overcome for such cold practicality for two minutes!"

"Sorry, I wasn't thinking," Bradfield said. Then, more fervently, "I'll have a damnable time replacing you. Just how many master illusionists do you think there are wandering around Meridon free as daisies?"

"None," Hetta told him primly. "You shall be forced to settle."

"I will." He sounded resigned. "Gods dammit, Hetta, I will miss you something fierce!"

"You had better. Oh, very well—there's a journeywoman illusionist called Ida Winters who might be willing to fill in for you at short notice."

"A journeywoman!" Brad groaned. "Heavens preserve me. Has she worked stage shows before?"

"No, but she's very willing to learn." It was hard for female illusionists to find work; Hetta was sure that Ida would move mountains if necessary to take advantage of the opportunity. After all, Hetta had. The thought was a sharp spike of ice in her belly, but she concentrated instead on how happy her illusionist friend would be at this chance. Ida had been in a depressive mood lately, despairing of ever putting her training to use. It was, however, difficult to feel particularly generous at the thought of giving her life's dream to someone else, no matter how much she knew Ida would appreciate it.

She gave him Ida's contact details, and he made her promise to have dinner with him when she came to pack up her belongings. Their conversation grew more stilted after that. She knew Bradfield wasn't quite sure what to say now that Hetta had delivered her bombshell and was anxious to get onto resolving what was for him a very pressing issue. It was a relief to replace the receiver in its rest. Yet the sound of Bradfield's voice had taken her away from her present self for a little while, and it was a shock to have to readjust to the world as it was again.

She dabbed at her eyes to be sure they were quite dry and smoothed her hair back into place before she left the gatehouse.

"Oh, Hetta," Marius said as she came back to the car, and guilt flickered in his eyes again. Hetta was too tired to call him on it. Instead, she deliberately turned the conversation to less painful topics.

The kineticar was a handsome black creature that looked entirely too modern for an estate apparently falling into rack and ruin. But how like her father, Hetta thought despairingly, to purchase the latest toys but decree that the elektrification and telephone wiring that had only gotten as far as the gatehouse must be put off.

"Have you met our new guest?" she asked as they began the drive back.

Marius had. "Although I'm not entirely clear on what, exactly, we are supposed to do with her. And Gregory is entirely too infatuated."

"You're immune to her charms, then?"

Marius averted his eyes, and some emotion she couldn't identify passed quickly over his face. "She's a pretty young thing, I'll admit," he said without inflection. "And innocent as a kitten—I can see why that would raise a man's protective instincts, but still, Gregory is insufferable."

"Love makes us all insufferable, I think," Hetta said mildly.

"Love," Marius said grimly, "has nothing to do with it. Greg's too young to tell love from infatuation."

"Have you ever been in love, Marius?" Hetta asked, suddenly seeing her brother in a different light. His romantic entanglements hadn't held much interest for her when she'd been younger, but it now occurred to her that she'd never known him to show a preference for anyone. Had that changed while she'd been away? Had he been disillusioned in love? He was, she thought with a sudden jolt, old enough that in a man who wasn't her brother, she might have expected him to be married with children.

"Not the sort that you're imagining, sister mine." A bitter smile twisted his lips. "And yourself? Fallen in love with your damned theatre director, I hazard?"

Hetta burst out laughing. "No. We've always been good friends, but even if I were interested in more, I am decidedly not his type." More than that she would not say. Bradfield's secrets were not hers to share.

A silence fell. Hetta looked back in the direction of the village as they drove. Stariel-on-Starwater wasn't visible at this distance and angle, but she felt it looming there, another thing that would need to be dealt with at some point. If she concentrated, the village pressed against her land-sense, like something very light brushing her skin.

"Did Father ever talk about his land-sense with you?" Hetta asked as they slowed to come into the converted garage next to the stables.

Marius looked startled. "I hadn't even thought about it, but I suppose now—"

But Hetta was already shaking her head. "It doesn't feel any different to me than before."

"Father never spoke of it, much," Marius said. "I suppose I just assumed that the connection sorted itself out, when you were chosen." He made a flailing gesture with his left hand.

"I admit I did too," Hetta said. "I was expecting something more dramatic. But now I'm wondering if it takes time to, I don't know, settle in?"

Marius shrugged as well. He parked the car, turned off the ignition, and drummed his fingers on the steering wheel before replying. "I could have a look in the family histories for you."

"I'd appreciate it."

Marius shot her a brief, searching look. "You're worried something's wrong. That the bond didn't take as it should."

Marius had always had an unfortunate habit of having flashes of insight precisely when they would be least convenient. Hetta considered dissembling, but eventually gave him an honest reply. "Yes. It may be that nothing at all is the matter—this might be perfectly normal, for all I know. But I would rather not find out that something has gone wrong with the bond from, say, Aunt Sybil."

Marius gave a short laugh, then reached to pat her reassuringly on the shoulder. "Don't worry, Hetta. I won't spread it around. And it's not as if me poking about in the library will make anyone suspicious." A touch of sadness crept into his voice.

"Would you still want to go back to your studies? I know Father prevented you from continuing."

Marius blew out a long breath. "I don't know. It's been such a long time—I have tried to keep up my interest, but it's been hard without access to the books and mentors I need." He looked at her fondly. "And I could hardly leave you in the lurch here." Before Hetta could deny that she needed him to stay, he held up a finger. "But maybe, once things are more settled here." He gave another laugh, this one far less bitter. "How strange, to no longer feel potential destiny looming over me." He seemed to realise what he'd said from Hetta's expression. "Sorry. I know it's not fair for me to revel in my freedom when you've just been unwillingly bound. But you've had years of liberty that I haven't."

"I know," Hetta said softly. She was glad that Marius seemed to be taking his new status rather well. There was an air of anticipation about him that she hadn't seen before.

"You know," Marius said slowly, "the one person Father might have talked to about his land-sense is Jack."

"The thought had occurred." She wasn't looking forward to that conversation.

Marius leaned forward, eyes fierce. "He'll come around. I know Stariel's not what you wanted, and it's not what you deserve, but I think that Stariel is lucky to have you for its lord."

Hetta had to blink rapidly at the sudden prick of tears this vote of confidence caused. “Thank you. I don’t know if you’re right or not, but I hope so.” She sighed. “Let’s go find Jack.”

15

CRYPTIC ADVICE

JACK WASN'T ANYWHERE to be found, and Marius's optimism didn't make a dent in the atmosphere of the house. Aunt Sybil simply treated any space Hetta filled as if it were empty. Since this was an improvement over her usual manner, Hetta made no effort to persuade her to abandon her cold shoulder. Lady Phoebe fluttered anxiously around, trying to pretend that everything was perfectly normal and that no one was displeased with anything or anyone. It was exhausting watching her do this, and Hetta retreated to her father's study to mull over the accounts further.

One of the maids brought her afternoon tea and simply shrugged when Hetta asked if she'd seen Wyn.

"Down in the village, like, dropping off the kiddies that brought us sloe berries today, my lord," she said. "They find the kineticar such a treat! Then he'll be helping Cook, I'll be bound; the kitchen-maid is still poorly. I'll tell him you want him, when I see him."

Hetta had thanked her, a little taken aback at the notion that she apparently had the power to summon Wyn as she pleased. That power was quickly shown to be imaginary, for Wyn didn't appear, and when she went in search of him, he was so legitimately busy that she couldn't reasonably interrupt him.

Hetta examined Miss Gwen in more detail at supper that night. She seemed a little fatigued, but she remained polite and grateful. There was nothing in the least alarming in her appearance, except for the odd notion Hetta got, after watching her for a length of time, that her manner was a little too perfectly ingenuous to be quite genuine. But, Hetta reflected, perhaps that was only natural given the situation.

Grandmamma didn't come to the meal. Hetta went in search of her after supper and found her in the stillroom, muttering darkly as she tied up fresh bunches of herbs and hung them. The stillroom's smell transported Hetta back in time. It wasn't unpleasant, but it was so strong that it took a while to adjust when one first entered. Hetta had spent many evenings helping Grandmamma here. The herbs hung just above head height for a lady, which meant Hetta had to stoop to avoid walking into some of the lower-hanging bunches.

Her grandmother thrust a large bunch of rosemary across the workbench at her. It had been a long while since Hetta had dried herbs, but her fingers remembered, and she automatically took the stems between her fingers and began twining a cord around them.

"We missed you at supper, Grandmamma."

Her grandmother gave an unladylike huff and hung her rosemary with unnecessary vigour, so that instead of the hook slotting neatly into the wire affixed to the ceiling for that purpose, it fell to the ground. Hetta hurried to pick it up. Grandmamma looked slightly mollified as Hetta handed it to her.

"I won't sit at table with that creature."

"I was meaning to ask you about that, actually. Will you tell me why you dislike Miss Gwen so much? Have you met her before?"

Grandmamma's eyes narrowed, and she pursed her lips, deepening the wrinkles in her cheeks. "I know trouble when I see it," she said eventually.

It was fortunate that Hetta was accustomed to her grandmother's opaque ways, or she might have grown frustrated at this inexact answer. Grandmamma set much stock in what she called 'portents' and Aunt Sybil called 'superstitions'. Then, in one of the abrupt changes of subject that was entirely typical of her grandmother, she said, "You've no plans to leave the estate, do you?"

"Leave?" repeated Hetta, surprised. "Well, I must go down to Meridon and arrange for my belongings—"

"Don't."

"Don't retrieve my belongings? Are you afraid I'm going to fill the house with truckloads of modern gewgaws? I will have you know that I own only a modest number of gewgaws, and certainly not enough to fill more than my own room."

Her grandmother waved this away as if it were entirely irrelevant. "Yes, yes. Of course you must tidy your affairs up. But not yet. Promise me you'll wait until we've seen off Miss Gwen, at least. You cannot be leaving while we have guests."

Hetta wasn't sure why this should be the case, but it was unlike her grandmother to make such a forceful request.

"Are you worried that Gregory is too taken with her?" Hetta pressed. Grandmamma was very fond of all her grandchildren, and it was possible that her reaction to Miss Gwen grew from this.

"Gregory is the least of my concerns. What worries me is that she could come here at all, if my suspicions are correct."

"What do you mean?"

Grandmamma considered her. "Talk to that lad of yours."

"You mean Wyn," Hetta said with a sigh.

Her grandmother gave her an approving look. "That's one thing I've always liked about you, Henrietta. You're not missish about straight-talking. And yes. Talk to Wyn." She rolled her lips like she'd swallowed something sour.

"Do you know where he's got to?"

"Checking the defences, I'll be bound."

Hetta stared at her, baffled. "Checking the defences? This isn't a fortress, and unless I'm quite mistaken, we're not under siege. Nor do we live in medieval times."

Grandmamma made an impatient noise. "He'll tell you what's what when he's ready. He's a good boy, that Wyn," she added fondly. Only her grandmother could refer so to a man nearly thirty years of age without sounding extremely silly.

"Well, until someone gives me a concrete reason to send Miss Gwen away, I can't help but take pity on her."

"Yes, it's a sad story she tells," Grandmamma agreed with maddening reasonableness, picking the petals off a late-blooming rose.

Hetta threw her hands up and was about to turn and walk out when her grandmother said, "And don't forget that the Frost Ball planning needs to be set in motion. And the estate's contribution for the Frost Faire."

Hetta sighed and took this as the peace offering it was intended to be, coming back to kiss her grandmother's cheek. "I have complete faith in you and Lady Phoebe to arrange things."

"Yes, parties are one of the few things Phoebe is good for," Grandmamma agreed.

Hetta chose not to answer this and left her grandmother to go back to her study.

She was congratulating herself on successfully avoiding confrontation over her new status for the entire day when Aunt Sybil swept into the room in high dudgeon.

"Where is Jack?" she demanded, striding across to the desk without waiting to be invited in. She frowned darkly around at the room. "Didn't take you much time to shift in here, did it?"

"I've no idea where my cousin is," Hetta said politely, not rising from her seat. "I haven't seen him since yesterday."

Since yesterday referred to the Choosing Ceremony, this understandably provoked Aunt Sybil.

"Since yesterday! Then you know that he has been missing since last night!" Aunt Sybil delivered this with terrible accent, but Hetta remained unmoved.

"I have to admit it doesn't surprise me. The others tell me it's quite usual for him to take his dog with him and spend a night or two out on the estate, and Shadow is as absent as her master. Apparently, many of the shepherds' huts are vacant at present, and Jack's been known to kip in one of those if he doesn't fancy coming all the way back to the house for the night."

"As though you care where he is!" Aunt Sybil said, her colour mounting. "He might be at the bottom of a cliff and you sit there, unmoved!"

Hetta raised an eyebrow and drew a pencil line through an entry in the accounts book with deliberate calm (she'd no idea whether it needed to be crossed out or not, but she liked the competent attitude the motion suggested. She could, after all, erase the line after her aunt had left).

"And have you any reason to suppose, Aunt," she said with slow civility, "that he is at the bottom of a cliff rather than in one of his usual haunts?"

"He has suffered an immense shock, as well you know! He shouldn't be alone at a time like this! Who knows what foolishness he'll take into his head!"

Hetta wasn't sure how sincerely worried Aunt Sybil was or whether her agitation was entirely due to her continuing pique over Hetta's new position, but she tried to give her the benefit of the doubt. She thought of Bradfield's manner when he was dealing with particularly high-strung members of the cast.

"I understand your concern, Aunt," she said, composing herself.

"And I agree that we should make sure Jack is well. I know my being chosen came as a surprise to him—almost as much as it did to me," Hetta added, then hurried on before Aunt Sybil could interrupt, "But that doesn't mean that I don't value Jack. On the contrary, I suspect he will be essential to the effective running of this estate. If he's still missing tomorrow morning, I will personally go in search of him."

Aunt Sybil would have preferred for a search to begin here and now, and Hetta tried to point out to her that Jack was probably fine and wouldn't appreciate his relatives coming to retrieve him while he was in a sulk, but to no avail. Eventually she was forced to summarily dismiss her aunt, which startled her enough for Hetta to get up and open the door, thus making it impossible for her aunt to remain seated.

After Aunt Sybil left, Hetta rested her head against the cool wood of the desk and tried to console herself with the thought that things couldn't possibly get any worse.

16

A TOUR OF THE ESTATE

THE NEXT MORNING at breakfast, Hetta enquired of her youngest brother whether Jack had, to his knowledge, returned. Gregory rolled his eyes, although the gesture wasn't intended for Hetta. He'd been grilled by Aunt Sybil the night before and was quite out of temper with the topic of his cousin.

"I've not seen him," he said.

"Could you hazard a guess as to where I should look for him? I know everyone says he's likely happily holed up in one of the shepherds' huts, but I admit I'd rest easier knowing he was well."

"Jack knows Stariel like his own hand," Gregory said scornfully. "You won't find him if he doesn't want you to."

"I was also thinking I need to tour the estate anyway. Will you come with me?"

Gregory looked torn, and Hetta noted with amusement the way his gaze slid to Miss Gwen, who was seated at the other end of the table next to Alexandra, quietly engaged in conversation.

The problem was resolved better than Hetta had hoped when Lord Angus Penharrow abruptly arrived after breakfast to pay his respects to the new lord. Hetta roped him into accompanying her with such efficient ruthlessness that they were mounted on Alexandra and Gregory's hacks and several fields away from the house before he could protest.

"Let me get this straight," Angus said, his voice rich with amusement. "*I'm* giving *you* a tour of Stariel Estate?"

"Let's say that you are enlivening my tour with your presence. I don't need a guide, per se. It's not as if Stariel is unknown to me." She smiled at him. "And if it wouldn't be terribly unprofessional to admit it, I would truly appreciate your opinion. I don't know what I should about land management, and you seem quite the expert."

"I've a weakness for damsels in distress," Angus confessed easily, nodding to her. "Especially ones that ride as well as you."

"Thank you for saying so, even if it is raw flattery, for I'm sadly out of practice," Hetta said frankly.

Whilst there were vehicle tracks through Stariel, the bulk of the estate was accessible only from horseback or on foot. Hetta had decided to tackle the Sheepfold first. North of the house, the Sheepfold encompassed the rolling foothills of the Indigo Range. It was a landscape of contrasts: steep hillsides that descended into narrow valleys criss-crossed by streams and the occasional small lake. The valley floors tended to be boggy, particularly this late in the year, and the soil was thin on the hillsides, making them treacherous.

The horses of Stariel were a local breed, stockier and less beautiful than their Southern counterparts, but much more sure-footed. The mare that Hetta rode was a mottled brown-and-white creature with a smooth gait and good manners. Lord Angus rode the larger horse, a grey gelding that already looked grubby about the hocks from mud-splatter.

Something deep and solemn in her settled as they picked their way up towards the higher hills where the more isolated shepherds' huts were located. As a child, she'd spent hours wandering these hills, certain she was the only one to discover particular overhangs and interesting tree formations. The landscape seemed shrunken, somehow, from her memories, but there was something reassuringly solid in the smell of damp earth, grass, and sheep leavings.

"You ought to drain some of the lower flats," Angus commented, scanning the area. "And put it to use for something other than sheep. There's good soil here in places."

"I'll have to take your word for it." She sighed. "I suppose drains are expensive?"

Angus cocked his head to one side. "In the first year, yes, but they more than pay for themselves in the increase in productivity."

"And that's what you'd do, in my place?" Hetta asked. "Won't it affect the waterways downstream?"

Angus nodded. "Aye, but you can prepare for that. If you design it well, you can reduce the effects of floods as well. I know this area is prone to flash-floods."

"Yes, it is," Hetta said. "And what else would you do, if you were in my place?"

Angus, it seemed, had put considerable effort into thinking exactly how to answer this question. "Well, Stariel is good land. It's a waste that so much of it is spent on low-margin goods, or not producing at all. The sheep are a reasonable use of some of the hill lands, but the flats would be better put into something else, with the proper drainage. And it's a crying shame to leave all the land to the south in forest."

"What would you replace them with?" Hetta prompted.

Angus frowned. "I've been thinking you should update your sheep breeds. Some of the newer breeds can still cope with the cold and produce higher wool yields. And I think I'd trial some orchard varieties to the south. You've tasted the fruits of Stariel's home farm—you should know they're something quite out of the ordinary. As I said, there's something in the soil here that makes the produce superior to that of the surrounding area. To be perfectly frank, I think that's the only reason the estate hasn't gone under. Not to mince words, but the management's been pretty abysmal for decades."

"Father was a great believer in tradition."

Angus shook his head as if this were an argument he'd had before. "There's tradition, and then there's refusing to take advantage of modern ways of farming that would be good for the estate."

"You sound like you've put a bit of thought into it."

Angus shrugged. "Don't like to see good land go to waste." He paused, then added, "Jack was of much the same mind. We got to talking about it a time or two."

"Well, if Jack is willing, I have a good mind to put him to work," Hetta mused.

Angus looked doubtful. "He loves this place, but he's always imagined it as his. I don't know how well he'll deal with being under your authority."

"Well, I am held to be persistent, if nothing else," Hetta said lightly, although privately she agreed with Angus.

Angus again swept the landscape with his gaze, and said without looking at her, "If Jack won't help you, I know of at least one neighbouring lord who will." He turned back to watch her expression, one eyebrow raised quizzically.

"You do, do you?" said Hetta, amused but also pleased. "Are you sure that you're not merely trying to bargain for a piece of Stariel for yourself? My steward tells me you've been making offers to my father for the last several years." It was understandable that Angus should be eager to buy a swathe of the eastern lands; the estate adjoined Penharrow Estate along much of that boundary. Stariel was far larger than Penharrow, but far behind it in terms of land improvements. When she'd asked Mr Fisk about the tenant farmers' views of the situation, he had given a noncommittal response. Hetta had added this to the ever-growing list of things she didn't know enough about.

Angus shot her a quick, brilliant grin. "Heard that already, have you? Well, I won't deny that it's true. I've been viewing those eastern boundary lands with avarice for some time now. Say the word and I'll make you a good offer."

"Given that I've been in my position for less than two days, I should think it somewhat premature to start selling off my inheritance," Hetta told him sternly, though she liked him the better for his honesty.

He laughed. "Fair enough. Don't mind waiting for you to come around." He looked her up and down as if he were taking the measure of a new horse, eyes twinkling. "It helps that you're easy on the eyes."

Hetta was decidedly glad that she'd taken Angus with her rather than Gregory. She wasn't quite certain whether his flirting was in earnest, but she was enjoying the attention from her childhood hero nonetheless.

She could see why he and Jack might have struck up a friendship. They shared the same abiding interest in the land and its people. They were both archetypal country men: broad shouldered, bluff, good humoured, and not too high in the instep to dirty their hands when necessary. There was a streak of deep patience in Angus that wasn't present in Jack, and Hetta wondered if this was an essential difference in personality or if Jack would mature into it.

They encountered a couple of the hill shepherds; rangy, introspective men who chose their words with care and seemed almost preternaturally aware of their dogs. The first denied any knowledge of Jack, although he didn't meet Hetta's eyes as he spoke. Hetta wasn't sure if this was because of discomfort at encountering a woman in what he might very well think was a man's place or if he was being deliberately evasive. The second was only slightly more helpful. He had seen Jack late the day before, but he hadn't spoken to him, nor had he seen where he'd gone to roost.

"You might try up in the Thornfield," he said at last.

They followed this shrugging piece of advice without much hope. They did find recent signs of someone's presence in the Thornfield hut, but there was no sign of Jack.

"I thought this might happen," Angus said. "If the man doesn't want to be found, we won't find him. Let him come back on his own terms."

Hetta sighed. "I fear you're right."

They made their way back via some of the northern pastures, and Hetta was interested to see that many of the tenant farmers they passed not only knew Angus but were known to him in return. They seemed rather more pleased to see him than Hetta. They paused briefly to greet the farmers they met. Some acknowledged Hetta as Lord Valstar; others only stared with disquieting silence or monosyllabic grunts.

"They'll come around," Angus said staunchly.

Even though they hadn't found Jack, Hetta didn't feel that the day had been wasted. Angus was good company, and besides having more of a feel for the estate, she felt exhilarated by the exercise, although she knew she would pay for it tomorrow.

They handed the horses back into the care of the head groom, and she walked Angus back to his kineticar. The garage was deserted, and she wondered if he'd repeat his impropriety of the previous week. He looked like he was strongly considering it. Did she want to encourage him? It had been a very pleasant kiss, and Hetta wouldn't mind repeating the experience, but things were different now. It had been one thing to kiss the neighbouring lord when she was leaving within a week; it was quite another now that she was staying. Hetta-the-no-name-illusionist could do what she liked with whomever she liked—that would not be the case for Henrietta Valstar, Lord of Stariel.

Before the issue was decided one way or the other, they were interrupted by Gregory, who besides wanting to plague Angus about his kineticar, demanded to know if they'd seen Alexandra and Miss Gwen.

"Don't tell me we have another runaway," Hetta said with a groan.

Gregory grinned despite his frustration. "No, just that the girls went out walking earlier this morning without telling me where they were going and I—"

"Felt like you were much in need of exercise," Hetta finished for him.

He laughed, unrepentant. "Well, yes, now you mention it!"

"Well, we didn't see either of them, so I'm afraid we can't help you," said Angus, not unkindly, looking somewhat bemused.

Hetta took her leave of them both and went back into the house. She made a mental note to order some books on drains and speak to Mr Fisk about making an appointment with the bank manager. Angus's advice had made her feel surer of her own instincts about the need to modernise.

Her steward proved elusive, so she made her way to the library with some thought of asking Marius if he'd found out anything about the lord's land-sense yet. The library was one of Hetta's favourite rooms at Stariel. The warm, high-ceilinged room was laid out almost like a hall, with staircases giving access to the upper level of books lining the walls. It was probable, Hetta thought, that it had once been a ballroom, but she applauded whichever of her ancestors had decided to build the east wing with its more modern ballroom and convert this smaller room into a library.

There was no sign of Marius, but before she could complete her circuit of the room, Aunt Sybil descended upon her.

"Are you going to tell me that you spent the entire morning off gallivanting with Lord Penharrow instead of looking for my son, Henrietta?" Aunt Sybil demanded. Evidently she'd come looking for Hetta for the express purpose of chastising her.

"I wasn't planning to tell you anything about my morning, no," Hetta said before she could stop herself.

Aunt Sybil swelled with indignation. "And I've heard you were seen being...*familiar* with Penharrow at Deeplake last week. It may have suited you very well to conduct yourself like a lightskirt back in Meridon, but here you have a reputation to uphold!"

"I wasn't aware I had any reputation left," Hetta said coldly. Then she buckled down her anger and said in more measured tones, "But you won't make me believe that you truly think I was in any danger in Lord Penharrow's company. Why, I've known him since we were children!"

"That is not the point!" Aunt Sybil seethed. "People will talk!"

"They always do."

At this point, the far door into the library opened behind Aunt Sybil, and Hetta's stepmother appeared with her youngest daughter in tow. Lady Phoebe eyed the two of them with alarm; little Laurel, with interest. Aunt Sybil didn't notice their entrance and continued her tirade. It was very passionate, if not entirely logical, and contained not only dark predictions of the fate that befell damsels whose reputations were sullied but also the conflicting sentiment that whilst Hetta did not at all deserve Lord Penharrow's attention, since she seemed to have got it, she'd better make sure not to put him off with her unwomanly illusory powers.

"Are you going to marry Lord Penharrow?" Laurel piped up interestedly.

Aunt Sybil jumped, and Hetta was hard pressed not to laugh. She turned to Laurel and said pleasantly, "I don't think so, no."

"Laurel!" Phoebe objected. "That is a very impertinent question!"

"Indeed," said Aunt Sybil, eyeing the now-mutinous Laurel with a frown. "One might think you were raised in a barn, Laurel! Shouldn't you be in the schoolroom?"

"I *was* in the schoolroom! But Mama said I might help her check the Wintersol decorations." She turned tremulous eyes to Phoebe. "You did say I might!"

"But surely it's too early for decorations?" Hetta said in surprise. Wintersol was still nearly two months away.

Phoebe shook her head. "Last year I thought so, and by the time we realised that rats had got into the chains, it was too late to order new papers from Greymark, and the only ones left in the village were horrid plain ones."

"I see," said Hetta, although she did not, entirely. "Well, I shan't delay you then." And with that, she took the cowardly route and fled.

17

EAVESDROPPING

WAS EVERYONE GOING out of their way to be as vexatious as possible, Hetta wondered? It certainly felt like it. Jack remained missing, and she could find neither Marius nor Wyn. Gregory sulked until Alexandra and Miss Gwen returned from their walk, after which he became extraordinarily thick-witted, gazing longingly at the object of his affection and offering to fetch and carry quite unnecessary items for her. In return, Miss Gwen blushed and stammered and disavowed the need for Gregory to put himself out. Watching the two of them was excruciatingly dull. Hetta spent some time trying to talk to Miss Gwen but found it far from easy. The girl reminded her strongly of a younger Phoebe, full of sensibility but not much sense. But despite her grandmother and Wyn's warnings, Hetta could detect nothing amiss about her.

Hetta had far more enjoyment from watching Alexandra sketch—her sister had real talent and, it became apparent, a fanciful imagination. She drew scenes of Stariel peopled with creatures from fairy tales—waterhorses, starcorns, and nymphs. But Alexandra grew self-conscious when she realised Hetta was watching closely over her shoulder and put her sketchpad away. Hetta sighed and left the three of them alone.

All that day, everyone seemed to want either to reproach her or request something from her. She sought refuge in her father's study, only to be interrupted by Grandmamma, who wanted approval for their contribution to the village's Frost Faire, and Lady Phoebe, who wanted to know what the Frost Ball budget was, and Mr Fisk, who wanted to take the accounts books back into his keeping and was most disapproving when Hetta said she wasn't yet finished looking through them. She went to the library and tried to discover if they had any of the books on drains or sheep that Angus had mentioned but found nothing younger than she was. Where was Marius when she needed his help?

Hetta was determined to find at least one sane person before the day was out and went hunting for either her oldest brother or Wyn late that night. Neither of them had appeared at supper, and since Gregory said he had seen Marius return to the house 'in a right state', as he put it, Hetta was beginning to be concerned.

She wandered the darkening house with increasing anxiety for some time until it occurred to her to check the same tower where she, Marius, Wyn, and Jack had drunk rather too much good wine what seemed like a very long time ago.

She cut across the courtyard to reach the tower, hunching in on herself as the cold, still air bit through her clothing. It was only marginally warmer inside the winding stone staircase. The small windows set around the tower let in dim rectangles of starlight. Glass had been added to them many years after the tower's original construction, the metal frames ugly and awkward against the grey stone.

About halfway up the stairs she heard voices, her hunch proving correct. Wyn and Marius were together, talking softly. Feeling slightly excluded, Hetta made her way up to them but froze when a few of Wyn's words penetrated.

"You should tell Hetta, you know," he was saying. "You do her a disservice, keeping this from her."

There was a sound very much like a strangled sob. She couldn't make out Marius's reply, but she could tell he was distressed. Her first instinct was to rush to his side and demand to know what was wrong, but she hesitated. What was Marius keeping from her?

"Well, if you will not tell her, I may be able to help." Wyn's voice grew too low for her to hear what he was saying, and Hetta had just decided that she'd better beat a retreat back down the stairs when she heard Marius say in surprise:

"I didn't know you could do magic, Wyn."

Hetta braced a hand on the wall to support herself, hearing Wyn's reply through a sudden daze. Surely she'd misheard?

"It is not something I like to have known. But, if you want to do this, come to me tomorrow, when you and I are both sober again, and I will do what I can."

Hetta stumbled back down the stairs, her mind in turmoil. Wyn could do *magic*? Marius had some problem that apparently only magic could solve? How long had this been going on?

Beneath the shock was rapidly rising anger. Wyn knew how alone Hetta's powers had made her feel at Stariel. He knew how she'd struggled to come to terms with them. For him to have kept a secret of this magnitude cast doubt across the depth of their friendship. Perhaps Hetta's friendship didn't mean as much to Wyn as his did to her.

Hetta knew she was reacting childishly, but it was hard not to march back up the stairs and confront them both. But, she thought bitterly, Marius had chosen not to share with her whatever it was that was causing him distress, and he'd been adamant that he didn't want Hetta to know it.

There are too many secrets at Stariel, she thought grimly as she went to bed that night. Her dreams were fitful things, full of never-ending chase scenes and strange, inhuman creatures.

18

COUSIN JACK

TODAY I AM going to pin Wyn down and wring some answers from him, Hetta thought upon waking. After all, as Mr Fisk was proving so obtuse, it surely fell to Wyn to instruct her on what was needed for the smooth running of the household. It was Wyn's *job* to help her. However, this intention wasn't so easily carried out. Whenever she tried to locate Wyn, he was either clearly engaged in some necessary task or else mysteriously absent. After the first few times this happened, Hetta began to suspect he was deliberately avoiding her. Although it was possible he was also avoiding Miss Gwen; Hetta hadn't yet seen them in the same room together.

In theory, as Wyn's employer, she could resort to tyrannical overlordship and simply demand his attention, but she was reluctant to do so. Her and Wyn's friendship had always been that of equals, despite the difference in their stations. She needed to tread carefully lest she irrevocably damage that. Of course, she reflected with no small irritation, this resolution would be much easier to stick to if the other party was not being so evasive. She was only slightly reassured when she found a comprehensive list of tasks requiring her attention on her desk. They were concise and businesslike except for the signature, which read, simply: *I will explain more later. My sincerest apologies for my absences, my Star—Wyn Tempest.* She huffed down at his handwriting in frustration.

Marius was a different story. He was entirely present and entirely preoccupied. He missed quite a few meals, and when he did appear, it was obvious to Hetta that something was very wrong and that he was trying very hard to hide it. He succeeded well enough, for the most part, with the rest of the family, who were not watching him so closely. But when he thought himself alone or unobserved, his gaze would turn inwards, his features heavy with sorrow. Others might have naturally attributed the sorrow to their late father's death, but Hetta didn't think so. This sorrow was new and of an entirely different sort to the more complicated grief that had been present before.

"Is everything all right, Marius?" she asked him bluntly at the first opportunity. He'd been staring morosely out the window of the dining room after everyone else had left. He started and coloured.

"What? Yes, um, everything's fine. I'll get along to the library now."

"That wasn't an attempt to prod you into action. You just seem… strained."

"No, no, it's fine. I'm fine. I've found some of the old family diaries. I'll let you know when I find anything useful about the lord's land-sense." And he sloped off, shoulders high and defensive.

Hetta stared after him, wondering if she should reveal her inadvertent eavesdropping. But maybe Marius was merely working through his own feelings about not being chosen. At least it was encouraging that he was still researching the land-sense for her.

The house slowly emptied of its extra relatives. Each farewell hit Hetta with a fresh wave of bitterness. For them, Stariel remained a comforting rock in a sea of adventure, a rock to which they could return at will but weren't required to live on. The house felt cavernous with their removal, although she knew the servants were relieved to have their workloads back to normal.

Unfortunately, Aunt Sybil remained. Her aunt's new favourite hobby was to loom in the background and interject snide remarks about the need for a man's hand on the reins. She would inevitably follow these up with some variant of: "Of course, clearly you don't think you need any help, since you don't care if your cousin breaks his neck out there alone!"

Hetta consequently spent a lot of time out of the house or locked in her father's study. She met the village councillors, who stared at her as if expecting a second head to sprout at any moment. *They will get used to me*, she told herself firmly.

She hated to take Aunt Sybil's side, but she was growing alarmed at Jack's continued absence. On Thursday, she was debating if they really *should* send out a proper search party when little Laurel burst into her study and cried gleefully:

"Jack's back! Look!" She pointed out the window, where two tall figures had just come into sight of the house—one with flame-red hair; the other palest blond.

They hurried to the front of the house to find Wyn returning with Jack in tow. Wyn's expression was very much that of a self-satisfied sheepdog who'd herded a particularly recalcitrant sheep successfully to its pen. Jack just looked resigned.

The awkwardness of Hetta's first encounter with Jack after the Choosing was relieved by, of all people, Aunt Sybil, who descended upon her returned son with so much exclamation and fuss that there was no need at all to find conversation other than, "I'm glad you're back." Jack gave her a very small nod as he returned to the house, submitting to his mother's fussing with ill-patience.

“How on earth did you find him?” Gregory asked Wyn, who stood beaming at the foot of the entrance steps.

“How did you persuade him to return?” Hetta asked, for this seemed the more important of the two questions.

“I told him he was needed at home.”

This was a very unsatisfactory answer, but before Hetta could question Wyn further, he nodded and strode away around the side of the house and towards the back entrance. She strongly considered shouting at him to come back, but before she could, Alexandra and Miss Gwen appeared around the other side of the house.

“Laurel told us Jack’s come home!” Alexandra said as the two ladies hurried towards them.

“Yes, and looks a right urchin, sleeping rough for four days,” Gregory answered her.

“But how relieved you must be to know your cousin is safe!” Miss Gwen put in, clutching her bosom.

“Well, yes,” Gregory said. “Although I don’t think anyone ever thought he wasn’t. Safe, I mean. Jack knows his own business pretty well.”

HETTA FINALLY CONFRONTED JACK alone in the billiard room later that day. Her nerves were strung tight, but it needed to be done. They couldn’t live in this house together without clearing the air between them, and the last few days had shown her how much she needed his help.

He glanced up when she came in. His appearance was tidier than it had been upon his arrival, although there were still circles under his eyes. His lips compressed into a hard line, and he looked away, taking up his position again and lining up a shot. Hetta didn't say anything but came to watch as he made it. The balls collided with a neat click that sounded abnormally loud in the still room. The shot was off, and the first ball rolled into the edge of the table and bounced off at an angle that put Jack no further ahead.

"Dammit." He glowered at the red and white balls.

"Indeed," Hetta agreed. "But the question is, how are you going to deal with it?"

Jack turned, mouth thinning. "Don't beat around the bush, do you, Hetta? Or, should I say, *Lord Valstar*."

"No, it makes me feel entirely too old." She ran a hand along the edge of the table and said firmly, "I need you to work with me, Jack. I can't do this on my own."

Jack's expression darkened. "You don't need to remind me of that."

"I take it Wyn already said something to you on the subject?"

Jack's brows went up. "Wyn? No. There was...another reason." He didn't volunteer what it was, and Hetta had the impression that he would refuse to answer if she asked. Hetta was getting very tired of secrets. She raised an eyebrow quizzically at him. He ignored her and turned back to the billiard table, body stiff.

Should she apologise? No—that would only hurt him more. Throwing it in his face how little she'd wanted the position he coveted would hardly make him happy. Besides, it wasn't her fault Stariel had chosen her over him. She was considering how best to ask him what he knew of the estate's financial position when he abruptly broke the silence.

"There was a flash flood in the upper reaches last night after all the rain we had yesterday." Hetta waited for him to go on, but he paused instead and scrutinised her expression. "Did you know that? Lucky no one was caught in it," he added. There was a forced casualness about him as he waited for her answer.

"I didn't know." She was about to add, *should I?* when it occurred to her that maybe she should have, bound as she was supposed to be to Stariel. She stared at Jack. Had that been what he was getting at?

Jack's mouth twisted bitterly. "Is there something you want to tell me about the Choosing, Henrietta?"

For a moment, Hetta didn't understand, and then with abrupt fury, she did. It was what Aunt Sybil had said the morning after the Choosing—that Hetta had the ability to cast illusions and perhaps she'd used them to her own advantage at the ceremony.

All thought of sparing Jack's feelings evaporated in the heat of her anger.

"You think I did this on purpose? You think I lied to you all, used my magic to fool you, all so I could stay here in this crumbling pile and let down my friends back in Meridon, who, I might add, were depending on me coming back as quickly as I could! You think I wanted to be saddled with piles of debt and love-addled teenagers and discussions about the best way to drain fields?" Hetta's voice had risen as she finally vented some of the emotion that had been building in her since the Choosing. "This was your dream, Jack. Not mine. How dare you think I would misuse my powers in such a way!"

She was so angry she wanted to hit him, but instead she clenched her fists tightly enough that her fingernails bit into her palms.

Jack flushed, his eyes bright and defensive. She strode out of the room and slammed the door with a satisfying thump.

19

THE STAR STONE

Anger always gave her energy, and she stalked through the house and clomped up the main staircase with unnecessary loudness. Aunt Sybil peered around the doorway of the green drawing room to see what was making so much noise but pulled her head back in with uncharacteristic silence when she saw Hetta's expression.

Hetta fumed her way up another flight of stairs and along the picture gallery, glaring at each of her assorted ancestors in turn. By the time she'd gone down the northern stairwell and entered the library, the initial white heat of her anger had begun to ebb, but then she encountered Marius perched in a windowseat and it flared up again, re-stoked when she recalled her brother's secrecy.

Marius looked up in surprise, holding a book open against his knee. He pushed up his glasses with one finger, blinking owlishly as she stomped over to him. The artlessness of his position made him look younger, and Hetta was reminded of seeing him in that same seat in that same long-legged way, years ago. It made it hard to stay angry.

"Hetta!" He slid the book beside him and folded his legs down off the seat. "This is convenient; I was about to seek you out." He frowned. "Is something the matter?"

"Jack is the matter," Hetta said ruefully, the last of her anger burning off. "I'm afraid he rather set me on fire with something he said. He and Aunt Sybil think that my illusory powers are responsible for my being chosen." She tried to make her tone sardonic, but Marius's expression turned unexpectedly serious. "Don't tell me you've been thinking the same thing!"

"No, no," Marius said immediately, but his expression didn't lighten. "But if I didn't know you as well as I do, I have to admit I might have."

"What?"

Marius held up the book he'd been reading. It was a worn, hand-written journal; the library contained a number of such chronicles, written by various Valstars, all of them poorly catalogued. "That's what I was coming to see you about. I've managed to find some more details on the Lord of Stariel's land-sense."

A small knot formed in her belly. "You're about to tell me that I was right, aren't you? My bond should have changed things. Something went wrong with the ceremony."

Marius looked grim. "It seems so. According to the family's accounts, you should be aware of Stariel in a much more heightened way. Things like rainfall, floods, forest fires, downed trees. You should even be able to direct energy to specific areas within the borders, encouraging higher yields, although that sounds more complicated. And you should be able to locate people within the borders," he concluded with an air of dreadful finality. "Especially anyone of Valstar blood."

"Which I can't," Hetta said, unnecessarily. "That's what Jack was getting at." Oh, that was irritating to admit, that Jack's accusation might have some logical basis. Anger stirred again; logic be dashed. Jack still should've known she wouldn't have misused her powers so!

"What?" Marius looked up from the passage he'd been re-reading.

"Before he accused me of rigging the Choosing, he asked me if I knew about a flash flood in the upper reaches last night." They both glanced involuntarily towards the view, where the Indigoes made dark shapes in the grey clouds.

Marius frowned, grimness sharpening the angles of his face. "When you touched the Star Stone, did you feel anything?"

Hetta shook her head. "There was just the blue glow and the lightshow that you saw. I was shocked, of course, but I don't think I felt anything from the Stone itself."

Marius became, if possible, even grimmer, pursing his lips. "I think you should try touching the Stone again."

Hetta was taken aback. "All right. What are you thinking?"

But he shook his head as they left the library. "I need more data."

They picked their way through the house, heading down the stairs to the understory. The understory consisted of the cellars, the ice room, the old dungeon that nowadays was used for storage, and the Vault. Hetta had the key to the Vault—it had been pressed upon her with some ritual words when she was still reeling in shock after the Choosing—and she opened the door and let them inside.

In their forefathers' day, the Vault would have been full of actual treasure. Nowadays, treasure was kept in banks, or at least it would've been if they had any. Instead, the Vault was used for items that were too valuable or too fragile to be left on open display. The small, uncluttered room held a strong smell of dust, making Hetta's nose itch. The box that contained the Stone when it wasn't being used sat neatly in one corner, entirely unprepossessing.

Hetta opened it. The object that had changed her life stared up at her. The Star Stone seemed less magical down here, less lustrous. Hetta hovered her fingers above its surface. What if, despite everything, she somehow hadn't really been chosen and touching the Stone now would seal her fate? No—she was being foolish. Stariel had chosen her, whether she liked it or not. No point being missish about it. She pressed her hands against the cool blue surface.

Nothing whatsoever happened.

She looked towards Marius and knew without asking that this wasn't what he'd been hoping for.

"I take it that wasn't the desired effect. What's supposed to happen?"

"Apparently the Stone should glow in response to your touch." He wrestled with some inner turmoil for a few seconds, then held out his hands for the Stone. Hetta handed it to him. Tension stretched between them, but nothing continued to happen as it touched his skin. Marius almost dropped it in relief but managed to catch himself in time. He let out a long breath, bringing the Star Stone up to eye-level, turning it this way and that. It glimmered dully, nothing like the hypnotising patterns it had had under the full moon.

He frowned. "This isn't star indigo."

"What?" Hetta said, although she'd understood his words perfectly.

"This isn't star indigo," Marius repeated. "Although it's a very good facsimile of it. Enough, with moonlight and illusion added in, to fool anyone. This isn't the Star Stone."

"Which means," Hetta said for them both, "that I'm not the Lord of Stariel."

20

THE PLOT THICKENS

Her words set two equally frantic but entirely separate trains of thought running, like shockwaves travelling in opposite directions from a single epicentre. One train of thought focussed on what this meant for the estate. This fake meant that there was currently no Lord of Stariel. Which meant they would need to hold the Choosing again. Except they needed the real Star Stone for that, and Hetta had no idea where it was. Someone had replaced it with a fake one. Someone had *wanted* Hetta to become lord. Who? Why? And what had they done with the real Stone?

The other train of thought was much more personal. If she wasn't the Lord of Stariel, then there was no reason for her to stay. She was relieved. Wasn't she? Of course she was. It was only that there was unfinished business here now, and it would be difficult to suddenly disengage from it. Could she really leave the estate without even trying to figure out who had done this and why? But she could, couldn't she? She could walk away right now and return to Meridon on the sleeper train tonight. But would Bradfield want her back after she'd so abruptly left him in the lurch?

Marius seemed to be on a thought track of his own, for he said in a soft, stunned voice: "This means it wasn't my fault you were chosen."

These words were bewildering enough to derail Hetta. "What?"

Marius went pale, as if he hadn't realised he'd spoken aloud. "I didn't touch it," he blurted.

Hetta stared at him. "What?" she repeated. She needed to stop uttering that monosyllable, but she felt unusually thick-witted.

Muted, everyday sounds travelled down from the house above, jarring signs that elsewhere, life was continuing as if the world hadn't been set on its end.

Marius swallowed. "At the Choosing. I didn't touch the Stone." He looked down at the false Stone in his hands. "I didn't want to be chosen. I thought Jack would be the next lord. I never meant to inflict it on you. But this means I didn't—that what I did didn't matter. It wasn't the real Stone." There was both guilt and relief in his tone, but his shoulders drew up around his ears, a hedgehog retreating into its prickles; he didn't want to talk about it.

Hetta felt there were entirely too many revelations happening in this tiny room. She closed her eyes briefly and then said evenly: "I can't deal with that now, Marius. Setting it aside, the main question here is what we do now we know *I'm* not lord."

They both looked down at the fake Stone, and Marius voiced one of her own thoughts. "Where is the real Star Stone, then?"

"With whoever did this, I imagine."

Marius's frown deepened. Evidently he hadn't gotten quite as far along that train of thought as her yet. "But why would anyone want to set you up as the Lord of Stariel?"

"Why indeed?" Hetta mused. "Is the Star Stone essential to the Choosing?"

"Yes," he said, then added, "but it's not irreplaceable. There have been times in our histories when it has been lost or damaged and a new one had to be crafted."

"Well, that's something," Hetta said briskly. She smiled at Marius, mainly in relief. "Otherwise whoever has it would have us quite at their mercy."

Marius didn't smile back. "Yes, but it's not a simple process. I was reading a bit about it before, and for one thing, you need a decent piece of star indigo. And for another, you need some fairly exotic ingredients. I think we should try and recover the old one first. And Hetta," he added with some force, "I don't think we should tell anyone there's something wrong until we do."

Hetta blinked at him in surprise. "I was resigned to taking up the lord's mantle when I thought it my duty, but I don't see how I can do so now, when I know myself to be an imposter. Besides, Jack already knows something is amiss."

"Tell Jack, then, if you must," Marius allowed. "But think, Hetta. If whoever did this finds out we've discovered the deception, they'll likely destroy the Star Stone, and we'll never find out what this was about."

"But we could openly make a new Stone," Hetta pointed out. "It will look far worse if we wait and then tell everyone that we need to re-do the Choosing Ceremony after I've been lording around here for ages."

Marius looked down at the Stone in his hand. "A few more days then. It's already going to be awkward. Surely it won't matter much either way, a few days?"

"In my experience, lying is never as simple as you think it is going to be." But he was right, and she could already see the train to Meridon disappearing into the distance, leaving her on the platform once again. Someone had taken the real Star Stone; that didn't suggest anything good about their motives. Could she really leave Stariel, leave a potential enemy to the estate behind, without making the least attempt to resolve the mystery? And there were those other balls she'd already set in motion as the new lord; she'd need time to tidy them up. "But you're right. I'd like to know who did this too, and what they meant by it. But if we have no leads by the end of the week, we'll have to tell everyone the truth. And I'm not keeping this from Jack if he accuses me again." It wasn't only that she couldn't bear the thought of him thinking she'd done this deliberately; mainly she had a fair knowledge of her own temper when provoked.

"It couldn't be his doing, anyway," Marius said. He added thoughtfully, "And it might actually be someone who had it in for him who did it in the first place."

She followed his chain of logic easily enough. The idea that Jack would deliberately appoint someone else as Lord of Stariel could clearly be discarded. That someone might have wanted to ensure Jack didn't inherit might be a plausible motive—but who held such a grudge against Jack?

"Why me?" Hetta wondered aloud. If someone wanted to punish Jack, there was Marius ahead of her, who wouldn't have been so unexpected a choice.

Marius paled again. "Maybe it *was* my fault after all. Maybe the illusion was meant to activate after a certain number of people touched it. And I didn't touch it."

The illusion. It galled Hetta to realise that Aunt Sybil and Jack were right; illusory magic *had* been used at the Choosing Ceremony.

"Perhaps," Hetta said slowly. "Or it could have been attuned to me personally. But setting a trigger for an illusion is difficult magic. It's much easier to cast in person." She picked up the stone to examine it more thoroughly, but the residue of whatever magic had been cast upon it had long since faded. Illusion required a lot of power to sustain for any length of time, and this spell had only had to perform just long enough to convince the crowd at the Standing Stones.

Marius was shaking his head. "I'm so sorry, Hetta. I never..." He bit his words back, guilt etched in the tightness of his lips. That deeper sorrow that had haunted him lately flickered in his eyes.

Hetta felt briefly impatient with him, tempered with sympathy for whatever wound he was still hiding from her. She put a hand on his shoulder. "Marius, if you have a breakdown about your role in this when clearly *I* am the one most seriously affected by it, I will be forced to lose my temper with you. You ought to be comforting me." She made her words light, but they seemed to help him.

He straightened a little, giving a weak smile. "Yes. Yes. I'm sorry. How terribly inconsiderate to make this all about me. How are *you* feeling, Hetta?"

"Angry." She stared down at the fake Stone. "That someone is pulling strings and making us all dance for them." She put the Stone back in its box, carefully closing the lid. "I need to think about how this might have been accomplished." And she needed to process what it meant for her, personally, that she wasn't the Lord of Stariel. She felt very much like a ball thrown up in the air, in that weightless moment before the pull of the earth began to drag it down. That it would come down was known and inevitable, but it was hard to know what she was truly feeling until it did.

They parted after discussing who they should question first and how it might be done without raising suspicion. She went to her father's study. It gave her a strange pang to think this would be someone else's study—probably Jack's—in not so very long.

But she wasn't alone. Wyn waited patiently by the window, sunlight glinting in his white-blond hair. He looked up calmly when Hetta entered and smiled.

"Well," he said. "I think it is time I explained myself."

21

MISS GWEN

HETTA PULLED THE door shut and said in a dangerous tone, "Oh you do, do you?"

"I'm afraid so." He gave an apologetic shrug.

It was too much. Hetta began to laugh, but she found that she couldn't stop once she'd started. Laughter choked out of her like bits of glass, bright and painful, turning dangerously close to tears.

"Hetta, Hetta, what's wrong?" He closed the space between them and put his hands on her shoulders. She hiccoughed and made the mistake of looking up. His face was so close that she could pick out individual eyelashes, the same white-blond as his hair, dramatic against his darker skin tone. *Like frosting*, she thought inanely. He smelled faintly of cardamom, as if he'd come from baking spice-bread in the kitchens.

She had a sudden urge to fold against him, but a treacherous thought swam up: Wyn could do magic. Magic had been used to fake the Choosing. She made herself take a step away from her friend. He didn't resist the movement, but he did cant his head and give her a small, sad smile.

"I'm not the Lord of Stariel," Hetta said, even though she'd promised Marius less than five minutes ago that she wouldn't reveal that to anyone except Jack. "The Star Stone is a fake."

Wyn's expression grew grave. "I was afraid of something like that."

Hetta stared at him with disbelief. "Does everyone in this household have some deep, dark secret they've been keeping from me in order to reveal it at the most dramatic moment possible?"

Wyn's lips twitched. "Probably. But this secret is my own—it is not my place to tell others'." He let out a long breath, running a hand through his hair. His gaze went to the window, to the view across the lake and beyond it the mountains. It seemed to steel something in him as he turned back, his russet eyes solemn. "I hardly know where to begin. I have been holding this one inside for so long, past the time when I ought to have shared it with you, my friend. I hope you will forgive me."

"This sounds like it's going to be a long story," Hetta said, alive with curiosity. "And in that case, I think I'm going to need a drink. Sit." She went to retrieve the decanter of whisky and glasses from the bottom drawer of her father's desk. She poured them both a generous measure, the amber liquid sloshing softly. Hetta pushed one across the desk and sat down behind it, deliberately putting the solid wood between them.

Wyn's long fingers moved restlessly on the surface of the desk, and he drew a circle around the top of the glass. "I suppose it begins with what I am."

Before he could say anything further, the door swung open. The delicate form of Miss Gwen appeared in the frame, saying:

"I'm so sorry to invade, Lord Valstar, but I wanted to speak with you—" She caught sight of Wyn and abruptly broke off.

If she'd actually changed form, the transformation couldn't

have been more dramatic. Miss Gwen's eyes glowed a bright, poisonous blue, and unholy glee dawned in her expression. It wasn't the face or expression of a young ingenue. It was the disbelieving smile of a shark discovering a bird has fallen into its watery domain.

"Hallowyn Tempestren Spireborn," she breathed. A little frisson of elektricity passed over Hetta's neck, a magic she didn't recognise. "Prince Hallowyn Tempestren, here, in mortal form." Miss Gwen gave a short, triumphant laugh, glittering with malice.

Wyn moved, so suddenly it didn't seem quite real. He was somehow, impossibly, across the room and looming down at Miss Gwen between one heartbeat and the next. "Gwendelfear of Dusken Roses, by your name, I command thee. Sleep." His voice was deeper than normal, and again, a strange power moved in the air. The room thrummed with the heavy pressure of an oncoming storm, and Miss Gwen collapsed. Wyn caught her, lowering her motionless body to the floor.

Hetta stood in frozen horror as Wyn left Miss Gwen and went to the open door, closing it after a quick glance in each direction. He blew out a sharp, controlled breath and turned to face her. The wildness that sometimes lurked beneath his surface was in ascendance, the dark planes of his face unnaturally sharp, his hair faintly luminescent, more silver than blond. His eyes burned, and she thought not of comparisons to the colour of horse-chestnuts, but of blood spilled across ancient wood.

He was terrifyingly beautiful and utterly alien.

Fear bloomed, just as alien, because this was *Wyn*, her oldest friend, but it didn't stop her reaching for her magic. It wasn't illusion she called for, the magic of fine control and steady imagery, but emotional, volatile pyromancy—a magic with no place in modern life. Fire simmered up beneath her skin, the warmth reassuring.

He met her eyes with steady resignation, waiting. Waiting for…

what? *For me to pass judgement*, she realised in a rush, and the fear snuffed out. She'd seen that expression before, on the night he'd come to them, half-dead and frightened out of his mind by a past he wouldn't speak of. He looked now as he did then, filled with desperate, aching loneliness, both pleading for help and wholly resigned to receiving none.

Hetta let her magic subside, unsure what exactly she'd planned to do with it anyway. "Tell me what's going on. What have you done to Miss Gwen?"

Wyn breathed in unsteadily, a little more humanity seeping into his appearance. He looked down at Miss Gwen's still form. "Her name is Gwendelfear, and I have forced her to sleep. It will not last. I do not know what to do with her now." He said the last almost wonderingly, and she recognised the mirror of her own blank shock earlier. "I do not know what to do." Apparently, she wasn't the only one who'd had the world change course on her without warning. It didn't give her much satisfaction.

"What did she call you? Hallow—"

"Don't say it!" Wyn brushed a hand through his hair, agitated. "My name, it leaves a kind of trace that others may track me by. I hope they may not already do so."

Hetta's mind had run ahead of her. What kind of names were Gwendelfear and Hallowyn?

"Who are you?"

Wyn met her gaze again and said quietly, "You *know*, Hetta. You know because that's not the question you want to ask. Ask it." He'd gone taut as a bowstring, that sense of *alienness* quivering through him again.

Hetta swallowed. "What are you?"

Wyn closed his eyes. "Yes. Yes, that's the right question." He wound, if anything, tighter, as if he would crystallise with sheer rigidity. "I am fae, and the youngest son of King Aeros, the King of Ten Thousand Spires. The short version of the tale is that many people want me dead. Particularly those of the Court of Dusken Roses, as Gwendelfear is. I have been in hiding from them for nearly a decade. Do you want the long version?"

He opened his eyes at the sound of Hetta's laugh and blinked, confusion washing over his features, bringing humanity back with it.

"Hetta?" He took a tentative step forward.

She waved her hands at him, stopping the giggles by sheer force of will. "You," she gasped as she tried to catch her breath. "You're a fairy prince. Of course you are." She'd thought that nothing could overshadow the revelation that she wasn't the Lord of Stariel; she'd been wrong.

"Yes." There was no mirth in either his expression or his stance. That one word contained such grim depths that it cut through Hetta's threatening hysteria like a cold blade. "I am a fae prince of the Court of Ten Thousand Spires."

She stared at him, a thousand half-formed objections on her lips.

He rolled his eyes. "Perhaps you want to say that the fae aren't real; that I can't possibly be one; that I must be joking; that one or both of us is insane; or possibly that this is all a dream and you will wake up any minute now. And those are all entirely reasonable sentiments to have, but I think they must wait until after I deal with Gwendelfear."

"What do you mean, *deal with Gwendelfear*?"

"I will bind her so that she cannot speak my name, and then once she has woken, I think we should try to find out what she knows about Stariel. The boundaries are weaker than they should be—that's why she was able to cross them with only Gregory's permission and still retain her powers, which shouldn't have been possible. If you were truly the Lord of Stariel then you could cast her out and prevent her from entering Stariel again, but as it is, I don't think rescinding your invitation will be sufficient."

"If Gwendelfear needed permission to cross the borders, how did *you* enter Stariel the first time?" This was the least of the questions Hetta wanted to ask, but it seemed as good a place to start as any. A *fairy prince*. She kept staring at him, but he grew, if anything, more human rather than less, that wildness folding away, leaving only Stariel's primly dressed butler in its place.

"Gwendelfear is of the lesser fae. The greater fae are able to resist such defences for a time, though it is not easy."

"You said they want you dead. Is that why Gwendelfear is here?" It seemed too extreme to be quite real, that anyone should want Wyn dead, or that the delicate-featured young woman could be an attempted murderess.

Wyn's hands moved restlessly. "No, I do not think so. That is what I was trying to find out, but I don't think she even knew I was here before today. There's something else going on. She crossed into Stariel from the mortal border, which should have been impossible." He paused. "I would leave you now if I thought it would keep you safe, but I fear there is danger here for Stariel even discounting my presence."

"What in Prydein is a 'mortal border'?"

"Ah—the estate's border on this plane. Such as that between Penharrow and Stariel," he added at Hetta's blank look.

Hetta looked down at the girl she'd given refuge to. "Is there any truth to the stories about iron harming fae? No, that's silly. I would've noticed if you—"

"It doesn't hurt us, but we can't work magic on it," Wyn said quickly.

"Then I think the old dungeon might be the best place to put her, for the moment. Then you are going to do your 'binding', and then you and I are going to come back here, and you are going to explain everything."

Wyn looked momentarily surprised, and then the merest flicker of a smile kindled in his eyes. "My Hetta. Ever pragmatic."

Hetta held out a finger. "Don't you 'my Hetta' me. I haven't forgiven you yet for lying to me."

Wyn nodded, acknowledging the reproof.

If previously asked, Hetta would have said it would be impossible to spirit an unconscious body through the house without anyone noticing, but this turned out not to be the case.

"Glamour," Wyn said succinctly.

Wyn's glamour was different to illusion. Illusory magic spun light, and masters of the art could render themselves effectively invisible, though only when standing still. It was almost impossible to sustain a convincing illusion while moving because of the need to constantly change the image. But this wasn't illusion as she knew it. There was no physicality to the glamour, except that as they walked it began to smell oddly like rain with a hint of spice. Hetta could see Wyn carrying Gwendelfear in his arms perfectly well. But no one else did; Wyn's glamour seemed to work on people's perceptions. It was deeply unsettling to meet Aunt Sybil in the hallway and have her gaze slide past Hetta and Wyn as if they were not present at all.

The old dungeon looked more like a storeroom than its namesake. After moving some boxes, however, Hetta discovered that the set of shackles she remembered discovering as a child was still there. The keys hung on a hook on the wall beside them. Wyn lowered Gwendelfear to the ground and pressed the tip of one finger to her forehead. "By your name I bind thee, Gwendelfear of DuskRose, not to speak my name."

Hetta felt the thrum of power in the air, and that alienness washed over Wyn again. She stared hard at him, certain that she'd seen feathers, but after a moment, she concluded she'd been mistaken.

"And it's that easy, is it, to bind someone not to speak of you?"

Wyn gave a low laugh as he shifted Gwendelfear next to the wall. She stirred a little but did not wake. "No. I am only able to with this one because my power so eclipses hers. She is one of the lowliest members of DuskRose. I would never try this on any of the greater fae."

As the shackles touched her, Gwendelfear changed. Hetta gasped, but Wyn didn't falter from his task. The girl—the fae—woke just as he finished, in a kind of confused panic, pulling sharply against the constraints and hissing. She looked up at the two of them with eyes that couldn't be mistaken for human. They were still blue, but now the colour filled the space where the whites of her eyes had been, and the colour was more vibrant than before. Her black pupils had become oddly deformed, with several symmetrical lobes, almost like the petals of a flower. Her skin had grown paler, with a greenish undertone, and her hair was no longer brunette. Instead it was the green of lakeweed, threaded through with lighter, yellowish tones.

Gwendelfear's blue, blue eyes fixed on Wyn.

"You!" She writhed. She started to say something else, but her voice failed, and her tongue caught in her mouth. "You dare bind me! You should run, Oathbreaker. DuskRose knows I am here, and they will find you. They will find you and they will *hurt* you." Her eyes flicked to Hetta. "And those who shield you."

Wyn shifted towards her, radiating menace. Hetta stopped him with a hand on his arm. He stilled but didn't take his eyes from Gwendelfear.

"How are you here?" he growled. "You crossed into Stariel via a mortal border. Do you openly flaunt the High King's law?"

Gwendelfear's eyes widened. "Oh, you don't know, do you, Oathbreaker? Did you think you would be safe here?" She smiled, showing subtly pointed teeth. "The Iron Law is revoked."

Wyn froze. Hetta added 'the Iron Law' to the list of things to ask about when they were out of Gwendelfear's hearing.

Recovering swiftly, Wyn narrowed his eyes at Gwendelfear. "Why are you here in Stariel, specifically?"

Gwendelfear gave a merry laugh. "As if I would tell you just for the asking!" She closed her mouth and smirked at him. And that was the last thing she said, despite Wyn's prodding. Hetta could tell he was reluctant to ask too much, lest he reveal information Gwendelfear didn't yet know.

"I welcomed you into my house," Hetta said after Wyn ran out of questions. She fixed Gwendelfear with a stare. "I welcomed you into my house and offered you shelter from your so-called persecution. And you've repaid me by threatening my friend and my family. Will you explain what your purpose is here?"

Gwendelfear's expression remained neutral, as if Hetta hadn't spoken. Apparently she had no conscience to appeal to. Hetta tried again. "What did you do with the Stone?"

A flash of surprise crossed Gwendelfear's face and she said, "What stone?" in a faintly puzzled voice before her eyes widened. "The Star Stone!" She glanced between Hetta and Wyn. "You have lost it!"

Hetta had difficulty reading her expression, but it was clear the fae was thinking rapidly.

"Are you saying you know nothing about it?" Hetta pressed, but Gwendelfear had now recovered from her initial outburst. She pressed her lips together, saying nothing, but her eyes glittered with interest. Hetta had the uneasy feeling that they'd given her far more than she'd given them.

Hetta gave Wyn a meaningful look. He nodded. They left the room, bolting the door shut from the outside. Wyn frowned at the doorway as if he could will its occupant to speak through sheer concentration.

"I wish you hadn't said that. Now she knows the Star Stone is missing, she'll realise something went wrong with the Choosing."

"Now we know it wasn't her who took it," Hetta pointed out. "Unless you think she faked that surprise?"

Wyn's gaze turned inward. "No, I don't. Although we already

know she's a reasonable actress, so I am not willing to bet heavily on it."

"No, I suppose we shouldn't," Hetta agreed. "How very inconvenient." She reached out and prodded him gently when he seemed about to get lost in thought again. "Now come upstairs. You have a lot of explaining to do."

22

THE COURT OF TEN THOUSAND SPIRES

"I SUPPOSE I SHOULD begin," Wyn said, "with the war between the Court of Dusken Roses and the Court of Ten Thousand Spires." He stood by the window in her study, staring outwards, as if he couldn't tell his story whilst looking at her.

"Gwendelfear called you Spireborn," Hetta observed. "And a prince."

"Yes. I am the sixth child of the King of Ten Thousand Spires. Nowhere near the throne in birth rank. Neither a great warrior nor a great mage. Unambitious. A liability in the Spires." He paused, and his expression grew pensive. "To understand the courts of Faerie, you have to understand something of our nature. Faerie and the Mortal Realm lie one atop the other, like two pieces of fabric, separate but together. In places, the boundaries are weaker, like patches in the fabric, and Faerie shines through. In others, the doors to Mortal are closed so firmly that you would never know what lies beneath the surface."

"I gather that Stariel is one of these places where the boundaries are thinner, then?"

Wyn shook his head. "Not precisely. Stariel is a faeland." At Hetta's frown, Wyn looked sheepish. "My apologies. I'm not explaining this very well." He crinkled his nose at the view and then began again. "Faerie is divided into kingdoms: the faelands. I come from one such—the Court of Ten Thousand Spires. Gwendelfear is from another—the Court of Dusken Roses. Stariel is another faeland, or, as we know it, the Court of Falling Stars."

At Hetta's blank look, he tried another tack. "*Lord Valstar.* It's a corruption of FallingStar."

Most titles were called after the places they came from. It was one of Stariel's peculiarities that the official form of address for the Lord of Stariel was 'Lord Valstar' rather than 'Lord Stariel'. It wasn't because of her surname; she would have been addressed so even if her last name had been Smith. However, any old estate came with a history of accumulated oddities, so Hetta had never given this particular one any thought.

"Am I to take it that my family are, in fact, fairies?" Hetta asked, pained. She'd been coping quite well with these fantastical revelations, but she thought that might be her limit.

He burst into startled laughter. The sound filled the small room, warm and touchable, and Hetta gave her heart stern instructions not to soften in response. *Remember how he's lied to you!*

"Don't you dare laugh! This entire tale is so fantastical that I wouldn't believe a word of it if I hadn't seen her change with my own eyes. How am I supposed to know what's a reasonable question to ask? I've only known fairies are real for half an hour!"

He wiped at his eyes. "Oh, I am sorry, Hetta. It was not really so unreasonable a suggestion. It was your tone. You are taking this much better than I'd hoped, despite my addle-brained telling of it."

"Well, get on with your addle-brained telling, then." Hetta eyed the whisky glasses on her desk, untouched from earlier. *No, better not*, she decided with regret. A clear head was required for this.

He sobered. "To answer your question: no, the Valstars are not 'fairies'. Or at least, not anymore. And I should correct your usage of terms. We are the fae; our land is Faerie. Your original suggestion was right, in some part. Stariel is a place where the boundaries between Mortal and Faerie are loose. This was even more so in the distant past, when one of your ancestors—a powerful mortal mage—laid claim to this land in both realms and was granted the right to hold it by the High King. He married a fae woman—so there *is* a smidgeon of fae in your bloodline—but the Valstar connection with Stariel traces back to him."

Wyn frowned. "But I am getting side-tracked. As I was saying before, you need to understand something of our nature." Hetta got the impression he was choosing his words with the kind of care a surgeon takes over his instruments. "We are...not human. In Faerie, time passes differently to the Mortal Realm. It means we can live to great ages, if we remain within its bounds. The oldest fae have much power and much knowledge, but they...lose something in that process. The oldest of us are cold, deadly, beautiful, and utterly without empathy."

Wyn's tone had become inflectionless, and Hetta rose to go to him, pulled by some small signal of distress. He took her offered hand and squeezed it, but only briefly, drawing back.

"No, let me finish this while I may. You need to know."

"Will you..." Hetta couldn't quite phrase the question, caught by what he'd said about 'great ages'. Would it be bad-mannered to ask?

Wyn threw her a slightly mischievous look. "I age like a human while I am here. And if I stay, I will die in something like a human span, although perhaps a generous one. The Valstars, too, are known for their longevity. Convenient, no?"

Hetta gave a burble of laughter, this one genuine. "You're

getting far too ahead of yourself. You were telling me about the war between your court and the Court of Dusken Roses."

"Hmmm." The light from the dying November sun lit up his hair in a pale halo, casting golden shadows over his brown skin, the contrast undeniably attractive. "Yes. Whilst political machinations and backstabbing and assassinations and so on are commonplace between fae courts, all-out war is not. For a long-lived race, we are mightily afraid of dying. But we also hold our grudges dearly. I do not know precisely the cause of the enmity between DuskRose and ThousandSpire; whatever it was, it had been firmly bedded down with blood and vengeance by the time I was born.

"As the youngest of six children, my father had no need of me. That kept me safe for a time. I was…careful, and I managed to avoid the worst of the traps that young, vulnerable fae can face." Hetta got the impression that his words covered a much darker and more complicated version of his upbringing than he was admitting to. "But by the time I was of age, the war between the courts had grown to such proportions that the High King intervened."

"You mentioned him before, to Gwendelfear. Something about an 'Iron Law'?"

"Yes." Awe tinged his expression. "The Iron Law is revoked. Storms above. I did not anticipate that."

"Yes, but what *is* this Iron Law?"

"The High King rules over all of Faerie. He issues few laws, but when he commands, Faerie obeys. You know what the fae are, Hetta, but you thought them a mere tale. The Iron Law is the reason for that. Centuries ago, he forbade any passage between Faerie and Mortal. I wondered, when Gwendelfear first came to us, but I did not know for sure until today that the law no longer stands. It is…a change so monumental I do not know what the full ramifications will be."

"You came here before it was revoked, though," Hetta pointed out. "Are you an outlaw of some kind?" He didn't look like an outlaw—or a fae prince, for that matter. He looked like a handsome but respectable man, waistcoat smoothly immaculate and bow tie crisp.

He grimaced. "It was not my intent. Stariel is a faeland, and I did not enter it from the mortal plane. I was prepared to argue that I had not technically broken the High King's law, if necessary. I was...very desperate." His amusement dimmed as his gaze went distant, remembering.

"Desperate? Because of the war between your court and the other one?"

"Not exactly. Sorry." He gave her another sheepish look. "I make a poor storyteller. As I was saying, the war between our courts—two of the most powerful in Faerie—grew to such proportions that it attracted the High King's attention, and he chose to intervene. He brokered an uneasy peace and decreed that the courts should cement it by uniting the two royal lines."

Hetta had a horrible sinking feeling that she knew where this tale was leading, but she said nothing.

"At the time, I was oblivious to politics, and the war, though ever-present, seemed a distant thing. But I was summoned by my father and informed that I was to wed Princess Sunnika of DuskRose. I was ambivalent about the match, but I resolved to do my best to honour ThousandSpire and the newly brokered peace. I vowed to marry Sunnika."

Hetta felt suddenly cold. Outside, the sunset washed the landscape with gold, but the warmth didn't penetrate her father's study. She wrapped her arms around herself and shivered as she waited for Wyn to continue. But he stared at nothing, lost in memory. Once more, she closed the distance between them and put a hand to his arm. He gave a start but didn't pull away. She could see it now, the fae prince lurking under his skin—that hint of something wild and alien she'd glimpsed flashes of before. She wondered if he was hiding beneath the same glamour as Gwendelfear, whether when it fell his eyes too would fill with colour, his hair and skin shift to some unnatural green shade.

Wyn stared down at her hand on his arm. "My father had finally found a use for me. Though he was outwardly compliant, he planned to have me murdered and frame DuskRose for my death, thus providing a neat excuse to continue the feud. Even the High King couldn't force peace under such circumstances. A retainer found out about the plan and warned me. I ran. I did not know what else to do. And once I had run, the honour of both courts rested on retrieving me, to punish me. Nowhere in Faerie was safe for me. And then I thought…the Court of Falling Stars, the faeland in mortal hands."

"But if Stariel counts as part of Faerie, why would—oh, the boundary," Hetta said in sudden realisation. "That's what you were trying to tell me before. Stariel has a border that you need permission to cross, not because it's an estate but because it's a faeland?"

Wyn smiled. It was the first proper smile she'd seen from him since Gwendelfear had confronted him. "Yes. The Mortal Realm has been something of a blind spot for the fae since our interaction with it has grown so very limited. And FallingStar has been so long in mortal hands that it is considered more mortal than fae. It was a risk to come here. As I said—a technicality that I only dared try because I so desperately needed sanctuary. But the High King's law did not stop me crossing over, so I assumed my technicality had held up. Then I had only to gain your father's permission to remain hidden within the protection of its borders."

"But because there is no Lord of Stariel at present, the boundary that protected you before is no longer there?"

Wyn shook his head. "The boundary is still there, just weaker. Greater fae will be able to pass unhindered. The lesser fae will need permission to cross, unless they forfeit their powers at the border, but at present any Valstar will do. Gregory must have let Gwendelfear in. I imagine she was sent on something of a scouting mission when the Iron Law was revoked, after Lord Henry's death, on the off-chance of gaining some kind of advantage over FallingStar. I do not think she knew I was here."

"Speaking of Gwendelfear, what in Pyrania's name are we to do with her? I can't keep her locked in the dungeons forever."

"I suppose not. For one thing, Gregory would probably object to it. And," he added thoughtfully, "probably Lady Sybil would not like it either. It would likely offend her sense of propriety." Wyn had always had a tendency towards levity when shaken, but Hetta didn't laugh, still struggling to come to terms with this abrupt expansion of the world. Wyn visibly reined himself in.

"There is a spell I know. A spell of forgetting. If we wait until nightfall, I cast it, and we take Gwendelfear back to her bed, in the morning she will wake with no memory of today and—hopefully—not realise that she has lost a day."

Hetta blinked at him. She'd never heard of that sort of magic outside of tales. But then, the fae *were* something from tales. "That sounds rather risky, letting her go. Won't she still recognise you if she sees you again?"

Wyn's expression had smoothed, revealing nothing of his feelings. "I am wondering if I should leave you. Leave Stariel, that is. Though I do not think Gwendelfear was here for me, her presence here and the weakening boundaries mean I may endanger you."

"If you think you can run away at such a time and leave me to deal with fairies and fake Stones and plots and bothersome relatives, then I am disowning you on the spot. Stop talking such idiocy and help me."

It hadn't escaped her notice that the kind of magic Wyn knew had deeply troubling implications, though she was trying very hard not to think of them. Preventing people from speaking?

Making them forget? He'd been hardly more than a child when he left Faerie—what kind of people would teach such magic to a child? What kind of child would need such magic?

Gwendelfear's blue, flower-pupiled eyes kept surfacing in her mind, and she couldn't help imagining Wyn with the same. She almost wished he would reveal his full nature. Surely the reality of it couldn't be worse that what she envisaged? But what if it was?

Still, she was dissatisfied with Wyn's plan, beyond the risk it posed. Abruptly she realised why. "I'm not comfortable hiding that creature in my household with my family oblivious to the danger she may pose to them."

Wyn nodded unhappily. "I confess I do not like it much myself. But between the two of us, we can keep an eye on her."

"No," Hetta said. "You've just been telling me that deceit and secrets are fae nature, and that's hardly a recommendation to resort to such methods. I think we should tell my family what's at stake."

If she'd slapped Wyn, he couldn't have looked more taken aback or more thoroughly disgusted with himself.

"You're right. Of course you're right. And you have a fae in the dungeon to prove it." He groaned and put his head in his hands. Then he made an active effort to shake his moment of temper away. He smiled weakly at her. "I am a fool."

An insight struck her. Was this what he meant when he said he had been 'careful' growing up? That he'd learnt to douse his temper before it could ever really begin to take hold? That he must always present this cheerful, mild-natured appearance? She found herself reaching out to grip both his shoulders.

"You don't have to swallow your emotions down like that," she told him fiercely. "It's me!"

"Of course, my Star," he said meekly, a smile twitching at his lips.

She knew he was teasing her to hide his fluster, so she shook him a little. It had about as much effect as shaking a tree, except that trees weren't warm enough that she could feel it even through his coat beneath her fingertips. His smile broadened, and his eyes warmed with some deeper emotion. It wasn't a *fae* look; it was a very *male* look. She swallowed and stepped back, flustered now as well.

"I can't say I relish the thought of telling Aunt Sybil that fairies may or may not want to take over Stariel," Hetta said in an attempt to redirect the subject to less unsettling waters. "But it's not fair to keep her in ignorance when doing so may leave her vulnerable, even to spare myself the unpleasant task of appearing to be a lunatic."

"Hetta," said Wyn slowly. "I don't think you should tell them you're not the Lord of Stariel. You'll have a difficult time getting them to grasp this fae business, but you'll manage it because, unwanted and unexpected as your appointment was, it gives you authority over them. They will not like it, but they will listen to you. If you admit you're not the lord, they will be leaderless, since there's no way to replace you without the Star Stone."

Hetta was forced to agree with his logic. "Fine. Let's go tell the Valstars they should believe in fairies."

FAIRY TALES

The Valstars, by birth and by marriage, bore a striking resemblance to a mob when assembled in Carnelian Hall—the largest room in the house—even with many of the family having left after the Choosing. Only the youngest members of the clan had been barred from the meeting. Little Laurel protested loudly that it wasn't fair, that there was something interesting happening, and that she wanted to know what it was, but Aunt Sybil shushed her so ferociously that she allowed herself to be bundled out of the room in sullen silence.

Hetta had never been one for giving speeches, but she'd watched Bradfield give them frequently enough to improvise. Of course, Bradfield's speeches had been mainly given to inspire good performances. Without thinking, Hetta caught herself taking on something of the theatre director's pomposity.

"I have called you all here to tell you something highly unusual and, in fact, unbelievable. Once I have explained myself further, I have no doubt that you'll all want proof of my assertions, so I say now that I have it and that you may all see it once I have laid out the facts of the case to you. I do this in the hope of preventing interruptions." Hetta met each of her relatives' eyes for emphasis. It probably wouldn't prevent them from interrupting, but there was no harm in trying.

Marius frowned and jerked his head in a fierce negative when she met his eyes. He thought this was about the lordship and the Star Stone. Wyn was trying his best to be unobtrusive at the back of the room. So far, no one had questioned his presence there. He wasn't using glamour to achieve that, was he? She didn't think so—there was no hint of that odd stormy atmosphere from when he'd used it before—but it was an uneasy thought nonetheless. He gave a resigned smile when her attention passed over him.

"I'm afraid that the lady we have been hosting these past few days is something of an imposter," she said.

Gregory made a sudden, indignant movement, but Jack spoke before he could.

"You mean Miss Gwen," Jack said calmly. The tiniest trace of amusement threaded through his next words. "I don't think many of us would be shocked to learn her name isn't Smith."

There was a wordless murmur of agreement from several family members, and Lady Phoebe spoke. "It's all highly irregular, but one cannot help pity the poor girl."

Gregory gave his mother an approving glance and once again would have spoken, but Hetta held out a hand to forestall him.

"No, Jack, as you've pointed out, I think we all know that Smith is an assumed name. I initially thought it was for her own peace of mind that she wouldn't tell us where she fled from. I was mistaken, however. She came to us with the intention of deliberate deception. I'm afraid Miss Gwen is not the innocent girl that she appears."

Aunt Sybil was nodding along to these words as if they confirmed her every suspicion, but her bobbing motion abruptly cut off at Hetta's next words. "She isn't a girl at all. She is not, in fact, human. She is fae, one of the fair folk."

A deep, profound silence fell, but Hetta had suffered much worse silences in the recent past. There had been far more people in the crowd at the Standing Stones, and she'd been far less prepared then. So she stood straight and unapologetic, letting the silence spill out, trying to give the impression that she was merely allowing everyone time to absorb her words before continuing.

"I thought as much," Grandmamma said cheerfully.

As if her words had granted permission, the room abruptly broke into incoherency, the general gist of which was disbelief. Hetta didn't attempt to reply to any of the demands flung at her. She waited as calmly as she could, though her heart beat rapidly and her stomach tied itself into knots. It took some time, but eventually, for lack of new material, her relatives simmered down again and looked expectantly at her.

"This evening, Miss Gwen—or rather, Gwendelfear, as her true name is—revealed her true form to Wyn and me and made a number of threats against this house. We...restrained her and attempted to ascertain why she was here, but she refused to say any more. This is why I'm telling you about it. We can't let her go free until we understand what her purpose was in coming here and if it poses a danger to us. But I can't conceal such a threat from you."

Aunt Sybil pinned Wyn with her grey-eyed gaze. "What nonsense is this, Mr Tempest?"

"It's true, what my Star says. Gwendelfear is fae. I saw it also," Wyn said quietly. He shot Hetta a faintly puzzled look. Even from this distance she could read the tension in him and knew he was waiting to be revealed for what he was.

Aunt Sybil's mouth thinned, but to Hetta's surprise she merely said, "Let's see the girl then."

Everyone took their lead from Aunt Sybil, although mainly

they bore the appearance of people humouring a lunatic as they traipsed down to the lower levels. Except for Jack, who looked very thoughtful indeed.

There was something inherently comical about the long line of Valstars making their way to the old dungeon. They couldn't all fit in the narrow space at the bottom of the stairs, and a natural hierarchy formed, roughly from oldest to youngest, with a few exceptions. Gregory defiantly pushed his way to the front, standing with Aunt Sybil and Jack. Hetta ignored him.

Gwendelfear was much as they had left her, but Hetta found her horror at Gwendelfear's strange appearance had dissipated. After all, while it might be startling, green-tinged skin and pointed ears weren't exactly frightening. There was even a strange beauty to her wide, flower-pupiled blue eyes, once you got used to them. The greens and yellows of her hair made Hetta think of summer grass. Was Wyn's hair like that, under his glamour?

But her family reacted to Gwendelfear much as Hetta had at first confrontation and recoiled. Hetta was pushed towards pity for the fae. It couldn't be pleasant to be looked at with undisguised revulsion. But if Gwendelfear minded, she didn't let it show. She kept silent throughout, her eyes burning with malice in her otherwise expressionless face.

When each and every age-appropriate Valstar had seen what there was to be seen, Hetta led the way back to Carnelian Hall. The cacophony of earlier had been replaced with dazed silence.

"Well," said Grandmamma briskly. "We can't keep the girl in the dungeon forever, fae or no. What are we to do with her?"

Hetta exchanged a look with Wyn.

"How," said Aunt Sybil slowly, "can we take the girl's appearance as proof when we know there is one here capable of casting illusions?" She'd been leaning against the mantelpiece for support, a kind of blank incredulity in her features, but as she spoke, her voice became firmer, her expression more assured.

Hetta's hands balled into fists. Wyn straightened, a flicker of anger clear for a split second before he damped it down. He opened his mouth to speak, and Hetta tried to think of some way to prevent him, but assistance came from a wholly unexpected source.

"The fae are real, Mother," Jack said quietly but clearly into the tense silence. "Lord Henry knew it as well. And, moreover, while Hetta can no doubt cast excellent illusions, I'm at a loss to know why she would want to do so in Miss Smith's case." He gave Hetta a faint, edged smile.

Aunt Sybil looked as if she'd just swallowed something very nasty. Her mouth compressed into a tight line, but she merely said, "I see."

Hetta was left with a complicated mix of emotions—relief being foremost amongst them, but beneath that, surprise. Jack, of all people, knew the fae were real? But then, Wyn had already said that her father had known, so perhaps it wasn't so surprising that he'd told his probable successor.

"There's the Tower Room," Jack suggested softly. When everyone looked at him, he shrugged. "Hetta is right—we have to know what this fairy girl came here for. The Tower Room's secure, but much more suitable than the dungeon. I didn't even know there were still shackles down there." He raised his eyebrows at Hetta. "Very resourceful, but rather barbaric, don't you think?"

"Indeed," she said quickly, too astonished to argue.

24

CONFESSIONS

WYN WENT TO move Gwendelfear to the Tower Room, and Hetta summoned Jack and Marius up to her study. Grandmamma invited herself along to this discussion, saying matter-of-factly, "You'll be needing my help in making the anti-fae talismans." Hetta found herself accepting this unexpected proclamation with a kind of amused resignation. If life at Stariel continued like this, she would become practically impossible to discompose.

Her study—or rather, her father's study, Hetta reminded herself—seemed much smaller with four people of taller-than-average height contained within it. "How foolish of me," she remarked as she entered with Grandmamma. "We should have convened in one of the sitting rooms. This is an impractical meeting room for four of us."

"Never mind that," Jack said. He had been leaning against the wall beside the window, but he straightened as Hetta came in, expression thunderous. "I can bloody well stand—" He caught sight of his grandmother behind Hetta and abruptly lost momentum. "Ah—Grandmamma. Forgive me." He flushed.

Grandmamma gave him a look of mild reproof. "I'm not made of glass, Jonathan, and if I were, it would take more than your daintily spoken oaths to upset me. Why, I've heard stronger swearing from milkmaids!"

Jack grimaced but didn't argue with her. Grandmamma, chastisement delivered, seated herself in the stiff leather visitor's chair next to the desk. Marius had risen from his perch on the settee under the window at their entrance but sank back onto it as Grandmamma waved at him impatiently.

Hetta closed the door and took a few seconds to compose herself as she did so. She was conscious of a strange tension within herself. She wasn't usually inclined towards deception, but for a fleeting moment she wished she didn't have to reveal her lordship as false. Partly this wish stemmed from the entirely natural desire to avoid the awkwardness that would follow. But beneath that superficial reluctance was another, deeper reason. For so long her life and her achievements had been quietly ignored by her family, and she was self-aware enough to admit, at least privately, that there was some satisfaction to be had from them being forced to acknowledge her.

"I have decided," began her grandmother before Hetta could speak, "that we had best distribute as many anti-fae talismans as we can about the borders until we find out what that creature was doing here and if there are more intent on coming." She frowned and added thoughtfully, "And how she got in with only Gregory's permission."

"Ah." Hetta fidgeted with her sleeve. "Well, I'm afraid there are further revelations to be had."

Jack's eyes narrowed, dark with suspicion. Marius was still somewhat shell-shocked from the news of Gwendelfear's identity, and it took him a second to process her words. Once he had, his mouth set in a resigned expression and he nodded. Grandmamma looked on with interest. When Hetta paused to choose her words, she prompted her with an expectant, "Well?"

"I'm not the Lord of Stariel," Hetta said in a rush. "I'm not the Lord of Stariel," she repeated, more confidently.

"Oh, well that explains it then," said Grandmamma. She frowned. "But why—"

Jack swelled with indignation, his colour rising, and he burst out, "What the blazes did you think you were about, Hetta? Was this some kind of poor jest or did you really think no one would notice?"

"Hey, that's not—" Marius protested, but Hetta cut him off.

"That's what you think of me, is it? That I was so desperate to rule that I used my powers to fake the Choosing?"

Jack bristled. "For Simulsen's sake, Hetta, it doesn't even matter anymore why you did it. The important thing is to set it right before more fairies descend on Stariel!"

"The Star Stone is a fake!" Marius rose and glared at Jack with a fierceness Hetta hadn't previously suspected him capable of. "It's a fake, and we don't know who did it or why, but it certainly wasn't Hetta. You're out of line, Jack."

Jack flushed, his stance still defiant, but doubt began to creep into his expression. "Why in the hells didn't you tell me that, then?" he mumbled.

"We *are* telling you," Hetta said. She found that her initial flash of white-hot anger had subsided into mere impatience. "It has, you will understand, been a rather busy day!"

Somehow the distance between the three of them had closed, and with them all glowering at each other, the study seemed much smaller than usual. The air between them fairly crackled with enmity.

Grandmamma got to her feet with all the stately grace of a sea liner coasting into port. "Well, I am glad that is all in hand," she said calmly. She navigated her way between the three of them with unruffled movements. "When you see Wyn, send him up to me. I'll be in the stillroom." She paused by the door and added, "And Jack, dear, do stop acting like such a pillock." The sound of the door closing echoed in the silence she left in her wake.

There was a frozen moment where it seemed they would be stuck staring daggers at each other, but Grandmamma's exit had made it somewhat difficult to maintain the serious demeanour required. Hetta let out an exasperated sigh and took a step back from Jack, who was beginning to deflate into sullenness.

Marius still roiled with righteous indignation, and Hetta just knew that he was about to demand an apology from Jack. She was moderately certain this would only make Jack less likely to apologise, so she prodded her brother sharply in the shoulder. Marius jumped.

"I think you ought to explain to our dear cousin what we found earlier today. Although he's jumped to some rather unfortunate conclusions"—she gave Jack a hard look—"he's not wrong about the seriousness of the situation and the need to remedy it."

"I'm sorry," Jack said stiffly after an awkward pause, folding his arms. "But you have to own it looked mighty fishy, Hetta."

Hetta said nothing but didn't try to hide what she thought of that. He turned away, flushing.

"Marius?" she prompted.

Marius related what they had found earlier with regard to the Star Stone. As Marius spoke, conflicting emotions chased across Jack's face: scepticism, worry, hope. Hetta didn't blame him for it. What man wouldn't be hopeful when presented with a second chance at something he'd thought permanently beyond his grasp?

"Well," said Jack when Marius had finished telling him about the Stone. "We shall have to make Gwendelfear tell us what the damned fairies did with it then."

"Actually," said Hetta, "setting aside how you propose to make

Gwendelfear do anything at all that she does not wish to do, I have reason to believe she might not be responsible for this particular incident. Gwendelfear was surprised when she learnt the Star Stone is missing, which doesn't make sense if she was involved in its disappearance."

"She could've been putting it on for show, to throw us off the scent," Jack pointed out.

"Possibly," Hetta acknowledged. "But it's difficult to fake genuine surprise. The reaction time is slightly slower when one is acting, for one must consciously think of the appropriate response. You *do* recall that I have spent a great deal of my latter years in the company of actors?"

They both blinked, as if they *had* temporarily forgotten this fact. Jack nodded reluctantly. "But if it wasn't fairies who took the Stone, who was it?"

Hetta had been contemplating that question ever since they'd discovered the fake Stone, in between such distracting occurrences as fae princes, and she hadn't yet come up with a satisfactory answer.

"I don't know," she said heavily. "And I'm not sure whether whoever was behind it was trying to target me, you, Marius, or just wanting to cause trouble for Stariel in general. It's most vexing to consider that my life may have been turned upside down simply to punish someone else."

"You mean," said Jack with a scowl, "that someone may have done this to prevent me from becoming lord."

Marius and Hetta shared a look. Jack wasn't entirely an idiot, and so when they turned their combined reproof towards him, each of them raising an eyebrow in gentle rebuke, he flushed but said staunchly:

"Well, I'm damned sick of us all dilly-dallying about the subject. I know it's immodest to own it, but I'll own it: I expected to be chosen."

"You shock me," Hetta said dryly.

Jack grinned, unrepentant.

"Are you going to tell everyone else?" Marius asked abruptly.

The levity drained from Jack's face, and he leaned back against the wall and contemplated the pair of them, a V forming between his eyebrows. "Why in the nine hells wouldn't I?" But his mouth thinned into a line and he answered his own question. "You think whoever is responsible will fly the coop if we show our hand."

"A rather mixed metaphor, but yes," Marius said.

Jack shook his head, but it was more in distaste for the idea than in disagreement. "Can we make a new Star Stone?"

Marius shrugged. "If you can find a piece of star indigo big enough, then yes. But it will still take time."

"Fine." Jack straightened. "Fine." He bit out the word. "But I'm not keeping up this pretence forever. The Frost Faire. We tell everyone after that, if we haven't found the Stone by then. That's a month away. I can keep my mouth shut for that long. But that's it." With that, he stalked out of the room. The door slammed behind him.

"Well that's nice!" Marius glared at the dark wood. "He could at least try to be helpful!"

"To be perfectly frank, that went better than I expected." Hetta sighed. "And Jack is right that this can't continue forever. We'll have to break the news eventually." Her heart felt oddly heavy. That wasn't going to be a pleasant conversation. "I suppose the Faire is as good a timeframe as any." She gave an impish smile. "How irritating that I cannot merely proclaim Jack my successor and run away to the city without further explanation. The thought is tempting."

"Is it, though?" Marius cocked his head to one side, grey eyes thoughtful.

Hetta chose not to answer this, instead saying, "Well, I suppose we ought to decide how we are to catch whoever is behind this."

She went to sit behind the desk. "I've been thinking about the illusion used. If it wasn't fae glamour, then an illusionist would be needed for the task."

Marius sighed and slid down into the chair that their grandmother had recently vacated. "Would they have had to be present?"

"Possibly. If they weren't there in person, the spell could either have been linked to me specifically if they had managed to get hold of some part of my physical essence—blood, hair, fingernail clippings," she expanded at Marius's frown. "Or the spell could have been designed to activate after a certain number of people had touched it."

"If it was meant for me, you mean," Marius said heavily.

"Yes. But there aren't many illusionists who could do either of those things—that's difficult magic." Hetta could have done it, but she hardly suspected *herself*. "It would be much easier to simply cast the illusion in person at the right time. And if someone did hire an illusionist, it probably wasn't someone local. How could you trust a local not to gossip, even if you could find someone local with the ability to cast something well enough to convince the crowd? And if it wasn't a local who did it, then our illusionist might very well be remembered. There aren't so many strangers passing through Stariel for them to go unremarked."

Marius was gazing out the window distractedly and didn't seem to have heard her excellent chain of reasoning. "Marius!" she recalled him. "You might at least praise my powers of deduction. Why, I sound just like a detective from a murder mystery!"

"Oh!" He started. "Oh, yes. Yes, I agree, Hetta. It's a good thought."

"Good—you may drive me to the train station tomorrow morning then. I want to ask the stationmaster if any strangers took a train out of Stariel on the days after the Choosing."

25

THE STATIONMASTER

THE STATION LAMPS—THE only elektric ones on the estate—were still on the next morning when they pulled up. Hetta made a silent vow to see the technology rolled out to the rest of Stariel, lord or not. The morning was cold and still, and the low-lying fog had made the drive a slow, cautionary exercise. She got out of the kineticar and marched briskly up to the ticket office. Marius trailed silently behind her.

The stationmaster spotted them coming and stood watching their approach. As they drew closer, Hetta realised with a jolt that she recognised him—not from her arrival weeks ago but from her precipitous departure six years ago. He'd been an old man then, but he appeared much the same now. He was of that leathery stock that doesn't change much between the ages of fifty and eighty.

He doffed his hat as they approached. The gesture hadn't been a personal one, for when they drew closer, his eyes widened and he made the same motion, this time with more intent. "Lord Valstar," he said. "Mr Valstar."

"I don't know your name, sir, but I recognise you," said Hetta. "I remember you helped me stow my trunk all those years ago when I left for Meridon." She gave a little laugh. "Though I doubt you remember me from then!"

"Indeed I do, milord. You've a strong look of your father to you, if you don't mind me saying, and I've a good memory for faces."

"Thank you for saying so," Hetta said, though it wasn't exactly a compliment. She put on her most charming smile and leaned conspiratorially on the counter separating her from the stationmaster. "I'm afraid I'm here hoping to take advantage of your memory for faces, sir. I wondered if you can remember any strangers leaving on the train the day after the Choosing."

The stationmaster's eyebrows shot up. "And why would you be wanting to know that?"

Hetta thought rapidly. She bit her lip, paused, and then said in a low voice: "May I trust you to keep a confidence?"

The stationmaster swelled with pride. "I know when to hold my tongue. I won't go wagging about it in the village, if that's what you're worried about."

Hetta endeavoured to look embarrassed. "I'm afraid it's a rather awkward matter. A valuable family heirloom was stolen, but it took us a while to notice and a while longer to pinpoint exactly when it had been taken. We now think it was probably taken on the night of the Choosing, when we were all distracted. One of our servants remembers seeing a stranger poking about with a town air to them," she invented liberally, "and I thought, as a long shot, that it might be worth checking if someone not from the area had departed the day afterwards. Or on the Monday?" She didn't look at Marius, but she hoped he had enough sense to keep his expression neutral.

The stationmaster had been nodding along. "Can't trust those not born and bred to the country life. Take their own mother if they thought it'd better their lot," he said sagely.

"But do you remember? I know it's a lot to ask."

The stationmaster thought, furrows forming in his forehead. "Just let me check. We keep a passenger manifest of departures." He drew an oversized book from a drawer and leafed back through it, his tongue between his teeth as he hummed. "Ah," he said, finding the relevant date. "You're in luck. Naught on Sunday morning—there's no evening train on Sunday—and only two people got on at Stariel on Monday morning. One was Mr Tidwell, who's been staying with his aunt in the village. He was only taking a short trip down to Greymark, I suppose. I remember him returning yesterday. The other fellow's likely your man—I've got him down as a Mr James Snickett."

A jolt of recognition ran through Hetta, but she tried to keep it from showing in her voice. "Do you remember what he looked like?"

The stationmaster screwed up his face. "Good-looking man," he said after a pause. "Blond. Thought he was a Southerner just from the look of him—might've heard him speak, though I can't be sure."

Hetta thanked him, outwardly composed, inwardly thinking furiously. James Snickett—there was a name she hadn't heard in a long time.

PHONE CALLS

SHE EXPECTED MARIUS to say something about her invented story as they made their way back to the kineticar, but he was silent. It was only as he was opening the door to get in that she noticed how mechanical his movements were.

"Marius?" she said softly once they were seated. The kineticar had a heatstone installed, and Hetta fumbled to activate it against the bitter chill.

Marius started. "Yes?"

"I recognised the name—James Snickett. He's an illusionist. He was at the Meridon School of Illusions, a few years above me."

Whatever had been distracting Marius, she had his full attention now.

"How well do you know him?"

She shook her head. "Not at all. As I said, he was a few years above me and left while I was still very junior. I'm not sure he would remember me at all—I remember him only because he was considered very talented." She gave a small, wry grin. "And he was a very handsome young man."

Marius snorted. "In this case, let us be thankful he was so handsome. But why would he want to fake the Choosing?"

"He wouldn't. Obviously, someone must have hired him. Which is excellent news—I can contact my friends in Meridon and get them to track down either Mr Snickett or a list of his recent clients. Can we stop at the gatehouse?" She checked her watch. "Bradfield should be up."

We must get phonelines installed at the house, Hetta thought as the gatekeeper nodded to them in bemusement when they let themselves into the office room of the gatehouse. The two-storey building was of more modern construction than Stariel House. It stood only a few hundred metres from the Home Bridge, the main accessway into the estate proper from Stariel-on-Starwater.

Bradfield picked up the phone, though he sounded flustered.

"The name's not familiar, but I'll see what I can find out for you," he agreed after she'd explained about trying to track down James Snickett, though she kept her reasons vague. "You holding up all right? How's the aristocratic life going so far?"

Well, someone stole the Star Stone and made me an imposter, she wanted to say. *Also, fairies are real, and my butler is one. A very attractive one, though Sweet Mother Eostre only knows what he's hiding underneath his skin.*

"Er—I'm fine," she said instead. Brad didn't notice her tone, distracted by the upcoming show.

"Hang fire—Ida wants to talk to you while I've got you," he said when she thought the conversation over.

Before Hetta could object, she found herself on the receiving end of effusive thanks from Ida for recommending her to Bradfield. "For you know what it's like, trying to find work as a female mage, and I've nowhere near your talent, Hetta!" There was a note of guilt in her friend's voice. Ida wanted reassurance that Hetta didn't resent her.

"Er—you're welcome, Ida. I'm glad you were able to help Brad out of the bind I put him in!" What was she going to do when she was ousted as lord? The space back in Meridon where she'd fit was already closing over. It was slightly lowering to realise her presence wasn't actually indispensable. She shook her head, annoyed at the direction her thoughts were taking. What had she expected—for Bradfield and the company to sit around pining for her? That would be unreasonable. *Even if apparently that's exactly what I wanted them to do.*

She asked Ida if she knew anything about James Snickett.

"James Snickett? Isn't he the good-looking one from a few years above us?"

"Yes," Hetta agreed with a laugh. Ida promised to try to find out who his recent clients had been.

When she hung up after agreeing to let Ida take her out for a meal next time she was in Meridon, she found Marius had lapsed back into abstraction. He leaned against the outside of the gatehouse, his focus as distant as the Indigo Mountains rising from the mist blanketing the foothills. His hair stuck out in all directions, a sure sign he'd been restlessly running his hands through it.

The salted gravel of the driveway crunched as she walked over to the kineticar.

"Marius?" she prompted. He came back to himself with a few slow blinks. "Are you all right?"

"Um—Yes. Yes, I'm fine."

"Well, you don't sound very convincing," she said flatly, but he shook off her question.

"How did it go? Do we know who hired our rogue illusionist?"

"Not yet, but soon, I hope," Hetta told him. The house came into sight as they curved the last bend around Starwater.

"It looks like something out of a fairy tale," she remarked. The fog was thicker here beside the lake, and it furled about the great monolith in slow-moving patterns. A curious feeling rose in her despite her frustration, a kind of child's wonder. There were many things she loved about Meridon, but this landscape of bleak fields and distant mountains and evergreens could not be found in that city.

"With real fairies," Marius added with a glance towards the west tower, where Gwendelfear was imprisoned in the Tower Room. What *were* they going to do about Gwendelfear?

27

BLACKMAIL

WHEN THEY ENTERED the house, Marius headed for the library while Hetta went in search of Wyn. The house was its usual bustle of people; there might as well not have been a fae in the tower for all the difference it made. The servants had so far been astonishingly incurious about the entire affair—something that Hetta chalked up to Wyn's glamour. It concerned her, and yet it was convenient not to have to deal with gossip on the subject.

Not that Hetta's family had shown much more reaction. There had been only one mention of the fae at breakfast—from the surprising source of Alexandra, who had said defiantly that she was going to visit Gwen and then deflated when no one tried to stop her. Hetta had merely requested that she take Wyn with her to open the door. Everyone else seemed to feel that fairies fell into that category of subjects considered gauche to speak openly about, and

Lady Phoebe had hurried to fill the silence with inconsequentials after Alexandra stomped out to find Wyn.

One fae locked away and another running the household, Hetta thought uneasily as she crossed the courtyard, where the shadow of the Northern Tower fell. *And an imposter in the lord's place.* How many other secrets were hidden within Stariel's walls, spreading fine cracks through the edifice? She lay her hand on an older section of stone wall beside the door that led towards the kitchens, the surface rough against her palm. How long had Stariel House stood, in one form or another, against all the world could throw at it? A low ember kindled in her stomach. How dare someone steal the Star Stone and threaten that?

She stepped away from the wall, shaking her head at the uncharacteristic rush of sentiment towards the building. *The stonework needs repairing*, she thought prosaically. Presumably due to her father's lack of maintenance budget. She made a note to discuss it with Mr Fisk—or maybe Wyn? Technically her land steward ought to be the one to advise her on capital expenditure, but it *did* relate to the house, and Wyn was currently head of the household staff. *And also a prince*, she couldn't help thinking, trying to fit those two pieces together, but they wouldn't click into place no matter how she rearranged them in her head.

Wyn was unexpectedly easy to find once she re-entered the house. She rounded the next corner and would have barrelled straight into him except that he dodged, quick as a cat.

"Good, I was just looking for you," she said as she recovered her balance.

He spread his hands in an apologetic gesture. "As it so happens, I was in search of you also, my Star. Lord Penharrow is here to see you."

That took the wind from her sails. "Oh." She searched his expression for a clue to his feelings but found none. He was every inch the dignified butler this morning, as buttoned-up as his immaculate suit. Even his hair, which had a natural tendency towards disarray, had been made sleek and extra-butlery. "Where is he?"

"In the green drawing room." A pause. "With Lady Sybil."

She narrowed her eyes at him. "Did you put him in with my aunt on purpose?"

"Her ladyship was eager to keep him company."

She couldn't help laughing. "That sounds suspiciously like a 'yes'."

He said nothing, but his eyes gleamed. *Prince Hallowyn Tempestren*, she thought. That's what Gwendelfear had called him.

She bit her lip. "Should I call you—"

"No."

She glared at him. "You don't even know what I was about to ask."

"Well, if you were about to ask if I want you to call me something different now that you know the truth about me, the answer is no. I would prefer you did not."

"Fine, go and do some work then, *Mr Tempest*, if you insist on pretending to be a butler. I'll track you down later."

He bowed, the slight curve of his mouth betraying him. "As you wish."

IT SPOKE WELL OF Angus, thought Hetta, that he looked for all the world as if he liked nothing better than to chat to acid-tongued aunts. His smile when Hetta entered the room was perhaps a shade more relieved than it would otherwise have been, but apart from that, his countenance showed no sign of irritation. He rose to greet her as Aunt Sybil lurked in the background, ready to swoop in and put a stop to any unseemly behaviour.

"I can't stop for long, but I brought you some of the books I mentioned," he said, nodding at a neatly bound stack on the coffee table.

"Oh." Hetta struggled to merge the mundane with the fantastical. "Thank you." How did books on sheep and drainage schemes fit into the same world that contained fae princes? Although, presumably, the fae needed to eat too. She and Wyn had once stolen a whole tray of cherry pastries, which he'd certainly eaten his fair share of.

She shook the thoughts away and focussed on the man in front of her. This wasn't the time to wonder if the fae farmed sheep. Angus was reassuringly solid, handsome as ever.

"I'm happy to lend you any book or periodical in Penharrow's library." He grinned. "Though I insist you return them in person." Would he still flirt with her if he knew she was a fraud? But Angus, she remembered, had shown an interest in her *before* she'd been chosen. That was heartening.

"A very generous offer, but Stariel really ought to develop some of its own resources." She'd already sent off for various dauntingly named volumes and subscriptions based on Angus's recommendations. She would argue with Jack that they were a necessary investment, if it came to it. Stariel shouldn't have to limp along on weak finances for simple lack of modernisation. "You shall have to come up with a less feeble excuse to invite me to tea, Angus." Aunt Sybil made a clucking noise, as if to remind them of her presence.

Angus grinned. "You're right. There's a new play starting at the theatre down in Alverness. Why don't we make a day trip, go to a matinee session?"

Her younger self swooned at the offer, and Hetta found herself accepting before she'd properly considered whether it was a good idea to encourage Angus with things as they were at present. But it was only a play—and far better to focus on someone like Angus, who was both human *and* clearly interested, as opposed to, hypothetically, certain butlers who were neither. Additionally, she didn't have to wonder if Angus was hiding an unsettling visage under his skin, although she quickly checked that thought, heat rising in her cheeks. She couldn't speculate about Angus's skin while sitting in the same room as her aunt. Even if a certain memory had risen, of a sticky-hot summer and a shirtless Angus helping to get a field of cut hay under shelter before a downpour. She quickly squashed the image, cursing her illusionist training that made it extremely easy to visualise the details.

Angus had to excuse himself after only a short time, and she took the books he'd brought up to her study. On her desk rested a tray holding a steaming coffeepot and all the necessary accoutrements. How, Hetta wondered, had Wyn managed to time that so beautifully? It looked surprisingly as if it belonged here, nestled next to her notes on the dark wood, though her father had never to her knowledge drunk coffee. Was it a peace offering? she wondered, unsure whether to be pleased or vexed. It didn't stop her from pouring herself a cup. The rich taste warmed her down to her toes, and she smiled with simple, uncomplicated pleasure.

Her smile faded as her gaze fell across the rest of her desk. Her *empty* desk. The accounts books had disappeared. Again. She let out a long breath of annoyance. Mr Fisk had taken them back again, despite her instructions to the contrary. He might have been her father's steward for years, but at this rate it was doubtful he was going to be Hetta's for even six months.

The thought pulled her up short. She wasn't the real lord; she wouldn't *be* here in six months. Ought she to be making staffing decisions on her successor's behalf? Ought she to be making *any* substantive decisions, when she knew she didn't truly have the authority to do so?

She drank the rest of her coffee and mulled over the thought and the ones that came with it, about phonelines, crumbling stonework, the shut-up Dower House, and drains. Standing next to the window, she could watch the fog over Starwater slowly burning off. It was a lovely sight, the remnants of frost glistening in the pale sunlight on the lake's edges.

She'd never asked for this role, but it was even worse to have all the trappings of it without any of the authority. It meant her hands were tied when it came to making changes to the estate. Or were they? Surely whoever came after her ought to be grateful that she was getting the ball rolling, as it were? Her time with the accounts and her conversations with Angus had convinced her the estate couldn't continue as it had been. Sitting twiddling her thumbs in agonised indecision didn't seem like it would benefit anyone.

She hadn't come to any firm conclusion by the time the coffee ran out, but she at least felt much more able to face the world.

There was a diffident knock at the door, and one of the housemaids came in carrying a bundle of letters. "The mail's arrived, my lord," she said to Hetta, handing her a sheaf of letters.

"Thank you, Lottie." The housemaid nodded and left.

She turned her attention to the letters, which were a mix of polite congratulations from neighbours on her appointment, bills, early Wintersol cards, RSVPs for the Frost Ball, which ought, really, to have been addressed to Lady Phoebe, and one last letter that did not fit into any of these categories. She thought it was another polite acknowledgement from one of the local gentry based on the quality of the paper and the neat handwriting, but when she opened it, she saw that it was something of another sort entirely.

> *Lord Valstar—it pains me to involve a woman in this matter, but I feel it is my duty to warn you that your brother's recent activities are such that would bring only scandal upon your house if they became known. As his younger sister, you must naturally look up to him,*

and it is to my sorrow that I must disillusion you so. Your brother is an unnatural predator who has used his position to lure innocent youths from the path of what is right and proper. I will not say more on this head in order to spare your female sensibilities, but I believe that you will agree that reparation should be made for the harm he has caused. Otherwise I shall be forced to lay information with the local constable.

Letters addressed to Mr T c/o Stariel Post Office will reach me.

Yours regretfully,

Mr T

Hetta dropped the note. She had a strong impulse to summon fire and burn the clumsy attempt at blackmail to ash, but she managed to check it. This was followed by an incredulous laugh as she recalled the phrase 'female sensibilities'.

What trouble had Marius managed to get himself into? She remembered, suddenly, the night she'd overheard Marius and Wyn speaking. Wyn had offered to help an upset Marius—help that had involved magic. It seemed probable that the two events were related. And maybe—related to the theft of the Star Stone? She folded the letter in half, slipped it into her pocket, and went in search of her problematic butler for the second time that day.

28

PEAR VARIETALS

Wyn was, as usual, busy. He stood at the back entrance to Stariel House, directing deliverymen to the storeroom, a large clipboard in one hand as he took stock of what had been delivered against what had been ordered.

The grocers' cart was nearly entirely emptied by the time Hetta arrived on the scene, and she judged that her interference would be both unhelpful and unneeded. Wyn flashed her a single brilliant smile in greeting, and she leaned against one wall of the house and watched him as he neatly toted up the last few items and thanked the men delivering the goods.

Hetta hadn't yet reconciled her new knowledge of him with the old, and it was hard to do so now, watching him engaged in such ordinary activity. He seemed to be on good terms with the deliverymen. The older of the two slapped him on one shoulder at some remark the younger had made. Hetta vaguely recognised the two men as locals from Stariel-on-Starwater. That people liked Wyn was something she'd already known—something she'd always attributed to his good nature and ready smile. Was it fae glamour, she wondered, watching the men? But she could detect nothing like the strange magic she'd seen Wyn use before.

As Wyn asked about the older man's wife and congratulated the younger man on the quality of the sausage the youth had apparently had a hand in making last time, Hetta reflected that it was possible a large part of Wyn's charm was because he was genuinely *interested* in people in a way that Hetta was not. Here she was, Lord of Stariel, and all she knew about these two men was that they were locals. Wyn knew the little details of their lives.

She came over when she judged the men were about to leave and introduced herself, thanking them for their efforts. They seemed surprised but pleased, and both doffed their hats in respect.

Hetta watched as the two men drove away. "Are you on such good terms with all the locals, Mr Tempest?"

Wyn considered the question. "On reasonable terms with most, yes." The morning sun revealed notes of mahogany in his dark eyes. He canted his head. "Is there something you want of me, Miss Hetta? More coffee, perhaps? I apologise if I misjudged the quantity."

She swatted his shoulder, and his eyes grew round and innocent. "But what have I done to offend you, Miss Hetta?"

She glared at him. "Well, if you're going to be like that, you could at least get it right. It's Lord Valstar to you."

"Of course, my Star."

"This is ridiculous," she said, throwing her hands up.

Wyn gave a slight bow. "I do my best."

"You know what I mean. This entire mess—fairies, nefarious plots, missing Stones. You."

"Which particular aspect of me is irking you this morning?" He tucked the clipboard under his arm. "Or am I merely the most accessible target at the moment?"

"The most accessible," she admitted. Partly to disconcert him, she added, "You know, you don't look at all like a fae prince."

He shrugged. "Good."

"In any case, there was something I wanted to talk to you about. Will you walk with me down to the Home Farm?"

He blinked, taken off guard, then replied easily, "As you wish."

The Home Farm was to the southwest of the house. The walk there took them through the woods along the lakeside, currently spartan without their leaves.

"Why do I suspect we are not going this way because you have developed a burning interest in traditional varieties of pears?" Wyn said lightly.

He was nervous, Hetta thought, though he hid it well. She didn't bother to answer the rhetorical question. The breeze rattled the naked arms of the beech trees around them.

"Tell me about Gwendelfear," she said, picking her words carefully. "How did you know who she was?"

He shrugged, his movements as graceful as ever as they walked, but she knew him well enough to see his tension. It was there in the way he held himself, as if every muscle was being individually directed, in the slight tightness around his eyes.

"I did not, at first, though I could tell she was of Faerie at a glance. It's difficult to explain how I knew that. It's..." She could tell he was searching for the right metaphor, his long-fingered hands making a rolling motion. "An instinctive thing. Another sense. The way you know coffee is coffee even before you taste it."

"You're saying that Gwendelfear smells fae?"

"It's as good an analogy as any."

"How did you know her name?"

"I read her—it's a gift of royal fae." There was a hint of bitterness in his voice, though his expression remained neutral. *Good*, he'd said earlier, when she'd told him he didn't look like a prince; it didn't take a genius to realise he disliked that his own magic was a mark of his birthright. "She refuses to speak to me. She hates me, although I am not sure if that is because of my court or because

I am responsible for her imprisonment." Another pause, and then he came to a halt, turning towards Hetta. "Do you want me to go, Hetta?" He was trying very hard to appear detached, but his voice betrayed him. The words had come out husky with emotion.

She studied him. He looked more natural here, amongst the stark browns and greys of the wood, than he had in the courtyard, cajoling deliverymen. Here, it seemed obvious he wasn't human, for what human had that sense of wild, contained energy, that alien beauty, that sense of absolute stillness? She wanted very badly to ask what lurked beneath his skin. Was he like Gwendelfear? She tried to imagine his eyes without whites, flower-pupils staring out at her from the russet irises. And yet she couldn't ask him, for she knew that it would hurt him to know his appearance was weighing on her mind so.

"You lied to me." She met his eyes steadily. "For years, you lied to me."

"Yes," he said. "I did." There was a long, sombre moment between them.

"You might at least try to defend yourself. It would make it easier to rail at you," Hetta said crossly.

Wyn gave a fleeting smile. "Very well. In fairness then, at no point during our friendship did you actually *ask* if I was a fae prince."

"That's a very poor defence."

"Yes." He turned his face away and examined the peeling bark of the nearby silver birch as if it fascinated him.

She scowled. It was like him to be flippant when nervous, but she was in no mood for his evasions today.

"I—" He swallowed. "Sorry, I'm being childish. Can you forgive me?"

Hetta sighed. The problem, really, was that she had half-forgiven him already, when he'd met her eyes across Gwendelfear's unconscious body with a frightened expression that said *please help me*. Remaining angry at him for keeping secrets seemed petty when set against things like threatened murder and wars. And yet, petty or not, she *was* still angry at him for it. "You'll have to give me time."

He made a loose gesture, as if to say that time was in plentiful supply. "But I doubt very much that the only reason you dragged me out here was to grumble at me. What's troubling you?"

Hetta debated for a few moments, and then drew the letter out of her coat and handed it to him. "This." She waited while he read it. His expression was pensive rather than surprised. "And," she added when he looked up, "I overheard you offer to help Marius out of some difficulty using magic—I don't know the particulars of it, for I didn't stay to listen—but it seemed unlikely that the two things weren't related."

Wyn handed her back the note. "The note is my fault—an oversight I can rectify easily enough." He hesitated and gave a short, tight smile. "I know you want more details than that, but this is not my secret to tell."

She gave him a long, thoughtful look, her mind shuffling through the possibilities. The fae magic Wyn had so far revealed had been troubling in its implications. "Are you going to work further magic on the person who wrote this letter?"

He met her gaze. "Yes."

"Is it—will it harm them?"

"It will cause them no small amount of frustration, I suspect, but in the sense you mean, no." This wasn't an entirely satisfactory answer, and Wyn clearly knew it. Hetta considered pushing but knew it wouldn't do any good. She didn't bother to hide her unhappiness with this state of affairs.

He let out a long sigh and straightened. "Shall we continue down to the farm or have you concluded your inquiries?"

"Well, we may as well, since all I've achieved so far today is to encounter a frustrating number of dead ends. At least this may count as some form of productive activity. I've been wanting to talk to the farm manager about the orchards since Angus suggested improvements for them." Mentioning Lord Penharrow had been a deliberate jab that Hetta immediately regretted, but Wyn took it without any noticeable change in expression. Hetta told herself sternly that she wasn't slightly disappointed by this.

Wyn smiled. "It appears I overestimated my importance then—you truly were interested in pear varietals." He shook his head, his expression comically embarrassed. "Arrogant, arrogant creature I am."

She laughed. "Well, it's more that I feel that I ought to be interested in pear varietals. Do we even grow pears?"

"We do, although not at present. The orchards will be fairly bare at this time of year, I'm afraid. Late-season apples may be the best you can hope for."

They walked through the woods in silence. The trees along this way weren't natives of Stariel. They had been planted by one of Hetta's ancestors who'd had a fondness for the great copper beech trees of the South. That ancestor had died before the trees were more than saplings, but the full glory of her vision was now realised some hundred and fifty years later. The copper beeches were not fully deciduous, retaining a significant mass of browning leaves on their lower branches through the winter. It made this part of the walkway very dimly lit, and Hetta summoned a ball of light without a second thought. Its amber glow bobbed merrily above their heads as they walked. Wyn smiled up at it but didn't comment. She dismissed it as the woodland came to an end, opening out to the fenced rows of the orchards.

Wyn had guessed aright. The ancient apple trees still bore a few late fruits in their upper branches. Hetta drew closer to the orchard and leaned against the gate, caught by a memory of a much younger Wyn squirreling his way up a gnarled apple tree.

"You used to climb like a cat," she remarked softly.

"Still do," he said promptly, coming to stand beside her.

"That does not seem like the kind of dignified behaviour one expects from fae princes. Or one's butler."

"Well—I am the only fae prince you have met. And perhaps you have previously been acquainted with only an inferior sort of butler." His eyes gleamed when she turned to look at him, brimming with mischief.

"No, you cannot possibly—" she said, laughing, for he was very properly attired in white shirt, bow tie, waistcoat, and neat tweed jacket, but before she could say any more, she was being handed said jacket and watching her friend leap nimbly over the fence to clamber up the nearest tree with the quick efficiency of a ferret. He paused when he'd reached a secure perch and plucked an apple from an outstretched branch.

"Catch," he called down, grinning.

She shook her head at his foolishness but couldn't help grinning back. She held out her hands obediently. He lobbed the apple gently, and it fell into her grasp with a neat plop. "Very nice."

She saw him turn and stare past her, amusement flickering through his expression before he composed himself. "Ah, Mr Brown. Well met."

Hetta turned to see that the farm manager had appeared behind them and was staring at Wyn, lost for words. Wyn made his way back to ground level, retrieved his coat from Hetta, and greeted him in a solemnly dignified fashion not ten seconds later, as if nothing at all unusual had just occurred. Mr Brown wasn't quite game enough to question Wyn's actions in the face of his slightly aloof manner, and Wyn would have carried them all successfully past the awkward moment if Hetta hadn't spoiled things by breaking into a fit of giggles.

29

THE MODERN MAN'S GUIDE TO SHEEP FARMING

THE DAYS TICKED away without any sign of resolving the mystery. The village's Frost Faire—Jack's deadline—was held on the first of December, and Stariel's Frost Ball for the local gentry would be the following Saturday, part of the month of festivities leading up to Wintersol.

The blackmail attempt and Marius's secret weighed on her mind. It seemed unlikely that Stariel had *two* enemies wandering about. She wondered how best to broach the subject with her brother while she went through and approved the list of supplies to be brought in as part of Stariel Estate's contribution to the Frost Faire. It felt fraudulent to sign her name against orders, but someone needed to do it, and it was, after all, hardly unreasonable stuff. She made a note to ask Wyn about the village council's attitudes towards illusions. She might as well offer her abilities up in the name of festivity if they weren't all as hidebound as her father. *Though it might also just make the villagers even gladder to be rid of me, if we announce my fake lordship soon afterwards,* she couldn't help thinking.

In a valiant attempt to put it out of her mind, she buried herself in one of the periodicals Angus had lent her, dauntingly titled *The Modern Man's Guide to Sheep Farming.* She was relieved to find it more interesting than its title would suggest, although unfortunately also tiresomely oblivious to the idea that anyone female might be reading it. Perhaps, she thought with a sliver of amusement, she ought to write to the editor.

Still, there was only so much one could read about sheep in a single sitting, and she found her mind wandering towards her older brother once more. It was a mixed blessing when he appeared at her study door, holding a nondescript wooden crate in a surreptitious manner.

"Oh, do come in," she told him, amused. "Anyone who sees you will immediately think you're up to something."

"But I often receive crates for my studies and tote them around the house for perfectly unobjectionable reasons!" Marius protested.

"It's not the box—it's your manner. This is why you always lose at cards, brother mine."

His face fell. "Well, I didn't want to bring the formal casket up, and the false Stone wouldn't fit in my coat pocket."

She refrained from pointing out that no one would have been bothered by him openly carting the Stone about if he had simply said he was studying the history of it for a paper he had in mind to write. No one enquired too closely into his scholarly activities, and everyone knew he often took odd interests. Instead, she asked if he had seen Jack today.

"No—he's in a mood." Marius emphasised the last word. "Or rather, a sulk. But he is at least being more useful than last time he disappeared. Grandmamma said he was out walking the bounds and distributing the defensive talismans that she made up."

There was beat of silence while they together considered the sheer strangeness of that statement. How one's perspective of the world could shift! Then Marius shook himself and placed the crate containing the false Stone on Hetta's desk. He undid the lid and lifted it out, handling it with his typical carefulness when it came to artefacts of interest.

"I think," Marius said, passing the fake from one hand to the other, "that it might be worth getting this analysed to see if we can trace how it was made."

"It's not magical," Hetta said swiftly, "or at least, not in any way I can detect. The substance itself, I mean. Obviously, there was a magical illusion cast upon it."

"Yes." Marius peered intently at the stone. Despite its dubious ancestry, it was still a pretty thing of iridescent blues and purples. "But someone must still have commissioned its manufacture. And there can't be that many places that could make something like this. If we can find out who made it, they should have a record of who commissioned it."

"Unless it was made by fae in parts unknown," Hetta pointed out. When Marius looked downcast, she added, "But it's still an excellent thought. I'm inclined to think Gwendelfear wasn't involved with the fake Stone, and in any case, it can't do any harm to pursue that line of inquiry."

"I wish we could send it to cousin Caro." Marius set the Stone down on Hetta's desk. "She's the chemist, not I."

"Well," said Hetta, patting his arm consolingly, "if we should find an unknown plant that looks like a clue, I shall know precisely who to turn to for their extensive botanical knowledge."

Marius rolled his eyes at her levity. "But if we send it to Caro, we'll have to explain the whole mess."

"We're going to have to explain it at some point," Hetta said with some reluctance.

But Marius was already shaking his head. "In any case, I know someone else from my time down in Knoxbridge who should do just as well. Better, perhaps, since his family is in the manufacturing business."

Hetta gave him an approving look. "Why, Marius, you dark horse. I didn't know you had connections with tradesmen! You must be careful with whom you associate." She tried to imitate Aunt Sybil's tones and was rewarded with a brief smile. It faded too quickly, and she wished she knew what was at the bottom of all this melancholy. "Are you well, Marius? You seem...distracted, lately." Should she tell him about the blackmail attempt?

"I'm fine," he said yet again, though his expression made a lie of his words. She knew he wanted her to drop the subject. She thought about pressing him on the matter, but he looked so miserable that she couldn't find it in her heart to do so. Instead, she surprised them both by rising and clasping her arms around him in a brief hug.

"Well, if you ever find that you are *not* fine, I'm here with a sympathetic ear."

For a moment, she thought he wavered, on the brink of releasing whatever was tormenting him, but then she felt him withdraw. "No need to get sappy, Hetta, or I'll begin to wonder if you are quite well," he said with false brightness.

She gave him a Look that she hoped conveyed that she could see through his facade, so he might as well tell her what it was about anyway. He ignored it and took his leave.

She spent an unsatisfactory hour with Mr Fisk, who didn't at all favour her proposal to even *talk* with the bank manager. "Risky business, loans," he said in an authoritative way.

"Well, I don't see how else we are to finance the expenditure that Stariel needs." Again, she suffered from a flicker of conscience. Ought she to be planning such outlays? But again, she consoled herself with the thought that she was only doing what was necessary, and she hadn't done anything irreversible yet. She would make Jack see that, if and when he succeeded her. It would save time to have inquiries already in motion. "And although there is certainly risk attached, I believe it to be a manageable one, with careful planning. It's not as if the estate produces no income, and the advice I have sought on the matter makes me certain that investing in Stariel in such a way is the only way to assure its future. The estate has been woefully neglected for decades now."

"Lord Henry—" Mr Fisk began.

"Spent money on trinkets like new kineticars while the cottages are badly in need of re-roofing, the house still isn't elektrified, and the shepherds are complaining that no money's been spent on new breeding stock in so long that our sheep are practically living fossils," she said tartly.

Mr Fisk scowled.

"In any case, there can be no harm in merely *meeting* with someone from the bank."

"If such expenditures are warranted, then why not sell the eastern flats to Penharrow? That would go a good way towards new roofs and suchlike, without the need for a loan."

"I am not selling my inheritance." That, at least, was a point she was sure any successor would agree on.

Mr Fisk tried his best to persuade her, and eventually she grew quite short with the man. "If I'm reluctant to take your advice, consider that it is you who have acted as steward of this estate during its decline. Why should I trust your instinct to steer us out of it again?"

The steward drew himself up to his full height, affronted. Since he wasn't any taller than Hetta, this wasn't especially impressive, a fact that seemed only to annoy him further.

"I have served Stariel in good faith for years. Your father placed utmost trust in me—"

"Oh, get out!" She rose. "You've put me in a temper, and I'll say something I regret unless you take yourself away this instant."

Bristling like an angry cat, he left. Hetta slumped back into her seat, abruptly ashamed of herself. Although, on the brighter side, she might have made life easier for her successor, since Mr Fisk would likely welcome them with open arms. The thought stung. Telling herself not to be so melancholy, she briskly put her papers back into their neat piles and made her way downstairs and out of the house, pausing only to don suitable outerwear.

She reached for Stariel as she walked, trying to settle her own restlessness, but the land was discontent too. She wondered if she ought to forgive some of Jack's bad moods—he was more sensitive to Stariel than she, and if he'd been living with the land's growing unease at its lordless state, then it went some way towards explaining his grouchiness. They couldn't go on like this indefinitely, even if Jack hadn't set his arbitrary deadline. She wasn't sure whether the thought was a cheering or depressing one.

ALVERNESS

TIME PASSED IN a mixture of sudden jolts and long, drawn-out hours. A strange atmosphere had fallen over Stariel House, an increasing sense of urgency and dread. Gwendelfear couldn't be kept a prisoner at Stariel forever; Stariel couldn't remain lordless. Hetta and Marius waited for the inquiries they had set in motion to bear fruit. Jack was often absent, roaming the foothills of the Indigoes in search of star indigo. Aunt Sybil worried over him as the weather turned colder, and Wyn spent an inordinate amount of time listening to her expanding on the subject and following her orders for preparing warming broths. Alexandra got into an argument with Gregory about Gwendelfear, with the result that Gregory took himself off to a friend's house for several days. Lady Phoebe fluttered around her children and managed to get a seething Alexandra occupied with preparing stall goods for the upcoming Frost Faire.

By the time Hetta's outing with Angus rolled around, she was eager for an escape from the strained atmosphere, but somewhat worried that she'd gotten in over her head with the neighbouring lord. Her conscience told her it probably wasn't a very good idea to flirt with someone who didn't know she would soon be leaving the district under a cloud of scandal.

Angus's reaction when he saw her made it hard to regret it very much though.

"Hetta," Angus said warmly at the sight of her. "You'll set hearts afire in Alverness."

She *did* look lovely. She'd even allowed herself some tactical use of illusion to make her hair shinier than usual. She did a little twirl, the layers of her pink dress making a satisfying swishing noise.

"Thank you." She smiled. "So do you." Angus did indeed look very well in his formal dress. His coat was well fitted and highlighted the broadness of his shoulders. She couldn't help some rapid mental speculation as to what he might look like divested of said coat, and then had to tell herself off sternly.

"We'd better take our leave, or we'll be late," Angus said to Aunt Sybil, who unbent a little in the face of such well-dressed masculinity and bade them an almost warm farewell as she shepherded them out of the entrance hall. Hetta spotted little Laurel peering down from the main stair landing above, her eyes huge and entranced. She almost waved but caught herself at the last minute. Laurel definitely wasn't supposed to be there and would not appreciate Aunt Sybil's attention being drawn to her presence.

ALVERNESS WAS AN HOUR and a half's drive south of Stariel, and notable for being the only town of much size this far north. Greymark was readily acknowledged as the true capital of the

North, being quite five times as large as any other Northern city—although still nothing compared to Meridon—but Greymark was four hours' train ride away.

They were going to a matinee—the days having grown too short to make driving in the evening desirable. It was a bright, crisp day, the sky a particularly brilliant shade of blue. Heavy frosts had become the norm over the last few weeks, but the ice had had time to melt by the time they set off, and Angus's driving inspired confidence.

"I've been meaning to learn to drive," she said without thinking. "It's impossible to get anywhere up here without being able to do so!"

"I'm very happy to chauffeur you wherever you wish. Indeed, I don't know how I could refuse you. You're devilishly charming, you know."

Hetta considered Angus thoughtfully. She was a little surprised that he hadn't offered to teach her himself. Not that she'd intended her remark to prompt such an offer—but the fact that he hadn't made her wonder. She had a sudden flash of insight that in his view it was unnecessary and undesirable for her to drive—as a lady she ought to commandeer a man to do so whenever needed. There were odd patches of old-fashionedness to Angus that Hetta would every now and then encounter.

Hetta felt the moment they passed Stariel's bounds with an intensity she'd never before experienced. Stariel pulled at her, as if the land was reluctant to part with any of its people without a lord to anchor it. But the car's movement was inexorable, and after a few dizzying seconds the sensation passed. Hetta felt lighter and strangely off-balance for it.

"Are you well?" Angus inquired.

Hetta nodded and forced a smile. "Stariel didn't want to let me go today, it seems. But we're beyond its reach now."

Angus's attention was primarily on the road, but she thought he looked thoughtful. "You don't much talk about it, your land-sense, as you call it. None of the Valstars do. Reticent to a fault, the lot of you."

Hetta laughed. "Hardly. It's just that to us it's a perfectly normal thing and to the rest of the world a highly peculiar one. And it's not fashionable to talk of magic, you know."

"It's real, though? I had thought it merely a quaint tradition."

"I'm sure the rest of the world thinks so," Hetta said. "But I'm afraid it is real, gothic and fairytale-like though it seems."

"And you all feel it?" Angus asked. "And you know when you've crossed the boundaries?"

Hetta nodded. "Yes, although some of us are aware of it more strongly than others. Jack has always been ascribed the strongest connection of our generation. When we were younger, he always had an uncanny knack for finding wild creatures, for instance. And he claimed to be able to feel storms when they rolled over the Indigoes, but that may have been exaggeration. Certainly my father could tell you what weather was about to come upon us." *When he was sober enough to pay attention to it.*

Angus was quiet the rest of the drive, and Hetta didn't try to coax him into further conversation. For herself, she was enjoying examining the countryside as they drove. The view was mainly farmland, a patchwork of mud-brown and green. The harvest had been some time ago now, but there were fields of winter crops sprinkled here and there: winter oats and swedes for livestock feed. Mostly, though, there were the grey blobs of muddied sheep. In the distance, the reddish brown of dying heather clothed the hills. Beyond lay the dark slopes of the mountains.

Angus recovered from his contemplative mood by the time they arrived in Alverness and became once more a charming companion. The theatre they patronised was called, unexcitingly, Alverness Theatre. Hetta hadn't been here before. In her youth, she would have been awed by the golden cherubs adorning the entrance way and the decadent swirls of the carved ceiling. After six years spent haunting the theatres of Meridon, it seemed almost quaint. Something like homesickness rose in her as they made their way to their seats, but when Angus inquired if she was feeling quite the thing, she laughed.

"It's only odd to see things from this angle, rather than the other side of the curtain." He didn't seem bothered by the mention of her old career, which was a refreshing change from her older relatives, who still treated it as something best not mentioned. She shook her head, some of her old anger returning. Why should paying people to raise sheep on your behalf be more respectable than performing magic with your own two hands?

The performance Angus had chosen was a reimagining of an old classic that Hetta had seen countless times before. Nevertheless, she enjoyed it. The actors were good, the set design well-considered, and Hetta was in a mood to be pleased. It was pleasant to take a momentary respite from the problems of Stariel in good company.

Angus took her out for tea afterwards. His manner was unusually serious as he offered her a sugared fig. "Sometimes I wonder if you aren't merely dallying with my heart, lass."

Hetta wanted very much to recapture the light-hearted tone of their previous communications. "I'm a highly incorrigible flirt. I fear I should have warned you!"

Angus accepted this sally with a brief grin, but all too quickly returned to sobriety. "You should have, if you're not at least a little serious about me, Hetta. What would happen, I wonder, if I tried to make an honest woman of you?" This last was said with a mix of sincerity and jest, as if Angus were trying to judge her own response before committing his own.

"I fear that might be impossible!" Hetta said valiantly, heart racing. This was supposed to be a blithe afternoon *away* from complicated problems!

"Hetta." Angus's voice was reproachful. "You must have thought about it? We make a good pair, you and I. And I know you've troubles aplenty with the estate. I could help, you know, if you would but let me."

He leaned forward as he said this and took her hand in his. Hetta blushed. She wanted very much to make a joke, but Angus deserved better than a vague misdirection as a response, so Hetta rallied and said lightly:

"I do care for you, my friend." She extracted her hand from Angus's. "And I do like spending time with you. But I have to admit I hadn't considered..."

"Things from so serious an angle?" Angus supplied. He gave a deep, frustrated sigh.

"Well—no. You must think me an incorrigible flirt. I'm sorry." *And I'm an imposter.*

"Well, I can't deny that I'm disappointed, but I have to respect your plain speaking." He smiled. "And you haven't told me to give up hope entirely." Hetta looked down at the lace tablecloth and tried not to fiddle with it. "But I don't wish to discomfit you—exactly the opposite. Tell me, how are the preparations for the famous Stariel Frost Faire progressing?"

Hetta grasped at the change of subject with relief, and no more was mentioned of Angus's declaration for the rest of the afternoon, nor as they drove back northwards. Fortunately, Angus, too, seemed to be deep in thought, and so she wasn't called upon to converse intelligently.

Thoughts chased each other through Hetta's mind. The play had reminded her of her old life—a life that she might soon be returning to—but that didn't make her feel as relieved as she'd expected. And then there was Angus's delicately phrased proposal. She wasn't sure whether Angus would have made the same offer to just-Hetta-the-illusionist as opposed to Lord Henrietta Valstar. She supposed she would find out after the Frost Faire. But did she even want to find out? She'd approached all her interactions with Angus with the giddy infatuation of an eighteen-year-old, but she'd just been forcibly reminded that she *wasn't* that eighteen-year-old anymore. What did she want, when that girlhood crush was set aside?

Again, Hetta was startled out of her reverie by the sensation of crossing Stariel's borders. She had the strong image of a friendly dog wagging its tail and trying to put its paws up on her in greeting. The sun had set by the time they drew up to the house, though it wasn't yet five o'clock. The days would continue to grow shorter until Wintersol, where the lengthening days would be balanced against the deepening cold. Angus gave her a considering look as he farewelled her, and she knew he was contemplating whether she would let him kiss her again.

Something of Hetta's complicated feelings on the subject must have been evident, for he merely gave her a wry grin and said, "Thank you for your company, Hetta." He paused. "I hope I have not worn out my welcome?"

"Not at all." On impulse, she rose up on tiptoes to press a kiss against his cheek.

He chuckled and nodded at her as he left. "Ah, you give me hope yet. Take care."

Hetta stared after him, conflicted.

31

THE BANK MANAGER

FOUR DAYS BEFORE the Frost Faire, Hetta received a note from Ida. Ida wrote with a genuine but slightly awkward gratitude, still fully aware that she'd taken a place Hetta coveted. But the letter didn't bring the information Hetta had hoped:

> *I'm afraid your quarry seems to have left the country for opportunities abroad. None of his intimates seem to think he'll be returning until after Wintersol at the soonest. And the man appears to have been remarkably tight-lipped about his clients. If I hadn't thought to ask his landlady, I wouldn't have found a soul among his acquaintance who knew he'd even been up north for a few days in October.*

"Whoever hired him chose well, then," Hetta mused aloud.

She rose from her desk and went to look out at the view towards Starwater. "I wonder if he was merely recommended to them or if they knew him more personally?" James Snickett was a Meridon native, which meant that if her hunch was correct, the pool of Northern locals who would have had an opportunity to meet such a person was limited. A school friend was the first idea that presented itself to her. James Snickett was well-born; he would have attended one of the prep-schools for boys of wealthy and well-connected families. She cudgelled her brain to try to remember whether she had reason to know which specific boarding school he had attended, but if she'd ever known it, she couldn't recall it now.

The grey weather outside perfectly reflected her frustration. The waters of the lake were choppy, tiny white caps creating a shifting pattern of white and deep green. She turned back and surveyed her study—it was becoming increasingly difficult to think of it as her father's. She'd removed the stag's head above the door without ceremony, relegating it to the attic. Her father might have been able to work cheerfully under its glassy stare, but she found the effect disconcerting. The racehorse painting had been similarly dealt with. In its place hung a bright watercolour of the Sun Theatre. Her gaze lingered on it.

Her introspection was interrupted by a polite knock at the door.

"My Star," said Wyn. "The bank manager has arrived. Where would you like to receive him?"

She flashed a look at the clock, surprised that the appointed hour had come so quickly. "Here, I think. Show him up."

Wyn nodded. "His name is Thompson."

She'd feared that Mr Thompson would be of Mr Fisk's ilk, but the man Wyn showed into the study couldn't have resembled her whippet-like steward any less. Mr Thompson was a short, stout man, dressed impeccably in a dark blue suit. Hetta was glad she'd chosen to hew to conservative fashion for today; even Aunt Sybil wouldn't have taken exception to her dress. Though she might object to the lipstick, despite the demure shade.

He greeted her with a smile, extending a hand. Hetta took it and shook. His grip was firm but not overly so. Hetta had met many men who were so determined to give a firm handshake that they rather overshot the mark.

"Lord Valstar," he said in greeting. "My name is Benjamin Thompson. I represent Gridwell's Bank."

"Will you take a seat?" Hetta waved at one of the two leather seats facing the large desk in the room. She took the other. It seemed ridiculous to sit behind a desk as if she were interviewing Mr Thompson.

After some preliminary pleasantries, Mr Thompson said, "I understand you're wanting to run elektricity and phonelines out to Stariel House?"

"Precisely," Hetta said. "I was hoping to arrange a loan to cover the additional expenditure. My steward tells me that the estate's accounts run at a very tight margin and has advised against additional capital expenditure at this time, but in my view, these new technologies are essential and the sooner we upgrade, the better. I am hoping you may be able to advise me how it could be managed. I thought perhaps the Dower House could be rented out." She considered for a moment and added, "I'm also considering whether investing in drains for some of Stariel's low-lying land could be worthwhile."

Mr Thompson's eyebrows went up, but he did not give her an outright negative. "Well, shall we go through the accounts as they stand, then?"

She bestowed a warm smile upon him and slid the main accounts book across the desk to him. "Be my guest."

Hetta wondered where Mr Fisk was. She'd sent Wyn to fetch him, but surely her steward hadn't forgotten that the bank manager was visiting them today? But time ticked on and still he didn't appear. A housemaid brought them refreshments, and Mr Thompson seemed favourably disposed towards the shortbread. He grew more engrossed in the accounts book, occasionally asking her for clarification. Hetta's own time spent with them hadn't gone to waste, for she found she was able, with some thought, to answer most of his enquiries. Mr Thompson's expression grew pensive as he worked his way through, and eventually he fixed her with a steady gaze and declared that he would need to review the whole in detail, if she didn't mind the time it would take. Hetta assented with some nervousness, busying herself with sorting through the latest house bills while Mr Thompson slowly turned the pages of the estate's accounts books, occasionally making a note in a column of the notebook he had brought with him.

It was very dull work. The only sounds were the rustle of turning pages and the tick of the study clock against the background of the steady rain.

Hetta stood up to stretch her limbs and paused by the window. A pale-haired figure was visible coming across the lawns. It must be Wyn, though it was impossible to discern any familiarity in the figure at this distance. He shifted and revealed a red-haired figure behind him. Their movements invoked those of hunting wolves.

Uneasy, she returned to her desk. Time trickled by with oppressive slowness. Mr Thomspon's expression grew increasingly serious as he worked his way through the accounts, every now and then making an annotation in his notebook. Eventually he sighed and glanced up.

"Lord Valstar, it grieves me to have to say this, but I fear your steward has not been doing his job as he ought."

Hetta blinked at him. "Oh?"

Mr Thompson shut the accounts book with a snap. "He was correct when he said that Stariel operates at a very thin margin, but the chief reason for that, I am afraid, is a certain amount of accounts fudging." He held up a stubby finger. "There may be some other explanation for it, but I fear that he may have been skimming from you."

"I see." Well, that certainly explained Mr Fisk's absence today and his reluctance to invite the bank manager to Stariel in the first place. She wondered if he'd made good his escape or if there was still some chance of catching him. "Thank you for alerting me to this. Will you take me through the details?"

He did so, and she made herself focus. "So in terms of the loan for upgrading the house?" she asked after he had shown her the deceit.

Mr Thompson considered her solemnly for several long moments. "We would need a more fully worked through set of financial plans, but, yes, I think the bank may be persuaded, once they are assured the accounts are under the control of someone appropriate."

Hetta's eyebrows shot up. "I assure you, I intend to employ a more honest steward as soon as I may, but surely we may come to some sort of preliminary agreement in the meantime?"

Mr Thompson looked faintly embarrassed.

"Oh. You mean that I am not deemed to be an appropriately responsible person, I take it?" Hetta said coldly. "Is this due to my qualifications or my gender?"

"Lord Valstar, I regret that…"

"My gender then, I take it." Hetta stood. "Very well. I will contact you again once I have secured either a steward or a husband. I will show you out."

Mr Thompson made several attempts to appease her as he packed up his briefcase, but she was in no mood for them.

THE HOUSE FELT EMPTIER than usual as she wandered the rooms, searching for someone to tell her where her steward had disappeared to. She supposed Mr Fisk had made a break for it and wondered if that had anything to do with Jack and Wyn moving like hunters over the lawns. She found it hard to care very much whether they had located him or not; it wasn't as if that would repair the harm he'd done to Stariel. It might be satisfying to yell at him for a while, but what then? Hetta supposed there would be an investigation, and policemen, and a whole lot *more* fuss that also would not do one whit of good for the estate.

Phoebe and Alexandra had been busy, she saw. Tinsel twined around the staircase banister, and holly and mistletoe hung from every appropriate outcrop, though it wasn't yet December. Drawn by a cobweb of memory, she followed the decorations through to the ballroom, summoning a tiny ball of light to softly illuminate the cold space.

She smelled the tree before she saw it, the pine resin taking her straight back to childhood. She used to sneak down at night to sit beneath the tree, letting the smell envelop her. The tree had been set up on the far wall. The northern edge of the ballroom was lined with glass doors that could be opened out in a concertina fashion onto the terrace along that side of the house. It made the ballroom difficult to heat when it wasn't packed full of guests, even with the large enclosed fireplace along the interior of one wall. It wasn't lit tonight, and Hetta hugged herself to ward off the drop in temperature as she made her way over the wood-panelled floor.

She paused to briefly touch her palm to a window. The glass was ice, cooling her hand instantly. The rainclouds of earlier had rolled away, leaving a clear, still night, and the glitter of stars spilled down on the terrace outside, washing everything in monochrome. Though she couldn't see far in the darkness, through her land-sense she could sense the immensity of the estate lurking out there: people and farms and wild forests. How could any one person be responsible for so much?

Perhaps she should ask Angus for advice on how to deal with Mr Fisk's defection. But that would require talking to him—something she'd been putting off ever since Angus had semi-proposed in Alverness. *I'll talk to him after the Frost Faire*, she promised herself. *After this pretence is done with.* If he still wanted to talk to her afterwards; he might not. The temporary state of her title was rubbing against her more and more.

She drew closer to the tree. It was a fine specimen of its kind, precisely the right height for the room, branches well-spaced. It radiated green vitality, though it was, of course, dying. It had been propped into position with the aid of a brass tub filled with water and stones. Hetta knew that the smell of the dying pine would spread through the house over the coming weeks, as would its slow-shedding needles. Already a sprinkle of fine green lines lay scattered around its base.

The tree was as yet undecorated, appearing oddly naked in its natural state. Hetta had reached out to brush the upright tip of one of the branches when the sound of a door opening made her turn. Even if the halo of white-blond hair hadn't instantly identified the dimly lit figure, the way he moved with the slow, graceful precision of a heron would have.

"They wanted to decorate it immediately, but I suggested they should wait for you."

Hetta rubbed one of the branches between her fingers, feeling the sticky pine resin cling to her fingers. "Thank you." She hadn't known it until she stood here, but she wanted to recapture that childhood memory. She'd always enjoyed decorating the tree.

A brief silence fell, in which Wyn paused in his movement. "Gwendelfear has escaped. We hunted for her, Jack and I, but she has passed the bounds." The words were so at odds with his quiet tone that it took Hetta a moment to process them. "How?" she asked eventually.

He came closer. "I cannot be certain."

"But?"

"I think she must have had help. Human help," he qualified. "I set my own spells against fae intervention, and there were the iron bracelets as well. But my spells are intact and the door was not forced."

"Who had the keys?" Hetta asked, although she already knew the answer.

"You. Me. Mr Fisk."

"I cannot think of any reason for Mr Fisk to be setting rogue fairies loose. Although I admit I don't understand the man. He has, according to the bank manager, been stealing from the accounts."

"The tower key is missing from Mr Fisk's set," Wyn said. "Though the rest of the keys remain. I checked. Mr Fisk himself is absent, along with his most valuable possessions. The stationmaster said he got on a southbound train." Wyn ran a hand through his hair, creating static between the fine strands, and gave a long sigh, full of frustration. It surprised but also pleased her, so rarely did he let himself express stress so obviously. "It seems I've failed in my duties. I've sent notices to the police in Greymark and Meridon of Mr Fisk, if he is seen there, but I do not have much hope of catching him without pursuing him in person."

"I don't suppose we would get the money back even if we did catch him, though we might find out what he meant by releasing Gwendelfear. I didn't think he was even aware of her imprisonment."

"Neither did I." Wyn's gaze turned inwards. "My spell-casting leaves something to be desired these days, it would appear. The glamour should have held against those who had not been directly told of her presence."

Here was confirmation of Hetta's suspicions regarding the servants' lack of curiosity about the Tower Room's occupant. Disquiet rippled through her. Wyn saw it show in her expression and accepted it without comment, although a certain heaviness crept into his posture.

Instinctively, she took a step towards him, shaking her head. "No, that was unfair of me. I knew what you were doing and gave my tacit approval. It was a sensible precaution. It would be the height of hypocrisy to reprimand you for it now."

Wyn's lips curved slightly, and he inclined his head towards her. "My Star." She knew she hadn't undone the damage her inadvertent reaction had caused, but he shrugged and deliberately changed the subject. "In any case, shall we give chase to our escaped steward?"

"No. He's caused quite enough trouble already that we'll have to manage. I say we wash our hands of him until and unless he emerges from whatever hideaway he's burrowed into." She examined his expression. "But that's not the escape that worries you most."

His voice grew quieter. "No. I cannot predict what will happen when Gwendelfear reports Stariel's affairs to DuskRose. I cannot decide whether it would be better for me to leave or not, whether my presence here will make the situation worse or if the aid I can offer weighs against that sufficiently." His eyes met hers, dark with worry.

"Don't you dare leave, Your Highness." A wisp of a smile crossed his face at the address. "And that's an order. I'm already down a steward for the day. I can't lose my butler and housekeeper as well."

He considered her with an inscrutable expression, then bowed his head. "My Star. If you wish it, I will stay until the lordship is confirmed, at least, and the boundaries back to full strength." Hetta wanted to object but hadn't figured out exactly which part of that statement she objected to most before he hurried on. "I had better check the defensive wards we placed." He made as if to leave and then paused, turning back. "What will you do when the Star Stone is found?"

She shrugged. "I suppose I shall endeavour to explain to my family why it is we need to re-choose a lord. That shouldn't pose much difficulty, should it?"

Wyn smiled. "I meant afterwards."

Hetta looked down at her feet. "I know you did." She blew out a long sigh. "I don't know. Everything seemed much simpler when I first arrived. I suppose I'll go back to Meridon, see if Bradfield needs two illusionists."

"Of course." Some inner debate took place, ruffling the smooth serenity of his countenance. Then, as if he couldn't help himself, he asked, "Will you miss me, Hetta?"

She looked up. It was a mistake. Their gazes locked. She stepped forward, or perhaps he did; she wasn't sure except that suddenly her hands were hovering half an inch from Wyn's chest. The warmth of him radiated across the space, the ghost of a touch.

Wyn froze as her hand lifted, almost of its own volition. Her pulse roared in her ears, impossibly loud in the quiet of the ballroom. When she rested her fingers gently against his cheek, he shivered, as if she'd plucked a violin string and sent it thrumming, his skin scorching against her chilled, ungloved hand.

The world quietened, became only the two of them and that single, feather-light point of contact. A sparking anticipation grew, flowing from Hetta's fingertips and curving around the space between them, and Hetta knew it wasn't only her own. Wyn's pupils were blown wide, the black nearly swallowing the russet of his irises.

And then Wyn jerked as if lightning-struck, stumbling back from her. His eyes were wide and unseeing. "No," he said hoarsely.

Hetta crossed her arms. "Well, you needn't sound *quite* so appalled."

He blinked down at her in blank incomprehension, and Hetta began to feel alarmed rather than annoyed when he did not answer, a slow, unfocused horror rising in him that had nothing to do with her. At least, she hoped not.

"Wyn? What's wrong?"

"I have to go. I have to stop it before it reaches the house."

"Stop what?"

He was already moving, quick and focused as a blade, but he paused before wrenching open one of the glass doors along the side of the ballroom. For a moment, he couldn't hide his chief emotion: fear. "A draken. My father—King Aeros—has sent one for me. One of the winged beasts of ThousandSpire."

And then he was gone.

32

DRAKEN

FOR A LONG second, Hetta stayed frozen, staring at the open door through which Wyn had disappeared. Then she swore and began to sort through her thoughts with cold rationality, fear clamped down as tightly as a snowball compacted into ice. There was no time for anything else. Wyn had gone to face a monster, a monster that had been sent to kill him. A monster that very well might kill him and would then, very probably, turn to the rest of Stariel's denizens.

Hetta thought of the guns locked in the gunshed but abandoned the idea even as it occurred. Her father had held strong opinions concerning women and guns, and while this had only made Hetta more determined to learn, no one had been willing to risk his wrath to teach her. Marius disliked the noise and recoil of the weapons and disliked even more the blood and gore involved in hunting with them, and he hadn't seen why anyone would want to know anything about them if they were not forced to. Jack had shared Lord Henry's opinions about guns' unsuitability for feminine hands. Hetta would be more danger to herself than any monster, wielding such a weapon.

The internal door opened, and Hetta whirled towards the sound. It was Jack. He came into the room bristling with suspicion and performed the briefest of double-takes at the sight of her. His shoulders came down a little.

"Oh. Hetta. Has Wyn told you that—why are you standing here in the dark with the door open?"

"Wyn just left through it," Hetta said to him, as calmly as if they had all been taking tea together. Keeping the same matter-of-fact tone, she said, "It seems he felt something cross over the wards he placed. Some kind of monster is on its way to Stariel. Wyn has gone out after it, and I believe I must go after him."

"A monster? What kind of monster?" Through the ice that had formed up around her, she noted that Jack sounded alarmed rather than disbelieving.

"A draken. Whatever that is. It doesn't sound pleasant, does it?"

"I'll get my gun. Which way did he go?" Then he stared out through the open frame of the doorway and said, "South," before she could answer.

He'd reached for Stariel for direction, Hetta realised with a jolt, doing the same herself. She wasn't expecting to feel anything, but to her surprise even she could feel something was wrong. Perhaps her land-sense was growing as she spent more time at Stariel. Or perhaps it was just a sign of how disturbed Stariel was by the threat. Something that should not be there was intruding, and Jack was right—it was southwards.

She took a deep breath. "I'm going with you." She jerked into motion. "We'd best not waste any more time."

Jack blinked at her. "You aren't serious? This is no time for your dramatics. You've no part in this. Now, I need to go." And he turned and strode away and out of the room. He'd intended to leave Hetta behind, but she followed him, though she had to trot a little to match his pace—Jack's legs were longer than hers. The possibility that she would disobey him hadn't crossed his mind, so he was both surprised and angry when he stopped in the entrance way to collect his coat and boots and found her right behind him.

"Hetta! Don't be stupid! And don't try to tell me you know how to handle a gun, for I know well you don't!"

Hetta ignored him in favour of digging a battered but warm-looking overcoat out of the coat bay. She had no idea who it belonged to. Fortunately, Alexandra had left her walking boots downstairs since she'd managed to get them caked in mud on her last outing, and Hetta had the same sized feet. She pulled off her house slippers and began to lace them. Only when she'd finished did she look up, to find Jack glowering down at her.

"You had best put your coat on, Jack. You're wasting time."

"You'll only get in the way," Jack said brutally, grabbing his own coat with a snarl. "Do you want to get Wyn and me killed?"

Hetta met his eyes coolly. "Trust me, I've no intention of getting anyone killed. And you're right—I've no idea how to handle a gun and no intention to try under such circumstances as these. But you forget that I have another weapon at my disposal." She focused her will and made a throwing motion. White-hot fire blossomed in her hand, and she hurled it at the door. It hit with a sizzle, leaving a black, smoking hole the size of a fist in the front door. With an effort, Hetta willed it to extinguish. Hetta was quietly impressed—she hadn't actually intended it to be quite that big—but she maintained a nonchalant attitude in front of Jack. *Control your emotions*, she reminded herself. *First principle of magic.* Or at least, that was how it worked when casting finely crafted illusions. Hetta frowned at the hole in the door and wondered if pyromancy might be different, if all you wanted to do was make a *lot* of fire.

Jack stared at the door, mouth agape. A strong, acrid smell of wood smoke filled the entryway, cold air rushing in through the hole.

Abruptly she laughed. "Oh, you made me lose my temper. However am I going to explain why I've made a hole in the front door?"

Jack still hadn't moved, so Hetta prodded him sharply, jarring him into motion. He scowled. "This is a bad idea, but I don't have time to argue. You do what I tell you—I won't have you taking fright at exactly the wrong moment." But he pulled on his boots and coat and didn't try to further dissuade her.

She could feel Jack's disapproval as he made his way down to the gunshed and armed himself with quick, efficient movements.

Hetta was perfectly happy to let Jack take the lead as they made their way along the edge of Starwater towards the southern forest. He handed her an elektric flashlight taken from the gunshed and availed himself of one also. Hetta didn't remind him that she could make her own light, not sure she had the control required after that fireball.

Along the edges of the lake, it would have been possible to make their way guided by starlight and moonlight alone, for the night was very clear and the moon was more than halfway to fullness. But once they were under the trees, they were glad for the flashlights.

The native forests of Stariel were a mix of deciduous and evergreens, and the thick green needles of the evergreens muffled sounds. There wasn't even the faint hooting of owls or the rustle of animals moving in the darkness. Everything felt caught in the same frozen stillness as Hetta, waiting for the axe to drop.

Now that she was outside and concentrating on it, Hetta felt Stariel's awareness as a weight on her mind. Jack didn't need to tell her that he was leading them towards the centre of that sensation of wrongness. Hetta stretched out every nerve, hoping as they rounded each bend of the path along the lake edge that she would spy pale hair glinting in the starlight, but there was no sign of Wyn.

The tension grew until Hetta felt that surely they must be nearly upon the monster. Just as she was about to risk opening her mouth to ask Jack, a screech pierced the night. The sound had something in keeping with an eagle's cry, but no eagle was large enough to make a sound so loud. Or perhaps it was only because the sound came out of silence and echoed around the surrounding hills, off the water, through the trees, that it seemed so unnatural. The sound came again, and Hetta struggled to find a direction for it. Then she saw that Jack was looking up. She followed his gaze and gasped.

The draken was visible only as a darker shape against the midnight blue of the sky. It was difficult to judge its size, but Hetta thought that it was larger than a carthorse—perhaps larger than several carthorses. Two sets of great feathery black wings stretched wide, and the creature shrieked again. Hetta realised that the sound was a battle cry, directed at its attacker.

For the draken wasn't alone in the sky. A much smaller shape swerved around it, darting in here and there, occasionally inflicting some small wound but for the most part barely managing to keep out of reach of the creature's claws and fangs. The smaller figure was man-shaped, with wings that were far more visible than the draken's, silvery white under the stars, the same as the figure's hair.

"Wyn," Hetta whispered.

Jack didn't appear to have heard her. He swore. "The idiot will get himself killed." He shook his head and raised his gun to his shoulder.

Hetta had no time to reflect on how strangely unsurprised Jack was to see their butler appearing in so decidedly inhuman a fashion

"No!" she cried. "You'll hit him!"

"Damned if I will." Jack took a careful line of sight. "I'm a better shot than you give me credit for."

Hetta wasn't willing to take that chance. "Wyn!" she screamed at the sky. "Get down!"

She wasn't sure he would hear her from below, but the figure faltered in his frantic dance. The startled pause was his undoing. The draken gave a roar of triumph as it caught one of Wyn's wings in its claws. Hetta's heart rose to her throat as Wyn managed to pull himself free, but he was wounded, his movements jerky. He did not fall to the ground so much as crumple towards it, a one-winged butterfly.

Jack fired the gun. The crack of it rang in Hetta's ears, the burst of flame temporarily leaving her night-blind. The creature shrieked, but when Hetta's eyes adjusted, she saw that it didn't appear to be wounded. Instead, it shifted its attention to Hetta and Jack and beat its wings towards them.

Hetta had time only for one quick, startled breath before it hit the ground where they had been with a thud and an irritated snarl at being denied its prey. Jack had had far better reflexes and had shoved Hetta out of the way, following her to the hard ground.

Now Hetta looked up at the monster, close enough that she could see its warm breath pluming out towards them. It folded its twin sets of wings tight against its body and resolved itself into the shape of something very like a gigantic black lion, all fur and muscle and grace, except for its beak-like muzzle. Its long ears twitched towards them.

Jack fumbled with his rifle, trying to reload. The creature's dark eyes gleamed in the moonlight, and its mouth opened in what Hetta could only describe as a grin, fangs glinting as it huffed out a breath. Fear boiled through her, quickening her heart, driving the breath from her lungs. She flung out her hands, and the fear flowed from them to the creature, white hot, uncontrolled, vast.

The monster had no time to move, no time to do more than

utter a cut-off scream as the inferno enveloped it. The fire burned white, blinding, briefly outlining the shape of the creature as a crumbling shadow, then burned away. The fire burned on after the shape of it had disappeared, fear overriding thought and urging her to keep burning, to burn until every shadow of the night lit up, to make sure that there was nothing hiding in the dark. She pulled on strength she hadn't known she had, strength outside herself, a tidal wave of fear and fire and magic pouring from her hands.

WINGS

SHE BECAME AWARE of someone shouting, and it distracted her enough that she managed to stop, the magic cutting off with painful abruptness, leaving her winded. She panted in the cold grass, tired beyond anything.

The dark and cold was a relief after the intense light, and Hetta felt a strong urge to close her eyes and drift off. Someone shook her, speaking words that it took her several moments to comprehend.

"Hetta! Hetta!"

It was Jack, and she opened her eyes to tell him to stop shaking her, but the pale terror on his face stopped her. In any case, he ceased his shaking when he saw she was awake. She sat up and looked towards where the creature had stood. There was a smell like roast meat. "Is it…?"

Jack swallowed. "It's dead." He was staring at her with more alarm than he'd wasted on the draken. "You…" he trailed off.

Hetta looked down at her hands as if they belonged to someone else. She'd had no idea she was capable of conjuring such destruction with her pyromancy. She couldn't quite comprehend it. She turned her hands over, searching for some sign of violence upon them, but there was nothing. She'd been worried about what Wyn hid beneath his skin. Perhaps she should have been worried about what lay beneath her own.

"Wyn!" she said, abruptly trying to stand. She managed it, but only when Jack offered her an arm to lean upon. She felt weak, each foot a lead weight.

"He fell in that direction." Jack pointed into the woods. "Wait here. I'll go and find him."

Hetta wanted to object to this manhandling, but as she was currently having difficulty connecting with her limbs, she was unable to do more than scowl after him as he hurried away. She stumbled over to the nearest tree trunk and leaned against it, taking deep breaths.

She wanted very much to be away from the smell of roasted meat. Her knees began to wobble less, and she found a stout branch to use as a walking stick. She was about to head in the direction in which Jack had fled when there was the crunch of heavy footsteps and the two men came into sight.

Well, one man and one fae. The recent aerial battle she'd witnessed hadn't prepared her for the sight of the great silvery-white feathered wings that rose from Wyn's shoulders, nor for the dark horns rising from his head. Her hand jumped in startlement, shining the flashlight directly into the two's eyes. They both flinched, and she lowered the beam with a mumbled apology.

Her attention was drawn back to the wings. They were folded unevenly behind him, the right one trailing awkwardly. He was bare-chested, but much of his exposed skin was covered by what Hetta recognised as Jack's scarf, which she assumed was binding his injuries, although it was impossible to assess the full extent of them in the darkness. He looked paler than usual, washed of colour, though his skin glittered with faint luminescence.

It was as if someone had taken the Wyn she knew and then stripped away at him to reveal some deeper, more concentrated essence. His hair was moon-white gilt with silver, swept back from pointed ears. The bones of his face were more prominent, cheekbones sharp as knives. His eyes gleamed with a brilliance of colour that shouldn't have been possible in the low light, but they were still human compared to Gwendelfear's whiteless gaze.

He seemed taller, although perhaps that was due to the two dark, spiralling horns growing from his head. He had one arm around Jack's shoulders, and it was evident that only through his support was he remaining upright. Weariness was etched in every line of him, but a ghost of a smile lurked in his eyes when they drew nearer.

"Well, this is not how I imagined you seeing me like this for the first time." He shivered. "My apologies for my appearance. I am afraid I do not quite have the energy to resume my more usual form just yet."

Jack made a low sound of disgust. "Let's get back to the house. Can you walk, Hetta?"

"Of course," she said, for she could see no other answer would be useful here.

The three of them made slow, limping progress back to Stariel House. No one spoke. Wyn seemed fully occupied keeping his feet under him, and Hetta was scarcely less so. Jack brooded, his expression dark. Only when they came in sight of the house, the light from its lamps spilling down to the lake, did he speak. "We'll go in the west entrance. Give you time to recover yourself." This was addressed to Wyn. "Unless you plan to reveal yourself to the rest of the family tonight?"

"I would not choose this moment, no," Wyn said lightly.

However, as they drew closer, a lamplight bobbed around and fixed upon them. Wyn gave a resigned sigh. "But we do not always get to choose our moments." He looked at Hetta as he said this. "So be it."

The light came rapidly towards them, and its owner was revealed to be Marius. He was clearly about to express relief at the sight of them when he caught sight of Wyn and his mouth fixed open.

"Surprise!" Wyn said faintly. "I'm fae!"

"Don't stand there gawping," Hetta said briskly. "Help us get him into the house."

With Marius's help, they got Wyn into the house and laid him out on a backless settee in the red drawing room. He went down with a groan and curled into himself a little, his wings shifting restlessly.

"Are you all right, Hetta?" Marius asked.

"I'm fine; just shaken." The amount of magic she'd used tonight had made her tired down to her bones. "Go and get some hot water," she instructed him, sitting down next to Wyn. He went with a worried glance at Wyn. She began to unwrap Jack's scarf.

"Again, not how I imagined you undressing me," Wyn said, his eyes gleaming.

She knew he was doing what he always did, using humour to distract, but she was impatient with this attempt to lightly skate over events. She met his gaze very seriously and quirked an eyebrow. "You did, however, imagine it?"

He blinked, colour rising in his cheeks. "Ah—" His eyes flickered past her, to Jack.

The charged intimacy of that moment in the ballroom lingered in her mind. It was the first sign she'd seen that the attraction she felt wasn't one-sided—an attraction that she still wasn't sure how to respond to. Wyn wasn't, after all, human, and tonight even less so than usual, she thought, looking at his wings.

"Perhaps this is not the time to discuss it," she agreed, pulling away the last bit of material from his torso. Jack's scarf was drenched in blood, but when she exposed the claw marks, they didn't seem deep enough to be responsible for such a quantity of blood. She frowned and looked up at him. He shrugged back at her as a response, then grimaced as the movement pulled at his wounds.

"I'm not human, Hetta. I can heal from wounds that would kill a mortal man." He fingered one of his horns meaningfully. "But it takes energy to do it, and that is something I have difficulty with in my mortal form. When I am greatly weakened, I revert to this state automatically." He made a thoughtful sound, and his feathers shifted with a silken rustle. "I haven't taken this form for years. I'd almost forgotten what it felt like."

Wyn did, indeed, seem better with each second that passed. Eventually he closed his eyes and…quivered. Between one heartbeat and the next, the wild fae prince disappeared, and Wyn, her old friend, was all that remained. He seemed not precisely diminished but, rather, compacted, as if he had furled part of himself under his skin. The power of it still leaked through.

"It's not an illusion or glamour, is it?" she asked him quietly. "When you change?"

His eyes were closed, but he answered her, just as softly, "No. I am greater fae. I can shift forms."

Marius came back into the room. He checked himself on the threshold and looked relieved, though whether it was to see Wyn relatively well or relatively human, Hetta wasn't sure. He had managed to retrieve the requested hot water and a cloth. Wyn's flinch was nearly imperceptible when she pressed it to the wound.

Jack spoke. "What in the hells was that, Wyn?"

Hetta started, having forgotten that he was there in her preoccupation with Wyn.

Wyn pulled himself a little further up, only the slow care of his movements and his paler-than-usual complexion betraying his pain. "A draken. One of the winged attack beasts of ThousandSpire.

My father must have sent it."

"But I thought Gwendelfear was from DuskRose?" Hetta said.

Wyn shrugged, then winced in discomfort. "There are plenty of spies in both courts."

Jack didn't seem at all surprised at this talk of fae courts.

Marius came over and sank onto the chair opposite. He raised an eyebrow at Hetta. "I feel almost gauche for asking, but what in the blazes is going on?"

"I'm fae," Wyn said mildly. "Your father knew when he took me on here." He nodded towards Jack. "Jack, also, has known for some years; Hetta only recently."

That stung, though Hetta didn't let it show.

Jack looked at Hetta accusingly. "You knew?"

"Don't take that accusing tone with me, cousin. Since it appears you too have been keeping secrets."

"Well, I certainly feel included in things, don't I?" said Marius bitterly. "A little more explanation would be nice."

"The fae are out for my blood," Wyn said. "They have been for a long time, but they have not known my whereabouts for the past ten years. They know now. But this business with Stariel and the missing Stone…I am not sure how they are involved."

"Well…" Marius was taken aback at Wyn's calm delivery. "Are we about to be overrun by fairies then?"

Wyn frowned and turned thoughtful eyes on Hetta. "I am… not certain. I think Hetta's disposal of the draken will have given them pause, at least. They will know that while Stariel is unclaimed, it is not undefended. But I do not know how long that will hold them for. We need to find the Stone—the lord will be able to fully reinstate the boundaries."

Although he gave this speech in perfectly normal tones, his skin tone seemed washed out from its usual warm brown, his breathing laboured.

"For goodness' sake, Wyn, lie back down. No one is going to be impressed if you faint," Hetta told him sharply. He gave a weak smile but complied.

Marius simply looked at the ceiling in despair. "This is madness. Fairies and charms and drakens." He turned back to Wyn. "Was it your people's doing, then, stealing the Stone?"

Hetta could tell Wyn was unhappy with the way Marius had drawn a line between them, human and not, but he didn't argue with Marius's description. It spoke of his fatigue that she could read him more easily than usual, but it was also something of a relief to know he wasn't inwardly as composed as his outward facade normally suggested. "I don't know. It would be very like them to do so, if they thought they could get away with it, but the fact that they have not made any movement to take advantage of Stariel's lordless state until now..."

"Well," Jack said, "I'll be damned if I can make tail or head of fairies, but if it wasn't them, then who else would want to set you up as Lord of Stariel, Hetta? I suppose your Meridon friends were delighted at your new appointment."

Hetta made a strong effort not to hit him. "It could be someone who didn't want *you* to inherit. I don't suppose you've made any enemies lately, Jack, with your elegant manners?"

"Then why not make it seem to go to Marius? Why bring you into it at all?"

Marius mumbled, "I didn't touch the Stone."

Jack rounded on him. "What?"

"I didn't touch the Stone! I didn't want it, Jack."

Jack was staring at Marius as if he had announced a desperate wish to become a ballerina or something equally improbable.

"So whoever it was could well have intended the illusion for me," Marius said. "I suppose. If the touching was the trigger for the spell."

"To hurt you or help you, though?" Hetta wondered aloud.

Jack looked disgusted with the pair of them. "What do you

mean, to hurt him? I've no idea what worm has gotten into your brain, Marius, but if you think someone meant to make you Lord of Stariel to hurt you, you're mad."

"Well, I can't think of anyone who would want to do either," Marius snapped, but Hetta frowned.

The sense that Marius was hiding something was also apparent to Jack, for he too gave his cousin a closer look and said, "You *have* thought of someone, haven't you?"

Marius shook his head, eyes alarmingly bright. "No, I haven't."

"This isn't a joke, Marius. With this draken...Stariel itself might be in very real danger. If you know something that you're keeping quiet for some reason..." Jack said.

Hetta wasn't convinced that pushing Marius when he was in a stubborn mood would do any good, but she was broadly in agreement with Jack's sentiments, so she said nothing. Her brother had been keeping secrets for far too long. But before the argument could go any further, the doors to the room flew open and Aunt Sybil burst in, followed swiftly by Lady Phoebe, Alexandra, Gregory, and Laurel. Aunt Sybil tried to pause on the threshold in astonishment, but the momentum of those behind her forced her to make an awkward shuffling motion and move out of the way. Still, she recovered quickly. "What is going on here?"

Little Laurel had spotted Wyn lying bandaged on the couch and burst out, "What's happened to Wyn?"

This had the effect of distracting everyone present for some minutes while Wyn reassured them all that he was in no immediate danger of dying and really, he was almost fine, and he really did not need tea, or his wounds rebandaged, or a doctor to be summoned on the instant. Hetta watched all this fuss with an odd lurch in her chest. She'd known that Wyn had ingratiated himself into her family quite firmly, but she hadn't previously realised what affection so many of them held him in. She was glad that he'd been able to assume his human form before they'd arrived—she doubted they would have been quite so solicitous of him in his other skin.

Eventually the fuss wound down and turned to demands for an explanation. Hetta kept quiet, wondering what the others would say. To her surprise, Jack, after a swift look at Wyn, said, "Well, we saw off a fairy monster, that's what." He nodded grudgingly at Hetta. "Hetta helped too."

Hetta did not much appreciate being the focus of her family's incredulous stares, but by now she'd had sufficient practice to not become completely speechless. She chose to merely nod back at Jack.

Laurel's eyes rounded. "What did you do, Hetta?"

This reminded everyone of her presence, and she was summarily banished to bed, the topic not being thought appropriate for children. Hetta felt sorry for her and managed to wink surreptitiously in her direction before she was hurried away, which made her perk up a little as she left.

Hetta felt the full weight of fatigue settle on her as the others turned back to her for more detail. She took her leave of them, heartlessly leaving it for Jack and Marius to explain. But, she thought as she mounted the stairs, Jack was right. This was serious now, and never mind Jack's arbitrary deadline of the Frost Faire. The draken changed things; it was no longer just scandal they faced. The time for a fake lord had come and gone; tomorrow they would have to tell everyone the truth.

34

CHANGES OF HEART

HETTA WOKE TO the image of a draken outlined in fire. It was a more vivid awakening than she was used to, but undoubtedly effective at destroying the last cobwebs of sleep. She lifted her hands in front of her eyes and fanned out her fingers. By rights, she felt, something so extraordinary ought to leave an indelible mark, but they were just as they always were.

This had gone far enough. Last night had made her fully realise that not having a proper lord wasn't just inconvenient but dangerous. Without a lord, there was no way to stop another draken crossing the boundary. She would need to call the family together and explain how matters stood. The thought did not inspire her to action, and she stared up at her ceiling. Really, it didn't warrant the intense examination it had been getting these past few weeks. The main conclusion Hetta had come to after scrutinizing it was that it could do with repainting. And how could such a mundane necessity exist in the same world as drakens and plumes of flame?

She was procrastinating. This would be a very awkward business, and it was natural to want to put it off. But the few moments of quiet contemplation had given her time to sketch out a plan. She, Jack, and Marius would present the news as a united front.

She walked the floors, searching for her brother and cousin, and eventually found Marius in the library. To her amusement, he had bundled himself up in a feather duvet but still kept to his favoured windowseat, resembling nothing so much as a dark-haired caterpillar. He looked up as she came in.

"How cosy you look!" she remarked. "What are you reading?"

Marius had activated only the lightspells near to his favoured perch, so the rest of the library was shadowed. Lightspells were technomantic creations. The fire risk of the library warranted their use over the gas lamps that dominated the rest of the house, though the spells were expensive, as they had to be recharged frequently. It was terribly old-fashioned; even the poorer parts of Meridon were getting elektric lights now.

The feathers in the duvet rustled as he shifted. "I've just been reading about how we ought to be able to sense the Stone when it's close, particularly in an unbonded state."

Hetta came to sit beside him, and with a sigh he un-swaddled himself and offered her a portion of duvet. She saw that he was dressed as if for a walk, complete with scarf and fingerless gloves, though the library was not, in her opinion, that cold.

"How close?" she asked, waving off his offer of duvet.

"Very close. In the same room, or so it says here."

Hetta pursed her lips. "Which is only useful if we knew very nearly where it was already! What are we to do if whoever took it merely buried it somewhere and forgot about it?" She sighed and rubbed at her temples. "Last night made me think we shouldn't stick to Jack's arbitrary deadline. We need to make a new Star Stone as soon as possible so that Stariel can have a lord to protect it from fae monsters."

Marius frowned and closed the book he was reading. "But I haven't heard back from my friend about where the fake Stone might have been made. That still might tell us something."

"Yes, but it might not, and what if there are more draken?" The word felt strange on her lips. "I don't even know how we survived last night's one, let alone more!" She told him about how she'd burned the draken with her pyromancy.

Marius wasn't as surprised as she'd expected. "It's probably because you were on Valstar lands. I've been doing some more reading, and I get the strong impression that Stariel historically gives a boost to those of us with magic." As Hetta blinked at him, he smiled and added, "You didn't really think you were the first Valstar to be magically inclined?"

"Well, Father certainly managed to keep that out of the family histories he was so fond of telling."

"Yes." Marius's expression took on a faraway look. "I'm beginning to think Father focussed on very select parts of our great and glorious inheritance."

"That's not exactly a surprising revelation."

"No," Marius agreed. "But it is oddly liberating to know that Father was not…"

"Not the sole arbiter of the proper way to be a Valstar?" Hetta suggested.

"Exactly. From my reading, Stariel gets ever more magical the further you go back. It seems to have been ebbing in more recent generations." He frowned, fingering the edges of the book. "I wonder if the change point correlates to when Wyn's Iron Law came into being? If being cut off from the rest of Faerie would have that effect?" His eyes took on that faraway look they got when he was chasing a hypothesis down a rabbit hole.

Hetta shrugged, a little disquieted by the idea that events a realm away might have been affecting her family and estate for years without them knowing it. "Maybe. You'll have to ask Wyn."

The abstracted look snapped out, replaced with one of sobriety. Marius drew in on himself slightly, and she knew he was preparing to say something he thought wouldn't please her. "I've been thinking about who would want you to be Lord of Stariel, Hetta."

"Don't tell me you're about to reveal whatever dark secret you've been keeping from me?"

She said the words lightly, not expecting the sudden change in Marius's countenance. He went pale and choked, trying to cover his reaction unsuccessfully. He pulled away from her, and she put a hand on his shoulder, frowning. "Goodness! I didn't mean to throw you into such a panic. I find it hard to believe that you have any secrets with the power to shock me, after all that we've seen lately. Unless you mean to sprout wings and horns and tell me you're a changeling?"

Marius gave a weak laugh but didn't meet her eyes. "It's—oh, it's nothing to do with this, Hetta. I *did* think of someone who wanted me as lord, but he couldn't have done it."

"What makes you think so?" She frowned, feeling she was missing something very obvious.

Marius ran a hand through his hair in agitation. "I've been thinking back to his reaction when I saw him the day after the Choosing. He would—it would've been different if he'd planted an illusionist to choose me." A memory came to her suddenly, of the blond-haired man who'd watched Marius with such intensity at the Choosing Ceremony.

Hetta couldn't help but remember how Marius's mood had swung from cautious hope to black despair in the twenty-four hours after the Choosing, and a wild suspicion coursed through her. Her first reaction was denial, but it *fit.* It fit with the blackmail note she'd received, and Marius's flushed cheeks and refusal to meet her eyes. She squeezed his shoulder where her hand still lay and said, picking her words carefully:

"I overheard you and Wyn speaking, not long after the Choosing.

He offered to help you in some way that involved magic. What was it?"

Marius had gone very still. It was the stillness of a cornered creature too overwhelmed with panic to act. She'd pushed him too much. She pretended she hadn't noticed and abruptly changed tack. She felt a little bad for her betrayal of a friend's secret, but she knew Bradfield wouldn't begrudge her it at this moment.

"You know, a lot of people assumed I was in love with Bradfield, my theatre director, or he in love with me."

Marius's frozen panic gave way to confusion. "What?"

She continued as if he hadn't spoken. "I've known for such a long time how entirely impossible an affair between us would be that I have a tendency to treat such accusations with levity. I sometimes forget that the rest of the world can take a more serious view of such matters than I do. It has always seemed to me that love cannot be controlled by reason, that we don't get to choose our attractions." She looked at her brother intently. If her instinct was wrong, she was about to offend him very greatly, but if her instinct was right, then such words needed to be said. She chose her words with care. "Bradfield has always preferred men to women, and I have never thought the less of him for it, nor considered that he is wrong to act on such attractions."

Marius's cheeks flamed red, and he looked at her with a kind of strangled disbelief. "Hetta—"

She met his gaze steadily, waiting. Her heart raced with sudden relief. She had, she thought, judged correctly. Her calm seemed to allow Marius to take a hold of his emotions. He gave a choked sound and looked out the window, the colour in his face fading a fraction. He took a deep breath.

"I cannot believe I'm having this conversation."

Hetta judged that the worst tension had passed. She gave a little huff of amusement. "No, I imagine not. And I'm sure I should be quite as embarrassed as you if you were to confront me with the details of my own past affairs. Some things one does not wish to discuss with one's siblings." She took a more serious tone. "But I cannot have you moping around over something so trivial."

"Trivial?" He looked at her sharply, eyebrows raised. "*Trivial*, Henrietta?"

She held her hands up defensively. "I meant the matter in general, not whatever specific heartbreak you've recently suffered."

He glared at her for a second and then made a sound somewhere between a laugh and a sob. "You're as incomprehensible as Wyn."

"I take it he knows, then?" Hetta tried not to be hurt by that.

"Yes," Marius said, shortly. He began to unwind himself from the duvet, and she knew he was thinking of escape. Every line of him declared how desperate he was for the conversation to be over. She had an inappropriate urge to laugh at him, for he did look very ridiculous, his serious expression at odds with his bundled-up appearance. Instead of allowing him to extricate himself, she leaned forwards and put both arms around him, pulling him into an embrace. He stiffened, and she hugged him more tightly. Abruptly he relaxed, letting himself be comforted. His arms came up to return the hug, and he let out a long breath of tension.

When she sat back, he was still flushed, but he met her eyes with a weak smile. "Wyn…helped me avoid a situation that would have been embarrassing for the family." His eyes grew sad and distant. "It seems I'm not a very good judge of character."

Hetta thought of the note and felt a hot spurt of anger towards its author. "Blackmail?"

He nodded stiffly. "Wyn knew a…a binding to prevent him from naming me."

"Ah." She reached out and grasped his shoulder again. "I'm sorry."

Marius gave himself a shake and sat up straighter. "Well. Never mind that." A thought seemed to occur to him, and he narrowed his eyes at her. "And what do you mean, your past affairs?"

She gave him a very impish grin. "Are you really going to lecture me on such a head? And do you really want details?"

His colour heightened again, but he didn't back down entirely. "I'm still your older brother! Don't think I haven't noticed the way you look at Wyn!"

She couldn't resist the temptation. "Well, he *is* a very attractive man." She gave him a sly look. "Don't you think so?"

Marius spluttered. "Hetta!" She only laughed, but his expression sobered. "I don't want to think this, but I feel I have to mention it..."

"What?" she asked as he trailed off awkwardly.

"The Star Stone. It occurred to me that..."

"Yes?"

Marius looked wretched. "Well, who do we know that can cast illusions and change their shape and who might have reasons of his own to want you to stay at Stariel?"

"No," Hetta said, immediate and fierce. "No, Marius. I won't think that, and you shouldn't either."

"I don't want to think it!" Marius said, temper flaring. "But—perhaps, perhaps he ought to leave."

"My Star!" came Wyn's voice from the library door. Marius and Hetta both started as they turned towards the sound, and Marius flushed again.

Wyn came towards them through alternating bars of light and shadow from the narrow windows. His slippered feet made no sound on the wooden floor, and he moved more slowly than usual, the bulk of bandages warping the fabric of his shirt. Hetta couldn't help imagining the arch of wings filling the space behind him. She wasn't quite sure what she thought of that. There had been that charged, breathless moment between them in the ballroom yesterday, and she wasn't quite sure what to think of that either. She tried to read her friend's expression, but it held no evidence that he was remembering that moment.

He paused when he caught sight of their faces, unnaturally grim. "I have come to say that I think it might be best if I leave Stariel. That draken last night was here for me. If I am not here—"

"No," Hetta said firmly. "Who's to say they wouldn't send another one anyway to try and invade us while the boundaries are weak? Gwendelfear didn't come here for you in the first place, and it can't be coincidence that someone stole the Star Stone at the same time as your Iron Law came down. You're the only fae we have on our side, and I'm not giving up that advantage just because you think now is a good time to play the martyr. Plus," she added, staring down at her hands, "I might not be lord, but I'm not exactly useless at dealing with fae monsters."

"Yes, sit down, you fool," Marius said. "Of course we're not going to throw you out."

Hetta cocked her head at her brother, who had the grace to blush and look at his feet. "Well, if we're about to be inundated by fairies, I'd rather have one we know on our side."

"Indeed."

"Hetta—"

Hetta flicked a hand up to stop him. "Enough. Wyn, Marius spoke correctly. Stop being so foolish, my friend. You said you'd stay until Stariel was safely re-lorded. Are you going to go back on that now?"

He canted his head to one side, and she could see him weighing factors. "Very well."

"Good. Now, do you know where Jack is?"

When she found Jack, he was engaged in cleaning the weapon he'd used the night before, along with several others, and his aspect was subdued. A strange expression flitted across his face when he saw her.

"Did Marius say anything more about who might want to see him as Lord of Stariel?" His face was turned towards the metal tools on the workbench. He had a rag in his right hand, and he folded it mechanically into ever-smaller squares, setting it down next to the rest of his kit with exaggerated care.

"Ah—no." Hetta decided that this wasn't her secret to tell, even if she could be sure of Jack's reaction. She suspected he might not be quite so blasé about it as she was. "I was actually coming in search of you." She took a deep breath. "I thought the announcement of the mistake at the Choosing to the family would go more easily if it came from the three of us. I don't think there's any point in waiting till after the Faire."

"No," Jack said, the word grudging but clear. His hands clenched into fists, rumpling the rag that he'd folded so neatly moments before. "No, don't do that." His next words were directed at the floor. "Stariel needs to be united right now, and it needs at least the appearance of having a lord."

Hetta froze. The urge to ask him to repeat himself was strong. "I'm surprised to hear you say that. Especially after last night, which for me rather highlighted the need to acquire a new Stone as soon as possible, since Marius and I have hit only dead ends so far trying to find the old one. I would assume the search for raw star indigo would go easier if we could search for it openly."

But Jack was shaking his head again, mouth twisted bitterly as he did so.

"After last night, I think it's bloody necessary we have someone here to scare off fairies if need be. And you…what you did last night. Bloody hell, Hetta, I didn't know you could do that." Jack turned away from her again. "I'll keep looking. You and Marius keep inquiring. After the Faire, if we still haven't found the Star Stone...but it does no good to air our dirty laundry for all to see in the meantime."

Hetta hadn't known her cousin had this deep vein of duty in him. His dislike of the situation was tangible, yet here he was holding it in check for what he saw as the greater good.

Hetta reached out and placed a hand on his shoulder, but he shook it off impatiently.

"Thank you," she said softly. He merely grunted, and she took that for the dismissal it was.

As she opened the door, he said suddenly from behind her:

"You did well last night."

Hetta paused on the threshold but couldn't think what to say. She left without speaking.

35

THE FROST FAIRE

DESPITE JACK'S WORDS and Hetta's intentions, they were no further along when the day of the Frost Faire dawned, with a truly impressive frost colouring the world white. A thin layer of ice crusted the shoreline of Starwater, but the sky was cold and clear, and the pale sun began to work at melting it away as soon as it rose.

In Meridon, winter faires sprang up along the banks of the river in the weeks before Wintersol like so many elaborate mushrooms. The Stariel Frost Faire on the first of December was necessarily a much smaller affair, but it was also a more intimate one. Hetta remembered, vividly, her first Wintersol away from home and how she'd felt both fiercely lonely and overwhelmed by the crowds. The years had turned the great city from stranger to friend, but she'd still felt the distance from her family in that season particularly.

Wyn was a veritable dervish of activity, both supervising, easing fraying tempers, and lending a hand where needed. Boards were put down on the village green to prevent the passage of feet from churning it to mud. Braziers had to be installed. Stalls were set up as per the plan laid out on a great sheet of paper propped up at the entrance. Cook prepared a mountain of toffee apples, all carefully wrapped in wax paper. These were transported alongside boxes of sloe gin and sloe jelly, the specialties of Stariel House.

Hetta's offer to use her illusory powers for the occasion had been cautiously accepted by the village council. She supposed they could hardly refuse such an offer when it came from their lord. Sweet Mother Eostre knew what they would think when the truth came out after the Faire, but she didn't much care. The satisfaction of showing off the full glory of her magic in her home village at least once was worth it. She knew the sceptics were in for a shock; they were judging her based on the lowliest of her profession. The isolated North had never seen a trained master illusionist of Hetta's calibre.

I have quite outdone myself, Hetta thought as she looked upon what she'd wrought. The village green had taken on the appearance of a great frozen lake, only without the cold or slipperiness of real ice. She'd based the stalls on those she'd seen once at a Meridon faire: the exteriors fashioned from rough-hewn wooden logs and icicles entwined with holly hanging from their A-frame roofs. Thickly furred spruces shed coloured snowflakes at intervals between the stalls. Around the whole floated magelights disguised as old-fashioned lamps, hanging unsupported in mid-air. She had, she admitted privately, perhaps gone a trifle overboard in her efforts to impress.

The locals were wary at first, tentatively placing their feet on the fake ice as if expecting an explosion. Some grumbled about this not being quite what they were used to, but they weren't immune to the charm of the scene. She caught one of the most vocal critics smiling with innocent wonder up at a floating lamp, though his expression quickly changed to a frown when he saw her watching.

The children were the most rewarding audience—but also the most demanding. They poked the floating lamps with long sticks and exclaimed when their attempts went straight through without so much as a ripple. They tried to catch the snowflakes in their fingers and laughed when they burst into clouds of green sparks on contact. Hetta smiled, pleased she'd thought to add that touch.

"This is impressive," Marius admitted as he came to stand next to her. Marius's concession to the festive season had been to wear a smart suit of green velvet and pin a sprig of holly to his coat. He looked more cheerful than she'd seen him in some time.

"Thank you. Although I'm not sure I appreciate the faint note of surprise in your voice. Where is everybody?" She'd come into the village earlier in order to make her preparations.

He laughed, the sound a welcome one that made her even more determined to shield him from the malice of his once-paramour. Marius hadn't laughed enough lately.

"Are you fishing for compliments?" he said cheerfully, joining arms with her. "Very well: I admit I had no idea you were capable of something like this. It's rather marvellous." He beamed up at the floating lamps. "Are those based on the ones over Riverset Bridge?"

"Yes." Hetta wrinkled her nose. "But I didn't think anyone would recognise them." She stared up at them thoughtfully. "To be honest, I'll own I didn't know I was capable of something of this magnitude either. I think you were right before, about Stariel giving a boost to Valstar magic."

Marius steered her along the stalls to the northern edge of the green. She could see her half-sisters and Lady Phoebe setting out their own offerings for the Faire next to Cook's goods. They had made up a number of sweet-smelling decorations: wire-bound heart-shapes caging cinnamon quills, star anise, dried orange rind, and pine cones.

They walked a circuit of the green, which had become a warren of narrow walkways between stalls. The locals greeted them cheerfully—Marius as one of their own, Hetta a little more cautiously. Marius bought an intricate wooden puzzle—"For Laurel," he explained at Hetta's questioning look—as well as a number of other little gifts, most of which Hetta was relatively certain he bought only to please the stall keepers.

"You're a soft touch," she teased after he'd purchased an extremely ugly sculpture made of bent spoons from an enthusiastic old woman.

He waggled a finger at her. "Now, now, I expect you to show proper appreciation when you open your gift. After all, you wouldn't want to offend me or the maker."

It was good to see his spirits somewhat lifted. "I'm sure I can find a dark cabinet somewhere to display it as it deserves."

He smiled, but then abruptly stiffened as he caught sight of something further down the row. She followed his gaze to locate the cause and saw a blond man, perhaps Hetta's age, well-dressed, and good-looking. Marius's reaction made it easy enough to hazard a guess as to this person's identity, so she squeezed his arm and said:

"You're a very poor escort, for you haven't purchased me any mulled wine and I'm half-frozen." The mulled wine stall was in the opposite direction to Marius's troublesome ex-lover.

Marius started. All the humour of the few seconds previous had been stripped from his expression. "What?"

"Go and get me some mulled wine, dolt. In fact, you should make sure Phoebe and the others have some as well. I'll find you at their stall." She gave him a gentle push in that direction.

"Oh—oh, yes. Of course." It was indicative of his distraction that he didn't quarrel with her summarily ordering him about.

Hetta waited until he was safely disposed of and then turned her attention back to the blond man. He didn't look much like a blackmailer. Nature had bestowed upon him a round, innocent face and fair complexion that made him look younger than he probably was. His expression, however, was at odds with his features. He was staring in the direction Marius had gone with narrow-eyed speculation. She saw the moment he realised she was watching him, for surprise and then swift calculation flickered in him before he composed himself.

He began to make his way towards her along the row of stalls. What course of action would be best of those available to her here and now? She didn't want him to think she took him seriously enough to pay attention to him. But on the other hand, she was curious about the efficacy of Wyn's spell, and she wanted to take the measure of this man who'd caused her brother so much grief.

She loitered in the space between two stalls, pretending to be very interested in the decorations on the evergreen there, and watched out of the corner of her eye as the man approached. She wished that Marius had shared his name with her—it seemed ridiculous to keep thinking of him only as 'the blond man'.

"Miss Valstar," he said when he drew near. "Forgive me." His accent was Southern and polished. Hetta didn't know where he and Marius had met, but the accent made her wonder if it hadn't been something to do with his Knoxbridge friends.

She made sure to take a long moment to turn. When she did, she treated him to an icy stare and spoke down her nose at him. The Valstar nose was particularly good for this sort of aloof expression, owing to its generous length.

He was even better looking up close, though also shorter than she'd expected, his perfect proportions misleading. His beauty was only dimmed by the fact that he was clearly extremely aware of it. *Oh, Marius,* she thought despairingly. *You should know better than to fall for a pretty pair of blue eyes.*

"Yes?" she asked coldly. "You are?"

He faltered in the face of this chilly reception but rallied quickly. "My name is John Tidwell. You do not know me, but I am acquainted with—" And here he frowned.

"Acquainted with?" she pressed, fascinated to see the binding spell in action. She wondered if he would find a way to refer to Marius, but if there was a loophole, he couldn't seem to locate it.

His brows drew together, and he flushed angrily. "The matter I wrote to you about," he burst out. She didn't think he'd intended to refer to his blackmail attempt so directly, but frustration had clearly overcome discretion.

"The matter you wrote to me about?" She made sure to sound puzzled.

"The matter that I'm sure you would not wish to be publicly known!" he said, then softened his voice. "I am sorry—I am overwrought. It is a very distressing matter, concerning as it does—" He frowned again as his words vanished on him.

"You wrote that rather spiteful note to me," she said flatly.

He affected an aggrieved expression, which she had to admit he did well. He had the right sort of face for it. "I do not at all wish to air the matter in the court of public opinion—as I'm sure you do not. The family's reputation—"

"I think you'd be extremely foolish to try," she told him. "Since I hardly see how you can do so without dragging your own reputation into it."

He gave an elegant shrug. "But I am not a local, Miss Valstar. What do I care what people say of me in the North?" His expression became guileless, his beauty piercing as an arrow, giving him an air of fragile naïveté. "And besides, I am but a remorseful victim, seeking protection from the law. No blame will fall on me for trusting—" He frowned as he lost his voice again.

But she'd heard enough. She could see exactly how he would play the situation, how he would use that boyish face, how Marius's status as a lord's son would be turned against him until he became a kind of monster preying on innocent youths. Or how he would if he wasn't spelled to prevent him from doing so, she thought with satisfaction. She cut him off with a sharp movement of her hand.

"As you seem intent on speaking incoherent nonsense to me, I will say good day to you. I don't wish to receive any more notes. And if I see you again, I'll report you myself for harassment." She turned and walked briskly away from him with great satisfaction. If John Tidwell had ever felt any real emotion for her brother, she'd eat her hat.

Her satisfaction dimmed as she replayed his words. "Miss Valstar" he'd called her. Was that merely a slip from someone unused to the way Northern titles worked, or did he know she wasn't Stariel's lord in truth? Marius had been convinced that his paramour had nothing to do with the theft of the Stone, but did they really know that for sure? She shouldn't have been so hasty to dismiss the man. If he had the real Star Stone, then perhaps it would be worth paying him in order to reacquire it. She rebelled at the thought; she didn't wish the man who'd hurt her brother to benefit by a single penny. *But I have to think of more than just my own preferences*, she reminded herself. Even if they told the rest of the family how things were, it would still take time to make a new Star Stone, assuming they could find enough star indigo; time in which Stariel would be vulnerable. It would be better if they could locate the old one.

She blew out a long breath to steel herself and turned back to confront John Tidwell again.

MULLED WINE

Mr John Tidwell had disappeared. Hetta's dismissal, unfortunately, had been every bit as effective as she'd desired. Drat. She shouldn't have let her temper get the better of her.

"If looks could kill, we'd have a bloodbath on our hands," Angus's voice said from behind her, and she whirled around to face him. "Whatever has offended you so, Hetta?"

"Oh, it was nothing of moment." She waved the question away. He tilted his head, a faintly inquiring look in his eyes.

"Clearly, then, you are vexed because no one has fetched you a glass of mulled wine." He held out his arm invitingly, and after a small internal debate, she took it.

She'd feared that her next meeting with Angus would be excruciatingly awkward, but he seemed to be taking pains to put her at ease. He told her an amusing anecdote about one of his sisters, followed up with an invitation from said sister—"For she's not seen you in an age, and company is thin on the ground here in this season"—and all in all managed to avoid referring to the fact that she'd rejected his proposal only a week before. He found her a glass of mulled wine, which made her spare a half-irritated, half-amused thought for Marius, who'd failed in the same task.

They walked the rows, and Hetta found herself in the unusual state of not knowing quite what she ought to do. She *liked* Angus, but she'd tried not to think too much about his proposal in the last few days. She'd told herself she wanted to see what happened between them after she revealed herself as a false lord, but was that true? Assuming the scandal didn't change Angus's mind, did she see any chance of a serious future between them? And it would be a very serious future indeed—there had been a few meaningful remarks from her family already reminding her that there were still certain expectations of young, unmarried women from 'the right sort of family'. Angus's proposal shouldn't have blindsided Hetta, but she'd grown too used to the freedom to be had as a person of anonymous background amongst the radically liberal theatre crowd. There was no room here for any more flirtation, if she wasn't serious. So—was she?

No, she thought with sudden and surprising certainty. *I think I just got carried away with getting so much attention from the object of my teenage infatuation.* But it wasn't Angus Penharrow that drew her as strongly as iron to a lodestone, and it wasn't fair to toy with the man when her heart sang for someone else—irrationally, perhaps, but there wasn't any point pretending it didn't. She'd just made up her mind to say something more definitively negative to Angus when they rounded a row of stalls and came across an unpleasant tableau. Marius was standing frozen with Phoebe and their half-sisters, mug halfway to his lips, as Mr Tidwell appeared around the corner.

Mr Tidwell's face blazed with the sort of anger that spells violence, and it was in his movements as he came towards Marius. Hetta felt a peculiar irritation with the man and his persistence, though his anger was understandable; he might not know about fae magic, but he knew that he was being thwarted somehow. His boyish good looks were rendered grotesque by his vengeful expression.

Hetta was annoyed but not seriously alarmed at the prospect of a scuffle breaking out, but that changed when Mr Tidwell stopped short of Marius and made a little throwing gesture that Hetta was intimately familiar with.

"Marius!" she cried, reaching out with her hands in a fledgling attempt to do something. She hadn't quite settled upon what when Alexandra shoved Marius out of the way of the impending fireball and the two of them went clattering to the ground.

The fireball wasn't an especially impressive effort, small and burning with a sluggish red flame. It hit a hanging scarf, sizzled, and then went out, leaving the sharp smell of singed wool in the air. It would probably have given her brother no worse than a minor scorch if it had hit him, though she was glad it hadn't.

"Really," she said, exasperated out of all patience. She marched towards Mr Tidwell, who was looking as if he'd shocked even himself with his pitiful fireball—probably the first one he'd even tried to conjure for such a purpose, she thought acidly. She was about to unleash her tongue upon him when a cry went up from her relatives gathered around the fallen figures of Marius and Alexandra.

Hetta shot Mr Tidwell a glare and then turned to push her way through the gathering throng of Valstars to find Alexandra lying prone, Marius crouched next to her. Alexandra was still crumpled where she'd fallen, her limbs sprawled in a worryingly boneless way. She must have caught her temple hard on the corner of the stall as she fell.

"Alex! Alex!" Marius was saying over and over, shaking his sister's shoulder.

Lady Phoebe had crouched on the other side of her, heedless

of her dress. She pressed her white handkerchief to her daughter's brow. Already it was stained cherry red.

Hetta dispatched Angus to fetch the local physician. "As soon as I can," he said grimly.

Alexandra roused after two horribly long minutes and was violently sick. Anxious relatives swirled around her and were more hindrance than help until Lady Phoebe took charge, sending some of them for ice and commanding the rest to take Alexandra back to the house. Alexandra seemed only vaguely aware of what was happening, complaining bitterly of her aching head.

"I know, dear, I know," her mother soothed.

Amidst the worry and confusion, Hetta spared a thought for Mr Tidwell, but he'd disappeared. Later, she promised herself, a burning nugget of anger flaring at the thought. Later, she would find that man and he would pay for what he had done to Alexandra, and Marius, and in all likelihood the Star Stone as well.

By the time Dr Greystark arrived, Alexandra's head was bandaged and she lay on her bed with ice on her head. Phoebe fluttered anxiously nearby, unsure what else to do for her now the initial crisis was dealt with.

Hetta remembered Dr Greystark from her girlhood. He hadn't much changed in the intervening years, apart from the increasing grey of his hair. He was a large man with a great deal of common sense, and his arrival did much to calm Phoebe. He commended her for her actions so far and examined Alexandra with calm, steady motions, though she flinched under his hands and said that her head was splitting. Her words were slurred and slow when she answered the doctor's questions, and she couldn't focus her eyes properly, her pupils blown wide.

Dr Greystark turned to the gathered party, his lips twitching in sober amusement to see so many of them. "It's difficult to make predictions with head injuries, so early on. The first hours are the most critical. She needs to be watched closely."

Hetta escorted him back downstairs and asked him what he really thought. He gave a grim smile. “I meant what I said, Lord Valstar. However, it’s a good sign that she is conscious. I’ll return tomorrow.”

Hetta saw him to his car and leaned against the doorframe, worry gnawing at her.

37

VENGEANCE

ALEXANDRA GREW WORSE during the night. Dr Greystark had told them to wake her every two hours, but each time she grew less responsive. She seemed increasingly unaware of where she was and who she was with. "I want to dance!" she complained, trying to rise.

Lady Phoebe pushed her down gently. "Later, my love, when you are well. You must rest!"

"I want to dance!" she whined, but she let Phoebe settle her again in the bed.

Daybreak left Hetta with a strange reprieve from the scene she thought she'd be facing the day after the Frost Faire. Jack didn't even discuss it. He simply scowled at Hetta on her way to breakfast, said, "Obviously there's no point making a fuss till Alex is better," and stalked out into the estate.

Hetta hadn't been looking forward to breaking the news, but she would have done so a thousand times rather than this...helpless waiting. With Phoebe, Grandmamma, Aunt Sybil, Lottie, and Dr Greystark all poised to do whatever Alexandra might need, Hetta's presence was unnecessary. Even Marius was better in the sickroom than she was. He could coax Alexandra to drink her barley-water or tonic when no one else succeeded.

Her younger brother Gregory felt similarly useless. She encountered him pacing the hallways or harassing Cook. Hetta tried to reassure him that he would have ample opportunity to demonstrate his affection for his sister once the worst had passed. "For then she'll need someone to keep her occupied as she recuperates." Gregory wasn't much impressed with this statement and, to be honest, neither was Hetta.

Her mind had too much time to turn, and she found it sifting through the encounter with John Tidwell. The name had rung a faint bell at the time, and now she realised that this was because she'd heard it once before: at the train station where the stationmaster had named people leaving Stariel after the Choosing. In her fear for her sister, Mr Tidwell had been pushed to the side, but now she wondered. Marius hadn't spelled out the details of their relationship, but she remembered his cautious hope the day after the Choosing, followed swiftly by black despair. It seemed a key piece of evidence, that Mr Tidwell had been angry or disappointed enough in Marius's failure to be chosen that he had broken things off between them. The expectation that Marius would inherit would be a natural one for a Southerner, where such things usually went to the eldest son, but Mr Tidwell might have had other reasons for expecting Marius to inherit. If he'd paid an illusionist to make the Star Stone appear to activate—if the activation had been linked to the number of times it was touched—then Marius would have appeared to be chosen if he hadn't made his own decision not to compete for the lordship.

She went and found Wyn, who was in the housekeeper's office. He looked up when Hetta came in.

"Alexandra?" he asked without preamble. He looked more tired than she'd ever seen him. The whole household was heavy-eyed today.

"The same," she said. "Dr Greystark brought a tonic for her but says otherwise there is little we can do but see that she is not agitated and wait."

"Oh, Hetta." He rose, concern creasing his face, but she waved him away. She didn't want sympathy just now; it made it harder to bear the waiting.

"In any case, that's not why I came to find you—what are you doing?" She was suddenly curious.

"Drafting an advertisement for a housekeeper."

"I was rather under the impression that you were filling that role." Her eyes narrowed in suspicion. "You're not arranging your exit from this house, are you?"

"I cannot do everything. Lord Henry was unwilling to hire new staff when the old housekeeper retired and encouraged me to expand my butlering duties to encompass both roles. But now we are also missing a land steward."

She felt abruptly selfish. It was easy to take Wyn for granted. He was always there, in the background, ensuring things ran smoothly, radiating calm competence. She remembered wondering about the news that he'd taken over the household management several months before her father's death, but Stariel had seemed so far away then and Wyn had never sounded less than completely assured. But it ought to have occurred to her in the time since.

"Oh, I am sorry, Wyn. I swear I've no idea how you keep up with half the things you already do. Of course we must hire more staff. Though, presumably, you were going to draw my attention to this?"

"That is why I called it a *draft* notice." His voice was very dry.

"I should have noticed."

"It's my job to tell you these things," Wyn said. "And I have told you at the appropriate time, ergo: now. Nothing is in any immediate danger of falling to pieces. I beg you not to look at me as if I am about to expire; it pricks my vanity. Tell me instead what you came seeking me for."

He came around the small desk as he spoke, and the size of the room shrank. The housekeeper's office wasn't generously sized and Wyn was a tall man. For a second, Hetta thought of feathers and filled the space around them with outstretched wings.

"My Star?"

Hetta gave herself a stern mental shake. "Do you know where someone by the name of Tidwell would be lodging?"

"Marius told you his secret, then."

"Yes, although even if he hadn't, I could hardly fail to have noticed his attack on Marius yesterday."

"I have put it about that it was a prank gone awry. An old school friendship from Knoxbridge, that sort of thing."

"I seem to be inordinately stupid today; it didn't occur to me that people would gossip. Thank you for coming up with a story."

Wyn's eyes gentled. "It's not stupid to be preoccupied."

They both mentally went upstairs, to the room where Alexandra lay. A cold lump formed in her stomach.

Though she'd noted how tired Wyn looked, closer up she could see it wasn't just a lack of sleep. There was a heaviness to him in place of his usual effervescence.

"I feel responsible for John Tidwell's actions," he said abruptly. "I did not anticipate that my binding would incite him to violence."

"Don't be foolish."

He sighed, and she could see the uncertainty in him. "Is it foolishness, Hetta?"

"Yes," she told him tartly. "So stop dwelling on it." His eyes were worn and full of secrets, and part of her wanted to shake him until they came loose. "I swear sometimes you're cryptic simply for the pleasure of seeming mysterious."

"It's a habit that's hard to lose," he said ruefully. "Shall we proceed to Mr Tidwell's lodgings, then?"

WYN DIDN'T ASK FOR clarification of their purpose as they stole out of the house. For that, Hetta was grateful, because she couldn't have explained precisely what she hoped to achieve. Or rather, she could rationalise it under the guise of following a lead that might end in discovering the Star Stone, but that was only part of the whole reason. The truth was much simpler and much less noble. Someone had hurt her family; she wanted to hurt them in return. She was fairly certain that Wyn knew this, but he said nothing as they drove into Stariel-on-Starwater. She really must learn to drive, but it had fallen to the bottom of her list of priorities in the wake of various other urgencies.

The remnants of yesterday's Faire were still scattered about, though the illusion had dispersed, and the stalls were in the process of being dismantled. Hetta caught Wyn assessing the work as if he were making notes, which, she supposed, he probably was. She found it hard to read his expression. There was a caution to him, the sense that he was watching her as intently as she was him.

Mr Tidwell had lodgings with a widow in Whitnow Street on the outskirts of the village.

"He might not even be here," Hetta said, looking up at the narrow two-storied stone house. It had a small garden at its front, bare in this season.

"He will be packing. His train leaves tonight."

"How very convenient you are." It occurred to her suddenly that the most terrifying person on Stariel Estate might not be whoever was behind the theft of the Star Stone, for in knowledge there was power, and no one knew more small details about the locale than her friend.

Wyn hesitated and then reached out, very briefly, to grip her shoulder in a gesture of reassurance. She stopped him from taking his hand back, resting her gloved fingers atop his. There was a charged moment, but beneath the sudden sensual interest that flickered in his eyes she could see worry. Everything seemed so very complicated between them, and she felt a strong urge to un-complicate. Seated as they were, he was, Hetta thought with sudden intent, within kissing distance. She wriggled closer, until their warm breaths mingled. He stilled, and she took the opportunity to walk her hand up his arm to rest gently on his starched collar.

"Hetta..." His voice was deeper than usual, vibrating with some strong emotion. "I don't think—" He broke off as she raised her hand further and traced his jawline. The heat of his skin seeped through her thin gloves. She considered herself a reasonably accomplished flirt, but this felt different, as if she hovered on the edge of a precipice, about to fall into an unknown land. Wyn leaned very slightly into the touch.

Dash propriety, caution, and fae. She would've kissed him then, but he was abruptly not there to be kissed. He moved away and exited the car in a swift motion, quick as a cat, while she still sat there, one half of an unfinished promise. She sighed, knowing he was probably right—now wasn't an appropriate time for such carryings-on—but irked all the same.

She got out of the car before he could open the door for her and glared at him. It was, she knew, entirely reasonable of him not to be sure of his own mind, but it was hard to hold on to this thought when he stood there, unrepentant and beautiful, smiling at her as if he knew exactly what she was thinking.

"How long are we going to dance around this thing between us?" she asked him crossly.

He ignored her question. "Mrs Eldervelt—the widow who lives here, and Mr Tidwell's aunt—is normally out at this time of day." He looked at the unprepossessing house. "She is elderly and possessed of an independence. I believe Mr Tidwell hoped that he might persuade her to make him her heir—from what Marius has told me, he has been quite desperate for funds since his father cut him off after he quit law school. Which is, presumably, why he was particularly anxious that Marius should inherit."

"Apparently we will be avoiding the subject until the cows come home, if left up to you," Hetta said, ignoring his words as he had hers. "You make me feel grossly lacking in subtlety, but tell me plainly whether you want me to stop. I don't wish to be foisting myself at you if you are in fact disgusted by me."

"Hetta—" He reached out towards her, stricken, but she backed away and fixed him with a stern look.

"No, Wyn. Tell me."

"I…you're leaving, Hetta," he said. "When we find the Stone. Even if there were no other considerations—and you cannot pretend there are not others—you will go back to your old life, away from Stariel, and I can't—I can't go with you." He drummed agitated fingers on the roof of the car, little metal sounds in the quiet street. "Storms above, I don't even know if you would want me to go with you. But I can't bear to be with you and then… not…" He trailed off, and the fierce emotion in his eyes knocked the breath from her lungs.

"Oh," she said uselessly.

His fae nature was close to the surface. She could see it in the prominence of his cheekbones, in the darker cast of his skin, in the brilliance of his irises. The soft scent of rain and spice coloured the air for a heartbeat, the thickening pressure before a storm—a combination she was starting to recognise as his magic, though why fae magic should have a scent, she didn't know.

Wyn exhaled, and the foreign magic dispersed as abruptly as it had come, leaving just her old, familiar friend in its place, all hints of non-humanness tucked neatly away.

"Shall we go up?" he said, as if nothing of importance had occurred.

"Oh, how I would like to shake you sometimes! But very well." She stopped him just before they went up to the gate with a hand on his arm. "I'm sorry."

He looked down at her, his expression as unhappy as she'd ever seen it. "So am I."

38

MR JOHN TIDWELL

HETTA HAD EXPECTED to feel a tide of anger at the sight of John Tidwell, but all she could summon when she and Wyn unceremoniously let themselves into his room was pity. Wyn's estimate had been correct—they'd caught Mr Tidwell in the middle of packing. A large trunk lay open in the centre of the room, and belongings lay strewn in the disarray necessary when one is attempting to confine one's possessions. Hetta had a sudden sharp thought for her own room back in the boarding house in Meridon.

John Tidwell looked up when they entered, a curious mix of alarm and guilt coming over him when he saw who it was. He'd been kneeling on the floor, wrestling with a case, and he rose in an undignified scramble.

"What do you want?"

"Aren't you going to enquire after my sister?" Hetta asked. He flinched.

"Surely it was just a fall." He looked from Hetta's face to Wyn's, and his voice rose, seeking reassurance. "Surely she must be fine?"

"No," Hetta told him coldly. "She's not fine."

He paled. "It was an accident. I never intended—"

"No, you intended to hurt my brother instead. Though I doubt you would have done more than singe him, with such a pathetic display of magic." She was abruptly tired. She'd come here out of a desire for vengeance, but there was no satisfaction to be had from this sorry creature. She waved away his attempts to explain himself. "I don't care," she told him. "Leave this house and this village and let me never see or hear from you again. I'm tired of you and your weak attempts at blackmail. But first, tell me what you've done with the Stone."

The man had been swelling with anger at her words, but this gave him pause. "Stone?" he repeated, genuinely puzzled. "What stone?"

She remembered suddenly what Marius had said about being able to sense the Stone when it was nearby. Mr Tidwell's confusion was very convincing, but still she reached for Stariel, sure that her land-sense would point her in the correct direction if the Stone was here to find. But Stariel had no light to shine on the situation, and she caught only a vague sense of ill-ease from the land, and that was nothing new. Stariel had been growing increasingly restless the longer it spent lordless. Wyn gave her an enquiring look, and she shook her head very slightly. The Stone wasn't here.

"There is a binding on you," Wyn told the man, to Hetta's surprise, "that prevents you from identifying Marius, that you may not set spiteful rumours about him."

"I knew it!" the man cried. "I knew it was magic devilry."

Hetta raised an eyebrow at him. "Magic devilry that you yourself used just yesterday."

"I will remove the bindings," Wyn continued, "on the condition that you never return to Stariel or seek to do further harm to any of the Valstars."

Hetta wasn't sure how she felt about this development. On the one hand, she couldn't quite be easy with the nature of Wyn's fae magic that made him able to constrain a man's mind so. But on the other, since the magic had already been done, the practical part of her thought it might be better to leave things as they were.

John Tidwell looked ready to bluster his indignity at length, but Wyn fixed him with an arctic stare. "Will you agree to those terms?" When the man would've tried to negotiate, Wyn grew distant and alien, implacable as a storm. "Those are my terms: agree to them and I will remove the bindings. Do not agree and I will not remove the bindings and I will still make you unwelcome at Stariel. And be warned, if you break your word, I will make you regret it deeply."

"And I will ruin you," Hetta added. She wasn't actually sure how one went about ruining people, but she was sure that she could if she put her mind to it.

"Very well," he said grudgingly.

There was a taste of magic in the air, lightning charged with spice, and then Wyn said, "It is done. You have until the train departs tonight to leave Stariel."

BEFORE THEY CAME BACK to the house, she made Wyn pause with a hand on his arm. "Do you—do you know of any magic that could help Alexandra?" she asked in a rush.

The warmth in his eyes dimmed. "Not that I possess. My gifts do not lie in healing. I am sorry for it."

Hetta patted his arm. "It was only a stray thought. I remembered the fairy tales I heard as a girl and..." She shrugged.

Wyn nodded and opened the door for her. Aunt Sybil was making her way up the main staircase as they entered.

"How is she?" Wyn asked.

Aunt Sybil didn't even reprimand him. Her expression was

grave and entirely without its normal hint of disapproval. "Worse, I am afraid. Dr Greystark is with her again. I am going to try to coax Phoebe to take a few hours' rest while he is here."

Wyn and Hetta exchanged glances.

"I'll come to you once I've changed out of my coat, Aunt," Hetta said. Aunt Sybil simply nodded and continued on her way.

Hetta went up to the sickroom after tidying herself and tried not to show how shocked she was at Alexandra's appearance. Her breathing had become laboured. The continual wheeze of her chest rising and falling was the only sound in the room. Dr Greystark was fiddling with various concoctions from his case, and Aunt Sybil sat in a chair by Alexandra's bedside, one hand resting on the coverlet. She was studying Alexandra's features with soft sorrow, and Hetta abruptly recalled that Aunt Sybil had lost a child to bronchitis long ago. Hubert, Jack's younger brother by two years, had died before he was three years old. Hetta didn't remember him.

Aunt Sybil hadn't been successful in persuading Phoebe to leave her daughter even for a few hours, but she'd evidently come up with a compromise. Phoebe was stretched out on a little trundle bed at the far end of the room, exhaustion ageing her.

Dr Greystark looked up as Hetta came further into the room, and his expression made Hetta feel as though a great clamp had wrapped around her chest, tightening. He gave soft instructions for administering the medicines he had mixed. Aunt Sybil nodded, her eyes not leaving Alexandra's face.

"Is there nothing else you can do?" Hetta asked quietly. She hesitated. "Perhaps a specialist we could send for?"

Dr Greystark didn't look offended at the suggestion, but he sighed heavily, brushing a hand through his grey locks. "You're welcome to try. Although I doubt they could do more than I have already." He looked at Alexandra, lines creasing his forehead as he frowned. "I will give you some names."

39

GREGORY HAS AN IDEA

MEALS HAD BECOME very quiet affairs since Alexandra's illness. Hetta made some desultory attempt at conversation, but it fell flat, and they ate for the most part in silence. Aunt Sybil hadn't come down to dinner, presumably taking it in the sickroom, and Phoebe made no appearance either. Gregory was also absent, Hetta knew not where, so it was only Jack, Marius, and Grandmamma at table.

Wyn had come to take their plates away—the maid had been co-opted by Phoebe for sickroom duty—when Gregory appeared. He came into the room with an air of defiance, which Hetta at first thought was merely due to his lateness. The wild burning of his eyes said otherwise.

"I know how to help Alex," he said as soon as he'd crossed the threshold. His words were addressed particularly to Hetta. "All she wants is your word."

Hetta frowned. "Gregory, what—"

"Gwendelfear. She says she can heal Alexandra."

There was a long silence, followed by Hetta, Jack, and Marius all firing approximately the same question at Gregory at once: just when and how had he been talking to Gwendelfear?

"I went outside the bounds and called her name three times," he said. Into the mildly astonished silence that followed this proclamation, he added, a little sheepishly, "I read about it in one of the books in the library. How to summon fairies."

Hetta's eyes automatically sought Wyn's. He had frozen, a tray piled with dishes held effortlessly in his good hand. He'd dispensed with the sling the day before, despite Hetta's protests. His gaze was turned inwards, and it took him several seconds to acknowledge Hetta's unspoken question. When he did, he looked thoughtful and inclined his head very slightly.

"You summoned Gwendelfear?" Jack asked.

"Yes," Gregory said, jutting his chin out. "I told her she owed Alex, since she's the one who set her free."

The room absorbed this information thoughtfully, and Hetta felt a sudden flash of exasperated wrath towards her younger siblings. Did they have no sense at all?

"Is it possible?" Marius asked Wyn. "Could she heal Alex?" Everyone turned towards him, although Gregory looked confused.

Wyn sighed and put the tray back down on the table. "Yes."

"But if Gwendelfear can, why couldn't you help her?" Marius asked. There was a note of accusation in his voice.

Wyn was already shaking his head. "Healing is not one of my gifts."

"What are you all talking about? Why are you asking Wyn like he's an expert?" Gregory broke in.

Grandmamma, Jack, Marius, and Hetta exchanged glances. There was no one else in the room but for them and Wyn, as Gregory had chosen a moment when the other servers were absent.

Wyn's lips twitched in a half smile as he turned back to Gregory.

"I suppose I *am* some kind of expert." He hesitated, then added, "I am fae myself, you see." He said it lightly, but Hetta knew him well enough to spot the tension behind his seemingly casual statement. She was coming to realise just how careful Wyn was about revealing personal information.

Gregory stared at him. "What?" He looked around the dining room for support. Marius looked embarrassed, belatedly realising his slip had inadvertently outed Wyn. Grandmamma was watching with every evidence of enjoyment.

Jack merely thumped the table impatiently. "Never mind that," he said, getting to his feet. "If Gwendelfear can heal Alexandra, then what are we waiting about for?"

"Wyn?" Hetta asked.

"Be very careful," he said. "The fae are bound by their promises, but they are very, very good at finding loopholes. Exact words are important."

Hetta's eyebrows went up. Wasn't that interesting?

"You all knew!" Gregory accused, pointing at Wyn. "How long have you known?"

"Does it matter?" Hetta said, shrugging and getting to her feet.

"I should rather think it does! How come it was fine to lock up Gwendelfear for being a fairy if Wyn has the run of the house?"

To everyone's surprise, it was their grandmother who answered. "Because Wyn swore an oath to protect those of Stariel when he first came to us, many years ago."

This time Gregory wasn't the only one who looked at Wyn accusingly. Wyn looked rather sheepish.

"Well. Yes," he said. "Lord Henry was no fool."

"Father knew about fairies?" Gregory said.

Hetta was also curious to hear Wyn's answer. It had always been peculiar that her father had so willingly accepted a strange boy into his household. He wasn't a flexible or warm-hearted man. She'd always presumed that it was a measure of Wyn's innate charm that he'd managed to thaw even Lord Henry's heart. But if there had been something rather more like a bargain to begin with, it made a great deal more sense.

"He knew enough to know how much he did not know," Wyn said finally. "Enough to take advantage of an opportunity when it presented itself."

Jack seemed neither surprised nor interested. "There will be time for nattering later," he said, striding to the door. "Where is she, Gregory?"

For the first time, Gregory looked a little ashamed of himself. "I—ah—I told her she could cross the boundary. She's waiting down by the copper beeches." In response to everyone's silent but intense rebuke, he added in a rush, "Well, it saves us a tramp to the boundary, doesn't it?"

FAIRY MAGIC

THEY FOLLOWED GREGORY's lead out of the house, pausing only to retrieve coats, hats, and footwear. Hetta put a hand on Wyn's arm to hold him back, and the two of them were the last in the procession.

Wyn looked down at her with an unreadable expression but didn't object when she tucked her arm into his as they walked.

"This oath business," she said in a low voice. "How does that work?"

"Fae cannot lie."

Hetta stumbled and gripped his hand for balance. It was warm even through their gloves, and she could feel his pulse racing despite his outward appearance of calm. He flashed her a fierce grin.

"You can't lie?" she asked, not because she doubted him but because she needed to speak the words aloud again to confirm them.

"No. I cannot." A hint of laughter in his voice. "It's a heavy burden to bear. Please endeavour not to take too great advantage of it."

It was too big a revelation to process all at once, so she asked the next obvious question as they made their way past the house and down to the woods bordering the northern edge of Starwater.

"Will Gwendelfear be bound by a promise to me, even though I'm not Stariel's lord?" Hetta conjured a string of lights without a second thought, though Jack had already switched on his flashlight. He shot her a narrow glance, annoyed and yet knowing he was being unreasonable. The woods that Hetta had walked through not so long ago with Wyn on their way down to the Home Farm were much less inviting in the dark, with the chill bite of winter bearing down upon them. Hetta hunched in on herself in an effort to preserve a little warmth. Wyn drew her to his side, as if to share a measure of his own, and she found it difficult not to give in to the urge to simply burrow into him.

"Yes. Our word is binding, unless we wish to lose a measure of our power."

"She called you Oathbreaker. Gwendelfear."

Wyn stiffened next to her but said nothing.

Hetta tried to put together what she knew of Wyn's past. "You said you ran from an engagement. Does that count as a broken oath?"

Wyn's answer was so soft she had to strain to hear it. "Yes."

She wanted to question him further, but Jack had realised that Hetta wasn't beside him and Marius and had swung around to find her. He scowled when he saw how close Wyn and Hetta were standing, and Hetta sighed and disentangled herself.

"Where is she?" she asked Gregory.

Gregory looked around. "She said—"

"I am here," said Gwendelfear, and, abruptly, she was. She stood before them in her fae form, her greenish hair flickering oddly in the yellow of Hetta's spell light. Hetta had become accustomed to Gwendelfear's whiteless, flower-pupiled eyes in the time she'd been here, but Jack, who hadn't seen her since her unveiling, was visibly repelled. The fae's dark green lips curved in a slight smile as she surveyed the party, though it disappeared for a second when she spotted Wyn.

"Hello, Gwendelfear," said Hetta. "You know why we're here."

It wasn't a question, but Gwendelfear nodded. "Alexandra." Her face softened slightly as she shaped the name.

Hetta saw no need to beat around the bush. "Can you heal her?"

Gwendelfear studied her face. "Yes," she said eventually. "I think so." Her eyes fixed unerringly on Wyn's. "I see you are still alive, Oathbreaker."

Hetta didn't realise she'd stepped forward until she felt Marius's hand on her shoulder, holding her back.

"I am," Wyn said steadily, his arms crossed as he looked down at the fae woman.

A dark smile whispered over her face before she said, "Ask what you have been wanting to ask," in a colder tone.

He frowned slightly but unfolded his arms. "How," he said, then added, "and why?"

A small smirk flickered on Gwendelfear's lips before she answered. "My father was a greater naiad."

Wyn blinked rapidly, evidently impressed, although Hetta hadn't found this utterance particularly informative. She dredged up some of her education. "Naiads are some kind of water fairy?"

"Waterfae," Gwendelfear corrected.

"They're known for their healing gifts," Wyn explained. "DuskRose is not known for such, so I was curious as to where Gwendelfear had acquired such a talent."

Gwendelfear narrowed her eyes at him. "Does it irk you that you, with all the magic of the mighty stormdancers behind you, cannot do this? That you must beg a lesser fae for help?" Her tone was mocking, but Wyn didn't rise to her bait.

Instead, he nodded to himself. "And why, Gwendelfear, would you offer this?"

"I want to be free of my obligation. The little Valstar girl freed me; I must repay the debt. But you would not understand such things, would you, Oathbreaker? Tell me, do your protectors feed you scraps from their table and tell you that you've been a good dog when you perform tricks for them?"

Wyn's expression didn't so much as flicker, but the air around him changed, becoming as charged as a looming thunderstorm, the taste of elektricity and spice in the air. Hetta had had difficulty seeing the prince in him before; she saw it now as he straightened, eyes cold.

"Do you have any other motivation for offering to heal Alexandra?" he pressed.

Gwendelfear glared at him, and Hetta realised that Wyn was trying to drive her into a corner. Clearly there was another reason and just as clearly Gwendelfear did not wish to reveal it.

"Does it involve bringing harm to Stariel or those who reside in it?" Hetta asked when it seemed like they were at an impasse.

"No," Gwendelfear ground out.

"Then I don't care what it is. You may keep your secrets, if you can heal my sister."

Wyn was still full of brooding menace, and said, "Speak the words," to Gwendelfear.

She tilted her head at him chidingly. "Of course. I am glad to make this bargain. I will attempt to heal Alexandra in repayment of my debt to her. I will even do you one better and promise to do no harm to those of Stariel from now until I cross the border."

Wyn still looked suspicious, but he nodded in answer to Hetta's silent question.

And then Marius said suddenly: "You care about Alex."

Gwendelfear glared at him as if sheer ill-will could silence him, but he appeared not to notice, repeating his words with increasing confidence. "Gregory told you how badly off she is. You're worried about her."

Gwendelfear said nothing, and that, in itself, was an answer.

"Well, in any case, let's get on with it," said Hetta, after it was clear no one else was quite sure what to say.

Phoebe was awake again and sitting with Aunt Sybil at Alexandra's bedside when the small army of Valstars approached. Her fatigue was such that it wasn't until they were all assembled around Alexandra that she frowned and began to form a question. By this time, Aunt Sybil had noticed Gwendelfear's presence and had begun to demand her own answers in a forceful whisper that was louder than normal speech.

Hetta explained as best she could, and the two women reacted predictably. Phoebe seemed ready to embrace Gwendelfear as a saviour; Aunt Sybil was suspicious but grudgingly willing.

Gwendelfear's gaze went past them to Alexandra's pale form in the bed, and something changed in her expression of self-satisfaction. Marius has guessed truly: Gwendelfear *did* care about Alexandra. The flicker of worry was gone in an instant, but Hetta had seen it.

"She will need to be in water," Gwendelfear said.

"Will a bathtub be suitable?" Hetta asked before any of her relatives could begin objecting.

Gwendelfear tilted her head to one side and considered. "Yes. The water should come from Starwater."

"The lake water is freezing!" Aunt Sybil objected before Hetta could stop her. "And you just expect us to carry buckets of it up here?"

Gwendelfear turned to her and said calmly, "Yes." Aunt Sybil drew in an angry breath. "This is magic, Sybil Langley-Valstar. It does not operate according to people's convenience."

"Can we heat the water?" Hetta too didn't like the idea of putting her sister into ice-cold lake water. But Gwendelfear shook her head.

"No. It changes the nature of the thing."

"Well," said Hetta, "I suppose we had best fetch some buckets then."

The serving staff were somewhat astonished when what seemed like every Valstar within shouting distance traipsed down to the kitchen in search of containers. It was something of a testament to the family's collective oddities that they acquiesced without fuss, although their eyes burned with curiosity. Wyn received many speaking looks, and Hetta knew that he would be expected to explain once they got him alone. She had no doubt that he would manage to come up with something but marvelled for the first time at the skill it would require to mislead people without speaking a word of untruth. No wonder he'd held that secret so closely; once people knew it, they would pay far too much attention to his precise words.

There was an icy wind straight down from the Indigoes, and its cold crept under scarves and pulled at hair. The reeds by the lake shore were blown nearly flat, and the surface of Starwater was ruffled, small white caps of waves slapping against the shore.

It was entirely unnecessary for them all to fetch and carry, of course, but somehow it had become a family affair. They all wanted to help Alexandra, and if this was the only way they could help, then so be it. Only Phoebe and—at Hetta's insistence—Jack had remained to watch Gwendelfear and Alex. Everyone else—including, to general wonder, Aunt Sybil—had taken hold of pails and water jugs and marched out into the blustery weather and down to the lakeshore.

Marius took one look at the water, removed his shoes, rolled up his trousers, and waded several steps out into the lake, gesturing impatiently for the others to hand him their vessels. Standing in deeper water, he was able to fill them more quickly. Hetta frowned at him as he took her pail.

"Don't you get yourself sick too." The water, she knew, would be only a few degrees above freezing at this time of year. His feet would be burning with the cold of it.

He handed her her pail impatiently and shrugged. "Best hurry along then."

No one needed to make two trips to fill the bathtub. The tub they'd chosen for the event was in a large if slightly dilapidated bathroom tiled in pale green. To this, an unknown decorator had chosen to add a row of large feature tiles circling the room at waist height, showing sprigs of lavender.

Aunt Sybil banished the men from the room, although she had to make a small concession for Marius, who carried Alexandra in. She was feverish again, thrashing weakly against his chest. He spoke to her in a low voice, trying to comfort her, but her eyes showed no comprehension. His mouth thinned into a line as he contemplated the cold, slightly green-tinted water. He glanced at Gwendelfear, who nodded impatiently, and he carefully lowered Alexandra into the water, still in her nightgown.

Alexandra hissed at the shock of the temperature and clung to her brother like a cat, splashing water everywhere. Marius's face whitened but he unpicked her fingers and stepped back, water dripping from his shirt. She sat, moaning piteously, her hands scrabbling at the tub's edges, too weak to pull herself up. After a moment, she seemed to relax slightly. Perhaps, Hetta thought hopefully, she was so hot that the cold water was bringing her relief.

Without a word of warning, Gwendelfear clambered into the tub, crouching over Alexandra. Aunt Sybil made a wordless noise of protest, but Gwendelfear shot her a poisonous look, and the sheer alienness of her wide blue eyes was enough to silence her. Gwendelfear turned back to Alexandra, her expression sharpening. She leaned forward and placed a hand on either side of Alexandra's head. Both of them stilled, until the surface of the water smoothed out again.

They made an odd tableau, Gwendelfear's greenish ankles emerging from the water on either side of Alexandra, whose head was now tilted back so that her eyes met Gwendelfear's. She looked confused but not frightened. Her rasping breaths were the only sound in the small bathroom.

Although Gwendelfear had been in her fae form the entire time, something about her shifted even further from humanity. Her hair took on the appearance of multihued lakeweed, shifting as if it were slick with water. The water began to…glow was the closest word Hetta could find to describe it, but it wasn't truly a glow. It was as if a sunbeam was suddenly filtering up through it, throwing the entire room into a greenish light. Gwendelfear's skin grew greener too, or perhaps it was merely the effect of the light.

Ripples began to form where Gwendelfear's skin touched the water, although she hadn't shifted from her crouched stance. Her pose was very like that of a heron poised above a fish. Soon the surface of the water was as ruffled as Starwater's had been earlier, though there was no wind or movement to cause it.

Small wisps of steam began to rise from the water. The light grew even greener, the waves even wilder, slapping against the edges of the tub. Alexandra made a small startled noise, and Hetta instinctively stepped towards them, but the light abruptly cut off and Gwendelfear sagged in sudden fatigue.

Gwendelfear released Alexandra's head and stepped out of the tub, her movements stiff. But everyone's eyes were on Alexandra, who was looking around the bathroom at her assembled relatives with a confused but entirely lucid expression on her face and pupils of the proper size.

"What's going on?" she asked.

Phoebe gave a sob and flung herself at her daughter, wrapping her arms around her, entirely heedless of Alexandra's soaked condition.

"Mama!" Alexandra objected, but Phoebe just gave another strangled sob and then began immediately to fuss about getting her out of the cold water and back into her bed, to which Alexandra said only, "But the water is quite warm, Mama. Why am I in my nightgown? And why are you all here?" Her gaze went especially to Marius, and she blushed.

They left Phoebe and Aunt Sybil to fuss over Alexandra, who said loudly that she was quite capable of walking herself back to her room, if someone would bring her a bathrobe, looking quite mulish when Phoebe protested.

Hetta caught Gwendelfear observing Alexandra with a look of tired satisfaction. She had faded casually into the background in the general rejoicing at Alexandra's recovery and would probably have slipped away without anyone being the wiser if Hetta hadn't caught her eye and made a slight gesture. Gwendelfear's eyes narrowed.

"I would have a word with you," Hetta said quietly to her.

The fae followed her out. Hetta led her into the hallway, down the stairs and into the green drawing room. Wyn ghosted along behind them. Gwendelfear ignored him entirely. When Hetta and Gwendelfear entered the room, he took up a position by the door, a silent sentinel.

The green drawing room had been decorated by Hetta's mother. Hetta had never met that lady, since she'd died giving birth to her. Hetta had come in here sometimes as a child, trying to picture her mother somehow in the space between the grandfather clock and the chesterfield. She'd never really succeeded, but the room had still come to mean refuge.

"Please sit," she said to Gwendelfear. The fae did so, her white-less eyes unblinking. Hetta wondered why she'd chosen not to adopt a human disguise. Maybe her magic was too drained to do so; there was a heavy weariness to her movements. Her appearance was even more jarring when contrasted with the ordinariness of her surroundings: upholstered chesterfield, country landscapes, aforementioned grandfather clock. Hetta tried not to show how much the woman's strange appearance bothered her, and not just because she didn't want to antagonise Gwendelfear. Wyn was watching her, and she knew that he would extrapolate her reaction to apply to himself also. He was as focused as she'd ever seen him, dark eyes intent on Gwendelfear, watching her as one does an untrustworthy dog without a muzzle.

"Thank you for helping my sister."

Gwendelfear made a movement much like a horse wriggling a fly off. "I did not do it for your thanks."

Hetta had seated herself across from Gwendelfear, the coffee table separating them. She felt a ridiculous urge to offer the fae tea. She wanted to ask Gwendelfear what she knew about the Stone and whether her court was involved but wasn't quite sure how to begin.

"Wyn," she said softly. "Would you leave us for a moment?"

He flashed them both looks: a warning to Gwendelfear and a request to Hetta to take care. But he left. "I will be outside."

Hetta wished she *had* offered Gwendelfear tea, for then she would have something to occupy her hands with. Consciously, she laid them together in her lap and met Gwendelfear's eyes steadily. "I'm rather out of patience with all this fae shilly-shallying, as my grandmother would call it. Will you tell me plainly why you came to this house and if my kinsfolk are in further danger from your people?" Taking a risk, she added, "You know the Star Stone is missing. Do you know its location?"

Gwendelfear was eyeing her oddly. "Do you truly expect me to answer your questions?"

"Well, I hope you will, but in any case, there didn't seem to be anything to lose by asking them."

Gwendelfear smiled. "Oh, I can see why he likes you, Henrietta Valstar." She paused to contemplate for a few seconds. Then she rose. "You were kind to me when I came here, though I came under false pretences. For that, I will grant you a truth." She paused to savour her next words and said with a cat-like smile, "The fae do not have the Star Stone."

LAND-SENSE

THERE WAS A certain apathetic quality to the atmosphere in the house the next morning. The family were, of course, relieved beyond words at Alexandra's recovery, but since they had all been subconsciously preparing for the worst, the sudden removal of that strain left them all fatigued. Hetta, Jack, and Marius all gravitated to Lord Valstar's study and Wyn showed up, with his usual foresight, complete with tea set and cake. Hetta told them, with resignation, of Gwendelfear's 'truth'.

Marius worried at his lip. "I just received a letter this morning, from my friends down in Knoxbridge. They identified the substance the false Stone was made of and gave me a list of manufacturers that could have shaped it, but it's a slim lead."

"Let's hear the list then," said Jack tiredly.

Marius obediently drew a folded letter from his coat pocket and read the list aloud. None of the possibilities shed any light on the situation.

"Well, it was always a long shot," Hetta consoled him when he'd come to the end of it.

"Well, that's it then, isn't it?" Jack said. "It's not fairies and no one has the faintest idea where else the damned Stone is. We may as well announce that the Stone is missing and take up the search for star indigo publicly. I'm sorry, cousin." He did look sorry, and there was no trace of triumph in his expression.

Marius looked to her for guidance. He would take her part, if she wanted to argue against Jack, but she could tell he didn't have much heart for it. Seeing their two faces turned towards her, both anxious, filled her with a bittersweet decision. Jack was right, and yet she couldn't regret the strange twist of fate that had kept her here for so long. Look at the three of them, come so far in such a short time.

Hetta breathed out slowly, coming to her resolution. She nodded. "It will be a scandal, but it won't be the first scandal attached to my name in the North. Unless anyone has any better ideas?"

They agreed to make the announcement to the rest of the family at dinner. "And we must make sure no one else is hiding any more pertinent information about fairies or secrets or suchlike," Hetta added, thinking of Alexandra and Gwendelfear. It was difficult to be truly angry at her half-sister, given that her actions might have saved her life, but cold fear filled her at the thought of what might have been. There wasn't much more to say after that, and they parted ways, each to be alone with their thoughts.

Hetta found herself wandering through the vast house, struggling with strange, unnameable emotion. Along the route, tiny details leapt out at her: the painting of Grandfather Marius at the top of the main staircase that Wyn used to hide notes behind; the long south hallway where a serious eight-year-old Jack had tried to teach Marius and Hetta how to bowl before being soundly scolded by Aunt Sybil; the door to her father's bedroom. She stopped outside this one. As a child, she'd been far too intimidated to intrude, but now curiosity plucked at her.

In more modern houses, it was usual now for spouses to share a bedroom, but Stariel couldn't be considered modern by any stretch of the word, and her father and Phoebe had maintained separate chambers ever since Hetta could remember. Obviously, there must have been some travel between the two, given the fact of Gregory, Alexandra, and Laurel's existence, but Hetta didn't like to dwell too much on the details of that.

She wasn't sure what she'd been expecting to find here, but it wasn't this quiet, clean room, bare of personality. Someone had been through and tidied away her father's things, and now the space might have been nothing more than a large and slightly shabby guestroom.

She went over to the windowseat facing north, out towards the Indigo Mountains. Her father's room was on the third floor, which struck her now as odd for an elderly and often inebriated man, but perhaps it had been worth it for this view. She sat down on the windowseat, walking her fingers along the ledge. What would her father have thought of all this? In his own way, he'd tried to do his best for Stariel, taking in Wyn, refusing to cut up the estate, and preparing Jack to take over the reins. He had always wanted Jack to inherit. The idea of Hetta becoming lord would never even have crossed his mind.

She'd never wanted this, this land of vast landscapes and idiosyncratic people and changeable weather, never wanted to research sheep varieties or drainage schemes or housing upgrades, never imagined a life spent buried in accounts books and arguing with tenant farmers. Why, then, was she so miserable at the prospect of giving it up? She reached instinctively for Stariel for comfort, but there was none to be had. The land was as unsettled as she.

She gave herself a little shake. She ought to do something

useful rather than this wallowing in self-pity. With this resolution in mind, she wound her way down to the housekeeper's office. Wyn wasn't inside and, after a query to the housemaid, she found him quietly turning wine bottles in the cellar.

"Are you hiding?" she asked, amused at the incongruity of this man, this fae prince, performing so mundane a task at such a time. His back was to her, his movements slow and graceful.

"No, actually." He turned. "I simply found myself too distracted to perform tasks requiring much intellect, and this still needed to be done." His mouth lifted when he saw her standing at the cellar entrance. "Hetta." He said her name as if he simply wanted the pleasure of saying it.

"Angus asked me to marry him," she said, surprising herself.

He froze. He did that under stress, went still as a deer in a hunter's sights. She watched him consciously un-freeze himself after a short pause, his shoulders relaxing in a display of sheer willpower.

"What was your answer?" His tone was mild, as if he didn't give two figs whether she married another man. His eyes told a different story, subtle but undeniable; she was getting better at reading him.

"I told him I wasn't sure of my own heart yet. Although after considering the matter, I don't think we would suit."

He let out a long breath. For a moment, she thought he was going to move towards her, but then he paused, his eyes widening at some inner revelation. He opened his mouth, looked at her face, and closed it again.

She crossed her arms and glared. "What?"

He paused and then said, carefully: "Lord Penharrow."

"Yes, we have now correctly established Angus's title."

"Someone with a motive to want you as lord," Wyn expanded. "Lord Angus Penharrow."

She narrowed her eyes at him. "If this is jealousy speaking—"

The air about him abruptly crackled with magic, bringing with it the smell of rain falling on dry earth. It filled the spaces between the dark wooded walls of the cellar for a breath before he drew it back into himself and once again was only her mild-mannered butler.

"Why would I be jealous of Lord Angus? You said you didn't want to marry him."

Hetta noted he hadn't actually refuted her charge. "For goodness' sake, let yourself be angry for once in your life. It's exhausting watching you tamp it down every time you threaten to lose your temper. No wonder you have so little faith in yourself—you never let yourself relax, really, do you?"

Wyn tilted his head. "Just to be clear here—are you instructing me to lose my temper at you, Hetta?"

"Well, I don't precisely encourage it, but you shouldn't fear that I'm going to break if you do." She paused. "And you're also allowed to be jealous, if you choose."

He shook his head, a smile tugging at the corners of his mouth. "Very well, then. But that isn't what prompted my accusation. We know it isn't the fae who took the Stone, and we know it wasn't Marius's lover. Who else stood to gain from your ascension? Lord Penharrow."

"On the off-chance that I would marry him and combine the estates?" she said sceptically. "A very long shot, surely? And besides, I don't even think combining the estates would work, with the land-sense." Although Angus hadn't believed in the land-sense, she remembered. She shook her head. "No. Out of the question."

JACK WAS JUST AS adamant in his reaction when Wyn had dragged them all together again in Hetta's study.

"No," Jack said. "He'd never do something so underhanded. And what would he stand to gain, anyway?"

"Hetta," said Wyn simply. "And land."

Jack's eyebrows went up. "What do you mean?"

"He's been after Stariel's lands for years."

Jack made a dismissive sound. "That's not a secret. And in any case, what good would it possibly do him to make Hetta lord?"

"He *has* been courting Hetta," Marius said slowly.

"*What*?" Jack looked so appalled at the idea that Hetta couldn't help but laugh.

"You needn't sound horrified at the idea of someone courting me, Jack. It's a little insulting. There *are* men who find me attractive."

"Yes—but, Angus and you?" he spluttered.

Hetta took from this that she wasn't the only person who had suffered a case of hero worship towards Lord Penharrow. "In fact," she said, needled, "he asked me to marry him."

This created a certain amount of uproar and the need for further explanations. When the initial reaction had calmed, Jack was still unconvinced

"I don't think that constitutes a motive."

"But perhaps," said Marius, "it would be worth checking Penharrow, to be sure. Any one of us ought to be able to sense the Stone's presence, if we get close enough."

They all turned as one to look at Hetta. She flushed and shook her head. "No. I cannot possibly visit Lord Penharrow given the circumstances. He will, quite rightly, take it as a sign of encouragement, which wouldn't be fair to either of us!"

"Why don't you want to marry Angus, anyway?" Jack asked.

"You can't be appalled at the idea that he would want to marry me and then equally appalled that I don't want to marry him within the space of the same conversation. Besides, it's none of your business." She couldn't help her gaze flickering beyond Jack to Wyn, who stood quietly next to the poster of the Sun Theatre.

"I don't see how it isn't my business," Jack shot back. "Given that he's our neighbour."

"We're straying from the point," Marius interjected. "Are we going to go search Penharrow or not?"

"On what basis?" Jack flared up once more in Angus's defence. "Angus has only ever been a good neighbour, and we've no evidence that he's played us foul other than his questionable taste in women." He gave Hetta a deliberately provoking look, and she might have risen to the bait except that a vague recollection bubbled to the surface of her mind. She let Jack and Marius argue while she tried to catch it. No evidence, Jack had said. It seemed an apt description for the entire mess. If Marius hadn't realised the Stone was a fake, there would have been no evidence of the crime at all. The false Stone was the only hard piece of evidence they had, for who other than the Valstars really understood the land-sense?

"Marius," she said, then—since he was involved in a passionate debate with his cousin—more loudly: "Marius!" The two of them broke off and turned to her. "Marius, what was that list of possible manufacturers again?"

She thought he would question her, but something in her tone alerted him, and he obediently fished the list from his pocket and read them out again.

"Smithson's Manufacturing," she repeated slowly.

"You recognise it?" Marius asked.

An image snapped into focus: a box labelled Smithson's Manufacturing. Where had she seen such an item? She frowned, searching, and abruptly her mind surrendered the memory. The train platform. A box stamped 'Smithson's Manufacturing'. A box collected by none other than Lord Angus Penharrow.

42

CONFRONTATION

THE OTHERS HADN'T wanted her to go alone to Penharrow, of course, once she'd explained. But Hetta was filled with an unpleasant mix of anger and hope, and she didn't want others to be party to her confrontation. Hetta had eventually pointed out that if they were relying on her to frighten away fae monsters with her pyromancy, it would be the height of hypocrisy not to allow her to face one mortal man by herself.

Marius drove her unhappily to Penharrow. Hetta drew in a sharp breath as they crossed the border between Stariel and Penharrow; again, there was that intense sensation of resistance, worse even than the last time. Marius shot her a concerned glance before returning his attention to the road.

"Don't you feel it?" she asked him. "Stariel—it doesn't want us to go."

He frowned. "Not specifically. All I've got from it these past weeks has been restlessness, like I can hear someone moving about in a distant room. But you know my land-sense isn't strong."

Hetta glanced back towards Stariel thoughtfully. She hadn't thought her land-sense was particularly strong either.

The midday sun might've been designed to show Penharrow Estate to its best advantage. Everywhere there were small signs of prosperity, obvious now that Hetta had been grappling with the lack of them at Stariel: cottages and roads and fences in good repair, fields neat and green. Even the sheep looked fatter.

Really, it was intolerable that Angus should be such a good landowner. It made it impossible to cast him properly in the role of villain, a concept she was still having difficulty with. Perhaps there had been some mistake. Anger warred with confusion.

Penharrow Manor was of more modest and modern construction than Stariel House, brick rather than stone and more coherent in design.

"It's probably fully elektrified too," Hetta grumbled under her breath as they pulled up. Marius gave her an odd look as he parked the car.

"You sure about this, Hetta?" he asked, grey eyes serious.

"Perfectly." She got out of the kineticar. "I shall be back shortly."

SHE'D KNOWN THAT ANGUS would be happy to see her and, indeed, had been conscious that he might take her spontaneous visit entirely the wrong way.

"Hetta!" he said delightedly when his butler announced her. He rose and kissed her cheek. "I had no idea I was to be so favoured."

She smiled, though it felt very false. "It's very good of you not to point out that I'm being abominably rude by calling on you without warning."

"Not at all!" he protested. "Please, sit. Will you take tea with my mother and sisters?"

"Perhaps," Hetta said, perching lightly on one of the chairs. "But I wanted to ask you something first. Something potentially rather serious, I'm afraid."

"You alarm me." Angus held a hand to his heart. "I hope you're not about to cast me off entirely?" He tried to pass this last remark off as levity, but there was wariness in his tone.

Hetta threw caution to the winds. "Angus, what do you know about the Star Stone?"

As soon as she'd said it, she knew. Angus covered his initial reaction well, but she'd been watching closely for it.

Angus frowned, continuing the charade. "The Star Stone?" he repeated in a confused tone.

Hetta sat back in her chair with a sigh. "Oh, Angus. Why would you do such a thing?"

"I'm afraid I'm rather confused as to what you mean."

Anger began to kindle in the pit of her belly. "I'm not a fool, though I think you've tried to make one of me. Does the name James Snickett mean anything to you? I suppose he was an old school friend of yours. That must've made things easier when you needed an illusionist you could trust. And Smithson's Manufacturing? I was *there*, Angus, when you picked up the dashed box."

This time even Angus couldn't pretend he wasn't startled. He blew out a breath. "How did you find out?"

"You think it's all superstition, which makes me slightly less angry at you. You have no idea what you've done, of the danger you put Stariel in. But that's of no matter right now. What does matter is this: what have you done with the Star Stone?"

"Hetta..." Angus held out a hand towards her.

She recoiled. "The Stone, Lord Penharrow. Where is it? Or will you force me to make a fuss about theft? I don't desire to make my affairs public, but you can be sure I will if I have to."

Angus abruptly gave up his pretence of innocence. He fixed

her with a very serious look and then said softly: "Whyever do you want it back, Hetta?"

"I wasn't entering into a debate with you, Lord Penharrow. I was demanding the return of a valuable family heirloom."

"I admit the theft doesn't sit well with me. But—"

"It shouldn't. And there is no but," she told him. "Where is it?"

"Come, Hetta, don't tell me you think that a pseudo-magic rock is worth all this fuss?"

"As a matter of fact, I do."

Angus scoffed. "You'd give up Stariel's lordship?"

"It's not rightfully mine."

And now Angus was leaning forward, his hazel eyes intent. "But why shouldn't it be? It took you by surprise, but you're thriving in the position. You have the ambition and the intelligence to make Stariel great again. More than any of your male relatives. You *know* that; you're not a woman of false modesty."

Hetta was silent. It was true that she'd been unable to keep from turning her thoughts to changes that ought to be made at Stariel, despite knowing the impermanence of her claim. And she hadn't fought terribly hard against Marius's suggestion that she maintain the fiction as long as possible.

Angus sensed her hesitation and continued, surer of himself. "What does it matter about the Star Stone or how you came to be lord? It'll cause a hell of an uproar if you try to change it. Why not continue as you have been? Make the best of things?"

"And you have only Stariel's interests at heart, of course," Hetta said, raising a weak protest.

Angus grinned, that same disarming smile that had made her younger self's heart skip a beat. "I'll admit I may have been looking out for my own interests too. It was wrong of me, but I couldn't bear to see such good land wasted. Your father's management was appalling—which ought to be evidence enough against the Star Stone's wisdom."

Hetta had sworn not to be drawn into a discussion, but she was finding that an increasingly difficult vow to keep. "And Jack, his likely successor? You assumed he'd be no better?"

"I assumed he'd be just as stubborn in his refusal to sell the land along the border," Angus said. His frankness was disarming. Hetta was fairly certain he knew that and was using it to win her over, but the realisation didn't lessen its effectiveness. One oughtn't to admire such ruthless practicality, and yet…

"But why me?" She dug her fingers into the arms of her chair. "I'm aware you're complimenting me for your own ends, Angus, but you can't make me believe you had any particular memory of me before I arrived."

"You were an impulse," Angus admitted. "I *like* you, Hetta. I had originally planned for Cecily." Hetta could see the logic in that. Her older cousin Cecily would've taken Mr Fisk's advice on the matter and that would have been that. With that thought came another sinking realisation.

"Mr Fisk was yours," she said dully. "Trying to persuade my father to sell, and then trying to persuade me. Making things worse than they already were." She closed her eyes briefly. "Did you know he was skimming or was that outside the scope of your arrangement?" Her voice came out sharp and brittle as hoarfrost.

"Hetta—" Angus began, reaching out a hand again, but he didn't deny the accusation, and she moved out of his reach. He took his hand back

"And you figured that if I wouldn't sell, then I might be persuaded into another arrangement. After all, I hero-worshipped you as a girl. How difficult could it be, to infatuate the woman?" Her lips tightened, anger swelling once more. "Where is the Star Stone, Lord Penharrow?"

"Hetta," he said again, and this time there was pain in his voice. "I spoke truly when I offered for you. I think we'd make a good pair. I still do. This doesn't have to mean the end of that."

"I think it does. Now, for the last time, where is the Stone?"

For all his compliments, Angus didn't appear to be able to take her demands seriously.

"Don't be hasty about this, Hetta. At least think it over." He made a conciliatory gesture and would have reached for her again, but Hetta's temper abruptly snapped. How *dare* Angus think he could simply smile at her and make all this go away! How *dare* he take what wasn't his! Fire flared within her—the same fire she'd hurled at a fae monster—and she let it swarm, flinging out her arm and casting it out. The fireball hit a section of wood panelling with a great crack, and it was an effort of will to squash the flames before they spread.

Angus stared as if he had never truly seen her before, the acrid smell of smoke heavy in the air. She looked down at her hands; she'd burnt through the palms of her thin gloves. She peeled them off, filled with a surging, furious satisfaction.

Then she stood, curling her hands into fists to keep them from re-igniting. "Don't push me, Lord Penharrow. Much as I might be tempted, I couldn't live with such a weight of falsehood on my conscience. I can't explain it to you, since that's obviously something you lack."

His mouth thinned. "Fine. I'll get it."

"You may take me to it."

Without a word, Angus rose and strode out of the room. Hetta followed him. He made his way up to what she presumed must be his office from the desk and papers there. He stalked over to a strongbox built into one corner of the room, fiddled with the combination lock, and wrenched the door open. Reaching inside, he pulled out something the size of a large, misshapen apple swaddled in cloth. He turned around, sorrow and anger warring for control of his expression as he handed it to her. "Take it. Damn you, Hetta."

Hetta ignored this, carefully pulling the linen wrapping away to inspect the item. The glittering blue of star indigo winked up at her. The tension thrumming through her eased a little.

"Thank the nine heavens." She re-wrapped the Stone and cradled it close. "I will take my leave of you then, Lord Penharrow."

Angus said nothing as she left. Hetta felt only a hollow coldness, as if the fireball had used up all her anger in its heat.

She nodded at Marius when she came out of the manor, and he relaxed infinitesimally, his gaze snagging on the wrapped Stone in her hands. She didn't release her hold on the Stone on the drive back to Stariel, hugging it tight to her body. It weighed more than its size would suggest, the solidity comforting.

Marius didn't seem to know quite what to say, and Hetta was glad for his silence, for this short reprieve before the storm rolled over them. It would be a mess, explaining to the rest of the family what had happened, having to hold the Choosing Ceremony again. Somewhere deep down was relief at finally finding the Stone, but it was buried under a huge, complicated emotion. It dug claws into her, a sharp, painful constriction in her chest that made it hard to breathe.

It was grief, she realised after a moment of internal self-examination; the grief she'd been waiting to feel since the moment she'd arrived at Stariel Station. But it wasn't grief for her father. The irony of this wasn't lost on her.

Jack and Wyn were both waiting in the entryway when they returned. Gods knew how they'd explained their loitering; Wyn had at least made some attempt to look as if he had a reason for being there, holding a clipboard vaguely. Jack was simply pacing.

"Well?" Jack demanded as they opened the door.

As answer, Hetta pulled back the wrappings from her burden. Her bare fingers brushed the Star Stone's cool surface.

The world shifted. The sensation grew outwards and downwards from her feet, as if she were a tree spreading roots deeper and deeper into the earth. She was no longer Hetta. Hetta was now just one tiny part of her. She was soil and roots, trees and mountains. Animals moved across her skin, and she was them as well. In her forests the leaves grew still, and she was a thousand thousand trunks slumbering in the cold. Blue squirrels and robins and blackbirds paused as she became them, tiny hearts skittering for a fraction of an instant as they and she adjusted. She felt the soft paws of a fox rearranging herself deep in her den.

In the sheepfold, the cloven hooves of sheep sank into her bogs and scrambled up her steep hillsides. Along the Indigoes, the cold wind swirled about her, caressing her, promising snow. And everywhere she felt the trickle and swirl of water, in her creeks and rivers and lakes, and beneath them, the slow, inexorable movement of the groundwater. And mightiest of them all, Starwater, its still surface broken only by the occasional shag.

She felt the weight of the house's stones upon her, felt the wriggle of the tiny humans inside and knew they were hers. Many of them held a spark inside, and she felt their connection to herself through it. She reached out and touched the sparks, gently, felt them flare in acknowledgement in the same way that the hearts of the tiny birds had as her awareness encompassed them.

She felt too the duality of her existence—Stariel and under-Stariel, two worlds occupying almost but not quite the same space. Tiny fae, native to Stariel, paused in their businesses to acknowledge her. She felt, too, the greater fae-spark who was not of Stariel, felt his solemn salutation as her awareness passed over him. And along her southern border, the smallest of testing intrusions by more fae who did not belong to her. She squashed them ruthlessly, turning them back. *You are not welcome here. You may not pass my borders.* She bore down upon them with terrible force and felt them crumple before her, fleeing.

She was so alive, more alive than she'd ever been; more alive than she'd known it was possible to be.

And then she was just Hetta again. It was like breaking the surface after having been under deep, cold water for a long, long time. The entryway had rearranged itself. Disoriented, it took her a while to realise that this was because she was lying on the floor, the Star Stone still held in one hand.

She felt the immensity that was Stariel lurking in the back of her mind. It wasn't the small burble of land-sense she was used to. She knew that if she chose to, she might plunge back into the connection again, but she knew also that that would be a very bad idea, that one could lose oneself entirely in something so old and vast. She felt, for the first time in her life, a wholly discernible emotion from the land.

It was satisfaction.

She opened her eyes to see three faces peering down at her, all of them with wild eyes.

"Well, that's convenient," said Marius when he finally found his voice. "Turns out you are the Lord of Stariel after all."

43

THE FROST BALL

Lady Phoebe had outdone herself for this year's Frost Ball. Hetta watched the throng of people whirling about Stariel's ballroom with a bittersweet mix of emotions. The mood in Stariel House had lightened, and if Hetta's stepmother chose to believe this was because everyone was excited about her party, there was no harm in that.

Nothing, she knew, would be as important to her as Stariel now. She'd known that since the moment the bond had clicked into place not quite a week ago.

She reached for Stariel, and the land responded. It was so intensely *alive.* She walked out onto the terrace, and Stariel hummed beneath the cool stones, wriggling with interest and a kind of eagerness to please. On impulse, she stroked her hand over a slumbering tree branch and felt the magic stir, green buds unfurling at shocking speed. *I probably ought not to do that,* she thought guiltily, pulling the magic back. It was deepening towards winter after all, and the buds would wither in the cold. But the irony of it hadn't escaped her: here was more magic than she'd found in all her years in Meridon. How could her father have been so indifferent to it? And just how much could she achieve by embracing it? She wanted to find out.

She made her way into the dark gardens with unnatural surefootedness, feeling each place to step without the need to look first. The gardens were still and silent but for the distant strains of music; there would be a frost tomorrow.

One of the advantages of her new bond with Stariel was that she knew where people were within the boundaries of the estate, if she wished. She paused next to the ornamental cherry trees. Wyn had been standing here alone for some time. Her new land-sense didn't enable her to read minds, but she didn't need to in order to guess the turn of his thoughts.

"You're thinking of leaving," she said without preamble.

He was nearly invisible until he moved, his slender form peeling away from the dark shape of the trunk. The sound of music from the ball carried to them clearly in the cold air.

"It will make things less complicated for you with the fae. I have drafted a notice for my replacement, and the applicants for the role of housekeeper will be here after Wintersol to be interviewed."

Hetta went to him. "Will you dance with me?" The band inside were playing a slow waltz.

"Hetta," he chided, but after a moment he held out his hand. "Here?"

"Yes." She stepped into his hold, her breath catching at the light touch of his hands on her waist. "Why do I want to make things less complicated with the fae?" she inquired as they began to move to the slow time of the waltz. Whatever had possessed Phoebe to pick such a solemn tune, she was grateful for it at that moment. It meant that she could lay her head against Wyn's chest and still move in time to the music. He made an inarticulate sound, half-protest, half-approval, before his arms tightened around her.

Wyn swallowed, and she felt the motion quiver through their bodies. "They will demand you turn me over to them. I do not know what they will do if you refuse. Nothing good, I suspect. I do not wish to bring that down upon you."

"What about the oath Grandmamma mentioned you made?" Hetta burrowed closer. "To my father?" He stiffened, and she looked up. "Oh. Oaths can be dissolved if the person who made them is dead. My father is dead. You aren't oathbound to Stariel."

"No," Wyn said. "I am not."

Their faces were nearly touching, the warmth of his breath intermingling with hers, but he remained silent.

"Do you want to stay?" she asked eventually. "While we're advertising for housekeepers, I'm in the market for a steward, if you happen to know someone who could fill that role."

He laughed, but his eyes were dark as forest shadows. She wanted to speak further, to command him to stay, and felt Stariel surge up in agreement with that desire. She repressed it; this had to come from him.

His voice was quiet. "Yes." A pause. "But I don't want to bring further trouble here. You can't ignore that, Hetta. You *shouldn't* ignore that."

She held his gaze. "I'm not inclined to let bad fairies dictate my actions out of fear of what *might* happen."

He smiled faintly at her description. "You make it sound so trifling." His gaze sobered as he contemplated the distant lake. The vast surface acted as a mirror, silver glittering in its depths. *The Court of Falling Stars*, she thought of the fae name for Stariel.

"I'm not afraid of the fae." She smirked, thinking of the fire she'd unleashed from her hands. "And I'll fight them for you if I have to."

He let out a soft huff of amusement. "Oh you will, will you?"

"That's settled then," she said. "Now will you stop brooding and, for the nine heavens' sake, kiss me?"

He stiffened, their slow dance coming to an abrupt halt.

Far away, the band began to play a fast-paced folkdance. Wyn stayed so quiet that she worried he'd stopped breathing. Then, as his still silence continued, she worried she'd offended him beyond recall. She was about to say something when Wyn abruptly threw back his head and laughed. It trilled out of him, silvery and delighted.

"Oh, Hetta," he said with such fond matter-of-factness that she blushed. He lifted a hand to cup her cheek. "How did I ever think I could resist you?"

"You are the worst—" she began, but the rest of her words were lost as Wyn abruptly lowered his head and kissed her. Her awareness narrowed to heat and the press of lips and the thunderous roll of her heartbeat. When he paused to draw breath, she squeaked, "You—" But he kissed her again, and after that she couldn't think of anything else.

"My Star," he said hoarsely, and kissed her again. Magic sang in her veins. "My Star."

He hadn't said he would stay, but for that moment, it was enough.

AUTHOR'S NOTE

Thank you for taking the time to read my book! I hope you enjoyed it.

The Lord of Stariel is the first book in the Stariel Quartet. The next book in the series is *The Prince of Secrets*. Keep turning the page for a sneak peek of the first chapter.

Please consider reviewing *The Lord of Stariel* on Amazon or Goodreads, even if you only write a line or two. Reviews mean a lot to authors, and I appreciate every one!

SNEAK PEEK: THE PRINCE OF SECRETS

THE CAT WASN'T in the linen closet. His Royal Highness Hallowyn Tempestren, the secret fae prince and newly minted steward of Stariel Estate more usually known as Wyn, frowned down at pristine and, above all, *unoccupied* white sheets. Crouching, he checked the lower shelves, but the closet remained conspicuously cat-free. It seemed unfair that the cat should *not* be here now, given the number of times she'd managed to sneak in to sleep despite his best efforts. Where in the high winds' eddies was she? Wyn could locate any mortal in the house in about thirty seconds, but the cat still eluded him after half an hour of searching.

Straightening, he clicked shut the closet door and considered where else in the labyrinthine Stariel House might appeal to a sly she-cat about to give birth. The long, empty shape of the hallway held no answers. Gas lamps cast a yellowish light, combining unpleasantly with the aged pink-and-green-striped wallpaper. A gap where one of the curtains hadn't been closed properly showed a thin rectangle of darkness. He straightened it absently, thinking.

Perhaps the bedrooms? Plumpuff—one of the children was responsible for the name—had a typical feline talent for inserting herself wherever she was least wanted. Wyn could readily imagine her choosing to have her kittens in the middle of one of the aunts' beds. Of course, the problem was that the house boasted an alarming number of bedrooms, in various states of habitability, spread sporadically over four floors and two wings. It would take time to search them all. Too much time.

He shifted from foot to foot, weighing his options, then sighed and with some reluctance reached out with his leysight. He rarely invoked it to such an extent, but it came easily, almost eagerly, to his call. The world sharpened, the lines of magic that criss-crossed this land sparkling with colour and the layers of Stariel and under-Stariel swimming before him, a beautiful and yet unwelcome reminder of the difference between himself and the people he served. They were human; he was not.

Stariel grumbled as he scanned the leylines for a hint of the cat's location. Wyn wasn't bound to this land and Stariel knew it. However, he had its lord's permission to be here, so usually it would simply cast a metaphorical eye over him, shrug, and move on. Not tonight, though. Tonight, Stariel crouched over him as he sifted through the currents of power, making them as stiff and uncooperative as chilled dough. He fought the urge to hunch under the unfriendly, disconcertingly focused presence.

It *could* be just the season affecting Stariel's mood. It was only six days until Wintersol, and it was natural for the land to be slow and reluctant to wake until springtime. It could also be that Wyn's magic was stronger at this time of year, and something about that had set Stariel bristling. Stormcrows knew faelands could be strange and arbitrary about such things. But had it been this bad in winters past? Had it felt this personal? He couldn't remember if he'd ever pressed the land for information near midwinter before.

Of course—there was one *other* thing that could explain a change in Stariel's attitude; its new lord. *Though I wasn't expecting*

Hetta's influence to increase Stariel's hostility towards me, he thought wryly. Perhaps his kissing skills could use more practice, in the slow, teasing wind of… He tugged his thoughts back from that distracting direction. Later. Right now, he needed to focus on finding the cat.

With an effort of will, he widened the net of his leysight, and his senses expanded through the house. Stariel resisted, frosty and intractable, only grudgingly giving up the locations of its inhabitants. The Valstars had ruled over Stariel for a millennium, and the land was far more attached to them than it was to Wyn, who'd been resident not quite a decade. Ten years was an eye blink to a faeland.

He pressed harder but still received only a hazy impression of the many lives within Stariel House. Most of the Valstars had returned to the family home for the Wintersol celebration and were spread through the interior like so many fireflies. The servants were largely down near the kitchen at this hour, though he didn't need Stariel to tell him that. If he strained, he could make out the no-nonsense tones of Cook giving orders.

But no cats.

Wait—the merest skitter of claws kneading at an already threadbare windowseat: the library. Wyn set off along the hallway with long-legged strides, as the library was at the opposite end of the house from the linen closet. There wasn't much time left. New life always affected the fabric of reality to some degree, and the atmosphere of the house had already begun to shift.

He caught snatches of conversation as he went. From the red drawing room came the sound of the aunts competitively comparing children. In the adjoining room, a good portion of the adolescents were playing cards, ignoring their parents' conversation. The crack of ivory balls distantly to the southeast told him that some of the older Valstar cousins were playing in the billiard room. He took care not to be seen, for he couldn't afford the potential delay. He didn't need magic for that: speed, stealth, and superior hearing worked just as well.

It took him only a few minutes to reach the library. The room's domed roof loomed overhead, the light-spells along the walls throwing ornate shadows into its curve. It was the only room in the house that warranted the use of the more expensive technomantic creations over gas lamps, because of the fire risk. They pinged oddly against his senses, like little blank spaces in the world, something he'd long since decided was a side effect of that specific branch of magic combining with the mechanics of mortal technology. Technomancy wasn't a magic the fae possessed.

He didn't need to guess who had activated the light-spells, for he could hear Marius Valstar speaking from the windowseat at the far end of the library. His stride faltered for a beat, but he mastered the urge to avoid Hetta's older brother and instead slunk towards him between the rows of bookshelves. Marius was reading to some of his younger relatives, voice warm with affection. Reading to children always put him in a good mood; perhaps he would forget to be angry at Wyn.

Wyn rolled his eyes at the over-optimistic thought. Of course Marius would simply *forget* that Wyn had lied to him for nearly ten years about who and what he was. It wasn't so much the masquerading as a human servant that had upset Marius. It was that Wyn had been deeper in Marius's confidences than anyone else, and the reverse had turned out not to be true.

Even if Marius *did* suddenly forgive him for that betrayal, there was another good reason for him to be angry at Wyn, though he didn't yet know it. Wyn's thoughts turned to Hetta again, and he couldn't stop the smile that came to his lips, even as a cold band settled around his heart. Perhaps it was better that Marius didn't know his sister and Wyn were...entangled. After all, it might end soon enough. It *should* end soon enough. The band tightened, the cold spreading over his rib cage.

Marius nestled into one of the windowseats, his dark head bent over a book and spectacles slipping down his nose. Two young girls sat together at the other end of the seat, Marius's cousins Willow and Violet. Their teenage brother Daffodil—their mother had a penchant for botanically themed names—evidently considered himself too old for stories, which he'd made clear by leaning against the wall as if about to walk away. His expression, however, was equally as enraptured as the two girls'.

A grey cat curled on Marius's lap, and Wyn's focused sharpened. It wasn't the cat Wyn was looking for. Stariel had deliberately misled him.

Wyn and Hetta's story continues in The Prince of Secrets. If you'd like to keep up with all my publishing news, you can sign up to my mailing list on my website ajlancaster.com.

ACKNOWLEDGEMENTS

THIS BOOK OWES SOMETHING of its final form to the following people:

Carla, for listening to me talk about imaginary people more often than anyone should have to, and for being the world's best sister.

Priscilla, for asking what was in the box.

Mum, for wanting 'another several books of pining' back when I thought this was a standalone novel.

The Oxford NaNoWriMos 2014, who were there when it began.

Marie and Steph, for so many Sunday afternoon writing sessions. I think the cafés know our faces now.

My many beta readers over the years, for all their feedback and encouragement: Anna, Chantal, Ellen, Erin, Karen, Kirsten, Mashayla, Rem, and Tony. Whichever version you read, I hope you like this one best!

And lastly, my wonderful and innumerable relations, none of whom appear in this book, I promise!

ABOUT THE AUTHOR

GROWING UP ON A farm in rural Aotearoa New Zealand, AJ Lancaster avoided chores by hiding up trees with a book. She wrote in the same way she breathed—constantly and without thinking much of it—so it took many years and a pile of finished manuscripts for her to realise that she might want to be a writer and, in fact, already was. On the way to this realisation she collected a degree in science, worked in environmental planning, and became an editor.

Now she lives in the windy coastal city of Wellington and writes romantic, whimsical fantasy books about fae, magic, and complicated families. *The Lord of Stariel* is her first novel.

You can find her on the interwebs at:

https://www.instagram.com/a.j.lancaster/
https://www.facebook.com/lancasterwrites
https://twitter.com/lancasterwrites

Printed in Great Britain
by Amazon